# Dragon Riders

# of

# Mirstone

## EDITED BY RICHARD FIERCE

Cover design by Keith Robinson
Anthology Editor: Richard Fierce

DRAGONFIRE PRESS

Dragonfire Press

Print ISBN: 978-1-958354-74-2

E-Book ISBN: 978-1-958354-73-5

First Edition: 2024

# CONTENTS

Introduction     i

Wanted: One Dragon Rider for a Persnickety Princess     1

Fire and Redemption     44

Final Night, First Dawn     65

Bloodrider     84

Unexpected Benefits     112

Riders of Ervum     151

The Night the Moon Fell From the Sky     186

The Lost Dragons of Mirstone     219

Dragon Unchained     245

Dreams of the Lost     269

Riders Rebirth     315

Rebirth     333

Wings Across Realms     365

# INTRODUCTION

Welcome to the third anthology set in the world of Mirstone!

In the first one, we did lots of world building, and with the second one, we explored magic and magical items. For this one, we're doing quests! Whether it's a journey to be rid of demons, or a flight on an airship to retrieve a friend, this anthology has quests of all kinds!

Happy reading!

-Richard

# Wanted: One Dragon Rider
# for a Persnickety Princess
### A.R. Cook

Quinn threw open the doors to the grand chamber, where a mountainous horde of gold, silver, and jewels shimmered in the torchlight like a million-starred galaxy. It was not the guardian's first rescue, which might have explained the slight sigh of tedium.

*A knight, a damsel, and a dragon. Like I haven't heard that one before*, Quinn thought. *I wonder if we all should just walk into a tavern...*

The tall, foreboding figure of Voranthian loomed large, and he turned to see who had intruded into his claimed domain. Iron-black scales clinked as he moved, claws clacked as he flexed his hands, and he raised high his head, atop which were two curved horns. "Ah, another fool challenges me. Quickblade Quinn, isn't it? I suppose the temptation of a dragon's horde is too much for even you to resist?"

Quinn tucked back a stray lock of brown hair. "Not really, Voranthian. You can have the horde. I'm just here for the princess."

Voranthian's dark eyes narrowed in confusion. "The... what, that pale, weak thing? Honestly, I was only keeping her around for the singing. Although she's quite shrill when prodded to sing."

From the corner of the chamber, a pair of wide, blue eyes peeked from the shadows. The sound of iron chains sliding against the floor accompanied the light grunts of struggling. An airy voice cried out, "Oh, Quinn! You see, you big brute? I knew my guardian would come for me! Now you're in for it!"

Voranthian laughed, a deep, abysmal bellow. "Am I? This pathetic whelp barely comes armored! And what measly dagger is that in your sheath, a blade of grass? Here I heard such rumors, that Quickblade Quinn can slay an army in one thrust, and what I get is some delusional performer playing dress up!"

Quinn stretched with a long, lazy yawn. "About those rumors… sure, I slay, but I'd much rather educate."

The black-scaled enemy paused. "Educate? Who, me? Oh, I see. Yes, there have been many that tried to coerce me into subservience. But I made quick work of them, as I will of you."

"Do what you will," Quinn drawled, gesturing *come at me* with one hand.

"Impudent cur!" With a roar of fury, Voranthian bore down on Quinn, claws outstretched in front of him to snare his quarry. Quinn easily side-stepped the bulky opponent, who barreled several feet passed and had to take a few seconds to turn around. Before Voranthian could fully pivot, Quinn retrieved a silver shield from the treasure horde and flung it, whacking the foe right in the head. There was a sharp, resonant clanging as the shield hit his horns, and Voranthian was both literally and figuratively rattled.

"Now, you see, I don't teach oversized swine like you for servitude," Quinn said, with a sharp crack of knuckles. "I just think you need to learn some manners. For example, locking up the poor princess for your own private serenades. That's rude."

Once he regained his composure, Voranthian raised his clenched fists high, planning to smash Quinn's skull. The swordfighter, again, dodged the attack as Voranthian's fists slammed into the floor, riddling it with cracks.

"Be careful, Quinn!" Princess Camellia called, as she tugged at the chains binding her to the wall.

From a secret tunic pocket, Quinn withdrew three long, silver pins. "Let me introduce you to my lessons. Lesson one: Bigger does not mean better. In fact, being bigger makes you react slower."

Quinn demonstrated this as Voranthian came in for another

blow, but his claws met only air. In an almost dance-like fashion, the guardian waltzed out of the way and snuck behind him. "Lesson two: stealing is a crime, even if it is a dragon horde. The royal dragon family took centuries to amass their fortune, and you have no right to take it."

Voranthian growled, turning to lash out again. "Who cares if I steal the horde of some stupid dragons? It's mine now! I don't have to serve my idiot king anymore. I can buy my own kingdom!"

"Lesson three: Always be a courteous host. Locking up the future dragon queen is a big no-no, even if you call yourself a knight."

This time, Sir Voranthian felt it – a small sting in his armpit, one of the few places his scale mail armor did not protect him. He realized, as Quinn raised two empty hands, that the pins were gone. No, not gone - stuck in the back of his neck (lesson one), the side of his knee (lesson two), and his armpit (lesson three). He faltered, realizing that the pins had been soaked in some drug. He fell limp to the ground, as his horned helmet fell from his head and clattered on the floor. His clawed gauntlets, which often proved to be as deadly as his sword, proved useless now as he landed face first with a heavy thud.

"Woo hoo! I knew you'd best that beastly knight," the princess called. "You'll have to teach me those moves someday, Mistress Quinn."

Quinn walked over to the captive, withdrawing a lockpick from her belt pouch. She located the rusty padlock that kept the princess in chains and began picking at it. "There's plenty you'll need to learn as a dragon queen, Princess Camellia. For one, don't take on a knight by yourself until you've grown a bit more."

Princess Camellia hung her equine head, which given her long, serpentine neck, was nearly down to her toes. Her cherry blossom-pink scales had not yet hardened with age, but her slender wings had recently grown in their flight feathers. Roughly the height of a moose at the shoulder, she was a far cry from the stature of her parents, but she could be a handful, nonetheless. "I know, but dragons are supposed to protect the family treasury. And with Mum and Dah away—"

"Don't worry, that's why they asked me to protect you," Mistress Quinn said, as the padlock to the chains clicked open. She gently unwound Camellia from her bindings. "You can help me drag this lug out of here. Traitors to the crown usually fetch a reward of 10,000 gold coins. After Lazulo and I turn him in, we can go goblin hunting. How's that?"

Camellia happily clapped her paws together. "Quinn, you are such fun!"

\*

The princess's happy demeanor, however, was not to last. She sighed as she laid languidly on the cushions in her bedchamber while Quinn sorted through their newly acquired bounty. The woman had just returned with Lazulo, her grey highland pony, who deserved a restful graze in the mountainside pasture after carrying the dead weight of Voranthian for almost a whole day to the city. The dragons of the Mooncrest colony knew to leave the horse alone, thanks to the Dragon King and Queen, so Quinn often made quick trips with Lazulo to nearby towns for supplies or spoils. The ex-mercenary had to make such expeditions by herself, of course— bringing Camellia into town would have done more than raise some eyebrows.

"Why are you moping now?" Quinn asked, not even bothering to look up at the dragon. She sorted the reward into thirds, two of which would go into the royal dragon treasury, and a third for herself.

Camellia grumbled irritably. "Mum and Dah will never take

me seriously if I can't even fend off one dumb intruder. Promise you won't tell them?"

"I won't tell, Princess. But don't be so hard on yourself. You haven't been trained to deal with knights, rogue or otherwise."

"Well, maybe I should be." Camellia lifted her head. "Until I can breathe fire, I should have other means to defend myself. Oooh, how about a mace? The spiky kind! You could get me one of those, can't you?"

Quinn gave Camellia a stern look. "No respectable dragon goes about smashing things with a mace. And you're a dragon royal. You have your duties."

"I *hate* my duties!" Camellia flopped her head back down on her cushions. "And I hate this stinky old mountain, with its stinky old caves, full of stinky old treasure. I wanna have fun."

Quinn repressed a groan. "You just knocked down twenty goblins in the underground caverns like you were playing skittles—"

"They're slow. Too easy." Camellia pouted. "Stinky, slow goblins."

Quinn sometimes regretted that she had read Camellia bedtime stories when she was a hatchling. The young dragon had formed an unusual attachment to fairy tales of princesses in high towers with beautiful singing voices and a penchant for flowers, pillows, and ribbons. She practiced singing during the times her parents were away to the hunting grounds, and she asked Quinn to teach her things like reading and needlepoint—which she quickly gave up on the latter after she poked herself with the sewing needle enough times. Quinn had, unintentionally, truly made a diva out of the reptilian royal, down to the princess changing her name to one she preferred instead of what her parents had in mind: "Gwaedlyd the Bloody Claw? Blegh, I hate it! I choose Camellia Cloudblossom, and I won't go by anything else! I won't, I won't, I won't!"

Quinn still remembered the look on the Dragon King and Queen's faces at this announcement. Why they hadn't devoured Quinn right there and then for putting those "human ideas" into Camellia's head was a mystery. She reached over to pick up a large leather pack sitting on the floor. "Then how about you help me sort through Voranthian's effects here? He conveniently left it behind. Might be something fun in here."

Camellia snorted in response.

Quinn rolled her eyes. She figured the one thing a mercenary and a dragon would have in common is the thrill of looting, but Princess Camellia was the least loot-loving reptile she'd ever seen. She started rifling through the pack. "Hmm… dagger, crossbow, bolts, spoon, socks, ew—flask, jerky, another spoon, comb, small spoon, long spoon, a scroll…" She unfurled the scroll, wondering if it might have any valuable information. She frowned. "Ugh, an invitation to the tournament? As if any dragon could hold that lug's weight. Anyway, spoon, spoon, what's with all the spoons?"

Camellia's head slightly raised. "An invitation to what?"

Quinn began shoving the loot back in the bag, finding nothing of interest. "Oh, a dragon riders' tournament. They hold one every year in Torvel."

The princess lazily reached over and picked up the scroll. She could read a little, thanks to Quinn's lessons, but it wasn't the words that caught her attention. The beautiful illustration of a mighty dragon soaring through the air, with a proud, caped human rider on its back, against a brilliant golden sun… she could practically smell the clean air, feel the cool wind, see the grand expanse of green world below.

"Aren't tournaments some kind of game?" Camellia asked.

Quinn shrugged. "I suppose."

"And the winners get pretty ribbons? Oooh, or a wreath of flowers? And everyone cheers and applauses and loves them?"

"Yes, I—" Quinn paused, and shot Camellia a hard stare. "No."

Camellia practically leapt onto Quinn, who managed to evade the excited dragon. "I wanna go! Pretty pretty pleeeeeeease? Come on, Quinn! Quinn Quinn Quinn Quinn Quinn—"

Quinn pushed back the princess, who was trying to give her an affectionate nose nuzzle. "Your parents would kill both of us if we did. What on earth do you want to go for?"

"Because it's exciting! And I'm tired of being trapped in the mountains."

"You want to watch a bunch of dragons and their riders fly around in circles? Honestly, it's one of the dullest things in the world. Besides, they don't exactly have dragon-sized seating in those arenas. There'd be no way for you to watch."

Camellia grunted, exasperated. "I don't want to watch. I want to compete!"

"Then *definitely* no."

The princess stuck out her lower lip in a pout. "Don't worry, Mistress Quinn. Mum and Dah don't have to know. They won't be back from the hunting grounds until the end of the month. And this…" She held up the scroll and shoved it in Quinn's face, "says the games are during the Springsfaire, which is the first day of spring, in five days."

Quinn raised an eyebrow. "How do you know spring starts in five days? You don't have an almanac."

"I can tell by the snow on the mountaintop. It's melted a few claws' lengths, and the moon crocuses are popping up. They always pop up one week before spring, and that was two days ago. So, there are five more days until spring." Camellia puffed out her chest and grinned from scaly ear to ear.

Quinn was rather impressed that the princess knew the terrain so well, it even told her what exact time of the season it was, but that cleverness still didn't convince her. "Listen, there is a litany of reasons you can't compete. First of all, dragon riders and their dragons take years to train. They practically start from the time the dragon has hatched. Second, this tournament is only for competitors of noble blood. Elites."

"I'm elite!" Camellia retorted. "I'm a princess, for roaring out loud!"

"The dragon *rider* has to be of nobility, not the dragon," Quinn said. "And, thirdly, a dragon needs a rider. And in case you didn't notice, you have no rider."

The words barely left Quinn's mouth before she knew what would happen next. Camellia gave her the biggest, shiniest, puppy-dog eyes a dragon could muster. "Yoooooooooou could be my rider!" Camellia said in a sing-songy, sweet voice. "Oooh, wouldn't that be so fun? And I hear dragons and their riders have close bonds, like, a soul-bond kind of thing. We'd be like… sisters! Don't you want to be my big sister?"

Quinn almost chuckled at the thought—*a dragon for a sister, I'd never hear the end of it*—but she retained her stoic expression. "I can't be a dragon rider."

Camellia stamped one of her feet, and it shook the room. "WHY NOT??" Her voice was no longer sweet.

Quinn rolled her eyes, shoving her hands into her trouser pockets. "Because… I can't fly dragonback. I'm scared of heights."

The dragon's anger quickly softened. "Oh. Well, then, I guess it wouldn't work. I'd hate to put you in a scary position. I won't make you do it, Quinn. Because I care about you, like I know you care about me."

"Thank you, princess."

Quinn thought that would be the end of it, but Camellia's composed façade dropped away a few seconds later, as she threw herself onto her cushions in a full-body tantrum. "BUT I REALLY

WANNA GO!!" She smashed her face into a pillow and started sobbing loudly, a little too loudly. She thumped her tail on the floor, and her whole body heaved with each dramatic blubber.

Quinn sighed. Camellia's theatrics were nothing new to her; if Camellia had developed her fire-breathing yet, the whole room would probably be torched by now. But the last time she threw a tantrum like this, she had caused an avalanche that covered the Mooncrest colony's nesting grounds for weeks until the dragons could melt all the snow, and if the King and Queen came back to that… "Look, I can't be your rider. But I know someone who could find you one."

Camellia's face became all smiles and adoring eyes. "Oh, Quinn, you're the best!"

*

"Are we there yet? My feet hurt."

Quinn rolled her eyes. "Does it look like we're anywhere yet?"

She rode Lazulo as he and Camellia trudged through deep woodland, where the ground had become boggy with soft peat. Barely any sunlight could penetrate the thick canopy above, where garlands of moss danged from branches like curtains of witches' hair. It was nowhere near the fairytale forests that Camellia had heard about—more like a place where icky ogres or trolls lived. Occasionally, a faint sound of scurrying animal feet or an ominous crow call made the dragon freeze, and she darted her gaze about in panic.

Quinn smirked. "You know there isn't anything out here that would be a threat to you, right? You're the top of the food chain."

"Well, one can't be too careful. You say so yourself." Camellia stepped into an especially goopy pile of mud. She swallowed back a gag as she shook the mud off her foot. "This would have been so much easier if I could've flown us to… wherever we're going. But noooooo, my brave guardian won't fly with me. I've never had to walk this much in my whole life! And now I'm dirty, and hungry, and cold, and—"

"You wanna play a game?"

Camellia perked up. "Oh, yes, you know I do!"

Quinn turned and gave her a pointed look. "Let's play the 'quiet game'."

Camellia's expression soured instantly. "I don't like that one. You always win!"

Somehow, for the next half-mile, Quinn managed to tune out the princess's complaints until she spotted it through the trees: a shanty, crudely built from driftwood, daub, thatch, and bits of broken metal. Attached to the shanty was something like a workshop but shaped like a giant chimney, square at the bottom and leading up into a tall stack built from clay brick and stone. Smoke billowed from the chimney, which had been the marker that Quinn had followed for miles to find the place—most travelers skirted around the boglands rather than pass through them, so the owner of this dilapidated home didn't worry about unwanted guests finding him.

Camellia wrinkled her nose. "I thought I smelled something awful. I figured it was swamp brimstone or something."

"There's no such thing as swamp brimstone, princess."

"Well, there is now! And it's coming from there!" The dragon pointed at the shanty. "Who lives there? Some kind of witch? A troll? A swamp beast with pus-filled boils?"

Quinn rolled her eyes. "I'm going to stop reading you those bedtime stories. They're giving you a wild imagination." She dismounted Lazulo and started to walk up to the shanty, but Camellia blocked her way with her tail. The dragon mewed anxiously, wringing her hands together. Quinn patted Camellia's tail. "Relax, there's nothing so beastly in there as you think.

Although 'troll' is a remarkably good guess."

The mercenary knocked three times on the wooden door, which trembled with each knock as the rusty hinges threatened to give way. A gruff, raspy voice barked from within the shanty. "Go away! If you're looking for the main road, you're so damned lost, even the Wayfarer Gods can't help you."

Camellia's body went rigid, and her ears flattened against her head. "We should leave."

But Quinn waved *it's fine* and called through the door. "It's me, Grandpa."

A long moment of silence passed, before the sound of a latch sliding came from the other side of the door. It opened an inch, and an eye framed by sallow, wrinkled skin peered out. "Dear Gods, ain't seen you in ages, Quinn." His voice suddenly dropped low, heavy with suspicion. "What's all this, then? Lookin' to pluck a few guilders from my pockets? Times is tough. I ain't a baron, you know."

"Last time I saw you, you were the one asking for the handout," Quinn reminded the old man. "Anyway, my friend here needs some help. She needs a dragon rider scout. And before you ask, yes, I'll make it worth your while." She reached into a pouch on her belt and withdrew a small coin purse, which she jingled enticingly.

The door opened farther, and what appeared to be mostly man stepped out. Mostly, since parts of him were not flesh and blood, but metal and glass. While his one good eye had an iris of dark brown, the other was made of amber glass with emerald-green swirled into it, set into an eye-plate of copper that covered the upper-right side of his face. His left hand was crafted from steel, with long spindly fingers compared to the bulky sausages of his fleshy right hand. One leg was an iron peg from the knee down. What else of him was flesh or fake, it was hard to say, as he wore a long-sleeved tunic, dark trousers, and a heavy boot on the good foot. An ash-gray cowl covered his head and shoulders, and a leather apron was tied around his waist. He was shorter than Quinn, although that might have been due to his hunched-over stance.

"As long as you're here," he grumbled, snatching the coin purse from Quinn, "Would you mind windin' me? It's such a pain in my arse to reach around to do it." He turned around to reveal, sticking out through the back of his tunic, a series of wind-up keys placed in spots down his spinal cord. Quinn turned each key fully around three times. A soft clicking came from within the man, and he slowly straightened up with a few cracks of bone and grinds of metal. "There we go. Now…" He turned back around, and only now noticed the dragon sitting a few yards away. "What's with the giant flamingo?"

Camellia stared at the clockwork man with wide eyes—it was hard to tell if her stare was in fascination or horror.

Quinn went to her and reached up to pat her shoulder. "Grandpa Edsel, this is Princess Camellia Cloudblossom. Her parents are the King and Queen of the dragon colony in the Mooncrest Mountains. She wants to find a dragon rider."

The old man pursed his lips into an amused grin. "Oh, has she, now? For one of her guard-dragons, I suppose. Not the first time those dragons have hired human help, eh?" He snickered, jabbing Quinn in the side with his elbow. "Those Mooncrest lizards are a funny lot."

Camellia cleared her throat, holding her head high and extending her head crest in regal splendor. "Actually, my good m…man? I am in the market—figuratively speaking, of course— for securing an experienced dragon rider from a reputable lineage for myself. I also require at least two references to vouch for their good character and work ethic."

Edsel gave Camellia a cock-eyed glare, and then he proceeded to laugh so hard he nearly hacked up a lung—or whatever might have been installed in place of a lung. "Ah ha, that's a new one! I ain't never seen any dragon so prissy in all my life! Barely out of the egg, are you now? And so proper-like. Usually, I just get a, 'give me what I want or I'll bite your head off' from you reptiles, but you're more snoot than snout, ain't you?"

Camellia grimaced and lifted her nose into the air. "You forget yourself. You are speaking to a princess, and I don't have to demonstrate patience with the likes of you, even if you are Quinn's grandfather. It is only because I like Quinn so much that I don't… uh… that I don't tell my Dah and Mum how rude you are to me!"

"Oooh no, you wouldn't tattle on me, would you?" The old man clutched a hand to his chest in mock fright. "Oh, poor old Edsel, being snitched on by the world's largest plucked turkey!"

"Okay, that's enough!" Quinn thwacked Edsel on the back of the head. "Stop it before you make her cry. Now, do you know anyone around here who might make a good dragon rider, or not?"

Edsel rubbed the back of his head, grousing. "Any reason her 'nanny' won't—"

Quinn shot him a death glare. "I'm not a dragon rider, remember? My fear of heights?"

Edsel raised an eyebrow at her. "Riiiight. So, what're you wantin' a dragon rider for? Looking to enlist in the royal troops? Or are you just lookin' for a pet?"

Camellia frowned. "If you must know, I'm going to compete in the dragon riding tournament in a few days, and I can't do that without a rider."

Edsel's amusement switched into bewilderment. "The tournament? Quinn, you've told this one she's loony, right?"

Quinn sighed irritably. "You can't tell her 'No' once she's dead-set on something."

"Well, ain't my business if she wants to bust every bone in her body." He rubbed his chin in thought. "There's a spot in Stonewell right outside these boglands that's a good place to start. But let me make something clear, *princess*," he said, his demeanor hardening as he fixed his good eye on Camellia. "This has nothin' to do with references, or good lineage. I've seen the most pathetic riders come from renown family lines, and the best come from nothing. This is about heart. I can spot a true rider from a mile away, so you trust my judgment and don't get all haughty with me, got it?"

The dragon gulped but maintained her poise. "Y-yes. But it's still my choice in the end, so what I say goes."

"Deal." Edsel gave Camellia a quick glance-over, up and down. "So, where's your harness and saddle?"

"My... what?"

The old man wiped a hand over his face. "By the gods... wait here, I might have something in the workshop that'll fit an overgrown prawn."

*

The sound of lances shattering as they clashed against shields made Camellia flinch. She had heard of jousting before but hadn't understood it was quite so... violent. She was watching from a safe distance, of course, at the tree-line of the forest that was a stone's throw from the outdoor arena down the hill. Quinn stayed with her, while Edsel had gone down to the arena to scout out the combatants of the day. He had told them this was an unsanctioned jousting arena, a place where anyone could train, noble or peasant—for a small fee, of course. One had to provide their own horses and armor, and the only weapons allowed had to be made of wood and be sanded blunt so as to avoid any fatal injuries. The peasant sons who saved up enough money for their own equipment would come here for a chance at jousting that they wouldn't get otherwise, and the noble sons enjoyed showing off in a more rugged setting away from their parents' invasive eyes—a bit of scandalous freedom.

"I hope they don't have any ale down there," Quinn groused. "If so, he won't be back for hours."

"This thing is so itchy!" Camellia complained, reaching around to scratch under the leather saddle strapped to her back. "It's too tight! And must it be so ugly? Maybe some leather roses sewn along the sides, or some silver bells—"

"Saddles need to be a little tight, so they don't shift during flight," Quinn said. "And it's purely for function, not a fashion statement."

"It wouldn't be a bad idea to make them a little fashionable," Camellia retorted. "After all, I want to look my best when I win the tournament."

"How about finding a rider before deciding you're winning anything?" Quinn narrowed her gaze on the arena. They could see the action well enough, but it was tricky to determine who was who. "See anyone promising?"

"Oooh, I like the one in the green tunic!" the princess said. Her eyesight could see farther than Quinn's, and she was watching the various pairs of fighters with keen interest. "He's very handsome, for a human. And he's a good fighter, which must make him brave. Or maybe the one with the red sash, he's the tallest. A tall rider would look good on me. But maybe the one in the light blue would match my scales better—"

"Dear gods, Camellia, you're talking about them like they're accessories!"

The dragon gave Quinn a curious look. "The dragon does all the work on a dragon riding team, right? So what else is a rider for?"

After a time, Edsel came trudging up the hill, which was no

easy feat for him with only one good leg. "Eh, it's slim pickings from this group of pups. I asked the proprietor who seemed the most promising warrior, and he says it's the boy Aeros. His father's Lord Valence, who comes from a long line of soldiers. Seems a bit green to me, but there's potential. Handles a horse like he was born in the saddle."

"*I* am not a horse!" Camellia reminded him. "But which one is he? Please say he's the pretty one!"

Edsel rolled his good eye. "He's the one in the armor, with the blue and yellow tabard."

The dragon lifted her head higher to look, and she eventually spotted the one. "He is… shiny. And tall enough. And he is quite good with a lance. Yes, I could make that work."

"But is he going to panic if he sees a dragon?" Quinn asked skeptically.

"No one will panic if they see *this* one," Edsel said. "But I'll talk to 'im. I'll tell 'im a dragon rider from the tournament can't participate anymore and is looking for someone to fill in. Say his dragon's got to compete in order to be considered for the King's Keep. I'll see if he's interested. And if he is, I'll bring 'im over, but for gods' sake, *don't say anything.*" He shot Camellia a stern look, then turned around and walked down the hill.

"Yeesh, your grandfather's a grump," Camellia muttered.

Quinn leaned her back against a tree. "Can't blame him much, given what he's been through."

Camellia knitted her brow in confusion, but then it dawned on her. "Oh, I see. How did he, you know, lose all those… parts? Was he in a war?"

"Actually, yes, but that's not how he got dismembered. You… probably don't want to know how."

"If you're going to put it that way, then *yes,* I want to know!" The dragon crossed her arms. "You can't say 'you don't want to know' and not expect me to want to know even more."

Quinn sighed. "Dragons."

Camellia placed a hand to her chest, her jaw dropping open in mortification. "Noooo! Which dragons? Not Mooncrest dragons!"

"No, not Mooncrest. But not all dragons are like you." Quinn stared down at the arena. "Keep that in mind when you're in the tournament. Those dragons are trained to win, by any means necessary."

Camellia's face paled a little. She took a deep breath and lifted her chin in resolve. "Thank you for the tip, but I'm still doing it. After all, I'm a princess. Trained dragons or not, they will know to treat a royal with respect."

Quinn shook her head but was silent. The tournament would be a lesson for Camellia, one way or the other. She'd either come out of it a little more humbled, or too frightened or humiliated to ever venture away from the Mooncrest Mountains again. And frankly, either would be good for her.

*

"Is that a… pink dragon?" Aeros Valence gawked at Camellia with pure awe. "Those are supposed to be extremely rare! Whoever caught her was extremely lucky, or blessed by the gods."

Camellia couldn't help but smile—*this boy knows a special dragon when he sees one!*—but she kept quiet while Edsel spoke to the young man, who couldn't have been more than sixteen years old. Aeros was of modest, sleek build, with cropped blonde hair and hazel-green eyes. His infectious smile was so pure, it could have turned pigswill to spring water.

"Nah, this one was acquired as an egg," Edsel said. "The owner says they thought they were buyin' an earth drake egg. It was a one-in-a-million chance. But you can see why they want this dragon in the tournament; no doubt the king would pay a handsome sum to have her in his Keep. But he wants to show she also has dragon riding potential—she's a bit on the young side, but she'll put on a show for sure."

Aeros glanced over at Quinn. "Are you her owner?"

Quinn huffed a laugh. "No one owns Camellia. She does what she wants."

Camellia gave a quick nod in agreement, lifting her nose in the air.

"I… see." Aeros grinned. "I've never ridden a dragon before, so I'll need some practice. Has she been trained?"

"Not a lick."

Aeros blinked in surprise. "And her owner wants to enter her in the tournament now? I think they should wait a few years until she's trained. How does Camellia feel about this?" He looked at Camellia. "You can speak, can't you?"

"She was born mute, the poor thing," Edsel quickly cut in.

Camellia shot him a dirty look.

"But I've been assigned to train you both," Edsel added. "Used to train new rider blood in my day. I can get you up to speed on the most basic challenges in the tournament. The flight course, the agility track, target shooting on dragonback. Easy stuff."

"That sounds fine by me, but it's still important to know how she feels about it." Aeros looked Camellia in the eyes. "I can see you understand what we're saying. Do you feel like you're ready? Because if not, then I won't agree to it. But if so, then I will work very hard over the next few days so we can both be as ready as possible. Nod for yes, or shake your head for no. Do you want to do this?"

*Oh, he's so sweet. But so young,* Camellia thought. *It doesn't feel right to give him so little time to prepare. But I want to compete so badly!* She nodded.

Aeros nodded back, and after a moment of thought, he took a

breath and smiled. "All right then. My family has lots of open field on our estate. We can train there. My father is away on business, so the timing is perfect. We'll start first thing in the morning."

"Glad to hear it, boy. Let us work out the details over some dinner at the local tavern, eh? My treat. Quinn, look after the… Fushia Fury! That's what her tournament name will be!"

Edsel and Aeros walked off down the hill towards town. Camellia gave Quinn a sour look. "The *Fushia* Fury? I'm not fushia, I'm pale rose!"

"Hey, you asked for this. What would you have called yourself, the Pink Princess?"

"Of course! The Pink Power Princess—that's so much better. I'll have to tell Edsel when he gets back."

*

Edsel returned later, lugging a parcel of tavern food for Quinn and Camellia, and they all walked back to Edsel's home for the night. Camellia managed to just fit through Edsel's front door, although she broke the door off its precarious hinges as she entered. Thankfully, the single-room shack was large enough for her to sit on one side of the room, while Quinn and Edsel sat across at the small kitchen table. There was a small bed against one wall, and Edsel had set down a thin mat and a quilt by the hearth. He had offered for Quinn to take the bed for the night, but Quinn refused. "I'll take the mat, thanks. It doesn't have old-crotchety-man smell."

Edsel started a modest fire in the hearth, and Camellia stared wistfully at the dancing flames. Soon, she'd be able to breathe fire, just like the other dragons in her colony. A thought occurred to her. "Fire-breathing isn't going to be one of the challenges, is it? Because… I could do it, I really could, except I have a bit of a cold, and I…"

"Relax. Wouldn't be fair to have a fire-breathing challenge. Dragons have all kinds of elemental breath, not just fire." Edsel took a jug of ale from the parcel and popped the cork for a swig. "We'll get you up to speed on the basics."

Camellia was quiet for a minute. "So… you said you used to train dragon riders and dragons. Was training dragons how you lost your—"

Quinn narrowed her eyes at Camellia in warning, but Edsel just shrugged. "Eh, you can't work in the Hatchery without losing a few pieces over the years."

"The Hatchery? Where's that?"

"In the King's Keep. It's sort of like a royal stable for dragons, where they're trained, bred, and cared for. Years ago, I was the caretaker of the Keep's Hatchery. Looked after all the eggs. I would be there when young dragon riders in training would come, once the dragons hatched, and the hatchlings would choose their riders."

"Wait, the *hatchlings* chose the riders? Wouldn't they be too young to know who'd be the right choice?"

Edsel gave Camellia a knowing glance. "But that's the magical thing. A bond between a rider and dragon is special. A dragon knows from day one who they're going to bond with. No doubts, no questions. If the dragon doesn't choose you…" His face softened, sorrow etched into its creases. "Then you ain't meant for it."

Quinn tapped her fingers on the table. "Maybe we should talk about something else—"

"No, wait, this is interesting." Camellia scooted closer to Edsel. "So, a dragon just knows who their rider will be? But… what if a hatchling doesn't choose anyone? Or, if someone who wants to be a dragon rider goes there, and none of the hatchlings chooses them? Then what?"

Edsel was quiet for a long moment, but then responded, "Then, you accept it. You can't force a bond. And you're happy for those who get to have one."

Something clicked with Camellia. She may not know everything about humans, but she could read the story in Edsel's face. Such sadness, such longing. She looked over at Quinn, and the woman nodded, confirming Camellia's suspicions. The dragon looked back at Edsel. "What if… what if it isn't the right brood? Or the right time? Maybe, if someone tries a different brood of hatchlings…"

"When you're there through twenty-five years, over a hundred different broods, and not a one even looks your way… you eventually decide to not let your heart be broken anymore." Edsel got up from the table and hobbled towards his workshop. "I better finish with the harness. You'll need it for tomorrow."

After he shut the door behind him, Camellia looked at Quinn and spoke in a hushed voice. "But that's not fair!"

Quinn shrugged. "Welcome to life, princess."

"But if someone wants to bond with a dragon that badly, they should be able to. They shouldn't have the chance taken from them!"

Quinn sat in silence, as if lost in thought. "Not everything is a fairy tale. Not everyone gets a happy ending."

"Quinn? You okay?"

"I'm fine. You better get to sleep. Big day tomorrow." She stood up and went over to the mat, and picked up the quilt. She brought it to Camellia, throwing it over the dragon's back, before going back to the mat and lying down. The dragon curled up on the floor, but she watched Quinn sleep, and listened to Edsel moving about in the workshop. She didn't like people being sad. And she didn't like feeling powerless to change it.

*

The first training session was bumpy, but both dragon and dragon rider made great strides for being completely new to the concept and partnership. Aeros proved to be an astute student, and his experience with horseback riding proved to translate well into dragon riding. Camellia, despite the constant look on her face that indicated she wanted to protest Edsel's strange teaching methods, managed to hold her tongue. The three of them spent hours in the fields of Lord Valence's estate, Camellia learning the proper gait while Aeros shot at hay bale targets with his bow and arrow. When it came to flying, the dragon princess was a bit shaky at first— getting off the ground with additional weight on her back was the hardest part for her—but instinct eventually kicked in and she was able to find her natural glide. She worked her way up to perform easy circles, figure-eights and even braved a vertical loop. Aeros, despite never having been airborne before, was clearly enjoying the thrill, with whoops and hollers of delights as the wind played with his hair.

Quinn stood by a fence at the edge of the field with Lazulo as he calmly grazed, while she watched the two students' progress. Only now, ever since Camellia's proclamation that she was going to compete in the tournament, did the woman feel like she could relax. Sure, Camellia and Aeros wouldn't win every challenge; there just wasn't enough time to learn everything. But it was clear the two of them were acclimating well, and they were having, dare she say it, fun. Even Edsel seemed to be in his element, shouting instructions and encouragement as if he had never stopped teaching.

The thought occurred to her… what if Camellia and Aeros actually bonded? She didn't even want to know how the Dragon King and Queen would feel about that. Not that they had ever expressed any opposition to Camellia ever bonding with a rider, but given how they had tasked Quinn with protecting the princess, how they hadn't wanted her venturing out into the wide, cruel world... given what had happened...

Quinn quickly dismissed the thought. No, they wouldn't bond, not in so short a time. The tournament would be over in a couple of days, then it was straight back to the Mooncrest Mountains, back to safety and the princess couldn't complain after that. Everything would be fine. Just fine.

By the second day, Aeros and Camellia were learning how to simplify and quicken their communication. The boy learned how to steer and guide the dragon without the need to tell her what he wanted—light tugs with the harness, or gentle taps with his heels against her sides let her know which direction to go. Edsel watched the silent communication for a while as Camellia performed a canter, but eventually shook his head.

"Stop, stop," he said. "That's all well and good for horses, but a dragon rider and his dragon need to be perfectly in sync with each other. You'll need to make split-second decisions that a tug on the reins or a kick won't be fast enough to communicate. We'll need to work on your mind-tether."

"I think I've heard of that," Aeros said. "But doesn't mind-tethering take years to develop between rider and dragon?"

"Eh, that's for deep mind and soul connections. Surface-level tethering will be easy. It's all about trust." Edsel gestured for Aeros and Camellia to sit down, across from one another. "Now, Camellia, you need to initiate. Once you establish the mind-tether the first time, the connection becomes instant after that. Concentrate. Try to visualize Aeros' mind like a string, and you want to tie the end of your mind-string to his."

Camellia closed her eyes and scrunched her brow in concentration. For several minutes, she strained, grunted, and clenched her teeth and she tried to focus. Aeros tried to focus as well, but he looked over at Edsel with a shrug. Right before it looked like the dragon might pop a blood vessel in her forehead, Edsel barked at her. "That's enough! Dear gods, you're going to break your brain that way. Hmm… we're going to need a catalyst to open your mind. Quinn, come here."

Quinn jerked slightly, unprepared for the order. "What? What do you need me for?"

"You've known Camellia longer than anyone. There's already trust there. You can help her ignite her mind-tethering ability, and that'll make it easier for her to connect with Aeros."

The mercenary stepped back a few paces. "No, thank you. You've worked with dragons, you do it."

Edsel shook his head. "Doesn't work that way. It's got to be you, Quinn."

Aeros looked over at Camellia, who was staring imploringly at the woman. He turned his gaze to Quinn. "It would be helpful to us, Miss Quinn, if you would. I bet it would make Camellia feel better to mind-tether for the first time with someone she knows."

The dragon placed the palms of her hands together, in a *pretty please* signal.

Quinn closed her eyes and rubbed her temples. "Fine, just to get her used to it." She took Aeros's place, sitting down across from Camellia. Both woman and dragon closed their eyes to concentrate—

Quinn instantly knew she was not alone in her mind.

"H-hello? Quinn?"

The mercenary could hear Camellia's confused voice in her mindscape. Everything was blurry at first, but Quinn focused and brought the dragon's visage before her. Around them was an ocean of stars and soft lights, like a purple and magenta aurora borealis. They stood upon a clear, ripping surface, a lake of liquid silver. The dragon looked around in awe.

"Wow, is this your mind, Quinn?" Camellia craned her head around in all directions. "That was so easy! This whole mind-tether thing is a cinch. I wonder why I was having so much trouble with Aeros…"

"Okay, now you know what a mind-tether feels like," Quinn said. "Now, break the connection, and you can practice with Aeros."

"Now hold on! I just got here. I want to look around."

Quinn could feel a hot wave of irritation, and it was starting to send ripples through the lake at her feet. "This is supposed to be for surface-level communication. You don't need to delve any deeper. If you don't break the connection, I will, and it could be jarring for you if you're not prepared for it."

Camellia leaned her head forward, narrowing her eyes. "What's that, way out there? A boat?"

Quinn turned to look, and yes, there was the faint outline of a boat on the horizon of the lake. She recognized it instantly. "Yes. Back in my mercenary days, I traveled a lot. Wherever there was work. But see, now you're nibbling at my memories. You need to leave."

The dragon grinned in amusement. "Oooh, I can see your memories while I'm mind-tethered? Do you have any of me? I mean, of course you do, but any fun ones? Wait, you've seen so much more of the world than I have. What's your favorite place? What was your favorite memory?"

The lake beneath them rippled more violently. "Camellia, don't ask me—"

*This is what we call mind-tethering.*

The voice was not familiar to Camellia. She looked around for the source of the voice, and she saw something—someone— walking across the lake towards them. The figure was tall, taller than Camellia, with turquoise-green scales and an orange-yellow underside and wings. Two long yellow horns sprouted from his head, and he had the brightest green eyes that Camellia had ever seen. The dragon, for indeed that's what it was, walked right up to Quinn. He spoke in a male voice, kind and gentle. *When we mind-tether, we can hear each other's thoughts. We can have hours of conversation like this in our minds, while time only passes a moment out there with our bodies.*

"Quinn!" The pink scales around Camellia's face flushed red. "Who's this? He's... kinda cute. Have you been talking to strange, cute dragons without me?" She turned to the dragon. "You, where are you from? I've never seen you before. How do you know Quinn? And why are you mind-tethering to her when I'm doing it? I'm a princess, so I get that privilege!"

The strange dragon did not regard her at all. It just kept staring at Quinn, almost... in admiration. Camellia turned to Quinn for answers, but she fell silent as she saw the tense anxiety on Quinn's face. Quinn's voice echoed around them, but it didn't come from her mouth. *Wow, this is incredible! I've heard of mind-tethering, from my Grandpa Ed. This way, I can always know where you are and that you're okay.*

"Quinn? What's going on?" Camellia felt a coldness in her chest, as Quinn turned her gaze to the water under her.

Quinn was quiet for a long time. Slowly, the turquoise dragon faded into little more than shadow. "That was a memory," the woman replied. "You asked me for my favorite, and it just sort of... bubbled up in my mind."

"A memory? Oh, so he's not really here." Camellia felt a sense of relief wash over her.

"GET OUT!" Quinn's voice turned harsh, forceful. Her face twisted in rage. "Camellia, you need to leave! I'm ordering you to leave! I can't seem to boot you out myself... it's been so long since I had to... get out of my mind, right now!"

The dragon jerked, stepping back from Quinn. She had never seen her guardian be so angry, so scary. Camellia almost did break the connection—she hated to make Quinn upset—but then she felt it. In her skin, her bones… anguish, sorrow, pain. It was Quinn's. And Camellia realized she couldn't leave Quinn like that. She had to fix it. "Who… was that? Why does he make you so sad?"

Quinn looked like she would admonish Camellia again, but she paused. She looked back at the shadow of the dragon beside her, and he slowly materialized again, all his color radiant. Her fury and pain seemed to subside for the moment—Camellia could feel it.

"You know," Quinn said softly, "It's nice to see him again. I haven't thought… I've buried the memories for a long time. But this is good, in a way. And… Camellia, you have a right to know."

Camellia tilted her head. "Know what?"

As Quinn spoke, what she described formed around them, memories dancing in color and light like phantoms made of sunsets. The boat from before was suddenly beside them, as a younger Quinn and a gang of people disembarked from it. Younger Quinn was dressed in pieces of armor and thick leather and packed to the gills in knives and weapons. There was also something about her eyes that Camellia couldn't place at first… they were hard. Icy.

"I've told you I used to be a mercenary, but I never told you what kinds of jobs I did," Quinn said. "It was all kinds of things, anything to make quick coin. But what I and my fellow mercenaries excelled at was tracking. Tracking down enemies of the kingdom, soldiers who deserted… and one day, we were assigned to track down a new threat. A dragon. He had been spotted near some farmland, and he was considered a threat to the king's livestock. My group split up, and I found the dragon first. He was hiding in a barn."

The image of the turquoise dragon materialized, but now he

was a hatchling, shivering behind a bale of hay. He looked out at Quinn, terrified.

"But I could see how young he was." Quinn's voice turned wistful. "I knew if he grew, he really could become a threat. But I just… couldn't. It was letting a lot of money go, but I made the choice to let him escape. Sometime later, I had a falling out with my team, and I was living on my own. Found an old cottage in the woods that was abandoned, so I started living there. I woke up one day, and he was there, right outside my house."

The hatchling, now grown into a young dragon, looked at Quinn. He looked at her like a puppy would gaze at their owner.

"He said his name was Balter. He found me, somehow, and he said he was alone. He told me he got separated from his colony in an avalanche, and he was lost. His wings hadn't developed enough yet for him to fly. He didn't know where to go, and I could tell he needed protection. So, he stayed… for years." Quinn watched the young dragon instantly grow into the dragon that had first crept up from her memories. "And we looked after each other, we figured out how to mind-tether, and once his wings grew, we even practiced flying together. I thought once Balter could fly, he'd go back home, but he didn't want to leave. We sort of… we *did*…"

"Bond?" Camellia couldn't help but feel jealous of this, but she kept calm and repressed her grumbling. "So, what happened to him?"

What happened next, Quinn didn't need to say a word. She couldn't. Camellia saw a memory form, the image of Quinn and Balter at their cottage. Quinn was preparing to leave.

*Now, Balter, you stay right here in the cottage. Don't let anyone see you, and don't go anywhere until I come back. Understood?*

Balter nodded dutifully.

The memory shifted to Quinn, in town, buying some food from

the marketplace. She seemed so happy, selecting what she needed from various stalls. She selected some golden apples, since they were Balter's favorite—

*QUINN!!*

Just one word. That was all Quinn had heard, one word screamed out to her. Pure terror. Quinn dropped her parcels and sprinted, all the way through town, back towards the woods. *Balter, run away! Whatever it is, run, fly! Balter!*

She arrived home... and Camellia saw what Quinn had found. The princess had never seen... couldn't even fathom... she had never known real horror before, but now she knew. She only saw the dreadful image for half a second, however, before it flashed out of existence, and Quinn turned away. She wouldn't—couldn't—relive it.

"He stayed because I told him to," Quinn said, her voice broken. "By the time I told him to run, I could feel the mind-tether was already gone. I knew it was the other mercenaries. They had tracked me down, but they found him instead. Dragon parts can be worth a lot of money. If he hadn't bonded to me, if I hadn't told him to stay until I got back, he could've escaped..."

The pain, the suffering, flooded back into Camellia from Quinn. It was excruciating. Camellia hung her head, her gaze downcast. "I... I'm so sorry," she said.

"I remembered he had described his colony to me," Quinn continued. "Up in the mountains. He said he had family there. I knew it was only right his colony knew. So, I went to report his death... to Mooncrest."

"Mooncrest?" Camellia raised her head. "He was from my colony?"

"I knew the dragons might tear me apart for entering their territory, but when I told them it was Balter, they didn't attack me. They sent dragons to retrieve what was left of him. I was brought before his parents... the King and Queen of Mooncrest. I had no idea he was the prince."

Camellia felt like an electric shock went through her body. "The prince? But that means... he was Mum and Dah's... he was *my...?*"

"I told the king and queen that Balter and I had bonded, and I would accept any punishment from them for failing their son. Honestly, I was fully prepared to die, and I deserved it. But they didn't punish me. Instead, they saw the love I had for Balter, and they gave me a great responsibility. As I had taken in and protected their son all those years, I could atone for my failing by protecting their next child."

The image of a pale, pink dragon egg in a nest popped into existence. The watermelon-sized egg suddenly cracked, and a tiny hatchling spilled out of it. The baby dragon, all pink and pudgy, took a quick look around, and spotted Quinn. The little one shakily got up on her feet, wobbling with every attempted step. She waddled—no doubts, no questions—straight over to Quinn, and rubbed her little pink head against Quinn's leg.

Camellia was quiet as she took it all in. "But... why didn't anyone ever tell me about Balter?"

"It was too painful, for everyone," Quinn replied, sighing. "And I vowed not to bond again, not to get too close. I had to protect you impartially and stay at your side as much as I could. But it wasn't right to keep this from you. You deserve to—"

Before she could finish, Camellia whisked Quinn into a tight embrace, lifting the woman off her feet and the dragon practically crushed her against her chest. Cascades of tears fell down Camellia's face as she bawled. "OOOOHH QUINN! You were in all that pain and you couldn't tell me! But I always want you to tell me things! You're my big sister, Quinn! I love you so mu-u-u-u-ch!"

In an instant, they were out of Quinn's mind. Yet Camellia was still holding Quinn in a bear hug, bawling at the top of her lungs. Edsel and Aeros watched in perplexed silence, for to them, it looked like Camellia had embraced Quinn and started crying at the very moment they had sat down to concentrate.

"So…" Aeros said awkwardly. "Did it work, then?"

*

The tournament in Torvel was nothing short of glorious grandeur. The parade of excited spectators flooding into the arena was a stream of brightly colored apparel, children waving ribbon wands and paper dragons on strings, and vendor carts selling every sort of themed food: dragon puff pastries, pretzels shaped like flying serpents, wyvern-shaped cookies, and cockatrice chocolates. The arena itself was a marvel of stone with crimson, gold, and emerald awnings providing the best seats shade from the sunlight, as there wasn't a cloud in the sky that day. Flags with family crests of the competitors hung from poles around the arena stage—the stage itself was massive, almost five times the length of a standard jousting list field. One end of the arena was a towering wall with two fifty-foot-tall wooden doors, a barrier so tall that no one could see beyond it to the field on the other side. In that field were twenty of the most imperial and imposing dragons in the kingdom—well, nineteen imposing dragons and one not-so-imposing pink one.

Each dragon and their dragon rider had a designated pen in the field, and Camellia sat in the one labeled with the Valence family crest. It had been a surprise that Lord Valence's son had entered the competition last minute, and already word had rippled through the arena about the young competitor and his unique dragon. Camellia looked around at her fellow dragons—*my my, they are quite…BIG*—and tried not to shirk as some of them locked eyes with her and stared her down. All shades of blue, red, and green dragons surrounded her, and they all smelled of ferocity. She thought she heard a silver dragon chuffing—laughter—as it walked past her with its rider. Her unassuming appearance was farthest from her mind at the moment; she listened as Edsel gave Aeros some final instructions and words of encouragement. She could smell Aeros's nervousness, or maybe it was her own.

Edsel came over to her and patted her on the shoulder. "You'll do just fine, lass. Don't let them scare you. They're all pampered pets. You and Aeros focus on what you need to do. I'll get you some water."

Camellia wanted to ask him something, something that had been nagging at her for the last few days of training, but she had to keep up her mute façade. He hobbled away, and Aeros waited for him to be out of earshot before he came over to Camellia. "How are you feeling, Camellia? All right?"

Camellia nodded, although her eyes said otherwise. She reached out with her mind-tether. *Can I ask you something?*

The boy nodded and lowered his voice. "Of course, but you can ask me out loud if you'd rather. I could tell when I met you that you could talk. I thought maybe you were shy."

Camellia raised her eyebrows in surprise. "I think Edsel thought I might say something stupid to scare you off."

Aeros let out a laugh. "You're anything but stupid. Is something bothering you? Are you nervous? I promise, I won't push you any harder than you feel comfortable with. And if you want to stop competing at any point, just tell me."

"I am a bit nervous, but that's not what's bothering me." Camellia took a deep breath. "I'm afraid if I tell you, you might be sore with me."

The boy rubbed the dragon's side gently. "I won't be sore, whatever it is."

"Well…" Camellia gave him a crooked smile. "There's something I need to do…"

*

Quinn sat in one of the cheap seats, trying to remain as inconspicuous as possible. She didn't like not being with Camellia, but only dragon riders and their trainers were allowed in the competitor field. She crossed her arms, trying to ignore the screams and cheers of the audience around her, as a peanut sailed through the air and bounced off her head.

"Quite a crowd today, eh?" said someone that sat down next to her.

Quinn tightened her lips, not wanting to engage in conversation, but when she looked over… "Aeros? What are you doing here? The tournament's going to start any minute!"

The boy smiled at her. "Camellia and I had a chat. And she felt like it was only right to have a different dragon rider. And I agreed with her."

"A different dragon rider? Who on earth…"

With a blast of trumpets and fanfare, the two giant wooden doors on the far end of the field slowly opened. In trotted the procession of dragons and their riders, each rider carrying a shield painted with their crest. At the very end of the line, the smallest dragon, head held high and rosy scales glistening in the sun, pranced in with a new rider on her back. There was confused murmuring mixed in among the cacophonous cheers of the audience. *Wasn't the pink dragon supposed to be ridden by Lord Valence's son? That's not Aeros Valance! Who is that? Isn't that…*

"Grandpa?" Quinn could barely squeak out the name. Her mortification was short-lived, however. Even from the cheap seats, she could see Edsel's face, for he pulled back his cowl to uncover his head. He scanned the cheering crowd, let the sunlight shine on his face and silvery hair for the first time since who knew when. And he smiled. Even his one good eye smiled. Quinn couldn't remember the last time—any time—he had smiled like that.

"Camellia asked for Grandpa to be her rider?" Quinn asked.

Aeros nodded. "You should've seen his face when she asked. You'd have thought someone had just asked him to be king."

Down in the arena, Camellia glanced back over her shoulder at Edsel and smiled. She touched his mind with her tether. *You ready, dragon rider?*

Edsel's mind was a jumble of thoughts, overwhelmed by the moment and the roaring crowd around him. Tears rimmed his eye, as it settled on him…*dragon rider*…the one thing he thought he would never be. The one dream he had surrendered so long ago. He forced his tears back and gave Camellia a nod. *Let's do this before my bones turn to dust*, he thought.

Somehow, above the crowd, above the excited gekkering of the dragons, above the trumpet fanfare, another sound boomed from above. A deep, thundering howl, a call that could have torn open the sky. A shadow passed over the arena, and everyone raised their gazes towards the sound.

Quinn's heart leaped into her throat. It was the largest dragon she had ever seen.

The giant reptile landed heavily onto the back wall of the arena, as its weight caused the wall to buckle and the parapet stones to fall. Charcoal-gray scales covered the beast, and eyes as red as garnets locked on the dragons in the arena. Spikes of obsidian poked out in a trail down its spine, from the nape of its neck down to the tip of its lashing tail that ended in a scorpion's curved stinger. It was a manifestation of nightmares, and its presence alone commanded all to freeze.

Edsel sharply sucked in air between his teeth. "Dear gods, Stormbreaker! I recognize that monstrosity anywhere. I was forced to match that beast to its rider, the spoiled son of that Duke Voranthian!"

Camellia's jaw dropped. "Voranthian? Big brute in armor, horned helmet, kind of dumb?"

"Exact—how do you know him?"

"Well, he tried to steal my family's gold, so Quinn whipped him and put him in jail for treason." Camellia grinned sheepishly. "Don't remember the dragon, though."

Edsel shook his head. "If Voranthian's in prison, he can still command his dragon through mind-tethering. He can even see through Stormbreaker's eyes. And my bet is, if Voranthian can't compete in the tournament, he's making sure nobody else can."

Stormbreaker swiveled its head from side to side in a hypnotic way, like a cobra. A strange sensation pulsed over the entire arena, and where everyone had been frozen in terror a moment ago, they now screamed and scrambled to escape. All the dragons in the arena, even the ones who had initially been prepared to stand their ground, suddenly shivered in fright and bolted, taking to the skies or plowing into the stands to evade the intruding monster. All except Camellia, who looked around in confusion.

"Why are they all running away? It's one dragon against twenty!" she called above the din.

Edsel was pale. He seemed to be struggling, sweat dripping down his face. "It's Stormbreaker... dragons of his ilk have a special ability to instill fear by their mere presence. His ability is especially potent. I've practiced for years in the Keep to withstand it, but..."

The ground rumbled as the gray dragon leapt down from the wall and landed squarely in front of Camellia. His head was nearly the same length as Camellia's body—he could have swallowed her in one gulp.

Quinn could feel the fear enchantment too, as it clouded her mind and willed her body to run. But seeing that beast so close to Camellia, its jaws mere inches from her ward, her fear was overruled. She jumped from her seat and made a beeline for the arena, drawing a concealed dagger from her tunic as she ran. Aeros willed himself to stay, but he couldn't uproot himself from where he stood; his heart pounded rapidly at the scene unfolding before him. He wanted to reach out with the mind-tether to Camellia, tell her to run, but his mind was too fogged by Stormbreaker.

Camellia stared into the red eyes of the leviathan. For a long, heart stopping moment, the two dragons locked eyes, the larger one looming closer. He growled venomously, pulling his lips back to display his long, stalactite teeth. Edsel couldn't read anything that was going on in Camellia's head—he figured she must be so frightened her mind went blank.

Until she lifted a hand and smacked Stormbreaker hard across the nose.

Quinn froze. Aeros froze. Edsel held his breath.

"I am the princess of Mooncrest!" Camellia declared, sitting back on her hind legs and placing her hands on her hips. "You don't growl, you BOW!"

Stormbreaker's jaw went slack, his eyes widening in shock.

Edsel rubbed the side of his temple. "Of course she's immune to the fear. Knowing you should run from danger takes common sense, and she doesn't have a lick of that!"

Stormbreaker roared, his hot stinking breath gushing out at Camellia and Edsel like a geyser. Before he could attack, he heard his master's voice in his mind. *Wait, that's that pink dragon from the mountains… if she's here, then that means…*

Movement from the far side of the arena caught the leviathan's attention. He spotted a woman with brown hair, wearing a leather tunic and a blue cloak, dashing toward him. Again, he heard Sir Voranthian's words. *It's Quinn! Forget the dragon and the old man. Kill HER!*

Without hesitation, Stormbreaker leapt over Camellia and Edsel, his focus solely on the approaching guardian. He opened his mouth as a crackling yellow light emanated from his throat, lightning dancing on his tongue and ready to fire forth. His attack was thrown off, however, as Camellia grabbed him by the tail and pulled with all her might. It was just enough to throw him off balance and cause the lightning to fly a few feet to Quinn's right. Stormbreaker twisted his neck around to lunge at Camellia.

Quinn sprinted, every muscle in her body firing, as she threw herself at the dragon's exposed side and drove her dagger between two scales. She knew it would barely do damage, his hide was too thick, but it gave her leverage to climb up his side to his back. If she could get close enough to stab his eye, or any soft spot…

Edsel mind-tethered to Camellia. *We've got to lure the beast away from here. We don't stand a chance fighting him on the ground.*

Camellia darted out of the way of Stormbreaker's snapping jaws. She didn't need to be told twice. She flapped her wings and was airborne, ascending above the arena. Stormbreaker followed, although it took him longer to take off due to his size and weight. Quinn clung onto one of his back spines, the rush of air threatening to knock her off. The two dragons soared high above the city, the larger dragon on Camellia's tail as she tried to outmaneuver him. Bolts of lightning blasted across the sky as Stormbreaker roared and spat at her, but Edsel steered Camellia artfully out of the way of each blast.

Quinn inched along Stormbreaker's back, clawing her way towards his head. The leviathan finally remembered he had an adversary on his back, and started to buck mid-air. Quinn grasped on with all her might, but a lash from Stormbreaker's tail thwacked her in the side and sent her flying. She tumbled head over heels through the air, the whoosh of air deafening her. She had always assumed her mercenary work was going to be the death of her, but she had never thought falling off a dragon's back would be the way she'd go.

Claws wrapped around her waist, and she stopped falling. Once Quinn realized she was now flying instead of falling, she looked up to see a familiar pair of blue eyes. "Hey, if you're going to dragon ride anybody, it should be me!" Camellia shouted.

Edsel reached down and pulled Quinn up into the saddle in front of him. "You take the reins, I'll watch the rear," he ordered. "Camellia, keep up the pace! You're slowing down!'

"Well, I'm sorry," the princess replied, her voice strained, "But… this is much harder… to do… with two riders… on my back!"

Quinn could feel Camellia's energy flagging. "Grandpa, we can't keep this up. Camellia can't carry us both and outrun that dragon!"

Edsel could see Stormbreaker was gaining on them. "Then we'll have to use the one advantage we have. Camellia, you're small."

The dragon huffed. "Yes, I know! You don't have to remind me!"

"No, you're small. He's *huge*. Bigger doesn't mean better."

A smile grew on Quinn's face, as she remembered now where she had learned the phrase from. "Bigger makes you react slower." She switched to her mind-tether. *Camellia, drop down and fly low, now!*

Camellia was relieved to oblige, dropping down among the city buildings and flying low along the streets, dodging the surprised people, carts, and horses along the roads. Stormbreaker flew down as low as he could, but couldn't fit between the buildings, so instead he circled high above, trying to keep track of Camellia as she wove through the city.

*Now what? Where do I go?* Camellia asked, her brain racing as she narrowly avoided a fountain in the square.

Quinn looked up and spotted it above the buildings. Right at the edge of Torvel and leading out towards the hills in the north were double-tiered aqueducts, sets of stone arches that supplied water to the city. The two rows of arches extended for miles and miles, and the archways were tall but narrow. But the aqueducts were across the far side of a field, which would leave Camellia wide open. Would she be fast enough?

*Head towards the aqueducts,* she ordered.

Quinn could feel Camellia's confusion. *What are you talking about? I don't see any ducks!*

*Not aque-duck, aqueduct! It's that structure that looks like a bridge,* Quinn thought back.

*Ohhhh...then just call it the bridge-thingy!* Camellia summoned all the energy she had left and took off towards the aqueduct, as she left the cover of the city streets. She flew low over the field, ten feet above the ground, hoping she could cover a good distance before being spotted.

But being a bright color was a disadvantage in this case, as Stormbreaker immediately spotted the pink blur rushing across the field. In seconds, he was behind her, zooming down towards the earth and gaining ground on her. The leviathan's focus was tunnel-vision, only the pink princess in his sight, as he opened his jaws to unleash a torrent of lightning.

At the last possible second, Camellia folded her wings against her body and flew like an arrow between one of the aqueduct's archways, skimming the walls as she barreled through. Stormbreaker tried to pull up, but being as giant as he was and as fast as he was going, there was no avoiding impact. He crashed face-first into the aqueducts, sending a cascade of stone and water down on him, as he tumbled in rag-doll fashion along the ground.

Camellia skidded into the earth, creating a rut in the dirt as she came to a halt. She lifted her wings over her head to protect her riders as debris and rocks from the aqueducts rained down around them. She yelped as a stone smacked into her wing's wrist with an audible snap.

"Camellia!" Quinn jumped off Camellia and examined the broken wing. "Oh gods, I should've never agreed for you to come here. I'm so sorry."

The princess grunted but beamed a huge smile at Quinn. "Are you kidding? That was the BEST! Did you see me out-fly that brute and do that air roll through the arch? I mean, of course you saw it. Wasn't that amazing? And with TWO humans on my back! I didn't know I could do that. And I never would have, if you didn't agree to come with me to this place. I'd still be stuck in Mooncrest, thinking I couldn't do anything."

"Um, ladies..." Edsel stayed sitting on Camellia's back, looking behind them. The three of them blanched as Stormbreaker, bleeding and bruised, pulled himself out of the rubble and staggered toward them. His eyes glistened raw murder, as he thundered a death roar at them.

Camellia's eyes bulged. Quinn readied some poisoned pins from her cloak, but she knew they would do little against this beast. Edsel, however, did not seem perturbed at all. "Camellia," he said with a grin, "how about giving this lizard a taste of your breath?"

"But I can't breathe fire yet!"

"Because you're a pink dragon. Pink dragons don't breathe fire. If all you think is 'fire,' of course your breath isn't going to work."

"But... what do I have then? I've never breathed anything but air!"

"Exactly. Take a deep breath, as deep as you can. Fill up your belly."

Quinn felt hot panic as she could see yellow lightning forming in Stormbreaker's throat. "Could you two hurry it up a little?"

Camellia inhaled, and inhaled, and inhaled as much as she could. Her sides ballooned out, and her face inflated like a pufferfish. She held it, turning purplish in the face as she waited for the next command.

Edsel nodded. "Now, think of protecting those you love. Think righteous fury. Focus, and..." With both his good leg and his peg leg, he squeezed against her sides hard. "Breathe!"

With a massive exhale—which erupted as a massive belch—Camellia opened her mouth. Something did, indeed, come out. A flurry of pink bubbles spewed forth, hundreds upon hundreds, each about the size of a cabbage. They surrounded Stormbreaker, dozens sticking to his scales and face, but all it seemed to do was confuse him.

"Bubbles??" Camellia whined. "That's rubbish!"

Stormbreaker apparently agreed, as a deep chuckle burbled in his throat. But one of the bubbles popped against his nose, and he instinctively licked at the sticky residue on his nostrils. He paused, as the black pupils of his eyes dilated wide, swallowing the red irises. Impulsively, he snapped at all the bubbles, gobbling and chewing until his mouth was stuffed with gummy pink residue. He kept chewing rhythmically, until he flopped lazily onto the ground with an earth-shaking thud. A strange noise hummed inside his chest.

"Um... what is happening right now?" Camellia asked. "Is he... purring?"

"Pink dragons breathe euphoria bubbles," Edsel explained. "Read all about them in my dragon studies. Your gizzard creates a sort of sap that is packed with endorphin chemicals, or 'feel-good' stuff. I'd say our friend here is as close to dragon heaven as he'll ever be."

Far across the field, Quinn could see a line of figures approaching—men on horseback. "I think the king's guard is heading our way. I'm sure two dragons flying through the city and destroying their aqueducts got their attention."

"Then I say we make ourselves scarce. They can take care of old Stormy here. He'll be more than compliant." Edsel extended a hand and helped Quinn onto Camellia's back. "Think you're up for a run, my dear?"

"If we must. I suppose fame comes with its drawbacks." Camellia sprinted away, heading towards the boglands, leaving Stormbreaker behind contentedly munching on his bubble gum.

*

As the three rested at Edsel's house that evening, where he was able to make a make-shift splint for Camellia's wing, they ate one final dinner together before Quinn, Lazulo, and the princess would depart for Mooncrest in the morning.

Sitting by the fire in the hearth, Quinn patted Camellia on the tail. "I'm sorry you didn't win the tournament, given there was no tournament. I know you wanted those laurels."

Camellia shrugged. "Eh, a tournament's all well and good, but compared to a real dragon fight, a tournament seems kind of dull now. But I hope Aeros can find his own dragon and enter the tournament again. He'd make a really great dragon rider."

Quinn smiled. "Speaking of dragon riders, how about it, Grandpa? You gonna be Camellia's rider from now on?"

Edsel hacked a laugh while rubbing his head. "Ha! After all that, this old man's had enough dragon riding to last the rest of his life. My heart can't take it. But I got the chance to be one, for a day. Thank you, Camellia."

The pink dragon giggled. "You're welcome, Grandpa."

Edsel's eyelid twitched. "I'm *your* grandpa too, now? One granddaughter was trouble enough."

"Of course! Quinn is my big sister, so that makes you my grandpa too. And that's okay if you've had enough dragon riding. I've got my own dragon rider. I always have." She looked at Quinn with a tender smile.

Quinn sighed. "Camellia, you know I would love that. But, Balter... it still hurts sometimes. It's hard for me."

"I know." Camellia nuzzled Quinn's cheek with her nose. "And that's all right. The hurt, I mean. Because that means you loved my brother. Maybe, when you're ready, you can share more memories of him with me? I'd like to know more about him, if that's all right with you."

Quinn smiled. "Of course, little sis."


## THE END

# Fire and Redemption
## Richard Fierce

The chill of dawn had barely lifted when Silas stuffed the last
of his provisions into his leather pack. His boots crunched over the
frost-kissed ground, a testament to the creeping cold that heralded
the changing seasons. Like many days before, Silas Marrow would
face the rugged mountains that loomed around his village.

"Silas," called a voice, tinged with worry yet steadfast as the
earth itself. It was Mira, his mother, standing in the doorway of
their humble home, her silhouette framed by the rising sun. Her
eyes held the warmth that he often found absent in himself.

"Keep your wits about you," she said, her tone firm but lined
with an undercurrent of concern that only a mother's heart could
weave into words.

"Always," Silas replied. There was a mountain to conquer and
prey to track, no time for lengthy farewells.

The mountains did not welcome him; they never did. They
stood indifferent, their jagged peaks piercing the sky with a cold
arrogance. Silas treaded lightly on paths that were more
treacherous than any foe he had ever faced. The wind howled its
warning through the narrow passes, and loose stones skittered
down cliffsides, eager to draw the unwary to their doom.

Every step was a silent battle against the mountain's will. His
muscles tensed and relaxed in harmony with the uneven terrain,
each movement a practiced dance with danger. A lesser man might
have faltered, but not Silas. Not when every arrow nocked, every
trap set, and every track followed was a step closer to…
something. Something that mattered more than just meat for the
table or coin for the purse.

The landscape was a desolate beauty, a canvas of stark
contrasts painted by nature's unforgiving hand. Snow-capped

peaks crowned the horizon, while below, valleys lay shrouded in the shadows of their towering guardians. The sparse vegetation that clung to life here was as hardy as the people who mirrored it— twisted pines and stubborn shrubs that refused to yield to the whims of the wind.

"Remember, Silas," Eamon's voice echoed in his mind, his words from the night before carrying the weight of an unspoken pact between brothers not bound by blood. "Don't let your anger consume you."

"Never does," Silas muttered to himself with a scoff, though he knew his friend spoke truer than he cared to admit.

Beneath the cloak of stoicism, his heart hammered with a rhythm that betrayed his collected exterior. Adrenaline coursed through his veins, a familiar fire that sharpened his senses and focused his resolve. This land was unforgiving, yes, but so was he. Every scar etched upon his skin was a lesson learned, every callus a tale of survival.

And survive he must—not just for pride, not just for the thrill, but for her. For them. For a future where the shadows of dragons didn't darken their days. With a steadying breath, he pressed onward, the weight of his bow a comforting presence in his hand, the mountain's challenge accepted without a spoken word.

The higher he ascended, the more the air grew thinner, colder, as if the very breath of dragons frosted the world around him. His fingers itched at the feather-fletched arrows in his quiver, each one meticulously crafted for this purpose—dragon slaying. Every shaft was a promise, a vow etched in yew and tipped with vengeance. They whispered of fire and scales, of terror that crept into dreams and turned them into nightmares.

"Revenge is a hunter's folly," his father had cautioned once, his words now lost to time and flame. But his warnings did not quell the hatred that seethed within Silas, a hatred born the day they found nothing but ash where their home once stood.

A gust of icy wind clawed at him, tugging at his cloak like the specters of past hunts, reminding him of the perilous path he walked. Yet beneath the cloak, his muscles tensed, coiled springs ready to unleash death.

"Focus," he chastised himself. "Remember why you're out here." The faces of those he loved flickered behind clenched eyelids—his mother's hopeful gaze, Eamon's steadfast nod. It wasn't just about revenge; it was about putting food on the table, securing another winter's heat, ensuring that laughter could still echo in hallways not yet burned.

"Can't falter now," Silas whispered, the words snatched away by the wind.

He scaled a ridge, movements precise and practiced, his hands finding holds on cold, unyielding rock. The hilt of his hunting knife pressed against his side. Always prepared, always aware— that was the creed of the hunter.

*Dragons took everything.*

The thought pounded in his head with every heartbeat. They had to pay. Yet, deep down, a splinter of doubt wedged itself into his resolve. With if vengeance only begot more loss? What if in his quest, he became the very monster he sought to destroy?

"Ridiculous," he snapped aloud, breaking the silence that had settled upon the peaks. "Monsters don't mourn."

A falcon's cry echoed from above, a sharp reminder of nature's ceaseless vigil. Silas's breath appeared as foggy clouds before dissipating like wraiths fleeing the dawn. An hour slipped by, then two.

At last, Silas reached the valley where deer were known to graze. He watched the sky, but there was no sign of any winged beasts. He crept among the tall grass, silent and unseen. A rustling sound, almost imperceptible, halted his advance. Ahead, he spotted his quarry. A deer, coat dappled in the light of dawn, nibbled on the grass, oblivious. Silas nocked an arrow, pulling the bowstring taut.

*Steady,* he told himself. *One. Two. Thre—*

The world around him fractured. A roar shattered the morning's calm, and the earth trembled beneath him. He whirled around, arrow forgotten, as a dragon descended upon the clearing. The deer bolted, leaving Silas to face the beast alone.

"By the gods…"

The dragon landed with the grace of a monarch, wings unfurling like sails crafted from sunlight. Its scales were an opulent cascade of gold, each one a coin minted by the furnace of the earth's core. They shimmered with a life of their own, reflecting the light in blinding flashes before his very eyes. Its presence was like a force that commanded the elements and bent them to its formidable will.

Silas stood his ground, though not out of any form of rebellion. His legs were frozen stiff and refused to obey his mind. The dragon was the embodiment of his hatred, the source of his deepest pain, and yet he could not deny the majesty of the creature.

"I feel the malice in your heart," the dragon rumbled. "It disturbs the peace in these hills."

"Dragons took everything from me," Silas said, surprised his mouth worked where his legs did not.

"Understand, young hunter, not all share the sins of those you loathe."

His head bowed slightly, a gesture that seemed impossible for such a massive beast, and Silas felt his resolve waver. The unspoken truth that not all dragons were the same gnawed at the edges of his conviction.

"Leave me be," Silas whispered. "I don't want to die."

"I do not intend to kill you," the dragon said. "Look beyond your sorrow and see me for what I truly am."

Silas's grip on the bow slackened, the weapon hanging limply at his side as he beheld the dragon in all its glory. In his gaze, there was a wisdom that stretched back eons, an understanding of the world that Silas could never hope to grasp.

"Your hate will consume you if you let it." There was a hint of something akin to compassion in his tone.

"Hate is all I have."

"Take this." The dragon extended a single golden scale toward Silas. It glinted like a captured star, a fragment of his own essence.

"Take it," he urged, his voice a command that brooked no argument.

Silas accepted it with a trembling hand. It was warm to the touch, pulsating with an energy that resonated deep within his chest. A name came to him then: *Aurelius.*

The dragon nodded once, solemnly, as if acknowledging a pact forged in fire. "We are bound now, you and I. Whether weal or woe, only time shall tell."

"Bound?" The word tasted like ash in his mouth. A bond with a dragon was not something he had ever envisioned, nor desired. Yet here he stood, a part of him irrevocably altered by the mere proximity of the magnificent creature. "Does your kind find pleasure in making chains with what you call gifts?"

The dragon, Aurelius, tilted his head slightly, a gesture so deceptively akin to human curiosity it infuriated Silas further.

"Pleasure is found in liberation, not in bondage. Your hated binds you, not me."

"Easy words for a beast who knows nothing of loss," Silas countered, feeling the sting of memories long buried clawing their way to the surface.

"Assumptions, young hunter, are the shackles of the mind. Your world is small, but it need not be so. Let the scale show you the expanse of possibility."

"Is it freedom you promise, or a form of servitude?"

"Only time will reveal the truth of your path," came the cryptic reply.

The scale burned in his hand, a sigil of connection he neither wanted nor could deny.

"I will leave you to wrestle with your feelings," Aurelius said. "The bond is unbreakable, but the journey is yours to shape."

With a powerful beat of his wings, Aurelius lifted himself into the azure expanse above, his departure leaving a silence so profound it thundered in Silas's ears. He stood there grappling with the gravity of an unwanted alliance, the seeds of change sown in the soil of his mind. His path forward was shrouded in doubt and uncertainty.

*

When Silas returned, the village lay nestled in the arms of twilight, a cradle of tranquility that mocked the turmoil within him. Each step toward his home stirred the dust along the path in soft, whispering eddies, as if the very earth could sense the discord he carried in his heart. Silas's encounter with Aurelius had seared itself into his mind, an unwanted brand that threatened to alter everything he knew about himself. He felt the stirrings of something unfamiliar—a curiosity that gnawed at the edges of his steadfast hatred.

"Cursed beast," he muttered, absently tracing the scale with his fingers. Its warmth seeped through his fingertips, beckoning him with an allure he couldn't explain. Lifting the scale, he studied the intricate pattern etched upon its surface. It was a slice of Aurelius himself; it was power, it was enigma.

"What am I to do with this?" he asked aloud, though no answer came save for the whispering wind.

The scale was the embodiment of all he had lost, and yet… it represented something more—a bridge to something he'd never dared to envision.

*Change is not a choice. It's an inevitability. Forge your path with care.*

Aurelius's voice resonated within his mind, a remnant of his presence that refused to fade. He could feel the tendrils of the bond Aurelius spoke of, winding their way around the fortress of his soul, unbidden yet unyielding.

The world around Silas continued, indifferent to his turmoil. A gust of wind howled through the valley, carrying with it the scent of pine and storm. He entered the town, and a familiar figure waved at him.

"Silas! Where have you been? Your mother was worried when you didn't return earlier."

"Dragon," he said, the word hanging between them like a portent.

"A dragon?" Eamon echoed incredulously. "Where?"

"Not here." He nodded toward the mountain. "There was only one."

"Are you hurt?"

"No." The lie tasted bitter. He was wounded in ways Eamon couldn't see.

"How did you get away?"

"I didn't. It let me go. And it gave me something. A gift."

"A gift?" Disbelief laced Eamon's words. "Since when do dragons give gifts?"

"Since today," Silas snapped, more harshly than he intended. The two fell silent as they walked, and Silas lost himself in his thoughts again. Aurelius had challenged every belief he held about dragons. The hatred that had burned for years felt diminished.

"Whatever it is, you don't have to face it alone," Eamon said.

"Alone," Silas mused. "Never truly alone again, am I?" He spoke more to himself than anything, and Eamon gave him a concerned look.

"We've all been through stuff."

"Have we?"

"Yes. You were there for me when I lost my family. Words can't express the pain I felt, but you were there as a friend. I'll never forget that. I'm here if you need to talk."

Silas nodded, letting Eamon's loyalty tether him to the present. Together, they navigated the winding dirt path through town, and Eamon splintered away as they reached his house. Silas continued on, the bond with Aurelius pulsing like a second heartbeat within him. It promised change, power, and maybe even healing.

His mother stood outside their home, working the meager garden. Warm light spilled out from the open door, giving her a halo.

"Silas, you're home," she greeted, her voice a soothing balm. Her intuition was a force unto itself, and her brown eyes searched his with a depth that suggested she already suspected the change that wrestled inside him.

"Mother," Silas managed, feeling suddenly like a boy lost in the woods. Her arms enveloped him, the scent of fresh herbs and hearth-smoke wrapping around him, grounding him in the familiarity of her embrace.

"I'm glad you're all right. I began to worry when you didn't come home earlier. Eamon said I didn't need to worry about you. I suppose he was right."

She pulled back and noted his stiffened posture. "What troubles you, my son?"

Her hand reached up, brushing a lock of dark hair from his forehead with a tenderness that belied the strength in her fingers.

"Change," Silas answered, the word tasting strange, foreign.

"Change is coming, whether I will it or not."

"Change is the only constant in this world," she replied, her expression unreadable. "But you are still my son, and always will be. We'll face it together."

*Together.*

The word echoed in the hollows of his thoughts, mingling with the image of Aurelius's golden scales and unblinking eyes. Could such a creature understand loyalty, or was it merely another facet of the enigma that was dragonkind?

"Go inside and wash up," his mother urged. "Dinner will be ready shortly."

*

"To arms!"

The calm of the night shattered like glass under a hammer's blow. A scream rent the air, a harbinger of chaos that spread through the town as quickly as the flames that followed. Silas was on his feet before he knew it, the last vestiges of sleep clawing at his consciousness.

"Silas!"

"Mother!" he bellowed, panic lending strength to his sleep-addled voice. Mira burst into his room, her face set with grim resolve. She pushed a sword into his hands.

"The village is under attack. Go, help the others." Before he could protest, she hardened her expression. "I'll be fine. Go!"

Silas's heart thundered in his chest as he dashed outside. The familiar streets were now a labyrinth of terror and confusion. Townsfolk were scattered, the elderly and young crying out amidst the bedlam. And there, among the havoc, Silas saw the source of trouble.

Raiders.

It had been many years since Spindlebrook had seen a raider

attack. Rage filled him, hot and fierce, driving back the fear. It was a rage born of helplessness, of watching everything he loved turn to cinders and ash. It was rage that demanded vengeance.

An explosion of pain sent him sprawling to the ground. A boot connected with his ribs, but he rolled with the strike, the pain manageable. His hands scoured the ground for his blade.

"Silas!" Eamon was suddenly there, his sword flashing, driving back the marauder. "We're outnumbered! We can't hold them!"

Silas knew he was right. "We need to get everyone to safety. The woods if we must."

Eamon nodded. "Fall back!" he shouted.

The whizz of an arrow cut his cry short. Eamon choked and gasped, and Silas's eyes widened at the sight of a shaft sticking out of his friend's neck. Eamon staggered and collapsed. Silas's heart clenched in his chest, and a raw, primal scream escaped his lips. He crawled towards Eamon, the chaos of battle fading into background noise as he focused solely on his fallen friend. Blood seeped from the wound, staining the earth beneath Eamon's pale face.

"No! Eamon, stay with me!" Silas pleaded, cradling his friend's head in his hands. Eamon went still, and Silas knew he was dead.

With a primal scream, Silas got up and charged the raider who had fired the fatal arrow. His sword sliced through the air, cleaving through flesh and bone as he cut down anyone foolish enough to stand in his path. The clashing of steel reverberated through the chaos, drowned out only by the anguished cries of the townsfolk.

Silas's heart pounded in rhythm with every swing of his blade, each strike fueled by a desperation that refused to succumb to defeat. He fought not only for his own survival but also for Eamon's memory and all those whose bodies now littered the streets.

Something heavy struck Silas in the back of the head, and the last thing he saw before darkness enveloped him was smoke coiling into the heavens, blotting out the stars.

*

When he came to, the copper tang of blood still lingered in his mouth. He retched and sat up. It was still dark, and the homes of Spindlebrook still burned. The raiders were gone. Silas let out a shaky breath and tried to process what had happened. His head throbbed, and he felt weak, but he knew he couldn't stay here. He needed to find others, to see if anyone had survived.

He staggered to his feet, his vision swimming with dizziness. His head pounded, and his side throbbed where he'd been struck. He searched for any sign of life among the wreckage, but all he saw were the charred remains of his once-thriving village. Forcing himself to move, he limped through the debris to his home, his gait unsteady.

Mira's body lie in the garden. Silas dropped to his knees, his heart wrenching at the sight of his mother, lifeless and cold. Tears streamed down his face, and he reached out to touch her, his fingers grazing her cheek. She was gone.

No more laughter or warm meals or stories by the fire. No more mother to hold him and remind him he was loved. The weight of loss crashed down upon him, and he crumpled onto the ground, sobbing.

He was unaware of how much time had passed, but when the tears would no longer come, he got up and numbly walked through the devastation. The bond with Aurelius hummed in his mind. Silas's path was clear. He had to find the dragon and seek its help. The creature told him their bond was unbreakable, and his only hope was to rely on the mysterious creature's power.

The village faded behind him as the jagged teeth of the

mountains rose to greet him, their silhouetted peaks clawing at the stars. The path before him was a gnarled serpent winding through boulders and scrub, and night clung to the crags and fissures, painting everything in shades of uncertainty and danger. His boots found purchase on the uneven terrain, each step a defiant act against the gravity that sought to pull him down.

Grit and sweat mingled on Silas's brow as he scaled the sheer face of a cliff. His fingers ached, finding precarious holds in the cold stone, while his feet searched for the next ledge to bear his weight. The mountain was a beast, indifferent to his plight, each jagged rock a snarl in its stony maw.

He never thought he would seek the aid of a dragon. The irony twisted in his gut, a bitter herb he was forced to swallow. His father's demise, the result of dragon fire and ruin, echoed in his skull, yet here he was, chasing after one like a lifeline thrown into a stormy sea.

*I'm a fool,* he chided himself, heaving his body over the crest of the ridge. *But what choice do I have?*

The sky, once a dark canvas studded with stars, began to pale, heralding a dawn Silas wasn't sure he wanted to see. He pressed on, driven by images of the village aflame, of his mother's lifeless body, of Eamon's head cradled in his lap in wordless farewell. Every memory was fuel, every heartbeat a drum pushing him forward. The raiders would pay, even if it took consorting with a dragon...

With each step, the dragon's visage materialized in his mind— Aurelius, golden and grand, a creature of myth made flesh. Could such a being understand the searing pain of loss? Would it even care? It didn't matter. Silas needed the beast's strength, not his sympathy.

The sun crested the horizon, painting the world in hues of blood and amber. Silas stumbled, catching himself on a boulder, the coolness of the rock a temporary respite against the fever burning within him. His chest heaved, drawing in the chilled morning air in great, shuddering gulps.

"I can't stop now," he whispered, his voice barely carrying over the wind that tore through the passes. A part of him yearned to collapse, to surrender to the overwhelming exhaustion that threatened to drown him. But there was a fire in his belly, an ember that refused to be extinguished. It was for them—for the people of Spindlebrook, for his family—that he would endure.

"Come on, dragon," Silas called out to the uncaring sky. "I'm coming for you, and by the gods, you *will* help me."

His legs trembled beneath him, but he willed them to move, to carry him onward. The shadows of the mountains stretched long across the ground, as if reaching to pull him back, but he was relentless. With every labored breath, with every pounding of his heart, he drew closer to the dragon—and to the vengeance that sang in his veins like a chorus of bitter spirits.

Silas's boots skidded on loose shale as he navigated the treacherous slopes, each step a gamble between progress and peril. The path ahead was a cruel joke, winding and narrow, with a drop so steep it would make the heavens dizzy.

A low growl rumbled from a nearby thicket, and Silas froze. Eyes narrowed, hand absently reaching for his blade, he suddenly realized he had no weapon to defend himself. A pair of yellow eyes blinked at him, attached to a creature that was all teeth and malice—the mountain's own sentinel, a rock panther with a hide as tough as the stone it prowled.

The beast lunged, and the two of them collided, rolling along the ground. The panther's claws slashed against Silas's arms, raking deep furrows in his flesh. Mustering the last remnants of his strength, he struck the beast on the snout with his fist. The panther yowled and retreated into the brush.

"I will not yield," Silas whispered. The words became a mantra, a shield against fear and pain. He struggled to his feet and clambered up a steep incline, muscles screaming in protest. Loose rocks cascaded down behind him, a reminder that even the very ground could be an enemy. His foot slipped, sending a jolt of panic through his body. He caught himself and pressed on.

*

As the sun dipped below the horizon, bathing the world in a bloody twilight, each shadow seemed to move, each rustle of leaves a whisper of danger. The ground leveled beneath his boots, and a silent hush blanketed the air as if the earth itself held its breath. Silas paused at the edge of the clearing where he'd met the golden titan the day before. How had it taken him all day to reach the place?

His heart thundered against his ribs, a drumbeat heralding the uncertainty of this meeting. "Come out, dragon!" he shouted into the silence, the sound of his own defiance stoking the fire within him.

A rustle in the distance tugged at his senses. Then, like the unfurling of a gilded banner, Aurelius emerged from the tree line, his scales catching the scant moonlight, alight with an otherworldly luminescence.

"Young hunter," his voice rumbled, each syllable a stone tumbling down a mountain. "Your anger is a beacon that none can ignore."

"Anger is all I have left," Silas spat. "It brought me here, to you. Are you going to make me beg for your help?"

Aurelius's great head tilted, his eyes—deep wells of ancient wisdom—considered him. "You are driven by revenge, yet you seek an alliance. This is a paradox only humans seem to relish."

"Help me," he said, not a plea but a demand. "Or watch as

more blood stains the ground."

"Blood has been spilled by both our kinds," Aurelius responded, a hint of sadness weaving through his authoritative tone. "But I see in your eyes a flicker or something more. Tell me, young hunter, what fuels your fire aside from vengeance?"

"Survival," Silas answered, the word tasting like ash on his tongue. "Justice. They took from me, now I will take from them."

"Such things are easily claimed, harder to fulfill," he countered, shifting his massive form closer. Each step sent a tremor through the earth, a sign of his power. "Our path will not be one of mindless destruction. There is enough of that in the world."

"Then what? What do we seek if not vengeance?" Silas's voice cracked, the weight of exhaustion pressing down on him.

"Balance," Aurelius declared. "And perhaps, understanding."

Understanding. The word echoed in his mind, a strange melody amid the cacophony of rage and grief. Could there truly be a place for such a thing in this shattered world?

"Enough of your riddles," Silas growled, feeling heat rise in his cheeks. "Will you help me or not?"

"Your journey is mine," Aurelius finally conceded with a slow nod, his eyes reflecting a wisdom beyond the mortal coil. "But the path we tread is one of peril and uncertainty. Are you prepared for what lies ahead?"

Prepared? How could one prepare for a partnership so incongruous, a tenuous thread spun between vengeance and the hope of redemption? Yet, there was no other choice.

"Lead on," he managed to say, the words scraping his pride like flint against steel. "Just... don't betray me."

"Betrayal is not in my nature," Aurelius replied, lifting his massive head toward the star-studded sky. "Come. The night wanes, and our enemies rest not."

The dragon set off into the darkened woods, the trees bowing in homage to his might. Silas followed behind, his heart pounding like war drums in his chest.

"Balance and understanding," he whispered to himself, echoing Aurelius's words. The concept felt foreign, yet it clung to him, a seed planted in the fertile soil of desperation. Had his hatred truly blinded him to any other way?

He glanced down at the dwindling sight of his ravaged home, then forward to where Aurelius's golden form forged through the night. In that moment, Silas understood that their fates were woven together, bound by a thread that neither fury nor flame could sever.

Eventually, they reached a cave, and Silas followed the dragon inside. The cavern was vast, with stalactites hanging like daggers from the ceiling and pools of crystal-clear water reflecting the faint moonlight from the entrance. Aurelius led him to a chamber farther within the cave, where he curled up on the ground and indicated for Silas to sit.

"Rest now," he said. "You will need your strength for what lies ahead."

*

Dawn had barely kissed the sky with its first blush of light when Aurelius summoned Silas to the clearing. His great golden wings unfurled, casting shadows that danced like specters in the early morning mist.

"Your prey is not just flesh and bone. It is wind, it is shadow. Become one with both."

Silas nodded, feeling the weight of the dragon's gaze upon him as he crouched low, the grass cool and damp beneath his fingertips. The hunt was second nature to him, but under Aurelius's scrutiny, he felt as though he was learning to stalk for the first time.

"Your anger is a tool," he continued, his massive head tilting as he watched Silas navigate through the foliage. "But it must be honed, directed."

Silas drew a slow breath, letting it out in measured silence. The dragon was right; the fire of his rage had often led him astray, blinded him. But now, as he moved with purposeful stealth, he began to understand the discipline required of a true hunter.

"Anticipate," Aurelius instructed, his voice a command that cut through the stillness. And so Silas did, predicting the path of the rabbit before it even sensed his presence. His muscles coiled, ready, and when he sprang, it was with a precision he had never known.

"Swift. Silent. Deadly," the dragon observed, approval warming his words like the rising sun. "You learn quickly, young hunter."

"I have a name," Silas said. "It's Silas."

"Silas," the dragon repeated. "I will call you by it, then."

With the catch secured, Silas could not suppress the swell of pride that rose within him. But there was no time to bask in success; Aurelius had more to teach, each lesson crafted from centuries of experience. He prepared the rabbit and ate, and the lessons continued.

"Balance is key," he said as they moved on to combat training. "Your body must be fluid, your mind clear."

He demonstrated, a whirl of golden scales and lethal grace, then beckoned Silas to mimic his movements. He stumbled at first, frustration nipping at his heels. But as the hours wore on, his motions mirrored Aurelius's own—more fluid, more purposeful.

"Good," came the simple praise from the mighty dragon. "Now again."

They trained until the sun hung high, until Silas's limbs ached with exertion and the clarity of purpose filled his every thought.

The teachings of Aurelius, once foreign and unwelcome, now coursed through him with the force of a raging river.

"Rest now," he finally commanded as evening approached. "Tomorrow, we continue."

Silas collapsed onto the ground, his chest heaving, sweat mingling with dirt. Yet, beneath the exhaustion, he felt an ember of something new: a focus sharpened not by hatred, but by determination—a determination kindled by the very creature he had once vowed to destroy.

Silas shifted his weight and watched the fading daylight dance across Aurelius's scales. The dragon lay sprawled across the earth, a living monument to an age-long gone. His golden eyes held stories untold, and as twilight embraced the sky, he began to unravel them.

"Once, we soared as guardians," his voice rumbled like distant thunder, "not as beasts to be feared."

Silas leaned against an ancient oak, its bark rough against his back, and listened. His mind, once a fortress against anything draconian, now absorbed his tales with a thirst he hadn't known he possessed. Aurelius talked of skies painted with dragon wings, of lands unscarred by human greed, and of battles fought side by side rather than blade against claw.

"Your people were once allies to mine," Aurelius said, his tone tinged with a melancholy that seemed too vast for one being to carry.

"Hard to imagine," Silas replied, his voice barely above a whisper, "when all I've known is loss at the hands of your kind."

"Loss," the dragon echoed, a soft snort sending embers dancing into the air, "is a language both our kinds speak fluently."

The night grew dense around them, stars peppering the darkness like flecks of silver. Yet within that shrouded silence, something within Silas stirred—a seed of understanding taking root in the fertile soil of their shared grief.

"Tell me," Aurelius continued, shifting so that the moonlight glinted off his hide, "what drives a hunter when the hunt loses meaning?"

Silas grappled with the question, the image of his home—of smoke and screams—surfacing like a specter from the depths. But alongside it rose another vision: a world where humans and dragons could exist without the pall of enmity between them.

"Maybe, the hunt could be for something more. For... peace." The words felt foreign on his tongue.

"Peace," Aurelius murmured, his tail sweeping the ground thoughtfully. "A noble pursuit, but arduous."

"Perhaps, but what worth is there in doing what is easy?"

"Indeed," the dragon agreed, a rumble of approval emanating from his chest. "And so, young hunter, we forge a new path—one of unity over discord."

That night, as the constellations wheeled overhead, their dialogue bridged worlds. Each word, each story, each shared silence wove a tapestry of camaraderie between dragon and human. And as dawn's first light crept across the land, painting the horizon in hues of color, Silas found himself no longer blind to the world Aurelius showed him—a world where vengeance gave way to a larger calling.

Together, they would chase that elusive dream of peace, driven not by the hatred that had once consumed him, but by a newfound resolve to mend what had been broken. With each passing day, the bond between them strengthened, tempered in the crucible of their combined experiences. And in the reflection of Aurelius's gaze, Silas saw not an enemy, but an ally—a comrade with whom he might stand against the coming storm.

*

Silas inhaled sharply, the cool air tinged with the scent of pine and an oncoming storm. Next to him, Aurelius unfurled his massive wings, the gold of his scales shimmering in the last light of day.

"Ready yourself," the dragon rumbled, his voice a deep thrum that resonated within Silas's chest. "The marauders draw near."

Silas nodded, feeling the weight of his bow in hand, the quiver bristling with arrows at his back. The familiar grip was a comfort and a reminder of past hunts, but this... this was different. This time, he did not stand alone, but side by side with a creature he now counted as a friend.

"Let them come," he said, his words slicing through the building tension like an arrowhead. "We'll be waiting."

Aurelius's great head turned towards him, those ancient eyes reflecting a wisdom that transcended lifetimes. He didn't speak; he didn't need to. The understanding between them was as palpable as the lightning flashing overhead.

With a swift glance, Silas surveyed the landscape: the rolling hills that led to his scorched town, the dark silhouettes of trees swaying ominously in the wind. They were protectors of this realm, guardians against chaos. Their alliance, once unthinkable, had become their greatest weapon.

"Through fire and shadow, we shall endure," Aurelius intoned solemnly, his voice carrying over the expanse.

"Through fire and shadow," Silas echoed, his resolve hardening like forged steel.

A cry shattered the night, the first of the marauders coming into view—a grotesque parade of malice and greed. They had razed countless homesteads, leaving only ashes and sorrow in their wake. But tonight, they would find not victims, but avengers.

"Silas," Aurelius whispered, his tone laced with urgency as he crouched, ready to spring into action. "Now!"

They erupted into motion, a fluid dance of dragon and human. Silas's arrows flew with deadly precision while Aurelius's flames carved a fiery swath through the enemy ranks. Each movement, each breath was synchronized in a ballet of defiance—a testament to what could be achieved when old hatreds were cast aside for a common cause.

The clash of metal, the screams of the marauders, and the roar of dragonfire filled the air, a cacophony of battle that threatened to overwhelm. Yet amidst the chaos, there was clarity. For every life they fought to protect, for every dream they sought to preserve, their bond grew only stronger.

As the dust settled and the echoes of conflict faded, they stood unyielding, a pair forged from the crucible of adversity. Their shadows merged into one upon the battered earth, a symbol of unity that no darkness could dispel.

"Side by side," Silas breathed, his gaze fixed on the horizon where new challenges awaited.

"Side by side," Aurelius affirmed, his voice a comforting rumble.

Together, they stood, their bond unbreakable, ready to face whatever may come—to bring justice to those who threatened his home and to defend a world on the brink of change. And in that moment, he knew the hunter and the dragon, once enemies, now friends, were united in purpose and unshakeable in their resolve.

## THE END

# Final Night, First Dawn
Jeremy Hicks

Axl cleared the jam in the spitballer with one of his two pairs of grasping appendages. The other pair reattached the pressurized hose to the weapon. It emitted a singular hiss as the retaining clip locked into position. The spitballer's familiar vibration informed the veteran Drover that it was ready for action.

Axl wasn't so sure about the fresh recruit that had glopped up the spitballer. Dwyzl kept shooting when the pressure was too low. The weapon would have been fine had he waited for its compressor to engage. Instead, the only Drover assigned to Papa Two-One was away from his station to assist their rookie. Again.

"Sorry, Axl, but I missed the warning chime over the noise."

The words passed seamlessly through the Tether. Their proximity strengthened the extrasensory bond through which the Mitra communicated with each other as well as their mounts. Neither wind nor rain nor screech of bird-of-prey intruded into it.

"Like I said about it the first time, don't say sorry. Do better."

"I know. I know. It's all so confusing. Not like the Clutch."

Axl placed one of his small graspers on the side of Dwyzl's neck. The recruit's pulse beat in staccato fashion, so the Drover exuded calmness until the young Spitballer's matched his own. The crewmen locked eyes for a moment and then nodded.

"You're not a larva anymore, Dwyzl. It's a weird, wild, and dangerous world above water. And it's fish-eat-fish out there."

"I can only imagine—"

"No, Dwyzl, that's part of being Mitra. You don't have to imagine. You don't have to worry. You just have to use the best tool you have."

Axl tapped the Spitballer between his black pupilless eyes, the carapace there as hard and unyielding as the exoskeleton of their massive flying mount. "It's all there in our ancestral memory."

"The Mind of the Mitra."

"The Mind of the Mitra." Axl responded as was customary when the All-Mind was invoked.

An abrupt change in the wing beat pattern of Papa Two-One cut through their reverie, shifting the winds buffeting them on the open back of the mount. Front and rear wings operated independently despite the Tether harness, their clear venation allowing the waning sun to pass. The light played in myriad patterns across the entire spectrum. Each beat birthed and killed a thousand rainbows, but he had no time to enjoy the spectacle.

Axl was sure there was some esoteric proverb buried in the All-Mind that might correlate with the afternoon lightshow, but his four lower appendages proved too busy threading the currents of air and other crew between him and his navigation station. What was happening and where they were at occupied his active mind. He could reach out with the Tether to a nearby unit, but that would alert Command he was away from his station.

Dwyzl's spitballer erupted into noisome action. Its mechanical *thump-thump-thump* an unnatural sound to Mitra ears, even after dozens of generations of Clutch-borne aircrews assigned bug mounts like their dragonfly. Papa Two-One flipped itself upside down, its tapering thorax and long, narrow abdomen visible for a brief moment as Axl glanced aftward. The Mitra's upper bodies wavered, but both remained fixed into position thanks to the suckers on the soles of their feet.

The recruit salivated with visible excitation as the gun launched ball after ball of acidic regurgitant—a fancy way of saying it fired condensed blasts of Mitra vomit. Disgusting to outsiders by all accounts, the technology was born from the biological necessity of their kind to feed on the blood of other species. Over a cycle of ages, his people had evolved from simple parasites to enjoy a civilization based on the symbiosis with their former hosts. The creation of Tether boosting technologies had brought them into better equilibrium, teaching them that groupthink and cross-species communication had its advantages.

Axl preferred the cleaner, shinier technology of the Drover's station to puke launchers. The Sunstone's prismatic effect rivaled dragonfly wings on a cloudless day, but the magnetic directional worked night and day thanks to a coating of bioluminescent paint made from a species of mushroom that grew near Logbog—the farthest clutch from Limewall—built at the base of a levee the size of a mountain range erected during the Age of Giants. Axl required only a few moments to determine their position with his maps and both instruments at his disposal.

"Heads up!" Flyer Kyndl's order rattled in the Drover's head, distracting him from his complex calculations. Cycles of encoding, training, and serving from Clutch to aircrew dictated his reaction. Order received. Order fulfilled.

Axl looked toward the watery surface of Pondhome. "Up" proved relative when one flew on the back of a Tethered dragonfly large enough to carry a half dozen adult Mitra without slowing. Papas were bred to be half again or smaller than Mamas. This meant a regular crew of four could work as aerial patrols while still having room for search-and-rescue duty too.

"Leaper, port side." Their fourth crew member, Blyx, called out as she charged their mount's only other spitballer. Their Tender was a true professional, serving longer than he or Kyndl. Her gun's rhythmic *thump-thump-thump, hiss, thump-thump-thump* steadied Axl's nerves until his eyes fell upon their target.

The frogstrosity's broad head broke the water's murky surface. Speckled yellow eyes with pupils taller than a grown Mitra disappeared as its toothy maw opened. Spitball rounds impacted

the lipless rim of its mouth and striking tongue. As the beast
cleared the pond, its damaged, smoking tongue unfurled like a
banner.

The dragonfly's barrel-roll maneuver dipped them close
enough to the water for the Drover's graspers to feel its spray. The
mount twisted its body, righting itself and its crew, and then
reversed course. The leaping frog sailed past where Papa Two-One
had been moments earlier. Kyndl's aerobatic tactics and Papa
Two-One's superior eyes and maneuverability prevailed.

For the moment, Axl reckoned.

Both spitballers pelted its mud-colored hide.

*Thump-thump-thump, hiss, thump-thump-thump.*

*Splash!*

Axl and crew lost sight of their target after it bellyflopped into
the pond. Papa Two-One circled in an expanding spiral as it was
trained. Spitballers fell silent, but the air compressors' noise rose
above all else.

All but the Tether.

When Kyndl spoke again, she sounded as if she were in Axl's
head. "Any crew have eyes on target?"

"Negative." Three responded as one.

"Should we call for reinforcements?" Blyx asked. Axl sensed
she was worried about Papa Two-One's safety more than hers.

They knew how much these new predators wriggling their way
into Pondhome enjoyed trying to eat their mounts. Countless
aircrew had ended up in the gullets of lesser beasts. They were the
first line of defense, though.

Any predator that made it past them could at best disrupt a
clutch's cycle and at worst devour the entire bed of eggs and larva.
The chances of any predator, or group of predators, destroying
every single Mitra clutch was small but contingencies existed for
such doomsday scenarios. Especially since The Rift had spread

from the depths to be visible to all Mitra.

The *thump-thump-thump* of Dwyzl's spitballer answered before any of them. The recruit's voice followed. "Port bottom."

Axl's neck craned to see the incoming threat. A blur of flesh and water exploded to his left as their mount dipped its port wings to give its Spitballers a better target. Turning into the target was going to be costly this time, the Drover determined before his dragonfly or its Flyer.

"Turn away, you blasted bug!"

Papa Two-One responded to the Drover's emergency command. In an instant, it flicked and flitted from port to starboard, bucking its Flyer about in her saddle. The frogstrosity missed out on its meal, but its tongue found purchase this time. As the beast flipped end over end in its fall toward the pond, the sticky appendage snagged the dragonfly's rear starboard wing.

Gravity and acceleration worked in tandem against the muscles securing the papery wing. Papa Two-One shuddered as the papery wing cracked, tore, and then ripped free from its thorax. The wounded dragonfly's body shuddered from antennae to anterior, and its head spun from side to side.

Its fixed multifaceted eyes were unable to emote, but its scream rang through their minds. Pain and fear filled the Tether connection like water poured into a cup. Axl screamed along with their mount, but more out of frustration than pain and fear.

"Station, Papa Two-One needs assistance. Repeat. Papa Two-One has been hit. We are airborne but ailing."

"Tether acknowledged, Papa Two-One. This is Station. We are dispatching the nearest Mama to assist. Can you provide exact location?"

Kyndl locked eyes with Axl who blanched and shrugged. They shifted their gaze aft to the freshie Spitballer that continued to waste ammo shooting at their submerged foe. When they looked at each other again, they grinned despite the danger and fear. They'd each been spit-happy rookies once upon a cycle.

"Negative, Station. Position is fluid. Repeat. Position not fixed. Drover will have to guide you in."

"Over, Papa Two-One. Mama Three-Three is on standby."

Axl prepared to work his literal magic, sinking into the Tether network and coordinating the positions of their local dragonfly assets, another of the Drover's primary responsibilities. When Blyx's spitballer joined Dwyzl's, he knew he was short on the one asset he needed: time. Axl reminded himself that he didn't need to reach every asset in his sensing range, just the closest.

He ignored his churning gut, the shifting winds, and other distractions as his mount evaded the frog again. The Drover's perception radiated outward. He pictured it like light from the sun. It washed over Pondhome. The light created a mass of shadows as it fell upon the Mitra and those symbiotic species Tethered to them. Among the dark shapes, he felt for—and found—the familiar shadow of a dragonfly. A mass of Mitra moved along its back.

"Mama Three-Three. This is Papa Two-One's Drover. Initiating Tether Positioning."

"Ready on our end, Papa Two-One," an unfamiliar but familial voice answered. "Mama Three-Three has you. Inbound."

The relativity of time was not lost on the Mitra. In fact, Axl found combat time to be the most relative of all. Most of a cycle could pass in a flash and then one agonizing series of unforgettable moments could dominate the remainder in such a way that it seemed an eternity. At least, that's how the All-Mind recalled this particularly fateful cycle.

Papa Two-One spiraled in the opposite direction, unable to bring its port side to bear on the target. Its three remaining wings worked overtime to keep it flying a rough circle around the target.

The frogstrosity swam for a stone sticking out of the mire, spitballs striking around it. Smoke rose from its blistered skin.

The beast hopped onto dry ground, smoke rising from its blistered skin. It clacked its teeth, shrieked, and leaped, using the stone to generate more force and speed than its previous attempts.

To Axl, time slowed as local space felt like it bent around them. One moment, the frogstrosity jumped at their mount. The next, the dazzling purples and greens of Mama Three-Three streaked between them. It appeared to the Drover that the larger dragonfly, easily the size of a sparrowhawk, formed a virtual wall between them and the persistent predator.

A moment later, however, Mama Three-Three accelerated, another blast of wind washing over the smaller dragonfly and its crew. The Mama's move-through maneuver had caught the frogstrosity midleap, all six legs catching the beast by its bumpy head. The giant dragonfly's jaws snapped shut and its razor-sharp teeth popped one of the beast's oversized eyes like an overripe grape. Its Mitra crew unleashed bursts of acidic spit from their array of spitballers, targeting the remaining eye.

Mama Three-Three dropped the flailing, maimed predator-turned-prey before it could damage the dragonfly or its crew. With its missing wing, Papa Two-One was not so fortunate. Unable to steer away from the path of the falling frog, it caught a vicious kick as the beast peddled for any purchase.

Axl's gut wrenched once more as their mount went into a sickening spin, spiraling toward the grassy edge of Pondhome. Whatever happened next escaped him as his vision spun from a blur of light to an abyssal darkness.

*

The veteran Drover was a novice at unconsciousness. Though he could not recall the experience, he did not think he had been bothered by it. He recognized it for what it was upon waking. Blessed was the All-Mind in that way.

Blessed were the context clues, too, like Dwyzl standing at the base of a bed so uncomfortable it had to be in a sickbay. Axl wondered about the whereabouts of the rest of the crew. Were they resting in another ward? Even as the Drover thought it, he knew it to be fanciful.

The Tether had answered with their absence. They were gone. He and Dwyzl remained, but the details remained hazy. Axl's head hurt. His heart did, too. His world shook around him, so roughly that it could have been literally. Surely it was a side effect of having his carapace bounced off a rock.

The Drover rolled over on the cot, but with four sets of appendages, he found no comfort on his side. The uncomfortable position did allow him to avoid Dwyzl's lingering stare.

At this distance, the Spitballer's noisome thoughts proved unavoidable. The freshie had not known the crew as long as their Drover, but his heart hurt for them nonetheless. Something more pressing, more fearful overshadowed Dwyzl's concern for his lost crewmates. He too showed concern for the shaking, which had lessened but remained constant.

Once Axl reached past the emotions exuding from the recruit, he discovered it to be infecting the Tether as far as he could sense. Fear, panic, and loss on a scale he'd never known washed over him.

He slid from the cot and stood on four wobbly legs.

"What do you mean The End? You all keep repeating it. So many Tethered that it's making my head ache all over again."

"You already know," Dwyzl moved closer and raised one of his graspers. "You just have to—"

"Recruit, if you tap me on my cracked carapace to make a cheeky point, I'm going to reduce you to spitball ammunition."

Axl opened his mouth and extended his feeding spike. The glands in his throat that supplied acid to his saliva clicked together to emphasize his point.

The Spitballer thought better of it and lowered his hand.

Retracting his spike, Axl said, "Glad to see you're learning, recruit. Now, let's go."

"Where? Thought you wanted to know what was happening?"

"We're going to get our orders. Fill me in on the way. The old-fashioned way, by telling me what the feck is going on here."

"In two words: We're evacuating."

While the crewmates hurried to the Harness Deck, where the dragonflies were prepped and launched, Dwyzl caught Axl up on current events. He repeated much of what cluttered the Tether. The Rift expanded, the shaking began, and now the dreaded Sundering was upon them, an event predicted—and ignored—for generations. Most Mitra had believed the giants that constructed the ancient levee between them and the Salty Vast would return to maintain it.

Their ancestors projected a symbiotic relationship onto another race of parasites, one with no idea the Mitra existed, much less staked an entire civilization on their engineering skills. The giants remained until the forest had been clear cut, the Salty Vast polluted with the runoff from their mills and towns, and the biggest species of fish and turtles pulled from Pondhome. Now, they had about as much chance of arriving in time to save the Mitra as the sun did of not rising the next cycle.

"None, you think?" Dwyzl asked, plucking it from the Tether.

"No, not at all. Look there." As they emerged onto the open upper deck of Barkback, field command for the Mitra Defense Force, Axl gestured with one of his longer graspers. "Station doesn't think so, either. Those Mamas are covered in larva and swollen with eggs. Thank the Ancestors the MDF took the Rift seriously."

Dwyzl peered past the growing assemblage of Mitra from every caste, from clutches near and far, to the dozen or more beautiful mounts with camouflaged harnesses bristling with spitballers fore, aft, dorsal, and ventral. Mama harnesses came complete with a sleek windscreen of pond-grown and spit-polished crystal to shield its crew from bitter winds on long flights. The screens shined in the moonlight as brightly as the expansive wings of the titanic dragonflies.

"Don't get too enamored with the ladies. We're Papa crew."

"Were. You've been reassigned." The Tether answered, rather the Mitra hustling over to them, who identified as Zyr.

"I am Clutch Adjunct Zyr, activated for emergency evacuation duty. There is little time to explain why but you have been reassigned to Mama One-Nine and scheduled to depart with the swarm at moonset."

The wooden deck beneath them shook and waves lapped higher and higher against the pond-facing side of the base. Shrieks, clicks, and buzzes from the mass of Mitra and mounts rose into the night. Zyr clicked three times and wobbled in visible excitement.

Skittering away from Axl and Dwyzl, the Clutch Adjunct said, "Report to your mount for Tether Attunement immediately. Your departure may be sooner than later."

Zyr's prophesy proved truer than those who prayed facing The Rift and awaited pale giants that would never come, not if the Mitra had another thousand cycles to enjoy Pondhome. Mama One-Nine's Relay had no sooner run the Tether Attunement for its newest crew when orders came to take flight.

"Where are you going?" Relay Sybl asked Axl.

"No offense, but I know a Drover's Station when I see one. I'll find my way."

"You're not our Drover, though. Myx is."

Axl turned to see the most bloated red mite he'd ever seen slide into *his* station. Swollen to twice the size of his compatriots, the Drover stopped when he found himself unable to continue. Still, it didn't stop him from trying again and again to wedge into the position. Finally, Myx stopped and sighed.

"I knew I should have donated before reporting. Stupid newborn adjuncts." Without another word, Myx stood with a groan, moved to the onboard Juicer, and vomited and vomited and then vomited some more, visibly slimming before Axl's eyes. Wavering like a deflated balloon, Myx slipped from the Juicer and back to the Drover's Station.

"Woo! The Spitballers should be good on ammo for now."

"This fool is my replacement?" Axl asked the Relay.

"Nope. Your Papa was pulled from active duty, which means you were reassigned, bub." Sybl clicked, her annoyance with the situation emanating from her like stink from a rotting minnow. "You're our new First Officer and Co-Flyer. Enjoy the promotion and listening to Abyl."

"The Flyer and Commander?"

"If you were going to Tether all of this, why did you ask?"

"No, I didn't. Haven't yet? Shit. I just did. Nevermind. What I meant was 'Mama One-Nine' sounded familiar. It's where one of my Clutchmates was assigned."

"Who was your Clutchmate, Axl?" Dwyzl asked, lingering between crewmates old and new.

"Spitballer, why're you not at your station?" Sybl interjected.

"Well, there's so many of them. Not sure which gun is mine."

"Easy. Hyx is on the ventral turret. He's down below already. Tender handles dorsal and First Officer takes the fore gun. You're aft. Tip of the taper, so watch your step and use the rail."

"Neat," Dwyzl said with the enthusiasm typical of those who had been hungry, predatory nymphs longer than binge-and-purge adults of the Soldier Caste. "Should be a good view."

"Yeah, don't get killed," a taller Mitra—wearing the snail shell belt typical of Tenders—said as he brushed by them. "Tail Spitballers have the highest casualty rates. No screen protection. I'm Syn by the way. If you need blood or bandages, reach out."

The Tender pulled one of the snail shells from his belt, the creature's foot coming away from its pad. "Speaking of blood, looks like you could use this, First Officer. Every limb is shaking with hunger."

"I do feel a bit faint, now that you mention it."

Axl patted his new Tender on the side of his neck and accepted the hard meal. Hard too was a relative term. His feeding spike punched through the snail's shell with ease, filled it with his acidic saliva, and then sucked down the delicious combination of their fluids. Warmth and nourishment filled his inner bladders.

"Thanks, Syn! You do the Tenders proud."

Axl's new crewmate clicked and returned the gesture.

"Heartwarming. Bloody heartwarming. Literally, am I right?"

Axl knew that animated cocksure voice but had not heard it this close since nymphhood. Abyl's voice had not changed in the slightest, but Axl hoped his Clutchmate had changed for the best.

"Commander."

"Is that all you have to say to an old Clutchmate?"

"No, I have lots that need saying." Axl recalled the time Abyl had disabled a safety net, allowing dragonfly nymphs into a Mitra nursery. The carnage still haunted him.

"You're angry about that silly old prank?"

"Prank? Half a clutch was eaten before they hatched."

"Well, we'll lose the clutch loaded onto this mount if we waste time discussing nymphhood naughtiness. Can we table this until after the end of civilization?"

Axl clicked and stalked past his commander.

"I know, Old Mite. I hate being right sometimes, too."

Abyl followed his Clutchmate, chittering with laughter.

Ever the professional, Axl slid into the forward turret—a bubble-like projection below the windscreen—and beheld the wonder of his new position. Silvery light twinkled across the countless facets of Mama One-Nine's two primary eyes. In contrast, her smaller eyes drank the moonlight, showing almost no reflection.

The reluctant First Officer felt her watching him, thinking to him in a way unlike any Papa. Her stress, worry, fears were palpable and paramount. Then again, the Mamas carried the weight of two dying civilizations and a crew of seven Mitra on their backs. He shuddered under the specter of that immense load.

By the waning light of their last moon at Pondhome, Axl made a wish. He hoped and prayed for a short assignment on Mama One-Nine. How that fateful wish came to pass would haunt him the rest of his existence.

*

Without prior authorization, Mama One-Nine and half the tarmac of Barkback launched. The flight of gargantuan dragonflies filled the night sky. Axl's digestive cavities lurched from the sudden acceleration, but he avoided voiding. Distant retching on the Tether indicated not everyone had been so successful.

"Crazy buggers." Abyl wrestled for control of their mount. Axl sensed something had stirred the entire swarm, so he joined with his co-flyer to calm her panicked ascent.

The rest of the dragonflies from Barkback took flight, almost too late to avoid the rising waters. The surge of sea water carried debris from the failing levee. A chunk of stone sailed by Mama, obscuring Axl's view. By the time it passed, their facility had disappeared into the briny mix. Over the Tether, Axl could not discern the cries of the ones trapped inside Barkback from the screams of those washed away.

A moment later, none of that confusion mattered. The sky cracked with an unnatural thunder. One of the Artist Caste might say that Magnificient Mirstone quaked, rattled, and rolled with the ferocity and frustration of a dog shaking fleas from its back. Axl knew the truth. Giants or no giants, the levee failed. The rest of the poetic meter held too true for him to comprehend. For his head hurt too much as did his heart, it was all too real, too raw.

A reverent silence fell over the Tether. Relays, Drovers, and every crewmate on a mount shared a version of what Axl felt. Ironically, he had never felt so alone, never experience so much silence, especially in the midst of utter devastation. His link to Mama One-Nine expanded his senses too much to handle it.

Axl pulled away but one voice begged him to return. Mama One-Nine did not want to be left alone in the midst of twisting, turning, flipping, and flying for her life, for the life of her eggs, and for the future of Mitra civilization. He assented and relief trickled into both their minds. It was not the cataclysmic flood they witnessed outside, but it might be enough to navigate their final flight from Pondhome. While Axl was neither dragonfly nor mother, he could empathize with Mama One-Nine on one level, veteran to veteran.

"We do what must be done."

*We do.*

From above, a rare compliment trickled down, too.

"Whatever you're doing seems to be working," Abyl said. "Controls are responding again. Keep it up, Old Mite."

"Where in bloody mess is the Drover?"

Abyl glanced behind him. "Overwhelmed, I think."

"Squeeze the berry too close to takeoff?" An unfamiliar voice asked. A quick check revealed it to be their belly gunner.

"It's likely, Hyx." Axl said. "Wouldn't be the first mistake I've seen these rookies make."

"Even I know not to make that one." Dwyzl chimed.

"Cut the chatter, Spitballers. Tender is seeing to Myx now." Abyl said. "You're guiding us until then, First Officer."

Axl would have asked "where" but he knew as soon as he reached for the information. Papas had scouted the diverse areas surrounding Pondhome for generations, though they had traversed the Salty Vast less than any other radial on their mental maps. The Drovers for dozens of Mamas, and a handful of Papas, conversed on the Tether. Others joined now and then, some with suggestions, others with lamentations, and too many with fears and doubt. Doubt was like loneliness. It was not common among those of the Tether.

In a span of wing beats, Axl and the others debated options, divided into camps, debated again, returned to their camps, and then collapsed into warring factions. Meadow, Marsh, and Ridge factions trumped the crazed minorities that either wanted to cross the Vast or linger near the toxic brine to await their oversized saviors, the Two-Legged Giants of Yore. All the while, Flyers struggled to keep the surviving swarm headed for their rally point, rocky ground where ridge descended to marsh.

When it came time to voice his stance, Axl stood for a fourth faction, one that made their opinion known through Mama One-Nine. *Parallel the ridgeline until morning.* Once he suggested the sunrise course as a compromise, a decisive majority of Mitra voices rose in support. They agreed that the sun would light and guide their way, even in the midst of darkness.

Axl thanked the sun for he was no heretic. He thanked the dragonflies, too, though, especially Mama One-Nine. Using the leechers on the bottom of his feet, the Mitra drank of her vital juices and thanked her for the nutrients, too. The dragonfly's blood would be the only warmth he enjoyed this bitter night.

Reverie and repast ended too soon for his taste. Fear waxed once more, brought into fresh focus as crew and mounts reported multiple contacts, all flying, furry, and fanged.

"Bats!" Axl cried and charged his spitballer.

Hyx's dual spitballer thumped into action which meant at least one incomer approached from beneath their mount. Axl imagined a path that spiraled upward, flipping Mama into a barrel roll before diving in a steep descent toward targets ahead and below. Abyl quibbled little, adding an unnecessary corkscrew here and there to their evasive maneuvers.

Mama One-Nine's crew targeted the interceptors that mistook her for an easy meal. Steaming spitballs filled the humid air around the maneuvering dragonfly, an aerialist supreme. Slowed by her precious cargo, she focused on quick turns and tight corkscrews, evading the snapping jaws of a furred menace. With its upturned snout and beady eyes burning from the hail of acidic rounds, the bat screamed and broke off its pursuit.

In the swirling mass of dragonflies, bats, and spitballs, other mounts and crews fought as hard but did not end up as lucky. Screams filled the Tether and died away, one after another. Mounts slipped from Axl's perception, but not being at the Drover's station meant he was unable to register specific callsigns or locations. Good luck finding any crew that went down in the marsh at night, he thought, aware it would reach the Tether. He hoped no one wasted time or energy on it. Confusion and carnage dominated their flight from Pondhome already. How many more would they lose if they stopped to look for the fallen?

Sanity or fear, perhaps a bit of both, prevailed.

"This is Commander Abyl, Flyer of Mama One-Nine. We're taking Lead. Full evasive and dive for the waterline."

Mamas and Papas executed a series of twists and turns that left the bats scrambling to locate their elusive prey amongst the constant assault of spitballs. The dragonflies accelerated faster, dove quicker, and disappeared into the dancing carpet of green. Mama One-Nine avoided the turbulent water of the flooding pond, rising and falling in rhythm with the waves.

Axl craned his head side to side, only catching glimpses of a dragonfly here and there among the feathery stalks of flora. Time and distance blurred as they flew under cover of the dense patches of towering water vegetation, enough of a span for Syn to return Myx to duty. Axl sensed Mama's unease but reassured her.

"Now, now, we'll be fine. I trust you to make that so."

"Don't worry, First Officer. I'm on station now."

"I wasn't talking to you, Myx. I trust in Mama. We'll see if you can earn my trust by doing your job. For once."

"Sir, I, uh, yessir!"

"That's better, Myx. Now stop talking and start droving."

"Exodus Flight, this is Mama One-Nine Drover Myx. Prepare for a Tether Handshake. All Drovers report."

Even without the Drover station, Axl didn't have to imagine what was happening. He had performed a similar check on flight after flight, patrol after patrol. However, he had never done so leading a swarm the size of Exodus Flight. In his mind's eye, Axl could see Myx moving a magnetic bead to his grid map for each Drover that checked in, one per mount. The math was easy. The implications of the changing equation were anything but as any subtractions would mean more loss to their peoples.

As Mama One-Nine soared through the night, the Tether hummed with activity as Drovers reported in from their respective mounts. Axl listened to the subtle fluctuations in the connection that signaled the presence of each Drover and their mount. He was frustrated with his current duty station as it did not have the maps available to note everyone's current position. Amidst the familiar voices and the reassuring clicks of acknowledgment, and growing list of missing, there was one absence in particular that sent a chill down Axl's carapace.

"Station, this is Mama One-Nine Drover Myx. I'm not receiving a response from Mama Three-Three's Drover. Repeat, no response from Mama Three-Three."

The Tether buzzed with concern, especially in the midst of the chaotic evacuation. Axl's mind raced with possibilities, his instincts urging him to take action.

"To whomever has them, relay their last known coordinates to Mama One-Nine," Axl said, volunteering them for search-and-rescue duty.

"We're going after them, eh? That an order?" Abyl commented from above.

"Mama Three-Three saved my mount and crew and turn about's fair play, Old Mite." Axl said, nearly choking on a nickname earned by behaving like an adult as a nymph. Abyl had never meant it as a compliment. The moniker, however, had instilled in Axl an unflinching sense of responsibility from nymphhood to this fateful night.

Without waiting for a response, Axl darted from his station, his four pairs of legs propelling him across the deck of Mama One-Nine. Dwyzl closed from the taper, his graspers filled with the woven spider silk rope used to help downed crews. They made their way to the edge of the dragonfly's thorax where anchors and pulleys were built into the mount's harness.

As they approached Mama Three-Three, Axl's heart sank at the sight before him. The mount lay still, its wings folded against its body, and its crew scattered across the surface of the water below.

"We're too late," Dwyzl said, his voice full of sorrow.

"For the mount anyway," Tender Syn said, joining them.

Axl nodded, his gaze sweeping over the fallen Mama and their crew. But amidst the despair, a glimmer of hope flickered in his mind. He reached out through the Tether, searching for any signs of life among the wreckage.

"I'm detecting faint signals from the crew. They're alive but injured. Requesting immediate assistance."

With practiced precision, Mama One-Nine's crew sprang into action, deploying ropes and harnesses to lower themselves onto the carapace of the slain mount. Their agile forms moved with purpose as they assisted in the rescue efforts.

One by one, the surviving crew of Mama Three-Three was hoisted aboard Mama One-Nine, their injuries looked after by Syn. Axl watched with a mixture of relief and gratitude as his fellow Mitra were brought to safety, their lives preserved amidst the chaos of the evacuation. The larva that had not been exposed to the briny water came next, carried two-by-two in the free graspers of Axl and Dwyzl.

Following a prayer for Mama Three-Three and those lives lost aboard her, Mama One-Nine and her inflated crew resumed its course. Surveying those clinging to survival aboard the back of their winged mount, Axl couldn't help but feel a sense of pride in their collective resilience. Despite the trials and tribulations they faced, they remained united in their determination to survive and rebuild.

Finally, after a long, deadly night, the first rays of dawn illuminated the horizon. Axl looked towards the future with hope, knowing that as long as they stood together, recruit and veteran, Mitra and dragonfly, they would weather whatever challenges lay ahead. In a world of myriad dangers, that was their collective strength: solidarity.

THE END

# Bloodrider
David Jones

Night lay heavy upon the land, shrouding the forested hills in shades of black and gray. The vampire Kelysen, perched upon dragon back, watched them pass beneath his cold gaze with indifference. A bell tolled some miles to the east, echoing through the mountains to call the hour from the city known as Laurelton. Hunger tightened Kelysen's throat at that sound. Bells meant people and people meant prey. How he longed to hunt, to lure, to feast. His body quivered with the need. And yet he sat, watching the land roll away beneath him, unable even to steer his gaze from his task.

*Does my blood thief hunger?* The dragon Stynaserian's voice crackled inside Kelysen's mind like the sound of thunder in a slot canyon.

"You know I do."

Kelysen was never certain if Stynaserian could hear his most private thoughts, or simply taste his emotions. At times, she displayed an uncanny ability to read his desires, but her penchant for keeping him half-starved robbed that trick of its mystery. Her twice-cursed blood, the only font of nourishment she allowed Kelysen, both empowered him to an outrageous degree, and kept him in thrall to her will. For though he possessed more strength and raw power than likely any vampire in all the world of Mirstone, Kelysen could not twitch his thumb without his dread mistress's consent.

*Serve well this night, blood thief, and I shall reward you handsomely.*

Such were her sweet promises, but her words rang hollow in Kel's mind. She never allowed him to fully slake his thirst with her blood. And she made him linger days between droughts. Already, three had passed since last he drank, and that only a meager sip. She enjoyed keeping him hungry, though whether from sadistic pleasure at his pain or fear of his growing strong enough to resist her influence, he could not say. Regardless, Kelysen loathed Stynaserian with a passion he had rarely experienced since his turning. Had he the strength of will to defy her, he would challenge the dragon. Kill or die, he would take his chances and be done with this deathless hell.

*There...* Stynaserian's feminine voice sliced through Kel's thoughts like a blade parting taut canvas. *Do you smell them? I scent horses and steel and wood smoke.*

"I smell them. I can't hear their hearts for the rush of wind, but I'd guess there are at least eight, perhaps ten in total."

Stynaserian's ponderous wings increased their beat, her anticipation at locating her quarry palpable. Kel could not fight her change in humor. A wash of giddy excitement ran through him, though he quelled it as best he could. Styn wouldn't allow him to drink from the knights they sought, nor even their mounts. She would order him to slaughter these men, and to do so without the least bit of finesse or art. He could take no pleasure in such killing, which benefited him not at all. The men, whom they were fast approaching, were likely mercenaries hired to seek out and kill the red dragon known as Stynaserian, the Mother of Mountains, the Thief of Souls.

No doubt these men had killed other dragons. Exterminating feral creatures brazen enough to terrorize human towns was, after all, a lucrative business. But these hunters didn't realize their peril. He almost felt pity for them. Especially since, deep within his most guarded thoughts, he yearned for them to slay the beast betwixt his legs. Not that they would ever come within striking distance of Stynaserian.

Kelysen would slay them before that could happen.

A thin stream of smoke rose from a clearing in the forest ahead where the Balanth's Blade river cut through the wood. Fire twinkled from a spot on a rocky beach where seven men reposed, cooking meat on improvised spits. Their armor, chain and steel and leather, stood stacked near the wood line, far removed from the river. A young boy sat near the stack, polishing a breastplate.

*Go, my blood thief. Kill them!*

Without hesitation, perhaps without even volition, Kelysen leaped feet first from Styn's back, the wind rushing past his ears, his black hair flapping above him, his loose jerkin and leather britches popping like sailcloth.

No sooner had one of the knights lifted his eyes at the odd sound than Kelysen, bloodrider and dragon thrall, landed amongst them next to the fire with a boom of impact that would have turned a regular man's feet, knees, and hips to dust.

Bereft of armor, and holding nothing more than a sharpened stick, the alert knight sprang to his feet only to have Kelysen punch him in the chest with such force it staved in his breastbone, collapsed both lungs at once, and hurled him into the river.

Had Kelysen been free he would have taken great pleasure in bleeding such a man. Now, however, suffering under Stynaserian's strict rule to drink no blood, he endeavored to kill without spilling a drop. For, no matter how his hunger burned, he would not be able to imbibe even that tiny amount.

The boy who had been cleaning armor hurled a sword to a knight across the fire from Kelysen and another to the man on his left.

"Good arm, boy," Kel called over his shoulder. "Thank you for giving these men an advantage. I would feel guilty killing them unarmed."

The man across the fire, burly and bearded and fully a head

taller than Kelysen, dashed forward screaming an incoherent battle cry. For sport, and he had to admit to himself, for the sheer pleasure of horrifying his enemies, Kelysen allowed the knight to run him through with his blade. The big man's momentum sent the cold steel through Kel's belly and out his back with an audible pop. Such a wound imparted little pain. He would compare it to his memories of getting pinched as a boy. It was well worth the look of shock on the knight's face when Kelysen remained standing face to face with him, a slight smile playing at his lips.

"What are you?" The knight braced his free hand on Kel's shoulder and moved to retrieve his sunken sword.

"I am a slave, dear knight. But also, I am death." Kelysen gripped the knight's hand, still holding the pommel, and squeezed.

The knight howled in agony as the pressure not only broke the bones in his hand, but minced the flesh. Kel studiously avoided bursting the skin so as to avoid bloodshed, but the knight would never again wield a sword with that hand.

Not that it mattered. He wouldn't be alive to practice learning with the other.

His partner, having watched this tableau without so much as lifting his sword, seemingly came to himself and rushed forward to menace Kelysen with his blade as if another through the gullet would make any difference to the vampire.

Moving faster than the human eye could follow, Kel spun and batted the newcomer's weapon aside before punching him in the throat. The knight collapsed, his sword forgotten, both hands clutching his flattened windpipe, struggling to draw in a breath that would never come.

The first knight, still cursing over his ruined hand, had dropped to his knees, tears glistening in his eyes and on his cheeks. In one smooth motion, Kelysen pulled the knight's sword from his belly and stove in the man's head with the flat of the blade.

Foolish.

Blood sprayed from the stricken knight's maimed scalp, some of it sizzling when it hit the campfire. The rush of Kel's hunger, like a burning ember lodged in his throat, pained him far more than any sword ever could. Almost, he broke with Stynaserian's commands and bent to drink from the dying knight. But the dragon's bond screamed inside him, twisting his thoughts to his task even over the demands of his craving.

The remaining knights, six of them, had each recovered weapons from the pile near the trees. Two carried long swords, three maces, and the last a pair of fighting daggers.

Such paltry implements would avail them nothing. With his hunger ignited, and yet obviated by his mistress's insurmountable orders, Kelysen sought only one thing: a quick end to these men's lives so that he might claim his boon from his mistress.

No more holding back.

A titanic scream shook the heavens which drew everyone's attention skyward. Seven dragons, none so large or majestic as their prey and yet deadly nonetheless, flew in a tightening circle about Stynaserian, closing now and again to rake her hide with claws, fangs, or horns. Each bore upon its back an armored knight in blackened plate armed with a likewise blackened javelin.

*Blood thief! Attend me! Defend your mistress!*

Stynaserian tucked her massive wings and dove for the river, briefly leaving her tormentors behind. At the final instant, before the earth might have done for her, she arrested her speed by spreading her wings wide, shaking the air with a rumble like thunder. Kelysen took three strides, bounded off a river stone big as the dragon's head, and leapt onto her back. Beating the air into submission, Stynaserian gained altitude, her great lungs laboring in her chest like the gods' own bellows.

*Distract these brigands so that we may escape!* Stynaserian commanded, thrashing the air with her wings so that she might match altitudes with their pursuers.

Despite his hunger, Kelysen was by no means weak. He was, after all, a vampire fed by dragon blood. Leaping from Stynaserian's armored back onto an emerald green beast twenty yards north and a dozen feet above him posed no obstacle. By design, he overshot the enemy dragon's rider, so that he landed between the wings, and thus safely out of the man's reach. The green dragon arched its neck to stare at Kelysen with an eye the size of an apple. It trumpeted its displeasure and wobbled in the air in a failed attempt to send its stowaway plummeting to the forest below.

Idiot creature. It could no more throw Kelysen free than it could shake loose its own scales. He considered stomping the dragon's spine in twain, he possessed the strength, but thought better of it. His hatred for his mistress notwithstanding, dragon kind were few in these lands. Slaying one without good reason seemed a waste.

Knights, however, were a different story.

The green dragon's rider, weighed down by his armor and his arms, only now made to interdict Kelysen. Moving with all the dexterity of a trout on dry land, he tried twice to catch his javelin on a hook attached to his saddle, before managing it on the third attempt. Kelysen sauntered closer to the man while the knight endeavored to draw a short sword from the scabbard affixed to his belt. He was still trying to rise to his feet when Kelysen took hold of his breastplate from behind and flung the knight up and out into darkness.

The green dragon bellowed a screech of horror as it curled it's neck to trace its rider's ascent into a blanket of low-hanging clouds. Kelysen hadn't meant to throw the man quite so high. He wanted the others to see the knight's trajectory. Fortunately, they had.

All six of the remaining dragons trumpeted their own alarms, mimicking the green's fearful call. Egged on by their riders, they scrambled after Kelysen's victim whose upward momentum had slowed to the point that he would soon begin a terminal race for the ground. The green dragon bellowed anew, flapping hard to intercept his rider, as did the others. If they weren't careful, they were all going to collide. And wouldn't that be a shame. Kelysen almost wanted to stick around and to see what would happen, but an insistent call from his mistress saw him leap from the green dragon's back in a long, arching dive that dropped him smoothly on the giant red's withers.

*A job well done, my blood thief.* Stynaserian climbed into the clouds, rising ever higher while pointing her muzzle ever eastward. She moved much too fast for so large a beast, but that was a facet of her magic. No dragon, aside from the smallest and youngest of their number, could have taken to the air without the inherent magic which flowed through their blood and through their souls. It was that very magic which had driven Kelysen to chance biting Stynaserian so long ago, reasoning that he could enlarge his power by tasting of it.

And he'd been right.

But what good was power without the freedom to wield it? No good at all.

*We have lost them. They're flying about in circles back there, trying to catch our scent. They never will.* Even in his mind, Kelysen could hear the smug satisfaction, even contempt, in his mistress's voice. *Fools. They sacrificed taking me to save one of their own.*

"Yes. Fools."

*Still, we cannot assume they won't suss out my lair. You must remain awake this day, my blood thief. I can't have dragon hunters coming upon me while I slumber. I've injuries to heal.*

Kelysen ground his fangs. He wanted to protest. He wanted to rail against her commands. He wanted to break *her* spine.

He could do none of those things.

"Yes, my mistress."

2

At some point in the distant past, Stynaserian's current lair had belonged to burrowing goblins. Most humans, elves too for that matter, would never believe such loathsome beasts capable of constructing a tiered city beneath one of the largest mountains in the western hemisphere. Even more ridiculous, they had managed to sculpt a magnificent capitol, hewn from raw granite, at the heart of their domain. And though many of its rooms were inaccessible to its current mistress due to her girth, the central hall boasted an open floor that could easily swallow three full-sized galleons with room to spare. Supported by twenty massive columns that ran along the periphery, each one wider in diameter than Stynaserian's neck and at least two hundred feet high, the great hall more than satisfied the dragon queen's needs for a safe place to slumber in peace.

Here she kept her hoard, a veritable lake of coins struck from platinum, gold, or silver, bearing the worn faces of kings long dead. Interspersed amongst them were untold numbers of weapons, pieces of armor, jewelry of every type, and myriad other trinkets which had caught the dragon's serpentine attention down through the ages for one reason or another. Kelysen felt certain Stynaserian enjoyed her riches. He would have to be blind and dimwitted to miss the gleam in his mistress's eyes as she waded into the hoard, sending mounds of treasure cascading in every direction. Kelysen set about lighting their supply of oil lamps all about the massive room. Their soft glow reflected from the treasure, giving the dragon's layer a buttery hue.

Kelysen knew the real reason Stynaserian had stolen such wealth. Whatever she secreted away in her lair could never be used by men. Simple as that. She needed no more motivation than pure, unadulterated spite, for Stynaserian hated mankind with a passion to rival a minor god. Any pain she might cause them brought her immense joy.

*Bring my salve,* Stynaserian ordered as she snuggled deeper into her piled treasure, the sound of tinkling coins echoing off the stone walls. *Those curs split my wing. Look! It hurts!* She stretched forth her left wing to reveal a tear in the fragile membrane between two finger-like bones.

"I already have it in hand, mistress." Anticipating her need, Kelysen had dipped into the warren of rooms at the rear of the great hall where he kept his few belongings along with a trove of magical ointments, powders, and other medicinal cures the dragon insisted he store there. Though her own magic saw her heal at an incredible rate compared to a creature of natural lineage, she put great stock in such products. More than once Kelysen had toyed with the idea of slipping poison into one, but he had never dared. Stynaserian's hold on his mind prevented him from causing her even the slightest direct harm.

Grimacing, he squeezed a dollop of foul-smelling, amber ointment onto a painter's brush and applied it to his mistress's wing. The wound bled little, thank the gods, though even this slight trickle sent a stab of hunger wending through Kelysen's guts. And yet, he dared not imbibe even so much as a drop until she gave him leave to do so. She would make him wait. He knew that. Stynaserian delighted in causing pain of every type. She wanted him to ask—to beg—for her blood, and well he might should the hours stretch too long. But he would hold out while he could. Even a slave had his pride.

*Careful!* She chided, her great wing trembling when the brush hairs passed over the open cut. *That hurts, you clumsy dolt. I can't fly if you shred my poor wing with your unskilled hands.*

"My apologies, mistress." Covering the tear with the disgusting salve helped to mitigate Kelysen's lust for the dragon's blood, though his hands still shook and his thoughts ran wild inside his skull.

Why she made such a fuss over this slight wound he couldn't say. She had taken far more damage in past battles and slept it off in a healing slumber. Kelysen allowed himself a sneer of contempt at her petulance, though he was careful to do so out of his mistress's sight.

"Where else are you injured, Great One?"

Gingerly, she folded her wing back and rolled on her side to expose her flank, her red scales glinting in the oily light. *I was gored across my ribs and I have a burn on my forelimb here.*

Kelysen painted these further wounds, neither of which had done more than scratch or blacken her scales, with utmost patience. How could so great and terrible a beast act the part of a babe with a stubbed toe? Perhaps her strength was waning now that she, at nearly two thousand years, approached middle age. She certainly wasn't the fearsome creature she had been in her youth, the wily red whose exploits had spawned myriad tales amongst the races of man, dwarf, and elf. Discolorations in her hide where newer scales, some of them misshapen compared to those around them, spoke of swords, maces, and javelins which had once pierced her natural armor. A brighter red than their older counterparts, these new-grown plates outlined scars in Stynaserian's flesh beneath.

The worst of these was not the longest nor, by its nature, the most impressive, Kelysen knew. For though she bore several bright red lines thick as a man's hand and long as a hose nose to tail along her flanks where knights had raked her with swords, the wound that had come closest to ending Stynaserian's life had left but a single dot of bright color upon her breast. Kelysen eyed the spot now as he caked ointment between the scales on her left forelimb. Deceptively small—no bigger than a large egg—the blemish marked the place where a knight once plunged an enchanted sword into the dragon's breast. By dint of fortune, good for her and ill for the man, his blade had missed Stynaserian's heart by a hair's breadth and he had paid for missing his stroke with instant, fiery death.

By her own account, Stynaserian had spent weeks afterward slumbering in a magical stupor to heal the wound. She had emerged from her lair a thin and withered ghost of herself, driven by hunger to hunt else she would have slept even longer. This was long before Kelysen unwittingly stumbled into her service, and she had been forced to remove the blade herself. She had tossed it aside to become a part of her hoard, a forgotten relic which had been, for a brief moment, the center of her world. It lay now at her tail, discarded and ignored, but powerful nonetheless. Its magic tingled in Kelysen's mind whenever he cast his gaze upon it. Not that he—

*Blood thief.* Stynaserian's thoughts sounded slow and languorous in Kelysen's mind. Both her body's natural inclination to heal and her blood's magical counterpart pushed her to drowse. Barring great need, she would not remain awake much longer. *You served me well this night. I shall let you sup. But you may take only five swallows. I have wounds to heal.*

Instant rage filled Kelysen, though it was tempered by his thirst. Five swallows? How was he to survive on such scanty rations? It wasn't as if he, given leave to drink his fill, could have consumed enough to harm so great a beast as she.

He would have railed against her, had he the will. Instead,

cursing the eagerness he could not hide, he hurried to a spot low on her neck where she kept a couple of her scales pruned back for the purpose of feeding him. She arched, giving him a space to sink his fangs, and Kelysen drank. As always, the magical elixir of dragon's blood clouded his head, drowning out all other thoughts besides the flow of power and the sweet taste that consumed his every sense. Nevertheless, Stynaserian's orders cut through even this fugue of ecstasy, for he could take no more than his allotted five sips before his limbs, moving of their own volition, pushed him away from her. And though his hunger remained, and the sight of blood seeping from his fang marks stirred it to a near unbearable crescendo, no amount of will power could make him return to it.

*Now go guard the entrance. And no sleeping until I wake.* Stynaserian yawned and stretched, digging her bulk deeper into the trove, before curling herself up, snout to tail like a dog. She drifted off in seconds, as was her wont after a flight let alone a battle. Her breathing slowed, as did the beating of her heart in Kelysen's ears.

Left alone to fume, he eyed his mistress, his tormentor, with a seething rage he could not quench. Many a time, he had tried to kill the beast, imagining the act in great detail in his mind. But the capacity to fulfill such desires eluded him, for he could no more lift a hand against Stynaserian than he could flap his arms and hie off to the moon.

His mistress never seemed to catch these murderous thoughts in his head. She appeared capable of gleaning only the surface of his imaginings, the gods be praised, for she would surely punish him had she any inkling of his secret fantasies. With her asleep, he feared to indulge them even less, and so he spent some minutes conjuring up various ways to dispatch the dragon by the most lurid means he could fathom. Tricking her into eating barbed caltrops was his current favorite. He would enjoy watching her languish in pain while they tore through her innards.

Still musing upon that glorious image, Kelysen's jaundiced eye fell again upon the sword which had so nearly ended his mistress's wretched existence. The blade, ensconced in a scabbard made of crocodile leather, lay now an arm's length from the dragon's curled tail. Its magic called to Kelysen whenever he looked upon it. A yearning pulled at his mind, calling for him to take up the weapon. Always before, the dragon bond had prevented him from doing so. Yet now, he sensed he could do it should he wish, so long as he avoided all thought of using it against his mistress. Had he gained enough power from drinking her blood to make this possible? Perhaps. He had lived as her servant, drinking nothing else, for more than a decade. Did that mean he might one day build sufficient strength to obviate his need to serve? Or, could he make better use of this reprieve and thus hasten the day of his freedom?

Kelysen, moving with the silence of the undead, took up the sheathed blade, holding it in both hands while he considered it. Perhaps it was the buzz of dragon's blood filling his mind, or the unrequited desire of a true slave, but the beginnings of a plan formed as he gazed upon the sword. One that would indeed see him escape Stynaserian's control, and through no direct attack of his own. What need had he of autonomy if someone else's hands were to strike his mistress down?

In the heat of the lair, yellow light glistening off his pallid cheeks, the vampire smiled, revealing twin fangs still coated in fresh dragon's blood.

3

Unable to immediately put his plan in motion for fear of the dawn, Kelysen waited out the daylight hours, guarding the lair as his mistress bid him do. Though its rays could not reach him deep inside the mountain, remaining awake with the sun aloft pained the vampire. Yes, he was more than powerful enough to tolerate such a trifle—he might even possess the strength to survive direct sunlight for a brief time though he had never chanced it—but doing so went against his nature. He wanted to sleep, yet every time he considered crawling into a night-black alcove deep in the goblin complex, his mind would skitter away from the thought. Thus he spent the day, aching, eager for nightfall when he might put his plan to work. At last, the sky darkened enough for him to venture out beneath the stars while his mistress snored.

With luck, he might never hear that hated sound again.

Locating the dragon hunters was child's play. Kelysen could pick out the stench of their armor, horses and, most assiduously, their dragons from across the valley that separated Styn's lair from the city of Laurelton. The knights had holed up in the wilderness north of its borders, at a bend in the river well away from the town proper. This suited the vampire just fine. It obviated his need to enter Laurelton, and thus endure the temptation of human blood he could not drink. Bad enough he must ghost through this encampment with the sound of so many beating hearts calling to his predatory nature.

Dozens of tents billowed in the night breeze while the camp slept. Five sentries, each wearing boiled leather and brandishing a spear, patrolled the outskirts. These were vigilant men, no doubt made all the more so since their company expected reprisal from the dragon they had failed to slay. Yet sneaking past them had been as nothing for Kelysen who moved like shadow. Their mounts might have been a different tale. Such magical creatures could sense the undead in their presence. But no sane person, even a knight familiar with the beasts, would sleep near a dragon. The creatures were known to flame in their sleep, and even if they managed to avoid setting fire to the camp, they might well roll over a hapless man, tent and all, in the throes of a dream. Thus, the company's dragons were settled some distance away across the river and, thankfully, up wind.

Only one of the many tents in camp warranted guards at its entrance, which to Kelysen's mind marked it as belonging to the group's commander. He avoided them by the simple expedient of rolling under the tent's loose back wall.

The camp commander was not asleep, which came as no surprise to Kelysen. He had heard the man's heartbeat, and the scratching of a quill, from outside the tent. His reactions, however, did surprise Kelysen. He turned on his camp chair to regard the newcomer with steely gray eyes.

"Ah," he said, his voice cool. "You are the vampire who killed my men yesterday evening." Briefly, his gaze darted to the sheathed sword in Kelysen's hands then back to his face.

Few men recognized a vampire without showing a speck of fear. Generally, Kelysen took a certain thrill out of watching humans quake in their trousers upon realizing their danger at his presence. Yet, this one's nonchalance came as a refreshing surprise. He hadn't even bothered to rise from his seat.

"I am Kelysen."

"I am Captain Nathanroy Sanderford. Have you come to kill me, Kelysen?"

When Kelysen first imagined this plan, he had known it would hinge on his complete belief in a simple precept: he had brought the sword here as a ruse. Giving it to the dragon hunter would engender this, Nathanroy, with false hope. He would think himself invincible, and therefore take chances against his better judgment. Thus, Kelysen was not aiding the hunter to slay his mistress. On the contrary, he was duping the fool into his own grave.

"No. I have not come to kill you, Captain. I have come to give you this." Kelysen handed over the sword, all the while whispering the lie in his mind.

Nathanroy took the scabbard though he continued staring at Kelysen for several seconds before inspecting it. Slowly, he drew the sword, his eyes growing wide as pure white light, dim but undeniable, spilled from the pristine blade. He held it before himself, his pupils contracting at the sight, and gasped.

"This is Lumos," he said, awe flavoring his voice. "The Day Sword. The Bond Breaker."

"It is magic. That is all I know." Kelysen kept his tone flat, his words measured. Hiding the truth from himself was proving harder than he had imagined. This sword, this Lumos, would lead to Nathanroy's destruction, not Stynaserian's. He was acting in the best interest of his mistress. He could do no other.

"Magic? This is one of the great wonders of Mirstone! There's not a blade of its like in existence. It dispels enchantments the way lye scrubs dirt. This once belonged to Harkerd Plunn, the greatest knight swordsman of his generation."

When Kelysen showed no sign of recognition, Nathanroy shook his head.

"He was called the Jackdaw. He bested men, dwarves, and elves from here to sea and back. Never was there his equal. How did you come by his blade?"

"Stynaserian ate him. You have the sword now. Perhaps, that makes you the Jackdaw."

"I could never—"

Kelysen held up a hand. "Put it to good use by slaying my mistress and it is yours. I am her blood servant and cannot do but her will until one of us is slain. Use that to free me, and I won't come to reclaim it after the deed is done."

It was all Kelysen could do to maintain the lie in his head. He did not, could not, want Nathanroy to kill his mistress. Otherwise, the triggers in his mind would make him kill the captain here and now. With all his dead heart, he willed himself to believe the ruse and by dint of sheer will maintained the lie.

"I must be away now," Kelysen said, turning to go. "I don't want my mistress to wake with me gone. Use that blade well, and strike true, knight."

Nathanroy nodded. "I will. Mark my word, she will not live one more week."

Kelysen started to leave, but froze at the back of the tent, a familiar WOMP-WOMP-WOMP tickling the furthest range of his hearing. He swallowed, and turned back to the captain who obviously couldn't yet hear the ominous sound.

"Make that one more hour."

"What's that? What do you mean, sir?"

"Stynaserian is here."

## 4

One of the sentinels blew a trumpet. Its shrill call split the night like a pickax carving ice. Across the river, a handful of the hunters' dragons roared in response, waking their fellows. In twos and threes, they leaped from their bed down encampment, beating the air with their wings in a manic effort to gain altitude and come to their riders' defense.

Kelysen rent a hole in the back of Nathanroy's tent in time to see Stynaserian fold her wings and stoop like a raptor, her body silhouetted against the silvery light of the moon. She barreled into a bronze dragon half her size from above, sickle-like fore claws digging into either side of its withers. Her position secured, she raked the unfortunate bronze with her hind claws as if she were running in place. The smaller dragon screamed in agony and surprise as Stynaserian rode it to the ground. Together, they plunged into the forest a quarter mile from where Kelysen stood to the tune of cracking trunks, breaking limbs, and an avalanche of dirt and soil thrown up in their wake. Of the twenty dragons who had taken to the air, five circled back to defend their fallen member, but the knight blowing the horn redoubled his efforts, and they broke off, abandoning the one Styn had driven to the ground.

A brief flicker of hope ignited in Kelysen's breast when he saw his mistress drop below the tree line. Perhaps, in her eagerness to attack, she had managed to break her own neck. But no. If that had occurred, the magical link between them would have been severed. Not only could he still sense her through it, an exhilarated thrill of triumph exuded through the link. Clearly, she had killed the miserable bronze, and took great pleasure in the act.

"You said before, you are that dragon's slave." Nathanroy, still bearing the naked blade at his side, had exited his tent behind Kelysen. A couple of guardsmen, entering from the front, hustled his way, but he waved them off before they could confront the pale stranger near their commander.

"Yes." Kelysen didn't turn, but continued watching the trees. He sighed and shook his head when Stynaserian flapped into view above the forest and roared.

"Will you help us slay her?"

Kelysen shook his head. "Had I my own will, I might. I hate that creature." He turned to regard Nathanroy, knowing his skeletal visage would appear gruesome to the human in the pale moonlight. "Instead, I must aid her. And I will kill you if I'm able."

The guardsmen drew their swords, but Kelysen ignored them. He turned his back and said over one shoulder, "Promise you'll return the favor."

With that, he sped away toward his mistress, moving faster than any knight could manage. Most of the men he passed, all of them scurrying about in a rush to don weapons and armor for the coming battle, didn't see him.

Stynaserian, however, was a different matter.

5

She dipped low, coming within twenty feet of the cleared field where Kelysen ran, and he bounded onto her back.

*Blood thief.*

"My mistress."

*You tried to betray me.* Stynaserian blew a torrent of flame at the hunters' encampment as she passed over it. Her fire engulfed three dragons and their riders making ready to fly. Given their natural armor, the beasts may have survived the attack with minor injuries, but the men died screaming.

"I came here as a ruse," Kelysen said. "I wanted the hunters to overplay their hand so that we might dispatch them."

Stynaserian's laugh shook Kelysen's mind like a typhoon trapped in a mug. He clapped his hands over his ears by reflex though that did him no good. The titanic booming made his eyes water bloody tears. He pressed himself low against her scales, eyes squeezed shut, enduring until at last her laughing receded.

*Liar,* she said, her tone still flavored with mirth. *Do you truly believe you could take any action without my knowledge? Fool, vampire. I gave you the idea of giving that sword to these dogs! I knew you would leap at the chance to betray me. And that your stupidity would not only lead me straight to their camp, but leave them vulnerable.*

Kelysen lifted his chin to gaze for a moment at the stars wheeling overhead. He was a fool. Never, since the day he first drank of her blood, had he been free to make decisions outside his mistress's control, not even while she slept. He had believed he could lie to himself, but all the while it had been his mistress lying to him. His play at moving against her from an oblique angle had been nothing but smoke and shadows.

*Good, you see things as they are. You will never be free of me, blood thief. I own you body and... whatever soul you might possess, you wretched creature. Now, help me destroy these hunters and their traitorous mounts. I'm hungry.*

Stynaserian turned in a circle made ponderous by her size, and bellowed a ringing challenge which rolled across the valley like a wave. She was a wily beast, old and well versed in aerial combat. Rather than merely turn about, she gained altitude, pumping her wings in great thrusts that kept her above the smaller dragons rising to meet her thunder.

Chagrined beyond measure, Kelysen fumed, but there was nothing he could do to gainsay the dragon's statements. She did own him, as she had well and truly proven this night. And he would kill for her, as he had so often done in the past.

He had no choice.

The first of the hunters' remaining dragons, of which Kelysen counted nineteen, reached Stynaserian's altitude seconds before she could pour fire upon the encampment a second time. It was a blue-scaled female, young from the look of her. The knight on her back wore leather instead of mail and bore a sword rather a javelin. Obviously, the man had dressed in haste and left his best weapons on the ground.

Stynaserian spread her wings at the last possible instant before the blue could attack, causing the smaller creature to overshoot her by half a dozen feet. She roared her frustration, but the sound morphed into a cry of pain as the giant red dragon seized her tail and bit it in half. Gallons of blood spilled from the wound, stoking Kelysen's hunger to new heights, not that he could do a thing about it.

The loss of a tail didn't necessarily impede a dragon's flight, but the instant drop in blood pressure left the blue weak to the point of languor. She plummeted from the sky, her rider adding his anemic scream to her howls of agony. Both cut off when they struck the rocky beach near the river's bend.

A sharp flick of thought from his mistress sent Kelysen diving from her back before he fully realized he was moving. He landed hard on the back of a red dragon which bore no rider. Likely as not, Kelysen had slain its rider the night before. Though he had no qualms against killing the beast, doing so at Stynaserian's behest grated the vampire's nerves. He fought the urge even as the young red waggled and bucked in an attempt to dislodge Kelysen from his back. But there was no fighting Stynaserian's hold over his mind. Try as he might, he could not prevent himself from raising his fist and delivering a full-bodied punch to the creature's spine, severing it with one blow. The red huffed out a fiery grunt and its limbs went lax, including its wings. Its neck drooped and it fell from the heavens like a hailstone.

Determined by a will not his own to finish his grim work, Kelysen leaped upward from the red onto the back of a formidable green almost as large as Stynascrian herself. As two more dead dragons fell past, dispatched by his mistress, Kelysen marched along the green's spine toward her rider. He stood betwixt the wings before he noticed the pall of magic streaming off the leather-armored knight seated before him. The man turned and stood and Kelysen saw that it was Nathanroy. The captain drew Lumos from the crocodile scabbard affixed to his belt. Its blade gave off a soft, pearly glow like a warning to all children of the night.

"It doesn't have to be this way," Nathanroy called over the wind. "Fight the dragon's will. Let us slay it together!"

"I am sorry I must kill you." Kelysen meant those words, which came as something of a surprise to him. He had never lamented taking a human's life since his first night as a vampire, but this man represented his best hope at freedom. Sad he must foreclose his own means of possible escape.

The sound of boots thumping down on scales made Kelysen

turn. Two of Nathanroy's knights, having spotted their captain in danger, had thrown themselves from their own mounts onto the green dragon's back. Neither appeared particularly dangerous, especially since they had to continually gyrate to keep their balance. But they were enemies. And while Kelysen might not be able to convince himself to forego slaughtering his mistress's would-be hunters, he could choose which to fight, even if that decision left him vulnerable.

Rather than strike with all his speed and thus end the two knights on the instant, Kelysen advanced upon them slowly as if fearing he might slip due to the green dragon's flapping wings.

The lead knight swung his blade, which Kelysen avoided with room to spare. It would have been the work of a moment to close the distance between them and twist the knight's head off his shoulders, or perhaps simply shove the both of them off the dragon, but Kelysen did neither. He instead took another step, showing his fangs.

Lumos's tip blossomed from Kelysen's chest with a sudden bust of light. Though a part of his mind had anticipated the blow, the pain came as something of a shock. He hadn't experienced physical agony in decades. Mundane weapons, while they might cleave through his tough skin and bones, imparted little more than a pinching sensation when used against him. The enchanted sword, however, sent a shock wave of searing agony up and down his spine. He screamed and convulsed like a fish wriggling on a spear. A blunt object, Nathanroy's boot no doubt, planted itself on Kelysen's spine, pushed, and sent him flying.

A spill of boulders along the banks of the river rushed up to meet him, and Kelysen spread his arms in a lovers embrace. His mistress had been wrong. She couldn't own him forever. Not when there was death to break his bonds.

## 6

Legends tell of only two ways to kill a vampire: a wooden stake, preferably elm, through the heart, and beheading. While the latter may well end the vampire's life, as it would most any creature, the stake, Kelysen knew from experience, didn't work. More than one would-be vampire hunter had driven a sharpened stick through his chest while he pretended to sleep. The expressions on their faces when he arose from his coffin despite the prescribed antidote to undead life was worth the minor discomfort it brought. Rending them limb from limb was even better.

A magic sword through the heart, however, appeared to be a different story. While Lumos's bite hadn't killed Kelysen straight away, his fall to the rocky shore had certainly loosened his grip on this mortal world. Though he couldn't be certain, he thought his spine may have broken, and his ribs were most definitely shattered. His left arm appeared to have grown a new elbow below his wrist and his jaw no long tracked true so that his lower teeth were misaligned with his fangs. Pain, like a rolling water wheel, creaked through his body, never slowing, never ceasing. On the bright side, his right arm at least remained intact. He could even move it.

Slowly, he opened his eyes. He wasn't supposed to have lived. Not only did he remain in Stynaserian's thrall, he also now lived in some forgotten pit of hell where agony served as the coin of the realm. He lay dashed upon jagged stones three feet from the river's edge. Moonlight shone upon the water where it babbled on in complete ignorance of the vampire's plight.

It was beautiful.

Further along, perhaps five feet upstream, lay a golden dragon of medium size, its body half in and half out of the water. Long, bloody furrows dug out of its scales and burn marks scored across its ruined wings spoke of Stynaserian's handiwork. She might well come out of this fight alive, and even if she didn't, she was at least giving a good accounting of herself without Kelysen up there to back her. Even now, part of his mind yearned to rise and return to that fight, but his body, too long starved on account of his sadistic mistress's evil whims, could not comply. He was too weak to heal from his injuries. Too weak to stand even to save his own hide. Soon enough the sun would rise, and he would finally find out if his new found strength would protect him against it.

Kelysen had his doubts.

*Vampire.* The male voice in his mind sounded weak, thready.

Kelysen lifted his head to find the golden dragon regarding him with one fist-sized eye. He seemed incapable of lifting his neck.

"Yes, dragon?"

*My name is Pelfare.*

"So?"

*We are dying, you and I.*

"Good." Kelysen shut his eyes. He could not sleep during the night, such was his curse, but perhaps if he feigned sleep the beast would stop talking to him.

*You are in thrall to the red. I feel it.*

Kelysen said nothing. He was done listening to dragons. Let the retch prattle, he had dying to do.

*I can help you break her hold over you.*

Kelysen held still for a long moment, intrigued despite himself. He had never considered seeking out another dragon to secure his freedom. Involving two of the cursed things had seemed an invitation to double his torment.

"I'm listening," he said at length.

*I teeter on the edge of death. Nothing can save me now. But while my heart beats and my fire burns, there remains magic in my blood.*

Kelysen's eyes snapped open.

*Do you hear me, vampire?*

"What trick is this?"

*No trick. A boon. Drink my life's blood before it flickers out and your bond to the red queen shall be destroyed.*

"Only to be replaced by a bondage to you."

*The dead hold no bonds.*

Hunger flared in Kelysen throat and his ruined body quaked with the need to drink. Using his good arm, he pulled himself across the rock, grasping whatever handholds he could find until he reached the creature's side.

*Promise me only that you will leave my compatriots alive. Do that, and my life is yours.*

"I will."

Pelfare, seeing that Kelysen lacked the strength to pull himself up to his neck, obligingly extended a forelimb, which the vampire used as a scaly ladder. Blood ebbed from the golden dragon's maimed flank, pressured out by his weakening heart. Almost sensually, the dragon pressed Kelysen to the widest of those cuts and the vampire drank.

Whatever reservations he may have held over trusting Pelfare, Kelysen lost them in the torrent of hot, magic-infused blood that filled his mouth. It washed through him in a torrent, spreading heat and healing through his limbs. His bones knit, his flesh sealed, and his body became whole. No longer limited at how much he could consume, the vampire drank without stinting. Even as the golden dragon's heart first stuttered and then stopped, he continued to feed, taking in more blood than he had ever done before.

When at last he rose, his face covered in glistening red, a fire burned within Kelysen. Dragon magic, suffused with that of his own, heated every cell in his body. His vision, already far superior to that of even an elf, became clearer, so that the night became like daylight. He could hear hares and deer and skunks traipsing through the brush half a mile away and distinguish each by their scent. And his strength… Kelysen couldn't be certain, but his body told him he was at least twice as strong as he had ever been. Such improvements likely wouldn't last, not at this intensity, but for the moment, he felt like a minor god.

A god without restraints.

7

High above, Stynaserian fought for her life. Eleven hunter dragons remained, most with riders still on their backs, though from the bodies strewn about the camp and the forest, it was clear she had dethroned many a knight. From the looks of things, Kelysen need not lift a hand against his former mistress to see her fall. The knights and their dragons had no intention of letting her live. They would fight sword and scale to the last of them if that's what it took.

But the vampire wasn't content to let his decade of slavery go unpunished. He owed the great red a debt of vengeance, and he would have it.

Moving like a sparrow through the trees, Kelysen shot into the burning encampment, eschewing the many bodies of dead men and dragons, and came to a stop at the end of the clearing.

"MISTRESS!" Driven by his newfound power, Kelysen's voice boomed fit to rival any dragon's roar. "TO ME!"

*Blood thief! I thought you dead! I need you!* The red queen thrashed and whipped her tail, dislodging herself from two smaller dragons bent on tearing at her abdomen with their gleaming claws. She fell and sped up her fall with a mighty pump of her wings, angling herself Kelysen's way, a storm cloud of pursuers fast on her tail.

Casting about, the vampire took up a discarded sword from a fallen knight, making no effort to conceal it. He moved as if he would run to meet his mistress and leap onto her back. She, seemingly too preoccupied to notice that their link had been severed, evened out her flight, her tongue lolling as she zoomed toward him.

At the final second, when Kelysen should have leaped onto her back, he instead jumped forward, sword outstretched to slash at the base of her right wing. Though his stolen blade carried no magic, the sharped steel bit into the dragon's shoulder with the force of a giant's punch.

Too late Stynaserian saw her peril. Kelysen's strike had already cleaved through her wing before she could jerk away. She screamed and belched fire even as she tumbled to her now-crippled side. Her momentum carried her through the copse of trees separating the hunters' former encampment from the river and into the water. Her impact sent a wave over the far bank.

Before she had even splashed down, Kelysen was on her. Without words or ceremony, he sprang onto her back and plunged his sword into her neck. She thrashed, craning to snap at him, but the angle was wrong and she couldn't reach. Her remaining wing threw off her balance and she stumbled about, kicking up splashes of cold mountain water.

She was still thrashing when Nathanroy's green dragon landed on her head, rear claws sinking into her neck where Kelysen had left his sword. The hunter captain sprang from his perch atop the green, Lumos flashing in the night, and chopped Stynaserian's neck in two.

The ancient red's body quivered and then collapsed into the river, her blood, strangely unattractive to Kelysen, colored the waters red in the moonlight.

Nathanroy, Lumos raised, turned to Kelysen who regarded him

from the dead dragon's back. Seven more dragons and their riders landed around them on the banks while the two stared at one another.

"Are we going to have a problem here, vampire?"

Kelysen shook his head. "No, Captain. I have no desire to harm you or your men. You have relieved me of a great burden."

Nathanroy hesitated and looked over at his mount before turning his attention back to Kelysen. "In that case, have you ever considered a career as a dragon hunter? We seem to be down a few riders and we usually hunt at night."

Kelysen laughed uproariously and stamped his boot. "Coming from a man who seems to fear nothing, that is a tempting offer. But I'm afraid I've had my fill of dragons for at least the next century."

"Come now." Nathanroy lowered his blade. "You have to admit you'll miss flying at least."

Kelysen coked his head to one side, a strange pull nipping at his hips and sternum. He smiled, showing his fangs. "No, my captain. I don't think I will."

With that, he spread his arms wide and shot into the heavens. No dragon needed.

## THE END

# Unexpected Benefits
pdmac

Resting his hands on the top of the shovel, Cullin stood gazing up at the dragon riders sweeping across the afternoon sky. *One, two, three…* He silently counted them as he studied each dragon and rider. Intently focused on the aerobatics, he startled when a hand waved in front of his face.

Dropping his gaze, he sheepishly shrugged to see his father frowning at him. His father raised his hands high enough for Cullin to watch him sign, *Stop wasting time. You've seen dragon riders before. If you want to see them again, finish what you're doing.*

Resting the top of the shovel handle against his shoulder, Culling signed back. *Sorry, Father. I got distracted. Can I go to the training center after I finish?*

*We'll see. Finish what you're doing first. That stump is not going to disappear by itself.*

Cullin nodded and looked down at the remnants of a stubborn stump that he had been trying to dig up since this morning. Between the axe and shovel, he had managed to get most of it separated from the deepest roots. There remained one tenacious chunk of the stump that probably had a thick root going straight down. Replacing the shovel with the axe, he paused to watch his father walk over to where Rusk stood on the plow platform tethered to two hulking oxen. Though he couldn't hear what was said, he knew by his father's arm pointing that he was telling his younger son to keep the rows straight. Cullin chuckled, knowing that his brother had likewise got distracted by the dragon riders and wasn't paying attention to the oxen.

An hour later, Cullin finally pried out the last remnants of the stump. Collecting the larger chunks, he carried them to the woodpile before filling a wheelbarrow with rich dirt from the pile next to the hogs' pen. Returning to the stump hole, he filled it until all that remained were scattered wood chips around a relatively smooth part of the field.

Walking back to the barn, he put away his tools and headed into the house, a stoutly built farmhouse made from the stones dug up from the fields, pausing to sit on the porch to take his boots off before going inside. His father opened the door and nodded at him, pleased.

*That was a tough stump. You did well. You may go to the training center. But,* his father paused signing to hold up a finger to emphasize, *stay out of trouble. You know what to do when they start their stupidity.*

*I'm not the one who starts it. All I want to do is see the dragons and riders,* he complained, signing back.

*I know that, but it doesn't stop them from being idiots. Avoid them as best you can.*

*I will, Papa. Do you want Rusk to come along?*

*No. He still has his own work to finish. Be back by dinner.*

*I will Papa.*

Happily relacing his boots, Cullin stood and headed down the footpath until it intersected with the cart path that undulated with the farm fields towards the distant walled city of Penred. In the far distance beyond the walls of the capital city of Lannraig, thickly forested mountains belonging to the Dragon Kingdom spread across the horizon. Snow-capped even in the summer, the mountains rose so high that the caps were often hidden in the clouds. He slowed down when he came to a pathway to another farmhouse. The door opened, and Kenzie emerged.

*Where you going?* she signed, taking off her smock.

*To see the dragons,* he grinned.

*Mind if I come?*

*I was hoping you could,* he replied, only too willing to spend time with her. Not only was she very pretty, she was the only one, besides his family, who made an effort to learn sign language. That she was as proficient as he and his family made him believe there was something more there than simply wanting to be friends. Then, several months ago, she surprised him by declaring that she wanted to be boyfriend-girlfriend and kissed him to seal the deal. Since then, he went out of his way to see her as often as he could.

Turning to toss her smock inside, she called out to her parents that she was going to see the dragons with Cullin. Not waiting to hear if they consented of not, she bounded down the path and stood on her tip toes to give him a kiss.

Cullin bent his head to kiss her, wanting to deliver a deep kiss but knew that her parents were probably watching from inside. Forcing himself to be satisfied with a brief kiss, he interlaced his fingers with her hand, and they walked off down the cart road, consumed with each other.

Anyone traveling along the road would have smiled to see the two. Cullin was tall, broad-shouldered with firm and thick muscles from the years of toiling outside. In contrast, Kenzie was slender and came up to the middle of his chest. Where Cullin would be described as rugged, Kenzie was graceful like a dancer, her thick auburn hair cascading down to the middle of her back.

Though excited to see the dragons and riders, they took their time, enjoying this time together. Yet all too quickly, they arrived at the landing and training field just outside the walls of the city. The field was the size of a small farm with tackle and armor sheds on the side next to the walls. On the side to the left of the sheds was the Governors Hall, a large imposing building of smooth white granite containing the Dragon Rider Governors' offices, assembly rooms, and other administrative offices. Opposite the tackle and armor sheds were the dragon sheds, large enough to give shelter in inclement weather. In between the sheds and Governors Hall, the level field stretched wide and far, giving ample room for any number or dragons and riders at one time.

Cullin and Kenzie positioned themselves as close to the dragon sheds as allowed, giving them an excellent view of the various riders and dragons. Leaning forward, Cullin rested his arms on the fence railing and breathed a sigh of contentment. The interaction between human and dragon was always exciting for him, especially when they talked to each other, though he could not hear the voices. It was something he yearned to do, though he knew it was impossible. He chuckled as he imagined a dragon moving his hands in sign language.

His gaze swept the level field until it rested on a dragon by itself over at the far end of the dragon sheds. The dragon was smaller than the usual flight-team dragons and seemed to be waiting for someone. Every now and then its head would perk up when a rider happened to walk by.

Kenzie touched his arm to get his attention and pointed to the other end of the training field where a rider and dragon had just landed.

Cullin's eyes immediately lit up when he recognized them. *That's Baran and Kriol.* To his surprise, Baran happened to look over and saw Cullin and Kenzie, giving them a friendly wave before resuming his conversation with the dragon.

Cullin grinned, his gazed focused on Baran. *He waved to us.* When Kenzie didn't respond, he twisted his head to see her looking behind them, her lips tight. Turning, he exhaled a frustrated breath.

There were three of them, smirking at him and leering at Kenzie. The one in the middle was tall and well-built like one employed as a physical laborer. He was the obvious leader as the other two hung back slightly. Though not as tall, they were built somewhat the same way except the blond-haired one had a little more heft to him. In contrast, the other, brown-haired with thin wisps of a beard, tended to the leaner side.

The three of them exchanged grins. The blond pointed to Cullin's head and said something then laughed. Cullin knew the point of the insult. His hair, though thick and curly, was white like snow, in sharp contrast to his bronze-colored skin from spending so much time outdoors. The other pointed at his eyes and wiggled his fingers pretending he was blind, mocking Cullin's deep blue eyes, insinuating that Cullin was both deaf and blind.

Though he couldn't hear her, he knew Kenzie was telling them to leave them alone. He watched the leader disdainfully tick his head at them and mouth the word 'Freak.'

The brown-haired one reached to grasp Kenzie's arm. Cullin slapped it away with one hand and slammed a fist into the man's chest, launching him into the air and propelling him back nearly a dozen feet.

Momentarily startled, the leader quickly recovered and threw a punch at Cullin who easily blocked it then delivered a bone crushing upper cut that snapped the man's head back and lifted him off the ground.

Rapidly assessing the situation, the blond man spun around and fled.

Cullin's hands clenched as he waited for either one to stand and resume their beating, yet neither tried to stand. He twitched when Kenzie touched his arm.

*We probably should leave*, she signed. *The authorities will be here soon. You know how it goes. The one who ran away will say it was our fault.*

*I've had it with everyone picking on us*, he fumed. *It's about time someone stood up to them. I'm not running away anymore.* Folding his arms, he defiantly leaned back against the fence, purposely waiting for the constables to come.

Two constables arrived much sooner than he expected, the third bully tagging along behind. Exuding their authority as law enforcers, they rapidly assessed the scene, especially the two men still on the ground, and crisply informed Cullin that he was under arrest for assault. Ignoring Kenzie's statement that they had started it, the constables started to reach up to grab hold of Cullin's arms when they suddenly stiffened to attention.

Turning, Cullin saw Baran, Prince Miach's son, standing at the fence. Confused, he frowned at Kenzie.

*He's telling the constable that he saw everything. He says that those three were bothering us and that the one man tried to harm me. Now he's telling them that if we don't, he will press charges against them.*

The constables respectfully nodded. Ignoring the protestations of the third bully, they manhandled the two on the ground and dragged them away.

Overwhelmed, Cullin turned to Baran and gave a voice to express his gratitude. "Thank you."

Then to his shock, Baran signed back, *You're welcome.*

*You know how to sign?* he said, his jaw dropping.

Baran smiled and nodded. *Yes. I have a younger sister who has hearing problems. No one knows except our family. You understand why.*

Cullin bobbed his head.

*I've seen you here a lot*, Baran said. *Would you like to meet my dragon?*

Cullin's eyes burst wide, and he quickly nodded.

Baran curled hand at them. *C'mon then.*

Cullin leaped over the fence then paused to lend a hand to Kenzie. As they headed towards Kriol who was talking with another dragon, Cullin again looked over to see the smaller dragon at the far end of the landing field.

*Who is that dragon waiting for?* he asked.

Baran looked to where Cullin pointed. *That's Gymi. He's waiting for a rider to claim him.* Seeing Cullin's furrowed brow of confusion, he said, *Nobody wants him.*

*Why?*

*He's unlucky.*

*Why?* Kenzie interrupted.

Baran sighed with frustration. *Because he's different. Come. I'll show you.*

He shifted direction and headed towards the dragon.

Seeing several people walking towards him, the dragon perked up only to realize it was Baran with two non-riders. His hopes vanishing, the dragon warily eyed them.

*How long has he been here?* Kenzie asked.

Baran rolled his eyes. *He's been coming to the landing field for the past year-and-a-half, hoping some rider will claim him. I admire his persistence, but he's wasting his time.*

The closer they came, the more Cullin studied the dragon. The first aspect he noted was the color, a drab green, so unlike the scintillating and vibrant colors of a normal dragon. And then there was the strange marking on its face that looked like a birthmark stretching from just below the left eye and ending below the left side of the jaw. It was when the dragon looked at him that he saw the different colored eyes, one a bright orange and the other an almost opaque black.

Then Cullin gazed at the dragon's face and the pained look of shattered hopes. Within that moment, Cullin saw the suffering of a lifetime of disappointment and abuse. His heart immediately went out to the dragon and stepped closer.

*I think he looks unique.*

Baran gave him a curious look then turned to tell the dragon what Cullin said, earning Cullin a cautious look in return.

Cullin shifted his gaze to fully take in the rest of the dragon and realized though it was a bit smaller than the normal rider-dragons, Gymi was very strong, with dips and curves of a muscular body beneath the scales.

*He looks like a very powerful dragon.*

Baran frowned and gave him a 'we-looking-at-the-same-dragon?' look.

"What did he say?" Gymi asked.

"He said that you look like a very powerful dragon," Baran replied.

"I am," Gymi confidently stated.

"That's all well and good," Baran firmly said, "but one of these days you're going to have to accept the fact that no one is going to claim you as a riding-dragon. Perhaps there are other positions that could better use your talents."

"I don't want another position," Gymi tartly replied. "I can match any riding-dragon in endurance and speed."

"That may be," Baran said, "but it still doesn't change the fact that no rider wants you."

When Kenzie finished translating, Cullin perked up. *I do.*

When Gymi saw Baran's disapproving frown, he asked, "What did he say?"

"He said that he wanted you, but that's impossible because he's neither trained nor approved to be a dragon-rider."

Gymi's eyes filled with excitement. "Where does it say that he has to be trained and approved?"

Baran shook his head. "There are two ways of doing things: the right way and the wrong way. We've had rules concerning the bond between dragon and human for who knows how long, especially for any human or dragon wanting to forge a bond as dragon-riders. You can't just up and say, 'I'm a riding-dragon and here is my human partner.' There are processes and procedures to go through."

"We'll see," Gymi cryptically replied, staring at Cullin.

Baran's look said Gymi's hopes were both unrealistic and foolish. "You can't change tradition just because it doesn't suit your wishes." He turned to Cullin and Kenzie. *I need to get back.*

*Thank you for your help back there*, Cullin said, ticking his head back towards the far fence. *I'd be in big trouble if it wasn't for you.*

*Any time*, Baran signed with a smile. He then turned to Gymi. "Don't get your or his hopes up." Without waiting for an answer, he walked away.

They watched him for a bit before Kenzie said, *I'd better get back.*

*Yeah,* Cullin sighed with disappointment, *me too.* Giving Gymi a warm smile and a 'goodbye' wave, he turned to go.

*Thank you for coming to see me.*

*You're welc–* Cullin jittered to a halt and spun around.

*What's the matter?* Kenzie asked with a puzzled frown.

Cullin stared at Gymi who returned his stare with what looked like a smirk. Shaking his head, he figured he was simply assuming that was something the dragon would say.

*That's true. It is something I would say.*

Cullin's mouth slacked open as he narrowed his gaze at Gymi, his thoughts overlapping and ricocheting in so many directions. *How… you're… but… You're in my head!*

*It's called mind-bonding and I'd appreciate it if no one knew about this.*

*What's going on?* Kenzie interrupted. *Why are you looking at him like that?*

*Make something up, but do not tell her of the mind-bond.*

Cullin relaxed as best he could, pretending nothing was amiss and gave Kenzie a limp shrug. *I was thinking it would be awesome*

*If I could be a dragon-rider.*

*That would be awesome*, she signed back. *Who knows… maybe one day.*

Repeating the smile and wave to Gymi, Cullin turned and started walking away, Kenzie beside him.

*Come back tomorrow and we'll talk more*, Gymi said.

*I will.* Cullen looked over his shoulder to see Gymi unfolding his wings and launching himself into the air. He stopped to watch and truly noticed how muscular and powerful the dragon was.

*

Cullin was back the next day, by himself. Gymi waited for him at his usual spot.

*I'm glad to see you*, Gymi said with a smile.

Cullin folded his arms and stared at him in wonder. *How is this possible? Can you read every thought in my head?*

*It doesn't work like that. Mind-bonding isn't me inside your head, although I suppose it is in a way. Mind-bonding is like having a silent conversation. I can 'hear' you when you speak to me, but only when you speak. In other words, unless you say something to me, I can't 'hear' you.*

*Can you do that with anyone?* He stepped closer to him.

Gymi thought for a moment then shook his head. *When a dragon agrees to mind-bond it is because there is something special between the dragon and the human. What most humans don't realize is that very few dragon-riders are mind-bonded with their dragon partners.*

*Really?* Cullin frowned and then remembered something from yesterday. *Do you know sign also? When Kenzie asked me why I was looking at you, you immediately said something to me.*

*Yes, I do. Just like humans, there are dragons born with certain… impairments. Long ago, when we discovered how you humans talk to those unable to hear, we copied it and adapted it to dragon hands. It's not something that dragons share, so it is knowledge you need to keep to yourself.*

*I will,* Cullin soberly replied, thrilled at this tidbit of knowledge. *You said that there has to be something special between a dragon and a human to mind-bond. How could you mind-bond with me? We never met until yesterday.*

Gymi narrowed his gaze at him. *I could mind-bond with you because you felt a kindred bond with me. I felt your heart go out to me. I knew you understood what it feels like to be considered abnormal. I saw those men harassing you yesterday. I also saw how you dealt with them. You are very strong.*

Cullin's lips tightened. *I got tired of being picked on.*

*I know how you feel.*

Cullin inhaled a slow breath. *So now what happens? I mean, we're mind-bonded, but is that it? What happens when some rider decides he wants you as his dragon?*

Gymi stiffened. *It doesn't work like that. A dragon and rider team is a mutual agreement. Both parties have to agree. The way I see it, you are my rider, if that is something you wish.*

Cullin's eyes popped wide, and his heart raced with excitement. *You mean it? Seriously?*

Gymi chuckled. *Yes. I mean it.* He then grew solemn. *Not everyone will like it. I expect push-back from both dragons and humans, more so from humans.*

*Why?* he said, though he knew the answer.

*First, you have not trained to be a dragon-rider. Second, it goes against centuries of tradition.* Gymi shook his head. *While I understand the need for a special breed of human to be a dragon rider, your human tradition of dragon-riders coming from certain levels of your society is stupid. There have been more than enough examples of riders who have no business being anywhere near a dragon, yet tradition dictates they are qualified by their position in your society.*

*Yet dragons go along with it,* Cullin pointed out.

Gymi sighed. *Yes. Tradition stupidities infect even us. But,* he brightened, *enough of that. Let's begin your first lesson in dragon-riding.*

*Now?* Cullin sputtered, his hopes leaping high.

*The first lesson,* Gymi said, ignoring Cullin's excitement, *is understanding how the whole riding thing works. As I'm sure you've noticed, you don't ride a dragon like you ride a horse. There are no reins attached to my head for you to jerk around. I'm not some ignorant brute for you to command and abuse.*

*I'd never do that,* Cullin objected.

*I know. The next part is the saddle. I had one made for me, even though they said it was a waste of time, that no one was going to want me as a riding-dragon.* He curled a lip in bitterness. *I'll show them. We're going to be the best team this kingdom has ever seen.* He bent down and reached behind him to lift the saddle and hand it to Cullin.

It was lighter than Cullin expected. *This looks like deerskin.*

*It is.*

Cullin studied the saddle, noting the grip-handles, side straps, seat, and especially the stirrups and fenders, all designed to keep a rider firmly in place while allowing him or her to wield a bow, spear, or sword.

*Here they come,* Gymi said, causing Cullin to pause his inspection and look to the right where three officious-looking men strode purposefully towards them. They wore a gold embroidered dragon in flight on the left breast part of their long overcoats, a symbol of their position and authority of office.

"Here now," the man in the middle called out. "What goes on here?" He was a lean severe man with an angular face.

Cullin pointed to his ears and shook his head.

Not understanding, the man stood to full height and repeated his demand.

*He's asking us what we're doing,* Gymi said.

*I know. I can read lips when someone is looking directly at me, but I'm not going to give him the satisfaction of knowing that, so I'm going to pretend I can't hear or understand. This should be fun.* He smiled impishly at Gymi.

Gymi snorted a laugh then coughed to cover his humor.

The man stiffened and jammed his hands on his hips. "I'll not repeat this again. What do you think you are doing?"

Cullin sweetly smiled and shrugged, pointing to his ears then shaking his head.

The man was about to upbraid Cullin when the man to his right, an older man with a thick metal-gray beard placed a hand on his arm, causing the man to snap his head to glare at him.

*He's telling him that you're deaf. Now he's telling him that they need to find someone who does sign language. Oops. Looks like they're going to confront me.* Gymi turned to face the three dragon-rider governors.

Cullin couldn't follow what was said, but from the body posturing and indignant faces, they were not happy with what Gymi told them. At one point, Gymi said something that caused the man in the middle to say, "Really? We'll just see about that." The three spun around in unison and marched off.

*That went well,* Cullin deadpanned, causing Gymi to laugh. *What all transpired? I was able to read his last comment of 'we'll see about that.' What did he mean?*

*I told him that it's not up to him or the other governors whom I choose. If I wanted a trained squirrel to be my rider, it was up to me.*

*Saddle would be awfully small,* Cullin replied, smiling.

Gymi chuckled then turned serious. *They wouldn't give me the time of day ever since I started showing up here. They figured no one would want me because I'm not a beautiful dragon like all the others. Well, I know my rights and I've read the rules and regulations and I know all about the traditions.* He focused an intense stare at him. *Do you want to be my rider?*

Cullin raised an eyebrow. *You have to ask? Of course I want to be your rider. Isn't it obvious?*

*Just a formality*, Gymi replied, *when they come back and demand to know if you agreed and are qualified.*

*Qualified?* Cullin's excitement suddenly dimmed. *I don't know the first thing about riding. And I'm not a soldier or a warrior or whatever like all the other riders. I've never studied combat.*

*But you know how to fight. I saw you take care of those three bullies the other day. You know how to take care of yourself. Can you shoot a bow?*

*Of course*, Cullin answered, wondering what that had to do with anything.

*Listen*, Gymi explained, *the riding part is easy because I'm the one responsible for keeping you safe in the air. It's the fighting while moving that's the hard part. It will take practice, just like all those other dragon-riders do. Do you think they could shoot an arrow and hit a target from the start? Perhaps one or two got lucky, but it takes practice... lots and lots of practice. These riders are out here every day, honing their skills. You'll have to do the same.*

Cullin's thrill returned and just as suddenly faded as his father's image invaded his thoughts. *What am I going to tell my father?*

*Tell him the truth*, Gymi replied as if the answer was obvious.

*But that would take me away from the farm and he depends on me to help out.*

*You're the only one who can help him?* Gymi asked.

*No. I have a younger brother, but he's not as dependable as I am.*

*And whose fault is that?* Gymi stared at him, watching him struggle. *If you could choose, would you rather be a farmer or a dragon-rider?*

*A dragon-rider of course,* Cullin said, *but my family depends on me.*

*And how many are in your family?*

*Besides my parents, I've got another brother and three sisters.*

*So there are six people depending on you,* Gymi said. *How many people depend on a dragon-rider?*

Cullin thought for a moment and shrugged. *I don't know.*

*Think,* Gymi said with some frustration. *How many dragon riders are there?*

Cullin wasn't sure. He knew there were two more dragon-rider centers, but this one here was the largest because it was close to the capital. *I don't know.*

*There are 126 dragon-riders in the kingdom of Lannraig,* Gymi answered. *53 are here and the rest are divided between the two centers near the borders with Shadwic and Mannkirk. So why are there only 126 dragon-riders?*

*I don't know,* he said, feeling like some dull-witted schoolboy.

Gymi shook his head. *Think. How many dragons are there?*

*I don't know,* he replied, starting to get angry. *I haven't had time to wonder how many dragon-riders there are because I spend all my time farming, helping my family.*

*No need to get testy,* Gymi soothed. *Dragons are not like you humans that give rabbits a run for their money in making babies year after year. There are 179 dragons in Drekwald. That number has changed little for the past 100 years. What that means is that being a dragon-rider is more than a privilege. It means being part of a unique group whose responsibility is to defend the* entire *kingdom, not just one farm… and not just your kingdom. Dragon-riders are also responsible for protecting and defending Drekwald. Have you ever wondered why there are no dragon-riders in Shadwic or Mannkirk?*

Cullin didn't have a chance to respond because a large shadow swept over them, causing them to look up.

A large, dazzling, metallic blue-grey dragon descended close by and ambled over. Towering over them both, he Ignored Cullin and addressed Gymi.

"Explain yourself."

"What's to explain," Gymi defiantly replied, all the while relaying the conversation to Cullin. "This human and I have agreed to a partnership as a dragon-rider team."

The dragon narrowed a stern gaze at him. "This is not how it's done." He slid a disdainful eye at Cullin. "Besides, he's not of the right class."

"Like me?" Gymi shot back.

"You're a dragon and should know better," he sniffed. "Though you have… um, certain undesirable qualities, that does not grant you license to do as you please. If you are so intent on finding a rider, perhaps something might be arranged, though I promise nothing."

"And nothing is what I've had this past 18 or more months," Gymi snipped. "You all were content to let me sit here, out of the way. In fact, you all forced me to this part of the landing field to keep me out of the way, knowing that no one would come by here to offer a partnership. And as long as nothing happened, you all were happy. Now that someone is interested, you're suddenly interested." Gymi stood to full height, though still forced to look up. "I've read the rules and regulations, and I'm entirely within my rights to enter into a partnership with a human. And there's nothing in there that says the rider has to be from a certain class of society. In fact," Gymi emphasized, "it wasn't all that long ago that dragon-riders came from the lower classes because they were better riders and fighters."

"That was quite a long time ago," the dragon loftily replied. "But your point is taken." He paused and for the first time acknowledged Cullin. "Do you wish to be a dragon-rider?"

"He's deaf," Gymi explained, causing the dragon to frown with consternation.

"This is foolishness. How do you expect to communicate when he cannot hear you?"

Gymi hesitated. "We are mind-bonded."

The dragon's jaw dropped, and he stiffened. "Are you mad? What possessed you to give this little-known gift to this... this mere human?" He flipped a dismissive hand at Cullin.

Gymi turned an affectionate gaze on Cullin. "Because we understand each other." He looked back at the dragon. "Besides, there are other mind-bonded dragons and riders."

"There is one," the dragon retorted.

"How do you know?"

"What do you mean?"

"How do you know," Gymi repeated. "There could be many more mind-bonded dragon-riders that you don't know about. Unless someone tells you... you don't know."

The dragon's face tightened, knowing Gymi was right. "You will persist with this arrangement?"

"Yes."

The dragon exhaled a slow breath. "You do realize that there is little chance of you being called to perform as a dragon-rider team. While he may look fit, there is far more to being a dragon-rider team than looking the part. Does he have any combat skills?"

Gymi shrugged. "Don't know yet."

The dragon shook his head. "You know little about this man and yet you willingly mind-bond with him. Is it any wonder that you are where you are, a square peg trying to fit into a round hole." He stood straight and peered intently at Gymi. "You have made your choice. So be it. You must now live with that choice. I will tell them. Do not expect to be treated any differently. Just because you have a rider does not make you a part of an elite group. That is something you must earn, and I highly doubt you are capable. That goes for your human, too." With that, he brusquely turned away and leaped into the air.

Stung by the criticism, Gymi watched in grim silence as he flew away.

*Who was that?* Cullin asked.

*That was Randar,* Gymi snarled. *We'll show them. Starting today, you will become the best rider in the history of mankind. Get that saddle on me and let's start training.*

*We do have one more little problem*, Cullin said, studying the saddle.

*Now what?*

*I haven't told my parents yet.*

*

When Cullin arrived early the next morning at the landing field, his father with him, he couldn't help but notice the frenetic activity over at the tackle and armory sheds.

*What's going on?* His father asked.

Cullin shrugged. *Must be some sort of group training or something like that.*

Crossing the field, Cullin noted that Gymi seemed nervous with pent up energy.

*What's going on?* Cullin asked, ticking his head at the dragon and riders forming up into units.

*Haven't you heard?* Gymi said, his eyes bright with excitement.

*Heard what?*

*Mannkirk invaded us last night. Their army is already laying siege to Obar-Kinnoch.*

Cullin relayed the information to his father whose eyes popped wide with worry.

*That's less than 150 miles from here,* his father said then looked at Gymi. "So it's true that he is your rider?"

"Yes. He and I are a team." Gymi studied Cullin's father, surprised that he didn't look at him the way other humans did.

"But he's not trained to be a rider," he objected.

Gymi shook his head. "They won't send us out until he's ready." Though he knew it wasn't true, that he and Cullin would probably never be a part of the dragon-rider command... unless they were desperate, he didn't want to give up hope or the impression that this was all just a waste of time. Now that he had a rider, nothing was going to stop him, not even Cullin's father. Though Cullin might not be trained like all the others, he was sure Cullin could be a great rider and fighter.

Cullin's father turned to him. *I didn't want to believe you, though I knew you'd never lie to me. I had to see for myself.*

*So you are willing to let me become a dragon-rider?*

His father smiled. *How could I not? This is a rare privilege offered to a select few.* He slid a glance at Gymi. *Though he's not the prettiest dragon I've ever seen, I have a sense that he has a great heart and it's what's inside a man... or dragon that counts.* He placed a loving hand on his shoulder. *I'm proud of you. I always have been. Remember, don't let the excitement of the adventure get in the way of wisdom. Listen and pay attention. Don't be reckless when you don't have to.* He gazed up at Gymi. "Take good care of him."

"I will protect him with my life," Gymi solemnly said.

Cullin's father nodded. "I know. And he will do the same. Let's pray that it never comes to that." He inhaled a deep breath and looked over to see the dragon-rider command launching into the air. Turning to Cullin, he said, *You'd better get busy. Who knows, they might need you sooner than you realize.*

\*

The siege at Obar-Kinnoch dragged on for the next month. In addition to siege engines, Mannkirk's army had brought along ballistae that they fired with devastating accuracy at Lannraig's dragon-riders. Yet the Kingdom's dire situation had grown more perilous when Shadwic invaded two weeks after Mannkirk. Lannraig's dragon riders were taxed beyond their capabilities as they now had to fight on two fronts.

Cullin and Gymi watched every day as bone-tired dragons and riders forced themselves into the air. Yet each day, a dragon or rider would return, wounded, incapacitated and unable to continue the fight. Occasionally a dragon and rider did not return.

Cullin and Gymi trained with frenetic urgency, using the same dummy targets and training areas that the Kingdom's dragon-riders used. With their attention focused on the war, no one paid them much attention.

*You're getting much better*, Gymi commented after Cullin placed three arrows in the strawman's chest. They wheeled away from the targets as Gymi positioned them for another pass.

*Do you think I'm ready?*

Gymi paused and hovered over the field. To their right, three dragon-rider teams returned. *See them?*

Cullin gazed down as the riders stumbled off their dragons. One rider flopped onto his back on the ground. *They don't look so good.*

*They're exhausted. We've lost eleven dragon-rider teams. If dragons ever want to continue as a species, we can't afford to lose any more.*

Cullin frowned. *What does that have to do with me being ready?*

*What it means is the longer we wait, the more dangerous it is for dragons. Whether you are ready or not, we can no longer afford to wait.*

*So why don't they just ask us?* Cullin huffed.

*It would prove them wrong about us.*

*Maybe we ought to show them how much they were wrong.*

Gymi curled his head back to look at his rider. *I've been thinking the same thing. Let's talk.*

They landed far away from the dragon sheds and Cullin dismounted.

*What's your plan?* he asked, stretching his back.

*I've studied how dragon-rider teams are used. Invariably, they attack from up high with the idea that they strike fear when they swoop down. While it's true that dragons are intimidating, especially breathing fire and such, once a dragon is brought down, they're not so intimidating anymore.* He shook his head. *But that doesn't stop them from continuing to use the same foolish approach. And here's a question for you; if the other kingdoms don't have dragons, why do we even* have *dragon riders? It's not like they're in aerial combat with an enemy. Our riders have a quiver full of arrows that they fire and once the quiver is empty, they return home to get more arrows. Why do we need dragons for someone who is nothing more than an archer?*

Cullin blinked at the revelation. *So why do we have dragon-riders?*

*Tradition*, Gymi answered with a sneer. *Tradition is going to get us all killed.*

*Do you have a better idea?*

Gymi grinned. *Of course. First, instead of attacking from high up, we swoop in low, so no one knows we're coming. Second, we drop in from behind them, attack their supply wagons. We hit and run. We use the same approach elsewhere. Keep them off balance so they don't know where we are or when we're coming.*

Cullin nodded, liking the idea, but knew the inherent problem. *They won't listen to you.*

*I know,* he slyly grinned. *That's why we have to show them.*

Cullin cocked an eyebrow. *How?*

Gymi gave him a knowing smile. *We attack on our own.*

Cullin's eyes blinked wide. *You crazy? You want us to attack by ourselves?*

Gymi laughed. *It's not what you think. What we do is sneak in, hit them and then disappear.*

*Oh yeah,* Cullin scoffed. *We just waltz into their main camp or wherever and fire a bunch of arrows and disappear.*

*Exactly.*

Cullin leaned forward and stared into Gymi's eyes. *You know I can never tell when you're teasing me or not.*

*I'm serious this time,* Gymi said. *Here's my idea. We sneak in at night—*

*At night?* Cullin exclaimed.

*Let me finish. We sneak down to where the supply wagons are, kill a couple of guards and disappear to another spot and do the same thing.*

Dumbfounded, Cullin stared at him, his mind a whirl with everything that could go wrong. Yet part of him liked the idea, and the irrational part of his mind began to win the argument. *So how do we do it? We need a plan... I mean a real plan that will work.*

*I already have one in mind. Here's my idea.*

It was after midnight when Cullin and Gymi lifted off from the landing field. Cullin shivered with nervous excitement, recounting the number of arrows in his quiver.

*How long will it take to get there?* he asked, thankful for the cloud cover.

*About an hour.* Gymi flapped his wings to gain altitude then shot off towards the Mannkirk encampment surrounding Obar-Kinnoch.

*You sure this is going to work?*

*If it doesn't, we'll have to try something else.*

*Very funny,* Cullin moaned.

*Relax,* Gymi encouraged. *I guarantee they're not expecting it.*

*Why?*

*Because it's nighttime. Full scale battles only occur in the daytime. It's tradition.*

*No one ever attacks at night?* Cullin said, his doubt obvious.

*Nope. The nighttime is for stealth and secret attacks.*

*Like what we're doing.* Cullin's confidence began to waver.

*Dragons only attack against a well-established enemy, someone in large numbers and someone they can see. The nighttime attacks I'm talking about are those stealth attacks like sneaking into the enemy's headquarters or castle and waiting for the right time to assassinate a leader or let down a drawbridge or something like that. What we're doing is creating distractions.*

Unconvinced, Cullin suppressed his concerns and focused on the task at hand. *How do we know when we're at the right spot?*

*We'll know.*

*That doesn't help me.*

*There will be lots of wagons with food and other supplies. There will be fewer fighters, if any. That's where we hit.*

That seemed like a safer environment than what he had first thought and Cullin relaxed as best he could, ready to get there. Yet when the lights of the city and the army in siege appeared in the far distance, his nervousness grew.

Gymi curved to the east to give the city and the surrounding enemy army wide berth. Cullin stared in fascination at the array of campfires spread out around the city below them. *I have a question.*

*Yes?*

*If dragons can breathe fire, why can't you all just light up Mannkirk's and Shadwic's armies and save us all the trouble of fighting them?*

*First,* Gymi replied, beginning to curve back towards the far side of the city, *while it's true that we can breathe fire, it's not like we have an unlimited supply. Think of us in terms like a poisonous snake. Once it releases its venom, it needs time to replenish it. That's why we dragons expel fire in short bursts so that we can do the most damage in between replenishing.*

*And second?*

*Secondly, we have to get close to use fire and there are nasty people down there with arbalests that make getting close a problem.*

Cullin was silent for a bit, gazing down at the scattered campfires dwindling in the distance. *Don't know why I just thought of this… and now is sort of a ridiculous time to bring it up, but… uh… if I can't hear them, how will I know when to attack?*

*You might not be able to hear, but your other senses have increased to make up for the lack of hearing,* Gymi answered. *Your sight is almost as good as a dragon's.*

*I doubt that.*

*Shush. Let me finish. And your sense of smell is like that of a wolf or any other wild animal. I noticed that when we were training. You could see and smell things that other humans can't.*

*So we're hoping these guys stink so I can smell them before they get to me?* Cullin smirked.

Gymi smiled. *You laugh, but you humans aren't exactly the sweetest smelling creatures. I've taken into account the wind direction for your ambush. Trust me; you'll know when the enemy is near.*

Cullin looked down to see a dark gap between the edges of Mannkirk's army and what looked like a line of torches in the distance slowly moving along the road towards the city.

*That's our target,* Gymi said. *Time to set up our ambush.*

*How do you know where to go?* Cullin asked, frowning.

*I've been here many times before tonight. I know the roads and terrain better than any other dragon.*

*What?* Cullin said with more than a hint of doubt.

*I made it my business to study the terrain and surrounding areas on the borders with Mannkirk and Shadwic. Just because I've been spending my time at the landing field these past months doesn't mean I've wasted my time. Let's face it, I've had plenty of time to study these areas and nothing much has changed in the past 75 years.*

Cullin blinked at the revelation, realizing that Gymi was much older than he was. His hands tightened on the saddle grips as Gymi descended to a small clearing.

*Now it's your turn,* he said and ticked his head at one edge of the clearing. *The road is that way about 200 paces. The forest is mostly pine, so the going won't be too difficult. There are plenty of places to hide. Wait until they all pass you then take out the ones at the end. I'll be waiting here for you.*

Cullin licked dry lips. Inhaling a deep breath, he shouldered his quiver and headed out to find a suitable ambush spot. Weaving his way through the underbrush, he was both relieved and concerned. The forest floor was mostly pine needles with excellent gaps between trees that allowed him to move quickly. It also allowed anyone an easy time of spotting him. Fortunately, the underbrush grew thicker the closer he came to the road. At one point, he almost stumbled onto the road before quickly catching himself.

Selecting a spot that allowed him quick access to the road as well as a hasty retreat, he anxiously waited. Time seemed to drag until he sniffed an odd odor and recognized it as the unpleasant smell of unwashed bodies. Shaking his head, he silently chuckled that Gymi knew what to expect. It was almost a minute before he saw the flickering lights of torches held high, casting dull shadows on the edges of the road. The first wagon passed. Though he could not hear, he could see the two drivers chatting, one obviously complaining by the exaggerated hand and arm movements.

A second and third wagon went by, then another four more. Cullin's hopes of surprise were beginning to fade. By the time the last wagon passed, he had just about given up hope. He was about to stand and step onto the road when movement to his right stopped him and a troop of soldiers marching with undisciplined footsteps suddenly appeared.

He watched them as they passed. They were bored and tired as they shuffled along, their swords and knives tucked safely in scabbards and their bows unstrung. After the main body passed there were a few stragglers struggling to keep up. One man, probably an NCO, harangued one plump soldier.

Cullin waited a few seconds more before poking his head out to look to his right. Seeing nothing, he stepped out onto the road, reached into his quiver, and notched an arrow. His first target was the NCO. Pulling back the string, he let fly, catching the man in the middle of his back, the force of the arrow penetrating deep into the man's chest.

The young man he had been harassing had little time to react as Cullin let fly another arrow that found its mark and another soldier of Mannkirk slumped to the ground, the men ahead of them blithely unaware.

Cullin unleashed four more arrows in the span of twenty seconds, felling four more soldiers. Suddenly aware that something was amiss, a cry that he couldn't hear caused the troop to jitter to a halt. By then, three more soldiers lay on the road. Confusion reigned as they sought to find their attackers. Three old soldiers spun around and charged towards Cullin, their swords drawn and ready to fight.

Two quickly fell, victims to Cullin's accuracy. The third dodged left and right hoping to avoid the fate of his compatriots, but Cullin's mastery gained from hitting targets while flying on Gymi's back proved too much and the third man fell. Seeing their comrades killed so quickly, the troop erupted into a race to save their lives and fled down the road.

Deciding he didn't need to stick around to see if his luck would hold, Cullin turned and retraced his steps back to Gymi.

*How'd you do?* Gymi asked as Cullin emerged from the woods.

*I killed eight.* As soon as he said it, a weird feeling swept through him. He had just killed eight men, some who might have had a wife and children. And all of them had families, a mother and father who loved them.

Sensing Cullin's sudden struggle, Gymi said, *Remember why we are here. These are Mannkirk soldiers intent on conquering Lannraig. How many of our own citizens have died because of them? Would you be as sympathetic if they had attacked your farm instead? How about Kinzie's farm?*

*I know you're right. I just never thought about it before.*

*Trust me,* Gymi said. *This isn't the first time Mannkirk had invaded Lannraig.*

Cullin exhaled a slow breath. *You're right. We wouldn't be here if Mannkirk had left us alone.*

*Exactly. You ready to go create some havoc over in the Shadwic camp?*

*Why not,* Culling boldly affirmed. *I've still got plenty of arrows left.*

The ambush on Shadwic's rear area might have been a nonevent had Gymi not spotted a lengthy wagon train just crossing Shadwic's borders. This time, instead of Cullin dropping down to let fly with bow and arrow, Gymi decided to employ a little fire. Swooping down at tree level, he let loose one prolonged eruption of flame that caught the entire line of supply wagons, as well as all the soldiers along with it. As they flew away, Culling twisted around to look back at the long row of flaming wagons.

*

For the next two weeks, Cullin and Gymi continued their hit and run tactics, hitting at different times at night, always at a different location. This particular night had been very rewarding with another Mannkirk supply train destroyed and eleven Shadwic soldiers killed. Though euphoric with their success, Cullin and Gymi were tired.

*I say we take a day off and rest*, Gymi said.

*No argument from me*, Cullin replied, glancing at the brightening sky. Dawn's morning light rimmed the mountains and they needed to get back before anyone noticed their absence. It was going to be close as they normally returned while it was still dark. Seeing some activity near the dragon sheds, Gymi chose to land at the far end of the field, hoping everyone would be too distracted to notice, or if they did, they would ignore them like they usually did.

Cullin dismounted then helped Gymi remove the saddle. Exhaling an exhausted breath, he scratched his head. *Don't know how much longer I can keep this up.*

*What's the problem?* Gymi asked as he gazed beyond Cullin's shoulder.

*My father's becoming a little more suspicious that all our training is at night. He suspects something is going on but hasn't said anything so far. I have a feeling he's gonna want to know the truth. Let's face it, I spend more time with you than I do at home... or anywhere else for that matter. When we're not doing this, I'm either sleeping the day away or here with you.* He frowned. *Even Kenzie is beginning to wonder what's going on.* He looked up to see Gymi looking behind him.

*We got company,* Gymi said.

Turning around, Cullin saw a group of men approaching, along with several dragons. He recognized Baran beside another older man whose determined march said he was someone in authority. He also recognized the large metallic blue-grey dragon from before, the one who had challenged Gymi's choice of human. The group stopped and formed a semi-circle around Cullin and Gymi.

Baran signed, *This is General Bradekh, the commander of Lannraig's army. The other men, as you probably already know, are the cohort leaders of the dragon-riders.*

Cullin dipped his head in respect.

The General kept his eyes on Cullin while Baran translated.

*He asks what you two have been doing these past few weeks.*

Cullin slid a glance at Gymi.

*Might as well tell him the truth,* Gymi said.

Nodding, Cullin addressed the General. *We've been ambushing the enemy.*

A slight smile curved the corners of his lips. *I know. We had reports that someone was causing havoc in the Mannkirk and Shadwic camps. I've also had reports of a young man needing a lot of arrows. Tell me what you've been doing.*

*It was Gymi's idea,* Cullin proudly replied. *He's brilliant. Not only does he know the terrain, he can read their reactions and future plans like a well-worn book.* He placed a tender hand on Gymi's side. It was a simple act yet one that bespoke a bond of deep friendship.

*Yes, yes*, the General said. *We know you two are close. How are you conducting your operations?*

*It would probably be better if Gymi explained them.*

For the first time, General Bradekh acknowledged Gymi. "Well?"

"We're doing hit-and-run operations," Gymi explained. "We use low-flying attacks so no one can see us or where we come from. One time it might be Cullin taking out a half-dozen or more soldiers. Another time I might light up a supply convoy. We target supply trains so that we interfere with their food and other supplies. We hit one spot then a different one for the next four or five days. Then we go back to the first spot. They've had several days where nothing has happened so they're not as alert. We also don't do a pattern so they can't predict where we'll hit. It keeps them off balance. You can't stay alert all the time. We've also hit them inside their own kingdoms."

General Bradekh turned to the others. Their response to his orders was met with reserve and some pushback.

*He's telling them to follow our example*, Gymi said. *Randar and the other dragons like the idea. It's the humans who have problems.*

*Who's Randar?*

*He's the one who told me I was crazy for bonding with you. Yeah... so how crazy am I now?*

Cullin watched General Bradekh point a ringer at another man and bark an order. The man stiffened to attention and saluted, spun around, and marched off.

Gymi silently laughed. *The man was arguing against our tactics and the General just put him in his place, telling him to immediately go and inform all the other dragon-riders that we will no longer use the high-altitude attack method.*

Cullin impatiently waited and watched as the General addressed the remaining military leaders and dragons.

Gymi's excitement burst. *He just told him that you and I are immediately part of the dragon-riders, that we will lead the next operation.* Turning to Cullin, he lowered his head to gaze into his eyes. *None of this would have happened without you. I owe you more than you will ever realize. I've waited decades to prove myself, but no one wanted me… not until you showed up and saw me for more than an ugly, hopeless dreamer, and useless fool. Because of you, these people now know that they've been wrong all this time.*

*Let's not get carried away,* Cullin said. *You're the brains of the outfit. I'm just along for the ride.*

*Now who's being silly?* Gymi said. *You're better than all these other so-called dragon-riders. How many have you killed?*

Before Cullin could answer, the General turned to address him.

*Do you have a rough idea of how many men you have eliminated?* Baran signed for the General.

"At least 101 that I know for sure," Gymi replied for him, causing the General's eyes to pop wide. "There were more, but by then they knew we were there, and we didn't bother to stay to find out."

"He's killed 101 of the enemy… in two weeks?" the General sputtered. The men with him raised eyebrows in doubt.

"Yes, General Bradekh. I've kept tally."

"But did you actually *see* him kill them?" a cohort leader scoffed. He was a tall man, well built with close-cropped blond hair.

Gymi turned a cold dark eye on the man. "You question the

word of a dragon?" He raised his head to look at the other dragons. "Do you question my word?"

"Of course not, Gymi," Randar answered. "You are a dragon. But perhaps it would be best to answer this human so that they may know a dragon never lies."

Gymi's lips tightened, and he curled a lip as he turned to the man. "Did I see everyone he killed? No. I only saw the times he took out eight or nine of them in less than a minute. I then added up the totals of the ones I saw. That came to 101. Were there more? Yes, a lot more. Tell me… how many have you killed?"

The man bridled as he stiffened with indignation.

Before he could respond, General Bradekh interrupted. "That's enough Cognan." He glared at the man and shook his head. "You've been around dragons for how long and you question them telling the truth?"

"But General," Cognan objected. "101 is an absurd number. There's no one in all the kingdom who can make the same claim… 101 enemy slain in two weeks."

"At least 101," Gymi corrected.

"If Gymi said it happened, it happened," General Bradekh stated. "End of discussion." He turned to Gymi and Cullin, noting their fatigue. "I know you're tired, but you're part of the dragon-rider cohorts now. Get some rest and report back to me this afternoon. We have a battle to plan."

*

Cullin still felt a bit thick and groggy, despite the seven hours of sleep. He looked up at Gymi as they crossed the landing field and headed to General Bradekh's temporary command center inside the Governors Hall. *Why do you look like you've slept for two days?*

*I'm a dragon*, he replied. *We don't need much sleep.*

*Not from what I remember*, Cullin snickered. *You're like cats who sleep nonstop except when they want food.*

Gymi laughed. *That actually sounds nice, especially if someone else is preparing the food.*

Cullin frowned the closer they came to the Hall. *Where is everybody? Seems awfully quiet.*

Gymi glanced around the fields and the Hall. *I see several dragons in the Sheds, but they're resting.* He turned back to Cullin. *Why do I not have a good feeling about this?*

Cullin abruptly stopped, causing Gymi to jerk to a stop. *If he wants to plan a battle, why does he need me?*

*You're the one who has been conducting the midnight raids*, Gymi pointed out.

*No.* We're *the ones conducting the midnight raids. And more to the point,* you're *the one doing all the planning. If he wants to plan, he needs to drag his butt out here.*

The main door to the hall opened and a younger man a little older that Cullin emerged. He was dressed in a clean crisp red and white uniform emblazoned with braided epaulettes, a shoulder cord, and magnificent golden buttons.

"Ah," he loftily said, looking down at Cullin. "Good. You're here. The General's waiting for you."

"And who are you?" Gymi asked.

The man straightened to full height. "I am Lieutenant Dathi, General Bradekh's aide-de-camp. But we've no time to waste. The General's waiting."

Cullin hooked a thumb at Gymi and stared at the Lieutenant.

When the Lieutenant furrowed his brow in response, Gymi said, "What he's saying is that I obviously cannot fit inside your building."

"Of course not," the Lieutenant replied, cocking an eyebrow. "We'll include you dragons when we're ready."

Cullin's face tightened when Gymi repeated the Lieutenant's word. *Tell him to stop being an idiot and fetch the General.*

*Perhaps it would be best if you went in,* Gymi suggested.

*Why? You're the one with all the knowledge of the terrain and battle plan. I go in there and my ignorance would be obvious. We're wasting time.*

Gymi nodded. *You're right.* Addressing the Lieutenant, he said, "It would be best if you informed the General that we should meet at a suitable spot for me to be part of the discussion."

The Lieutenant stiffened with indignation, giving Gymi a look of cold arrogance. "What? You? What makes you think that you can just waltz in here and think that you're equal to any other riding dragon?"

Gymi's head bent down, and he thrust it at the man's face, causing him to scramble backwards. "Listen you insufferable little toad, tell the General that we're here and if he wants to plan anything to get himself out here. Now."

The Lieutenant leaped back through the door.

*I may have been a little rough on him,* Gymi sighed, *but I'll no longer put up with anyone's insults. We're more than equal to any dragon-rider team and it's about time we were treated like it.*

The door opened and General Bradekh stepped out, followed by the smug Lieutenant, Baran, and the other cohort commanders.

Baran gave Cullin a stern stare and signed, *What are you doing?*

*Saving time,* Cullin signed back. *Gymi is the one with all the knowledge. He's the one who planned our operations. He's the one who knows the terrain. He's the one you should be talking to.*

When Baran repeated what Cullin said to the General, Bradekh nodded in understanding. "He's right." He thrust a finger at his Aide. "Find Randar. Have him meet us at the Sheds."

"Yes Sir." Saluting, he bounded down the steps.

Curling his fingers at the others to follow, General Bradekh descended the stairs and headed across the field to the dragon sheds. "You three walk with me," he said to Baran, Cullin, and Gymi. The others drifted to the sides and out of the way as Gymi moved in closer, his pace relaxed and slow so the humans could keep up.

"You ready to lead another attack tonight?" Bradekh asked Cullin.

"He says that's not a good idea?" Baran said, reading Cullin's sign language.

The General's lips tightened. "Why not?"

"He says that he has obvious problems communicating and it would hinder the operation. He says that it would be better if one of the cohort commanders led the raid. He says that he and Gymi would be more than happy to do their part."

General Bradekh nodded. "A wise answer. Gymi."

"Yes General?"

"We want to hit the enemy at as many locations as possible. Do you have suggestions?"

"Yes General. We need to take into consideration where Cullin and I have hit already."

"Then you need to be the one planning this."

Gymi hid his satisfaction. "Yes General."

By the time they arrived at the Sheds, several dragons had stirred and stood waiting for them. One was already in the air and on her way to fetch Randar. While they waited for Randar to arrive, General Bradekh got the attention of those present, both dragon and human.

"Gymi is in charge of planning this operation. Commander Finten will lead the raid. Any questions?" When no one said anything, he crisply nodded. "Good. Then let's get to work."

When Randar arrived, he and General Bradekh went off to

another part of the field to talk overall strategy, leaving Gymi and Cullin to deal with the rest. While the dragons might have been doubtful of Gymi's planning abilities, they kept their doubts to themselves. On the other hand, most of the humans were downright antagonistic, questioning and belaboring each idea, Commander Cognan being the most vocal. It got to the point where Gymi finally had enough and called out to General Bradekh.

"If they're not going to listen, I'm wasting my time."

In one smooth motion, Bradekh turned and marched over, stopped and jabbed a threatening finger at his leaders. "If you can't keep your mouths shut and make this work, I'll find others who can."

"But Sir," Cognan complained. "His ideas are unworkable."

"How do you know?" Bradekh snapped.

Cognan shook his head. "We always attack from high up. It gives us the advantage of speed and power while instilling fear at the same time." He hooked a thumb at Gymi. "He wants us to fly at treetop level which makes us easy targets."

Bradekh turned to Gymi.

"It's what Cullin and I have been doing these past two weeks," Gymi said before turning to Cognan. "That's why we attack at night, in the dark, when it's hard to see, when you humans are tired and prone to confusion, when weapons like arbalests aren't positioned where they need to be, when—"

"That's enough," the General interrupted. "You've made your point." He turned a cold glare at Cognan. "Hasn't he?"

"Yes Sir," Cognan replied, slipping a hateful glance at Gymi and Cullin.

The look did not go unnoticed, but the General had more critical matters to worry about than to salve the ego of a stubborn subordinate. "What time to we start our attack, Commander Finten?"

Though initially doubtful, Finten had warmed to Gymi's battle plans. "We leave here after midnight. There are enough assembly areas throughout the surrounding forests and fields to allow all of us to be hidden until we attack."

"How many dragon-riders are involved?" Bradekh asked.

"All of them," Finten replied. "We're going to overwhelm them and hit hard and fast."

General Bradekh crisply nodded. "Good luck."

\*

Dawn was yet hours away when they returned, euphoric from an overwhelmingly successful campaign. Not one rider or dragon suffered so much as a scratch. In addition to supply trains destroyed, whole encampments were incinerated as dragons swept back and forth bellowing flames that caught their enemies unaware. The speed of the attack surprised even the attackers as they landed one after another, dragon riders rapidly dismounting to gleefully recount their exploits and success.

Commander Finten landed and quickly found General Bradekh. Together, they received individual reports. As more and more riders recounted their successes, Bradekh realized that in all probability, they had won a resounding victory. When Cullin and Gymi ambled over to give their report, Finten shook his head in amazement. "Don't know why we didn't do this from the beginning. Your strategy was brilliant."

Bradekh likewise was more than impressed but held his finger up for them to wait. Turning to Finten, he said, "Send a rider to tell the two field commanders to launch attacks—immediately."

"Yes Sir." Finten hustled away to inform two scout riders of the General's orders.

Bradekh turned to Gymi and Cullin. He silently gazed at them for a moment. "Well done. In all likelihood, you two have just saved the kingdom. I will inform King Hedryk of that point. Now go get some rest. This isn't over yet."

Gymi respectfully nodded and together he and Cullin headed across the landing field. Baran met them midfield.

Though extending a hand to Cullin, he spoke to Gymi. "I was wrong about you, about both of you. I won't make that mistake again. I'd be honored if you'd consider being members of my cohort." He then signed the same request to Cullin.

Cullin looked up at Gymi who smiled and nodded. *We would like that very much.*

*Good. Then, like the General said, get some rest and report back to me this afternoon.*

*Yes, Sir,* Cullin replied with a crisp salute, imitating the palm open to the side of the head salute he saw so frequently with the soldiers.

*None of that now*, Baran gently said. *You're part of the elite dragon-rider cohorts. Likewise, as a deputy cohort commander, you'll be commissioned a lieutenant. Now go get some sleep. You and I have a lot to discuss later*. With that, he turned and headed off to find Kriol.

Cullin stood immobile, his jawed slacked open. *What just happened?*

*You've just been elevated to the ruling elite*, Gymi replied, his eyes surveying the still frantic activity of dragons and riders making their way to various resting spots whether in the town, sheds or back in Drekwald. *You know what that means?*

*What?* Cullin looked up at his friend.

*It means we still have to prove ourselves.* Gymi gazed affectionately at him. *Some people are not going to like you being an officer or me being your dragon, people like Cognan who publicly embarrassed himself and will blame us because he was wrong. All that means is that we have to prove we're better than they are.* He bent his head down to get closer to Cullin's face. *There's nothing we can do about the way we look or who we are… and you know what? I'm glad we can't.*

## THE END

# Riders of Ervum
## A.G. Porter

### *Chapter 1*

Velis stood like a silent sentinel, his lean form cloaked in the shadows at the edge of the chamber. The soft luminescence of magical crystals cast an ethereal glow upon the circle of Elders gathered in the heart of Halacritas's most sacred sanctum. Their murmurs wove through the air, a tapestry of concern and resolve. Each Elder's visage, weathered by the passage of centuries, was etched with the gravity of their conclave.

"Brothers and sisters," intoned Elder Mirael, her voice carrying the weight of the ages, "we stand upon a precipice. One of our last dragon eggs finally has a rider, the young prince of Levaria, Prince Leryn. We must bring the egg to him, for he has been called by the ancient prophesies to bring about the new age of dragons."

The chamber resonated with the hum of agreement, the very stones of Halacritas vibrating with the power that coursed through the room. Velis's keen elven senses, honed through years of vigilant service, caught every inflection of urgency. His hand rested lightly on the pommel of his sword—a sword that had sung through the air in defense of Halacritas more times than he could count. As the Elders spoke, his green eyes remained locked onto the iridescent shell cradled within an arcane nest at the chamber's center. The egg pulsed with a life of its own, a heartbeat of potential awaiting the chance to soar.

"Together with the elves, the dwarves, humans, and the witches, we have protected the egg for eons," Elder Mirael continued. "They have sent us their strongest warriors to take charge of the egg, to protect it, and bring it to the young prince."

"Velis." The Elder's voice sliced through the chamber, and he stepped forward, his long brown hair cascading over his shoulders as he approached the revered circle. His presence commanded silence, and the Elders turned their ancient eyes upon him.

"Guardian of the Egg, your prowess is known to us all," Elder Caius said, his gaze piercing into Velis's soul. "Your blade has kept the darkness at bay, but strength of arms alone will not suffice in the trials to come."

A ripple of energy surged through the air, and Velis felt the call to action ignite in his veins. He bowed his head slightly, acknowledging the honor and burden of his calling. "I stand ready," he declared, the timbre of his voice resonant and clear. "The egg shall not fall while breath remains within me."

In that moment, Velis embodied the unyielding spirit of Halacritas—their past victories and their future hopes. His duty transcended mere allegiance; it was woven into the very fabric of his being, just as the fate of this dragon egg was entwined with the destiny of their world.

"Bayon of Halesford," Caius called. "Human in blood and hero in soul. Your bow has pierced the heart of many enemies of Halacritas, but you must lean on your brothers and sisters in times to come."

Bayon, clad in armor that had seen countless battles, its steel plates glinting even in the muted radiance of the enchanted crystals, carried an air of solemnity. His dark hair was pulled back from a face etched with the severity of war, yet his brown eyes burned fiercely with an unquenchable fire—the same fire that had forged his bond with Velis on bloodied fields.

He bowed his head. "I stand ready."

"Hyan of the Ash Mountains, prince and future leader," Caius turned to the dwarf. "Your axe has protected more kingdoms than your own. Your ability to see good in all will serve you well, but you must also rely on your faith for what you cannot see."

The stout dwarf stood tall. His long auburn beard was tied and braided in the design of his people. His armor was shiny, the best and strongest to be found in Halacritas. And while he looked polished and clean, there was a fierceness in his brown eyes.

"I stand ready," Hyan said, bowing his head in reverence.

"Euphenia, witch of the Iylis Coven and protector of the lost," Caius said to the slender and imposing woman. "Your spells and potions have cured the sick and healed the brokenhearted. You must be ready to depend on your mind as well as your soul."

Her long black hair flowed like a river of night, and her piercing yellow eyes seemed to hold the mysteries of the cosmos.

"I stand ready," she bowed her head, her dark hair falling in her face.

"Will you accept this charge?" Elder Iyara asked, her piercing eyes reading the depths of their resolve.

"We will." Velis' voice was a whisper, yet it carried the strength of ancient trees, rooted deep within the earth. His green eyes gleamed with an inner fire; the ember of an oath ignited.

"By steel and by spirit, we shall deliver the egg to Prince Leryn," Bayon added, his tone leaving no room for doubt nor fear.

The chamber held its breath as the warriors accepted their quest. The Elders exchanged solemn nods, their faces etched with lines of age and wisdom, each crease a testament to the gravity of the moment.

"Go with the blessings of Halacritas," Elder Thalor intoned, raising his arms high. A cascade of light spilled from his fingertips, showering them in a spectral glow that seemed to fortify their very beings.

"May the winds guide you, and the shadows flee your path," Elder Iyara whispered, her incantation weaving around them a subtle armor against the dark forces that would surely hunt them.

## Chapter 2

The night sky, once a tapestry of stars, now bled with the crimson hue of destruction. Flames erupted from thatched roofs as the once-peaceful village, on the outskirts of Halesford, convulsed under the onslaught of the Hass Mara. Their silhouettes, dark against the firelight, moved with ruthless efficiency, torches in hand, setting the world ablaze.

A woman's scream cut through the chaos, a chilling reminder of the human cost beneath the roar of fire and the clash of steel. Villagers scrambled in all directions, clutching children and whatever meager possessions they could carry. But their frantic efforts were no match for the encroaching terror that consumed their homes, their memories, their lives.

Amidst the pandemonium, a single figure stood out, commanding the malevolence like a maestro of madness. Lakara, the leader of the Hass Mara, towered above his minions, his presence as unyielding as the stone walls of Halacritas itself. His face was a map of old battles, scars etched deep into his skin, but it was the cruel smile that played upon his lips which truly marked the man. In his eyes, the reflection of the fires danced with a fervor that mirrored the darkness in his heart.

"Spread the flames! Leave nothing but ash!" His voice boomed over the clamor, each word punctuated by the crackling of timber and the collapsing of structures. His orders were not shouts of desperation, but commands issued with cold, calculated precision. The Hass Mara moved at his behest, a deadly choreography of destruction enacted with terrifying grace and one goal: find the dragon egg.

*

The warm halls of the Elders' stronghold had receded behind them weeks ago, giving way to the untamed expanse of Halacritas. Velis led the caravan, his eyes sharp, picking through the bramble and brush as they made their way towards the woodlands that bordered the realm. The dragon egg was secure in front of him as he rode his trusty horse through the dense forest.

The group pressed on, silence their companion, save for the crunch of leaves and the occasional caw of a distant crow. Hours slipped into each other, the monotony of the journey broken only by the occasional pause to navigate around a fallen log or a sudden dip in the terrain.

As afternoon waned into evening, a sudden shift in the wind brought an unease that crept up Velis's spine. He raised a hand, halting their advance with a swift gesture. The group froze, blending into the foliage as if by instinct.

"Something's amiss," Euphenia whispered, her voice barely carrying to Velis's ears.

No sooner had the words left her lips than a volley of arrows sliced through the leaves, embedding themselves into tree trunks with deadly precision. The Hass Mara descended upon them like a storm.

"Fan out!" Velis commanded, drawing his sword with a metallic ring that sang of battle.

The group sprang into action, each moving to their assigned roles with practiced ease. Bayon ducked behind a tree, releasing a flurry of arrows that sought out their assailants.

Velis pushed forward, his blade parrying and striking with lethal grace, a deadly dance of combat. The Hass Mara, cloaked in garb that blended with the forest, emerged from their cover, steel glinting in their hands as they charged.

"Protect the egg!" Velis roared over the clash of metal, his voice carrying the weight of their sacred charge.

Hyan moved like a force of nature, his axe's arcs of destruction keeping the enemy at bay, ensuring that no harm would come to the precious cargo they guarded.

Euphenia's incantations filled the air, her hands weaving patterns that pulled at the fabric of reality. Though the Hass Mara were relentless, the group stood firm, repelling the ambush with a ferocity born of necessity and the unspoken knowledge that the fate of Halacritas rested in their hands.

Velis lunged with the precision of a striking serpent, his elven blade singing as it met the steely resistance of a Hass Mara's sword. Each movement was a masterful display of martial prowess, a weaving dance of attack and defense. His long brown hair whipped about his face, yet his green eyes remained locked on his opponents with an unwavering focus that spoke volumes about his experience in past battles.

"Bayon, cover!" Velis called out, ducking beneath a vicious swing aimed at his neck.

From behind a gnarled tree, Bayon nocked arrow after arrow, the tension of the bowstring a familiar comfort in his calloused fingers, a silent promise of protection. With each release, his arrows cut through the space between them like dark whispers, finding their targets with deadly accuracy. His aim was true, each shot finding its mark amidst the shrubbery where shadows would have obscured the view of an unseasoned warrior.

Amidst the fray, Hyan's stout form was a stubborn stone against the encroaching danger. His axe, a blur of shimmering metal, cleaved through the air with a force that belied his size. He grunted with effort, auburn hair matted to his forehead, but his blue eyes shone with a determination as unyielding as the mountains he hailed from. Each step he took was calculated, positioning himself to shield Euphenia as she focused on her incantations.

"Stand back," Euphenia warned her friends, her voice a resounding echo that seemed to shake the very leaves from their branches.

Euphenia's silhouette glowed with an otherworldly light, her yellow eyes reflecting the fierce flames that began to swirl around her outstretched hands. The air itself crackled with the power of her spell, a dance of fire that grew into a protective barrier around them. Her long black hair billowed as if caught in a tempest, and the arcane words that left her lips were a symphony of ancient power. As she conjured the fiery shield, it roared like a dragon's breath, repelling the agents who dared draw near with its unbearable heat.

The Hass Mara faltered, their coordinated attack disrupted by the elemental fury that now stood between them and their quarry. The group's resolve was a palpable force. The scent of singed earth mingled with the metallic tang of spilled blood, painting a vivid portrait of their steadfast defiance amidst the chaos.

In the moment of heightened battle, Velis and his companions were more than just warriors—they were the living embodiment of Halacritas's last hope, the guardians of a legacy that would shape the future of their world.

Velis's blade hummed through the air, a silver arc that met the dark iron of his adversary's sword with a resounding ring. The Hass Mara agent before him was relentless, a shadow among shadows, but Velis moved with a dancer's grace, each parry and thrust an answer to the rhythm of death whispered by his foe's blade.

The Hass Mara's numbers dwindled, their assault broken upon the unyielding will of Velis and his comrades. As he continued to slice his way through assailants, a thunderous noise shook the ground, sending them all flying back. Velis's head hit a rock with a loud crack, black dots swimming in his vision.

When he sat up, he saw a man in a long black robe appear in the middle of the fray. When they made eye contact, the large man began moving through the sea people, his eyes focused on Velis.

## Chapter 3

Bayon tried to stop his advanced, but the man quickly out maneuvered him and shoved him into Hyan with his magic. Stopping in front of Velis, he pointed a long sword at him, one made of dark metal, the pommel encrusted with rubies. Power leeched from it, filling Velis with dread.

"Your journey ends here, friend," he said as he stood before Velis. "Hand over the egg and we might let you and your companions live."

"I've grown rather fond of the egg… friend," Velis teased. "I think I'll keep it."

"I am Lord Lakara, leader of the Hass Mara," Lakara raised is sword into a fighting stance. "You stand no chance against me."

"Well, I am Velis of somewhere I am sure," Velis raised his sword as well as he stood. "I have been in more precarious situations than this, probably. I think I'll do just fine."

Lakara didn't seem distraught over Velis' declaration. In fact, he looked thrilled and eager to go toe-to-toe with Velis No-Name.

Velis was not lying when he said he had faced his fair share of foes, but he was sure that none of them were as formidable as Lakara, nor as determined to get what he was after.

Lakara swung his blade without remorse. The hit reverberated through Velis's body, shaking him down to his boots. There was magic behind that hit, power that he had never felt before, not even from Euphenia.

He tried not to let the shock show on his face, but he wasn't sure how successful he was. Still, he deflected each hit with all the resilience he possessed. How he was standing, he didn't know.

The pressure of the egg in the bag on his back reminded him of his mission. He had to be willing to give it all to ensure this dragon did not fall into the wrong hands. That thought pressed him forward, brought forth strength and he was able to gain some ground in the fight. With another swing, he pushed Lakara back, slowly, but he was gaining some traction.

The fight brought the duo toward a cliff and Velis moved as far from it as he could. Heights had never bothered him, but he did not fancy being kicked off into the depths by a member of the Hass Mara. He wouldn't mind if Lakara took a tumble, though.

"You don't think you can push me off, do you?" Lakara asked as if reading his thoughts.

"No," Velis said. "Not until I sever your head from your shoulders."

Lakara laughed again and lunged forward. Velis matched each blow even though he could feel his muscles ache and tire. He wasn't sure how much longer he could stand against this foe. Still, he was standing, somehow. To both of their surprise, Velis knocked the sword from Lakara's hand. The beast of a man looked at Velis in shock.

"The dragon gives you it's power," Lakara said.

"How can that be when this is not my dragon and it is still inside its shell?" Velis asked. "Perhaps you are not as strong as you think."

Velis pointed his blade at Lakara's throat and the man stiffened.

"Your people will never have this dragon," he declared. "We have the protection and the blessings of the Elders of Halacritas."

Lakara sneered. He brought his hand up and a ball of red magic began to form. Velis took a deep breath, realizing this could be his last moment. The magic was thrown and Velis brought up his sword as if it could protect him. He closed his eyes, waiting for the dark spell to hit him. When nothing happened, he looked through squinted eyes.

A wall of white light stood between him and Lakara. His foe looked at the wall in utter disbelief, mouth hanging open in shock. Velis took the distraction and stepped forward, plunging his sword deep into Lakara's chest.

He stared at Velis. "The dragon… it cannot be…"

Velis didn't take time to ask Lakara what he was trying to stay. Instead, he kept good on his promise and removed the man's head from his body. Velis kicked Lakara's chest and sent him over the cliff and into the water below.

Euphenia came forward and set the remains of Lakara on fire. It was no mystery to her that those who wielded dark magic could find a way back if their body was intact.

When the Hass Mara members witnessed what happened to their leader, they began to disperse. Hyan and Bayon chased a few down, but the others escaped. Velis dropped to his knees and quickly pulled the bag around to check on the egg.

He pulled out the large, golden egg. There was a crack on the surface, causing Velis's heart to drop.

"Euphenia," he whispered breathlessly. "What have I done?"

The witch moved forward, taking in the sight with a worried expression. Bayon and Hyan returned and immediately realized something was wrong.

"I have failed." Velis held the egg close and hung his head.

He could feel tears burn his eyes. After all these years, the egg was lost. The return of dragons has ended and it was all because of him.

"Gods," Hyan said in disbelief.

"I will return to the Elders and confess." Velis began to stand.

"No, you bloody elf," Hyan said gruffly.

"Look!" Euphenia said excitedly.

Velis opened his eyes and watched as another crack formed on the egg. Tiny, white lines appeared rapidly across the golden surface.

"It's hatching!" Bayon announced. "Put it down! Put it down!"

Velis placed the egg on the ground and took a step back. Euphenia rested her hand on his wrist, her excitement pulsing through them both.

Another hairline fracture appeared, and then another. They jumped when something, a foot, poked through.

"By the gods!" Hyan said in disbelief.

A white head popped from the top of the egg and then the rest of the body followed. The water of life rushed forward as the newborn dragon lay on the rock underneath the brightest moon they had seen so far on their journey.

They could tell the dragon was breathing, but it lay there, unmoving. Slowly it began to shuffle around on unsteady legs and unfurled its wings. It was the purest white Velis had ever seen and his father's people were the fairest in all the land. It opened its eyes and he took in their deep, black color. It was darker than an abyss and vaster than the night's sky on a clear night.

Its gaze held a silent vow. It would protect this land, its people, with every fiber of its being. They all watched it in awe and wonder.

"It is beautiful," Euphenia said in a whisper. "So much power for such a small thing."

Small was relative. It was already the size of a large house cat, and even bigger when it spread it's massive, leathery wings.

The dragon waddle over and sniffed around Velis's boots. It did the same to the others as if trying to familiarize itself to their scent. When it was done, it returned to Velis, looked up at him, and gave him a tiny roar.

Velis nearly smiled as he picked the dragon up and cradled it in his large arms. The dragon snuggled against his chest and closed its eyes.

"I don't know what to do," Velis confessed.

"We continue on our journey," Euphenia said to him. "We have to assume the Hass Mara has tracked our location from all the magic that was at play here. We have no more time to dawdle."

"I agree." Bayon still had not taken his eyes off the dragon. "We continue on our journey, get the egg… err, dragon, to the prince."

They all agreed, mounted their horses, and took off into the night.

## Chapter 4

The days turned into weeks as the group moved across Halacritas. The small dragon was growing at an exponential rate. After the first week, it learned to fly. At first, Velis was fearful it would fly away from them, but it seemed to know it was supposed to stay close and never strayed far. The next week, it could blow small flames from its nose and mouth. It singed Hyan's beard when the dwarf was standing too close while it practiced.

Hyan was distraught as his beard was very important to him. The dragon brought him a dead rabbit and left it at his feet the next night, and the dwarf patted its head in forgiveness.

Velis spent as much time as he could explaining to the dragon who he was meant for. He told the dragon it had purpose in this world and they were there to ensure he reached the faraway land of Levaria.

"Your rider is a prince," Velis said to the dragon.

The group stopped next to a riverbed to rest and refill their canteens. The young dragon played in the water and even caught a couple of fish, gulping them down quickly. It was already the size of a small horse and Velis wondered how big it would be by the time they reached their destination.

"I should have known I'd find you with him," Euphenia said as she sat next to Velis.

She had removed her shawl and laid it behind her, relaxing on the dark fabric. Velis noticed the slender curve of her shoulders and the way her small but taut muscles stretched the length of her arms.

Euphenia was a beautiful woman and they had known each other for a long time. This wasn't their first mission together. They had been in more life-or-death situations than not. Velis had always felt close to her and if he were ever to allow his emotions to rise to the surface, he would admit that he cared for her.

"He is growing so fast," she said, looking at the dragon.

"How do you know it's a he?" Velis asked.

"It's a feeling," she said, moving her yellow eyes to him.

Velis felt a nervousness move within him as she stared deep into his eyes. He recalled the first time he had seen her. It was in the middle of a fierce battle. The Elders has sent him to the covens to help them with troll raiders.

Euphenia was hurling her magic at the invaders, her raven hair whipping around her like tendrils of smoke. Velis was facing off against three trolls when her magic swiped through them like a blade, cutting their feet out from under them. They shared a moment of gratitude; he thanking her for saving his life and her thanking him for lending aid.

When he returned to the Elders, he told them of Euphenia, her power and her heart. It was not long before they called for her, recruiting her into their small faction.

"I wish I could ask it," Velis said. "Then I would know for sure."

*Ask.*

"What did you say?" he looked at her.

"I said nothing." She furrowed her brow in confusion.

*Ask.*

Velis stood up, looking around, "I heard it again."

He drew his sword thinking he was being mentally attacked by a nearby sorcerer. Euphenia stood with him, looking around in concern.

"What? What is it?" she asked.

*Ask me.*

"I hear…" Velis looked around and then his eyes landed on the dragon.

It was looking up at him with those dark orbs. Velis didn't want to voice his thoughts out loud for fear that he was wrong and that Euphenia would think him mad.

"Did you…" He walked toward the dragon.

Crouching down in front of it, he placed a hand on his broad chest. Closing his eyes, Velis relaxed, wondering if he were indeed losing his mind.

*Did you speak to me?*

*I did.*

Velis' eyes popped open, and he smiled. Looking back at Euphenia, he waved her over.

"What is going on?"

"He is speaking to me," Velis said in excitement.

"By the goddess!" Euphenia stared at him, then at the dragon. "So, he is male."

"I don't know," Velis laughed. "I'll ask."

*I am Ervum. Dragons can choose who we want to be.*

*What do you want to be?*

*I am Ervum.*

*Right.*

*Does it matter what I am?*

*No, I suppose not.*

*If I went with how I feel, then I am male. Euphenia felt this as well.*

*How do you speak our language?*

*I have been learning, listening to you speak.*

*You're only a few weeks old.*

*Dragons do not age and grow the way humans and elves do.*

*I can see that.*

"What is he saying?" Euphenia asked impatiently.

"His name is Ervum," he answered.

"A lovely name," Euphenia smiled at the dragon. "'Connected to nature' is its meaning."

*You are right, Euphenia, meaning 'good omen.'*

"Goddess!" Euphenia stared at the dragon in shock.

"What are you lazy lot doing?" Bayon asked, walking up with a few fish.

*Bayon.*

Bayon stopped in his tracks and nearly dropped his tackle gear.

"Why are you standing about staring?" Hyan asked.

The dwarf had returned from bathing down the stream. His red beard was still wet, but had been freshly braided.

*They are looking at me, Hyan, prince of the Ash Mountains.*

Hyan quickly moved to Ervum, placing a hand on top of dragon's head. Tears pricked the dwarf's eyes. He had never believed dragons would return to the land and now here one was, finding him worthy enough to speak to him.

They set up camp for the night there beside the river. Velis and the others stayed up late into the night telling Ervum all that had taken place while he was in his egg. Velis explained they were taking him to Levaria to meet his rider.

*Is he a good man?*

*I have never met him, but if you are meant to be his dragon then I would like to think so.*

*I would like to think so as well.*

Ervum said that while he was new to this world, he had spent over 100 years in his egg. He had heard and learned much about the Elders. They were good people with their hearts in the right place.

When the others fell asleep at last, Velis stayed up talking to Ervum. He couldn't suppress the wonder he felt talking to the dragon. Truth be told, he felt as if he could talk forever.

*Was it lonely? Waiting?*

*At times. The Elders were kind to me. They would visit me every day, making sure I was growing and safe.*

*It hardly seems fair that you had to wait.*

*It is my lot. I am not angry about it. I am out now and learning much and for that I am thankful. And I am excited by what I have seen in this world. It is beautiful. I cannot wait to explore more.*

Velis finally laid back on the bed he had made for himself. He thought of all they had discussed and explored through conversation. Ervum was marvelous and he knew that soon he would be with his rider, and for some reason, that filled Velis with unease.

## Chapter 5

After only a few days, they entered Aduceus, where Euphenia was born and raised. Its name came from a time when witches

166

were persecuted for being wielders of magic. After years of war and fire, the once lush fertile land was now a tangle of weeds and bogs. However, there were patches where the earth was healing itself and that was where they hoped to find a few days of rest.

Velis could only imagine what those days must have been like for Euphenia. Like elves, witches had long lives. Euphenia was a young girl during the times of the Purification. She lost her family, her home, and nearly her life.

They moved slowly through the bog, having to dismount their horses so they could maneuver the narrow roads. One slip and they would find themselves in the thick mud. Many people who travel through Aduceus end up victims of the bog, falling into the boiling soup, never to be seen again.

"Almost there," Euphenia told them. "It is just beyond the trees."

The trees she spoke of were merely dead remnants of what were once massive oaks. Velis could recall when their branches reached for the sky and their leaves blocked out the sun. The witches would often live within the trunks for they were large enough to contain an entire family.

Now, unable to part from the magic and shelter that was once given to them from the trees, they lived beneath, working endlessly to treat the roots and bring them back to life.

Euphenia walked ahead of them, standing before one of the corpses of a home and recited a few words from the ancient language. A door appeared and a set of stone stairs descended into the ground. Ervum landed beside her, rubbing his head against her leg. She smiled at him and walked through the opening, Ervum following behind her.

They descended the stairs, horses and all. It was dark, but Euphenia used her magic to conjure a ball of light to guide their way.

Soon the dark was pricked with light in the distance. As they moved closer, the light looked like the sun, but it was an artificial light made of magic and raised to the upmost point in a deep cavern. It was big and bright, casting beautiful beams upon the rows of vegetation and homes.

Velis had visited the Coven of Iylis many times throughout the years, but it always took him by surprise when he saw what they had created. The world had taken their home from above and the coven recreated it below. It was vast and spread through several cave systems. The people of Iylis were many things, but they were not weak.

The group walked through the village, many of them stopping to welcome Euphenia back home and then dropping to their knees when they saw Ervum. They gave worship to the goddess of their namesake, Iylis, for blessing their lifetime with the return of the magical beasts.

The canopy of people parted like the final curtain at a grand play, revealing a grove that shimmered with an ethereal glow. As the group threaded through the last clinging people giving their praise, a figure emerged from the luminescence, her presence as commanding as the light that seemed to bend around her form. She was Kenyis, the High Priestess of the Iylis Coven, garbed in robes that flickered with the essence of living flame.

"Welcome home, daughter," she intoned, her voice a melody woven with power and grace. "Velis, as always when I see, you bring my heart great joy. And of course, we welcome our brethren of the dwarves and humans. I hope you can find rest here."

"Thank you, Priestess." Hyan bowed, and Velis could see he was taken in by her beauty.

"Good day to you, dragon." Kenyis walked to Ervum, bowing low. "It is an honor to have you in our home. Please, feel welcome and safe here."

Ervum bowed his head in return.

"I expected you to bring an egg, Euphenia, not a dragon." Kenyis chuckled. "You are always outdoing yourself, young one."

Before them, Kenyis raised her hands, palms upturned to the cavern top, and the air thrummed with latent energy. A warmth cascaded over the group, washing away the chill of the swamp and the fatigue from their bones. It was as if the sun itself had descended to kiss the earth, bathing them in a golden radiance that whispered of hearth fires and sanctuary. The light coalesced into a dome above their heads, a shield from the darkening world, wrapping them in the safety of its embrace. It disappeared slowly, but Velis still felt the magic in his soul.

"Rest here," Kenyis offered, her eyes reflecting the flicker of her coven's elemental affinity. "The fire of Iylis is your ally, and within this coven, you shall find respite."

After bathing and enjoying a meal, the group sat in the common room of a hostel. Kenyis had given them refuge here and Velis's bones were thankful. Ervum lay curled up next to the hearth, content with a belly full of goat meat. Velis watched him for a while, amazed at his growth and intelligence. Once more he was filled with dread at the thought of leaving him in Levaria.

Levaria was ruled by a noble king, *his* king. Velis had served in the army for years until the Elders called him into their service. While he had never met the prince, if he were like his father then he would rule with justice. Velis knew that royalty had a different view of the world, but they always ruled fairly.

"Good evening." A young woman entered the hostel.

She was tall with red hair and shimmering yellow eyes like the rest of the witches in her coven.

"Palis!" Euphenia stood and rushed to her. "It is so good to see you, sister."

The two embraced, and Euphenia closed her eyes, smiling deeply. When they parted, the two women looked at each other with love and affection. While they may only be sisters in the sense of loyalty to the coven, the bond was just as true.

"Kenyis sent me here to accommodate any need you may have," Palis said to Euphenia, then looked at everyone else. "Please do not hesitate to ask."

"First, I need you to sit and tell me all I have missed," Euphenia said, pulling Palis next to her on a soft seat.

The two women spent the next few hours talking about the coven, the progress they had made on the roots of the tree, and the hope of new life.

"Marl is with child?" Euphenia asked in surprise.

"She is," Palis smiled. "She has wed as well. It was a shock to us all as you know it is not our custom to do so. However, she met a human man and fell in love. Kenyis welcomed him to our fold. He took the oath."

"Does that mean he's a witch, too?" Hyan wondered, finding their way of life interesting.

"In a sense," Palis said to him. "He will not have the powers we do. You are born with magic. Those married into the coven will be blessed by the goddess. They may be given divination or become a healer, but they will never be able to wield magic as we do."

"What of the child?" Bayon wondered.

"The child will be a witch," Euphenia said. "If the goddess has blessed their union and he took the oath to protect and serve our coven, their child will be a witch."

"Male or female, it doesn't matter?" Hyan asked.

"Our male witches sometimes refer to themselves as wizards, but it is still the same type of magic," Palis explained.

"Fascinating," Bayon nodded, deep in thought.

"I find how inclusive your people are to be refreshing," Hyan said to them both. "It is not often to find those so welcoming to those unlike themselves."

"We welcome all here," Palis smiled at him. "Even dwarves."

Hyan shifted under Palis's gaze. His ruddy cheeks, if Velis wasn't mistaken, turned just a bit brighter.

## Chapter 6

Euphenia was sad to say goodbye to her home once again, but they had many more miles to go. Palis gave them parting gifts of bread, dried meat, and full canteens of water. She also kissed the top of Hyan's head, which made the dwarf fumble over his words as he bid her farewell.

Evrum glided above them as they left Aduceus, the rhythm of his expansive wings coinciding with the beat of Velis's own heart. Once more he felt the pang of loss, knowing soon he would not have the comforting presence of the dragon's consciousness nestled against his own. He wondered if the others felt the same.

*They do.*

*I did not realize you were listening.*

*I suppose I always am, in a way.*

*That makes sense, though that is very strange. What if I were thinking about being relieved to be rid of you?*

*Why would anyone want to be rid of me? I am a powerful and trustworthy ally.*

Velis chuckled at Evrum's obliviousness to sarcasm. Dragons were truthful creatures; it was not in their nature to speak half-truths.

"I see you two are still in communion," Hyan said, guiding his horse forward. "If you ever tire of the elf, Ervum, I can entertain you with fascinating stories of the dwarves."

"He's jealous," Euphenia whispered with a small laugh.

Velis looked at her with affection. If he weren't mistaken, she shared the emotion, if only fleeting.

Velis glanced over at Bayon who was chewing on a piece of dried meat with a silent smile. Velis merely glared in his direction and pushed forward, his dark eyes scanning the horizon for any signs of danger. They entered the ancient forest that bordered the land of Levaria. The air was thick with the scent of moss and pine, and a sudden rustling in the bushes ahead brought their group to a halt.

Velis unsheathed his gleaming sword with a swift motion, his senses honed for any potential threat. Euphenia's hands crackled with magic as she murmured an incantation under her breath, ready to unleash her formidable powers at a moment's notice.

Out of the shadows emerged figures cloaked in dark hooded robes, and the group readied themselves for battle.

"Peace, friends," one figure walked forward. "We are here to welcome you to Levaria. I am Fein, Prince Leryn's personal guard. Please, lower your weapons. We mean you no harm."

As Fein came into view, Velis and the others could see he wore the Levaria emblem on his metal armor. Fein was a fair elf with long, white hair that was pinned back at the crown in a delicate braid. His blue eyes were bright, and he looked youthful and vibrant.

"We apologize, brother," Velis said to him, sheathing his sword. "Our journey has been long and treacherous."

"I am sure you speak the truth," Fein replied, walking to the group.

He and Velis shook hands and embraced, the customary elven greeting. Fein clasped Velis on the shoulder and smiled. "You have traveled far, but you are in the realm of Levaria. Rest easy. Come, the prince awaits his dragon. A dragon I see that has hatched. What joyous news! We were afraid it would not come to pass."

"This is Ervum," Velis pointed to the dragon as he landed next to him.

In just the three days at Iylis, Ervum had grown another foot. When he sat back on his hunches, his head was above Velis's, putting him close to seven feet in height. His wingspan had also doubled in size, and his girth and muscles were large and strong.

"The creature told you his name?" Fein looked at Ervum in wonder. "It is a pleasure, dear dragon. Welcome to Levaria."

Fein bowed as did the other guards. Ervum inclined his head in return after a moment of staring them down.

"He says thank you," Velis told them.

"He speaks to you?" Fein snapped his head toward Velis.

"He speaks to all of us," Euphenia informed them.

Fein's eyes widened in amazement at the revelation that Ervum could communicate with them. The guards around him murmured in astonishment, clearly taken aback by the special bond between the group and the dragon.

As they made their way through the enchanting forest of Levaria, guided by Fein and his guards, a sense of awe washed over the group. The trees seemed to whisper ancient tales, and the very air hummed with an otherworldly energy that invigorated their spirits. Ervum flew overhead, his scales shimmering in the dappled sunlight that filtered through the canopy above.

Velis felt at home. It had been many years since he had been in Levaria, but he knew the woods like he knew his own name. The air smelled the same, and the way the ground felt beneath his felt was like walking on a fond memory.

Before long, they arrived at the grand gates of Levaria, towering high and adorned with intricate elven runes that shimmered in the sunlight. The city beyond was a marvel to behold, with elegant spires reaching towards the sky and cascading waterfalls that added a gentle melody to the surroundings.

As they approached the castle gates, guards in gleaming armor stood at attention, their expressions a mix of curiosity and respect. Fein spoke a few hushed words to them, and the gates swung open soundlessly, allowing the group to pass through.

Inside the castle walls, they were greeted by a lavish courtyard adorned with blooming flowers and sparkling fountains. Prince Leryn stood at the center; his commanding presence undeniable even if he were young for an elf. The king and queen stood in wait nearby, and Velis could see how much Leryn looked like his mother, though he had the stern eyes of his father, deep and dark blue.

Ervum landed gracefully in the courtyard, his towering form drawing gasps of awe from those gathered. The prince's expression shifted from one of anticipation to pure wonder as he beheld the majestic white dragon, his pitch-black eyes gleaming with a mixture of reverence and excitement.

"Welcome, honored guests," Prince Leryn spoke, his voice carrying a regal tone that echoed through the courtyard. "I am overjoyed to see that the dragon egg has hatched and brought forth such a magnificent creature. We have long awaited this moment."

The king and queen stepped forward, their faces alight with joy at the sight of Ervum. The queen, her features graceful and serene, reached out a hand towards the dragon in a gesture of welcome. Ervum lowered his head, allowing her to caress his snout gently, a rumble of contentment escaping him.

"We are forever grateful for what you have done," the king addressed Velis and his companions. "Tonight, we will celebrate this victory. The bonding ceremony will take place, and then we will feast. For now, please enjoy the amenities we have to offer here as reward for what you have done."

"Uniting Ervum and the prince is reward enough." Velis bowed to the king. "But we will graciously accept your offer with a sincere heart."

"He has been named?" the prince asked.

"He named himself," Velis told him. "It was his choice."

"How marvelous," the queen smiled.

Prince Leryn eyed Velis curiously and then looked at Ervum. He walked over to the dragon and reached out a palm. Ervum sniffed the air and then touched the boy's palm lightly. A smile transformed his face from a serious prince to a curious child.

If Ervum was happy with the prince, then Velis should be happy for him. That was what friends did for each other. Velis realized the dragon had become just that over the course of their journey, a friend. He wanted what was best for his friend. He had to question, though: if he was supposed to be happy for his friend, then why did it hurt so much to watch him with the prince?

*Chapter 7*

The palace was a fortress of strength and protection. It stood as a beacon of hope to all in Levaria, and to many in Halacritas. The elves had overcome their initial hesitation to share the realm with different species. It had taken a war to get to this point, and while they still had more wrongs to right, Velis knew that with Ervum, they were on the right path.

With all of the hope the moment had brought, Velis could not shake the odd sensation in his soul. He paced around his luxurious room in the palace, unable to overcome the feeling that something was off.

Velis's nerves were on fire. The group had been given a grand lunch, fine new clothes, and enough coin for them to retire and never have to work a job again. Velis cared nothing for the coin. The Elders always made sure his needs were met and that was all he could ask for.

As they sat at lunch, a hush had fallen over them. He knew they felt the same way he did. Or maybe he hoped they did. When he couldn't sit there in silence any longer, he excused himself and was shown to his chambers by a servant.

His saw Euphenia's eyes as he left. They were full of questions and worry. He knew she was worried for him. He was constantly worried for her. There was no doubt in his mind she could save herself. She was no damsel, but that didn't mean his heart didn't pain him when he thought something might happen to her.

Velis kept these thoughts to himself for many reasons. He never wanted Euphenia to be used as a means to hurt him by his enemies. Also, there was that fear that maybe those glances meant nothing to her. Perhaps he only imagined her eyes lingering on his lips and her hands remaining on his shoulder a moment longer than was polite.

As much as he had tried to push away his feelings and avoid her over the years, fate had a way of bringing them back together.

Velis threw himself on the plush bed, but it was more to stop pacing than anything. After weeks of sleeping on the ground, one would think the bed would be comfortable enough to lull one to sleep. That was not the case. His mind swam with thoughts of the future, of Ervum's future, of Euphenia's eyes across the room stirring dormant emotions.

As he lay there, looking up at the painted ceiling, he prayed to the gods something would explain his strange feelings, but there was no answer at the other end of his prayers. That was the way with gods, their timing was not always in line with his.

A knock on his door made him quickly rise. Picking up his blade, he moved toward the door and stood to the side.

"It's me, Velis," Euphenia said to him. "Put down your blade."

Velis opened the door to find her standing there in a deep purple gown that had been given to her by the queen. She was breathtaking in anything, but the new dress accented her figure. He tried to be a gentleman and not stare. She grinned up at him as if knowing she made him nervous.

"What is it?" he asked, clearing his throat. "Is something wrong?"

"Somewhat," she admitted. "May I come in?"

Velis moved out of her way and she walked by him, filling his nostrils with the scent of lavender oil. Euphenia walked around the room before sitting on the edge of his bed.

"What... seems to be the problem?" he asked, trying not to notice the dark skin of her legs pecking out of the slit of the dress.

"I have a sense about this place," she told him. "I feel like something is amiss."

"I do as well," he confessed.

"Thank the goddess it is not just me," Euphenia breathed out heavily.

"I think we should keep a close eye on the prince and Ervum tonight at the banquet," Velis told her. "I do not doubt the Hass Mara had followed us. It may seem unlikely for them to try anything within these walls, but they are so close to their prize."

"I agree." She stood and walked over to him. "You do not think that Hass Mara would actually attack Vealkesh?"

"I think they are capable of anything." He looked down at her. "We must be vigilant."

"Right, of course," she nodded. "I shall go and tell the others."

She made to leave, but Velis gently grabbed her wrist. Euphenia turned and looked back at him quizzically.

"Velis? Why do you hold my arm?" she asked.

"I… I don't know." A blush burned his cheeks. "I just want you to be safe and… I…"

*Tell her.*

He heard Ervum speak to him.

*Not now, Ervum. I can't.*

*Elves. You have long lives, but you do not live forever. Do not spend you years longing for her when you could spend it with her.*

"Velis?" Euphenia broke his connection to the dragon. "I can take care of myself. You do not have to worry."

"But I will," he said plainly. "I have no doubt you are more than capable, but I will worry because…"

"Because…?" she prodded, still confused.

Fragile was a heart that longed for someone who didn't want them in return. Or was he wrong? Was Ervum right? Should he say something? Velis was a war-hardened soldier and did not like to show his weaknesses as it could be used against him. Yet, something had changed within him in the past few weeks.

He wanted more to life than war and fighting. There was a slim chance that would ever happen given his oath to the Elders. A wife and children were not something he could have, even if he wanted it, but her… he wanted her.

Velis gently pulled Euphenia close until she was flush with his body. Her warm face suddenly took on a rosy hue. She looked up at him with questioning eyes. There was a mixture of hope and desire there that made the entirety of his body shake.

Velis took her face in his hands and leaned down, his face hovering over hers for just a moment. He wanted to make sure she wanted this as much as he did. When Euphenia did not move, he pressed his lips to hers, kissing her deeply. Euphenia gave in to the kiss, wrapping her arms around him. Velis let all of his pent-up feelings for her pour into that kiss. He wanted her to know how he felt for her, how he had always felt for her.

He took her in his arms and led them to the bed. For years he wanted her to know. He wanted to say something but was too afraid. Now, all that fear was gone.

Suddenly an alarm sounded in the distance. They froze before Euphenia bolted up.

"The palace has been breached," she said in a frightened whisper.

Velis grabbed his sword, and they bounded out of the room. Hyan and Bayon met them in the hallway, weapons in hands. Bayon was already stringing his bow.

The group raced the halls of the palace, passing guards on their way to their battle stations, their weapons drawn and ready for what lay ahead. The once peaceful night now echoed with the sounds of chaos as they reached the grounds outside. The Hass Mara agents in dark cloaks flooded into view, their intentions clear as they stood in a fighting stance.

The Halacritas defenders formed a fighting circle, radiating fierce determination. The intruders hesitated at the sight of the formidable group, but their mission's objective outweighed their fear.

With a battle cry that shook the air with an explosion of energy, Velis lunged forward, his sword slicing through the air as he engaged two enemies at once. Hyan followed suit with his mighty axe, his dwarven strength unmatched as he swung it in calculated arcs. Euphenia's magic coiled within her and exploded forward, killing at least nine of their foes.

As many as they cut down, more and more came. Velis knew the Hass Mara were a legion, but their numbers here were greater than he had ever seen before. They were doing well defending themselves, but he knew they could not last if this onslaught continued.

A mighty roar erupted, echoing across the sky as Ervum landed with a force that shook the ground. The prince ran up to his side, drawing his sword. The sight should have brought Velis relief and hope, but the uneasy feeling that had been brewing all day welled up inside him.

Bayon suddenly took a sword to the shoulder and cried out. Velis went running toward him, but suddenly a sharp pain penetrated his back.

"You have failed, brother," a voice said in his ear.

Velis turned to see Fein, a sneer marring his unblemished face.

"You have sided with darkness?" Velis snapped.

Leryn sauntered forward; his blade pointed at Velis's throat. The guard forced the dagger deeper into his back. Velis wanted to cry out but bit down on his tongue. He didn't want to give these traitors the pleasure.

"We have sided with the victors," Leryn told him.

"The king will not stand for this," Velis grunted out.

"The king his dead," Leryn replied. "So is the queen. All of Levaria is mine. We will bring in a new Halacritas soon. One that is under one rule. Mine. Finally, we will be at peace."

"You're a fool," Velis said. "You cannot stamp out darkness with more."

"No, brother," Leryn stepped forward. "You are the fool to believe those ancient idiots up in the mountains have any control over this kingdom or me. The dragon is mine. It has been written. Ervum. Come."

Ervum looked over at the group and made his way to the prince. He sat back on his haunches next to Leryn. He gave Ervum a strip of meat as a reward. Ervum was not a dog or any animal that could be trained. The dragon was something more than a mere beast. He was the magic of Halacritas.

"With this dragon, we can begin a new era in Halacritas," Leryn said, giving Ervum another piece of raw meat. "I feel like you should know before I kill you, since you did bring him here and you are one of the superior beings. We will find the other dragon eggs. They will be bred. We will have a fleet of dragon riders in a few short years. No one will be able to stand in our way. And you, Velis, you will be too dead to stop it from happening. Ervum, as your rider, I command you to kill Velis. I am feeling benevolent, so make it quick."

Ervum moved forward immediately, bearing down on Velis, danger in his dark eyes. Velis had experienced an array of pain in his long life. He had been shot with arrows and stabbed with daggers, dragged by a horse, and thrown from a cliff. Still, he thought death by dragon would rank highest on the list. Not because of those sharp teeth, but because it was Ervum.

He had grown fond of the dragon. They had become friends, companions, and he wanted that to mean something. There was nothing like the bond between a rider and their dragon, though.

"We have the others," a guard said.

Euphenia was thrown down at his side, her face bloodied, a magic shackle around her neck. A member of the Haas Mara stood over her. He had to be a strong wielder of magic to get that band on her. She looked up at him and the pain in her eyes filled him with rage. He made a move to go to her and the guard shoved the dagger further into his back. He felt his breath leave his body and cried out in pain, falling back down.

Hyan and Bayon were shoved to their knees in front of the prince. Bayon looked the worst of them all. He had a gash that ran the length of his face and he cradled a broken arm. None of them were unharmed.

"This is the end for your group, Velis," Leryn said. "I do owe you for bringing me Ervum. So, again, I will make your death swift. Any last words?"

*You do not need any last words*, Ervum said to him as he stepped forward.

*Ervum, please.*

*Please? Why do you beg?*

*I know you are in there. This is not you, my friend.*

"Well, speak now!" Leryn demanded, unaware of the conversation taking place.

*In where? My own head?*

Ervum asked looked down at Velis, tilting his head.

*This frail prince has not tricked me into doing his bidding! Here I thought you were smarter than that. I only played along until I could find you again. It took parting with you to realize the prince is not my rider. It is you. It is all of you. You are my family.*

Velis felt a surge of hope rush through him as he realized Ervum's true intentions. Despite the pain in his body, he managed to flash a defiant grin at Prince Leryn.

"You've underestimated us all, Leryn," Velis said, his voice strong despite the agony.

In a sudden burst of movement, Ervum twisted his massive body, knocking Leryn off his feet with a powerful swipe of his tail. The prince went tumbling to the ground, his sword clattering away. The Hass Mara member holding Euphenia was distracted for a split second, long enough for the witch to summon a burst of flame that disintegrated the magic shackle around her neck.

A brilliant burst of energy erupted from Euphenia, knocking them all down. The blade in Velis's side dug deeper. He sucked in a breath as pain shot through his body. It took what felt like an eternity before he could see clearly again, and when his vision cleared, Prince Leryn was standing over him, his blade high over his head and rage in his eyes. Velis knew his intent was murderous and brought up his arm to try and deflect the blow.

As Leryn brought the sword down in a wide swing, Ervum's form came into view, opening his massive jaws wide. His mouth clamped down, devouring the prince from his head down to his chest. Ervum picked him up and gave him a violent shake, tearing his body in two.

Blood splattered the dragon's white scales and Velis's fallen form. Ervum spat the prince out with a roar and breathed fire into the night sky. Velis watched in awe as Ervum unleashed his fury on their other foes, first Fein and then the Hass Mara, his power and might on full display.

He tried to stand but fell back to the ground. The blood loss was making him weak and stealing his vision, and he found he could no longer breathe.

*Ervum… Ervum, keep them safe for me.*

## Chapter 8

### One Year Later

The wind was crisp and cold. Velis had awoken early in the morning and walked out to watch the sun rise over the mountains. He took in a deep breath, letting the freezing air cleanse his lungs. He could still feel the sharp sting where the blade had pieced flesh and bone from time to time, but he had made a full recovery thanks to Euphenia. She came out of the small house they shared together, wrapped tightly in one of his furs.

"I have been sent a message from the elders," she said, kissing his cheek. "They have a mission for us."

Bayon and Hyan emerged from their own huts as if her words had summoned them. It was possible they had. They all shared a bond with Ervum that had formed them into a sort of family. That was mostly why they had built this small place at the base of the mountains, close to the Elders, but something for themselves, too.

The Elders hadn't known what to do with them once they had returned, Velis nearly on death's door. Euphenia had been their voice, explaining to them the treachery of the prince and how Ervum had claimed them all.

In all of Halacritas's history, a dragon had never had more than one rider at the same time. It was unheard of—until now. After the Elders consulted with Ervum, they found Euphenia's recount of events to be true. Not that they could have stopped them from being bonded; it was just new territory.

Ervum's shadow covered them, filling Velis with a tingling that started from the center of his chest. Seeing the dragon always gave him a sense of hope for the future. He had grown to his full height and strength since then. Ervum was a formidable beast that would instill fear into all of their enemies—and they had many.

The Hass Mara had been scattered, but they were still out there in the shadows. Velis would not rest until he had rid Halacritas of their evil and he knew the others felt the same.

"Well, let's go," Hyan remarked gruffly.

He had still not gotten used to flying. The dwarf would grumble that he was meant to be beneath the land, not flying above it. Still, Velis could feel his love for Ervum and knew that Hyan wouldn't have it any other way.

Ervum nudged Hyan, making the dwarf smile. He rubbed the dragon's large snout. Bayon was always the first to climb Ervum's large wings and wait impatiently for the others.

"How you carry us all, I will never know. Especially the dwarf," Bayon joked.

"Keep eating those meat pies, Bayon, and he'll have to hold you in his claws," Hyon said.

"Tell your lovely lady to stop sending them, then," Bayon remarked. Hyan blushed.

*I would never carry you like that, Bayon. No matter your girth. I am strong. But Palis must always send meat pies. They are my favorite treat.*

Velis and Euphenia looked at each other with a grin. They were an unlikely family and it was even more unlikely that all of them had been chosen by Ervum. Still, here they were and they would live this long life doing all they could to keep the people of Halacritas safe.

## THE END

# The Night the Moon Fell From the Sky
## Selah J Tay-Song

The night the moon fell from the sky, Jun was perched on top of the tallest stalk in the bamboo forest, watching Noct hunt nighthawks.

The dragon had come to Jun in the late winter, for help with a stoat who was trying to steal her eggs. A stoat could hardly best a dragon in a fight, even a tiny dragon, but Noct had to sleep sometime, and every evening she woke afraid to find her nest plundered. For six cold weeks, Jun sat outside a small hollow in a rocky hillside above the forest, guarding her nest sunrise to sundown. The stoat came twice, and Jun gave it a fierce drubbing with his bamboo staff each time. The stoat was incredulous that such a tiny creature as Jun could be so ferocious, but after the second beating it did not return.

In spring Noct's eggs hatched, and the nest was full of squirming dragonlings even more tiny than Jun. By midsummer, they were gone, dispersing over the valleys on wee wings, in search of their own territories. But Noct remained and allowed Jun to climb on her back. She flew him all over the valley, from his home, a hollow in a stalk of bamboo, to the lakeshore where he gave offerings to the dead twice every day. At first Jun thought her transport was repayment for his protection of the nest, which he would have offered freely, but she remained with him well into the first frosts of autumn.

The night the moon fell from the sky, Jun sat in a crook of knotted stalk, contemplating the dark silhouette of the valley far below. The steep hills wore their dark cloaks of bamboo like shrouds. The lake lurked distant on the valley floor, the full moon reflecting on its surface like a giant eye.

Jun shivered and looked toward the heavens. Noct flitted and dashed across the moon's silver face, snatching nighthawks from mid-air. Occasionally, the resident colony of bamboo bats crossed her path, a tiny dark cloud of swift, furry hunters. She chased them for sport, but to Jun's relief she didn't try to catch them. The last thing he needed was an angry swarm of bats descending on his home in the bamboo.

Jun sat back in the crook of the highest branch and leaned against the stalk. The hard skin of the bamboo was smooth against his hands. Even though the stalk was thin, it supported Jun's minuscule weight easily. At just under three inches tall, he was tall for tiny folk, but still small enough to navigate the world far easier than the pitied big folk.

From time to time, one of the big folk came tromping noisily into the valley, snapping branches and sending forest creatures scurrying. Ruan was a dwarf who peddled various supplies to mountain folk of all sizes, trading for unique crafts he could sell as curiosities in El Tal. In return for Jun's pottery, which he sold as doll-house furnishings to other big folk, Ruan provided Jun with supplies he needed to live in the bamboo forest; rice, copper thimbles for cookpots, fabric scraps to make clothing, and incense and candles for the rituals.

When Ruan visited, he marveled at Jun's intricate cups and bowls, tiny and fragile as eggshells in his giant hands. He peeked into Jun's house, built into the bamboo stalk at just the height of Ruan's eyes. He crouched down by the tiny pond and peered into the cave, not much bigger than his fist, where Jun turned his pots and fired them in a kiln that, to Ruan, was like a toy oven.

And Jun, in turn, pitied him. What must it be like to be so huge that a few grains of rice were not enough to fill you? No wonder the big folk were so hungry, and so intent on consuming all of Mirstone. No wonder they ate up entire valleys with their thirst for lakes.

Jun had nearly drowsed off when the moon began to fall toward him. One moment it was up in the sky like a shining coin, the next it was falling steadily in his direction, growing bigger every second, and pale as a ghost. He jerked fully awake, stood on the branch and strained his neck, tilting his head back to see.

When it seemed the moon would crush Jun, it suddenly veered and drifted down the hillside toward the lake. He blinked. The shining coin was still in the sky. But the pale ghost of a moon was still falling, falling.

As he watched, stunned, the ghost moon struck the surface of the lake. It was too far away to hear the splash, but Jun could see the ghost moon floating on the water, a second eye beside the moon reflecting from the sky, both glaring up from the vast lake.

He whistled. Noct turned and hurtled through the air to him, coming out of friendship, not obedience. They had learned to communicate, crudely, through whistles and shrieks when they could not see each other's eyes. Jun jumped off the stalk and landed between her wings. Gripping her spiny crest, he guided her down to the shore of the lake, where the ghost of the moon had fallen into the watery grave of his family.

*

Ten years before the night the moon fell from the sky, the valley floor had been a vast wetland, traversed by a pleasant, winding river. By its banks, Jun's family tended tiny rice paddies and raised minnows in a bustling little village. They were known to the other mountain folk as the Valley Folk.

Jun had never been satisfied with life in the valley. All through his childhood, when Ruan brought tales of the vast cities of big folk and the tiny folk who lived in secret among them, Jun listened intently. The day he became a man, he shouldered a knapsack and cut a bamboo twig for a walking staff, and set out over the hills to find one of the cities the peddler spoke of, El Tal. When he reached the rocky crest of the hill that overlooked the valley, he stopped and looked back for one last time at his childhood home.

Later, Ruan would explain that the officials of El Tal had ordered the dam built to turn the valley into a lake to store water for the city. He could not explain why they decided to close up the dam in spring, when the river was high. On that fateful day, Jun knew none of this. He only saw the river rising, spilling its banks, churning with mud and broken bamboo. It all happened so swiftly, and looked so strange, that he thought he was dreaming as the lake rose from the mouth of the valley and swallowed up his family village in a torrent of violent water.

Later, after the shock wore off, and for years, Jun was haunted by the thought that he might have done something that day. He had watched the water begin creeping hungrily up the valley. He might have rushed back down the hill and warned his family. Instead, he had stood rooted in place on the ridge, watching the carnage. Doing nothing.

When the lake stopped rising, he still had not quite registered what happened. He left his pack on the ridge and ran through the forest to the new lake shore, a jumble of muddy rocks dragged along by the rising river, lined with floating stalks of shattered bamboo. He expected to find his family, wet and bedraggled but alive, on the shore. But the rocky shore was empty and eerily quiet, save for the lapping of the lake. Jun made a little raft out of a bamboo leaf and poled to where he thought his family village had been. A few things had floated up and were bobbing in the dark water. His sister's doll, with mouse-fur for hair. A bamboo staff with a piece of fish skin tied around it; that had belonged to his grandfather. His father's rice straw sunhat.

Everything else was gone, preserved in a watery grave forever.

After the lake swallowed his village, Jun lost all desire to leave the valley and seek his fortune in the city. He was the only one of his kin left alive, and now he had a duty to steward their graves. He went into the bamboo forest and made a home high in the thickest stalk he could find. He found a spring-fed pond lined with clay, and a small cave set in the roots of a tree above it. He began throwing pots at first because he had nothing to cook or eat on. But soon the act of sitting in his little cave, throwing pots while the rain dripped noisily on bamboo leaves, became the only thing that soothed the deep ache in his heart.

When Ruan came to the valley looking for survivors, he was surprised to find Jun alive. He explained what he had learned of the dam. Jun had suspected the sudden arrival of the hungry lake had something to do with the big folk, and he had planned to hate them all forever. But with Ruan there in front of him, his hate crumbled.

He told Ruan what he had seen. Showed him the doll, the hat, the staff. Ruan was sorry. He said he would have warned them, if he had known himself. He offered to take Jun with him to El Tal, and introduce him to the tiny folk he knew there. When Jun refused, Ruan was generous, giving him freely enough supplies to keep him well-fed until Ruan next came to the valley.

A few days after Ruan was gone, the surface of the lake came alive. It was if a ferocious wind blew across it, only there was no wind. Jun cooked some rice and made moon-cakes. He brought these to the edge of the lake and set them on rock just within the spray of the lapping water. He lit some incense Ruan had left and sang songs his grandfather had sung when one of the Valley Folk left the world of the living. The lake calmed, and Jun began to give offerings at sunrise and sunset, to keep the spirits of his family at peace. After that, his life attained a steady rhythm. Seasons came and went, but nothing really changed in the bamboo forest.

Until the night the moon fell from the sky.

Noct landed on the rocky lakeshore and Jun stepped off her back into a pile of incense ash, a deposit from years of offerings. Noct, who disliked the lake, crouched by the lapping waves and growled low in her throat at the fallen ghost moon, a huge disc of pale fabric floating like a skin on the water some twenty feet from the shore. The lake was placid, but the disc was wriggling, as if something was trapped under it.

Jun kicked off his sandals and plunged into the cold, dark water without thinking. It wasn't until he was over his head, treading swiftly toward the fallen moon that he realized he was walking on the grave of his family.

A chill even colder than the lake water ran through him. He thought he could see the ghosts of his family looking up at him through the dark waters. He almost turned back, but kept plunging forward instead.

When he reached the moon, he saw that it wasn't a moon at all. It was a moon-boat, a giant sphere of silk that puffed up like the moon and rose into the sky when a fire was lit under it. Jun had never seen one himself, but Ruan had spoken of them, while recounting other wonders from tiny folk in other corners of Mirstone. He said some tiny folk rode the winds in moon-boats, traveling much farther than their feet could take them. Jun had listened raptly, but he hardly believed such a marvelous thing actually existed. Ruan had a tendency for flair in his stories, and you couldn't always tell when he was being straight and when he was making believe.

But tonight, Jun saw the marvel of the moon-boat with his own eyes. The big white disc that had fallen into the lake was a sphere of pale silk. It was tied with ropes to a basket, which was now sinking, threatening to pull the entire thing under, down to the depths where Jun's family rested.

And something was moving there in the center of the fabric. Jun pulled himself along the mass of silk until he reached the center. He drew his belt knife and cut into it until a tiny woman came spluttering to the surface, coughing up lake water.

She struggled against the fabric, and Jun gripped her torso, helping heft her head above water. Trying to get a better hold on her, his fingers found something hot and slippery, a contrast to the cold, hard lake water. His fingers came away from her ribs slick with blood. Noct shrieked from the shore, distressed by the smell of violence.

Jun whistled, both to call and to comfort Noct. He knew she feared deep water, but if the woman was injured, he could hardly drag her all the way back through the cold water.

After a few more shrieks of protest, Noct came. Jun lifted the woman out of the water and delivered her to Noct's waiting talons. When they were safely aloft, he fought his way out of the mess of silk and followed them to shore, swimming with all his might. He staggered through the shallows and collapsed beside the woman on the rocky shore.

But he could not rest yet. He was shivering and he thought the woman, who had been in the water longer, must be in danger of freezing to death. "Noct, a fire," he pleaded, and made the whistle he would sound when he wanted her to ignite his kiln with her breath. Noct was hopping from foot to foot on the slippery rocks, trying to shake the water from her talons. At Jun's request, she shrieked and flew off into the night.

Under the watery light of the moon, Jun sat up, shivering, and crawled closer to the strange woman who had fallen from the sky. He could not see her well, so he felt his way along her torso to her wound. He felt the slickness of blood on the skin in the hollow of her hip, then a splintery stub of wood. An arrow, broken off. When Jun's fingers reached it, the woman jerked upward. She grabbed

Jun's hand with uncanny strength.

"Please," she whispered. "The scroll. Please. Take it."

She pressed a roll of parchment into his fingers. It was wet with blood. "Please. They must know—"

Noct dumped a jumble of wood from her talons next to Jun, and ignited it with a whoosh of flames from her throat. In the sudden light, Jun saw the woman's face. She was older than he, in a uniform of padded white silk that was stained dark with her own blood. She was beautiful, and Jun fell a little in love with her in that moment. But her face was drained of color, and death was in her eyes.

"Know what?" he demanded. "Hold on, hold on! Know what?"

He dug into a pouch he carried at his waist, a small cloth bag full of sachets of herbs. His grandfather had taught him the craft of medicinal herbs, and isolated as Jun was, he had gathered what herbs he recognized from the forest, in case he fell ill. The bag was soaked from his foray into the lake, but he did not think that should matter. He dipped his finger into a powder of nightbane, an herb for shock and to ease pain, sodden to a paste with lake water. He stuck the paste into her cheek. "Hold on," he said again. "I can get the arrow out."

In truth he had no idea how to do this, or even if it was a good idea, but he was ready to try anything to save her. Noct watched beside the fire, quiet and intent. Jun gave the woman more nightbane. How much was enough to dull her pain? His grandfather had used a whole bowl of paste once for a child who fell into a fire. Jun nudged at the broken shaft again, and she didn't flinch this time.

But she looked into his eyes, and he saw death still lurking there. "It's too late," she said. "Please give them the scroll. They must know…"

Death came forward and took over her eyes, until they were

still as glass fishing floats. Jun looked away, unable to stare death in the eye with the grave of his family at his back. One moment her fingers were still gripping his, pressing the scroll into his palm, and the next moment her hand was a limp object resting on his skin.

Noct shrieked at the moon, a wild keening scream of mourning.

*

The next day Ruan came and found Jun curled against Noct's belly on the rocky lakeshore, beside a dwindling fire and a dead woman. With Ruan's help, Jun rose, changed into warm, dry clothes, made a skiff and poled out to bring in the moon-boat. They sewed a shroud from the voluminous silk, weighted it with rocks, and dropped the woman in the lake, so she could rest with Jun's family. They sang songs to the dead together, lit incense, and left rice, since Jun had not had time to bake mooncakes.

Jun did not know if burying the woman in the lake was the right thing to do. His glimpse of her in life had made him think of eagles and rocky high places, and he thought she might want to rest somewhere airy and light, not at the bottom of a deep dark lake. But Ruan said she would have the company of his family's ghosts, and they could share news.

Later, in his hollow in the bamboo stalk, Jun knelt by the fire and unrolled the scroll, hoping to find some answer there, but the lettering was completely strange to him. He showed Ruan the scroll, but he could make no sense of the lettering, either. He offered to take it to a scholar in El Tal, but Jun was reluctant to part with it.

"She said, 'they must know.' Who must know, and what?" he wondered to Ruan. "She was bringing a message somewhere, but where, and what is the message?"

Ruan stayed a few days, until Jun had somewhat recovered from his shock, and before he left, he copied a few of the characters onto his billfold using a tiny charcoal stick from Jun's kiln, using a piece of glass to make out the miniscule lettering on the tiny scroll.

When Ruan left, Noct returned. Ruan always made the dragon nervous, which Jun assumed was due to his being much bigger than her. Noct slithered into the pottery cave in the early evening, when Jun was throwing pots. Her pitch-black scales shimmered in the light of the grease lamp. She wriggled her long, sinuous body between pots and around the lamps and vases littering the floor of the cave. Here and there she flicked or bumped something slightly, making the whole place rattle, but she never caused anything to break. She settled into the warmest place, in front of the kiln, and seemed like she would sleep, but after a few moments a peaceful breath she rose and paced around the cave again. Jun cringed as her tail flicked a vase and made it shudder back and forth until it settled again. She nosed up against a pot toward the back of the cave. Jun had leaned the scroll in it after Ruan left. She nipped her teeth delicately onto the top of the scroll and plucked it from the pot, dropped it on the smooth stone floor of the cave, and began pawing at it.

"Hey!" Jun stood, releasing the pedal and sending wet clay flying. "Stop that!"

Noct turned and Jun met her eyes and found wildness there. She was not like a pet, to be ordered to obey, and in that moment both she and Jun knew it. It always happened when they looked into each other's eyes, that they understood one another. But today, she seemed to be ignoring Jun.

Jun changed his tone quickly. "Please." He held out a placating hand. "That's important. Please don't destroy it."

Noct shook her head back and forth and the action rippled along her whole body and through the cave. She returned her attention to the parchment and began pawing it again. Jun watched, helpless to stop her.

She inserted a talon along the top fold of the scroll and drew it down, flattening out the parchment. She sniffed at the lettering, and Jun feared she would devour it with a gulp, or turn it to ashes with a breath of fire. But instead, she flicked her long, forked tongue gently along the characters. When she had touched each letter, she raised her head to the ceiling of the cave and shrieked so loud a shelf of cups came crashing down. The sound of the crash startled her and she wriggled herself backward out of the cave, knocking over everything on the floor on her way out. She shrieked despair and anger into the twilight of a falling night, until distance faded her cries and erased them altogether.

Jun stood in the ruins of his potting cave. The only thing Noct hadn't destroyed was the scroll. He knelt on the ground and stretched it flat again and wished he could make sense of the characters. What about it had upset her so? Had she found some meaning in the ink? Or was she merely smelling the woman's scent on it, and grieving her?

*

Dawn was approaching when Jun tossed the last shard onto the midden where he threw all his failures. He was tired, but he made the journey to the lake's edge to light incense and set mooncakes on the rocks, along with some red autumn berries he had found near his pottery cave. He was about to head back to his hollow for a nap when he heard the beat of Noct's wings.

Noct shrieked with excitement and slammed her wings against the forest floor, sending up a flurry of debris. She dropped something heavy at Jun's feet and shrieked again. When he did not pick it up, she inclined her head toward it several times, shrieking all the while.

Jun had not seen Noct so animated since the last time the stoat had threatened her nest. Hoping to ease her distress, he bent and picked up the item she had dropped, a small, flat oval stone, carved with a single rune. The stone was dark with blood.

This character he understood. Along with the rituals for the dead and herb craft, his grandfather had also taught him several of the runes. When Jun was a child, he had carried a similar stone with the same rune, painted instead of carved. The character translated to "Danger is Imminent," but the working of the rune was to protect its carrier.

Jun looked up a Noct in shock. "What is this?"

Noct wriggled her whole body, shimmying her scales and shaking out her spines. Jun first registered her excitement as relief that he had picked up the stone, but when she started to beat her wings, he realized she was trying to communicate something new.

"Where did this come from?" Jun wondered aloud.

She shrieked again and crawled near Jun on her forelegs, laid her wings down flat away from her back and shimmied again.

"What does it mean?"

Noct stopped her wild shimmying and captured Jun's gaze in hers. When their eyes locked, Jun felt understanding roll over him in waves. "You want me to come to where you found this stone."

She held his gaze, piercing him deeply with her golden orbs. Jun stood frozen, captivated by her stare but terrified of what it meant. She must have found the stone somewhere beyond the valley. Jun had never left the valley, not since the rising lake crushed his dream to visit the wider world. He had to stay, to tend the souls of his family. And now he had one more soul to care for.

"Who will leave the offerings?" he pleaded with Noct. "If I leave, who will burn the incense and sing the songs to ease their souls?"

Noct held his gaze relentlessly. Her only motion was a faint impatient twitching of her tail. Jun stroked the rune stone in his hand and wondered why Noct was so insistent that they leave the valley. Was she warning him of danger coming to the valley? Or bringing him to someone in danger?

Jun did not feel capable of helping anyone, if that was the case. He had failed to save his family. He had failed to save the woman in the moon-boat. He was useless at anything but throwing pots, and even that he failed at again and again before his pots began to take adequate shape.

Trying to break Noct's gaze, Jun's eyes fell on the tiny notch in her wing, where the stoat had bitten her in her sleep once before Jun chased it off. He thought of all the days she had spent peacefully sleeping, while Jun watched over her and her nest. Even though they did not share a common language, she had trusted him enough to sleep in his presence.

With growing anxiety, Jun realized he was being called to trust her now. He did not need to know where she was taking him. He would go, because he owed her the same trust she had shown him.

As soon as he made the decision, Noct broke her gaze and shrieked excitedly. He climbed onto her back as he had done a hundred times since spring. This time, his legs shook so hard he could hardly get purchase on her slippery scales.

Noct flew high over the valley, up over the ridge that Jun had once stood upon and watched his home be swallowed by a lake. They were so high that he could see El Tal shining in the distance. Jun felt a stab of regret, that he had never followed his heart and traveled there. But before he could dwell on that, El Tal sank out of sight as Noct flew over a series of grassy steppes. When the smokey spire from a tiny chimney in a village on a high plateau spiraled up to Noct's talons, Jun felt a jolt of nostalgia and sorrow, remembering similar spires of smoke rising from the valley floor.

Noct set Jun down in a clearing of worn-down grass in the middle of a scattering of hide-covered huts with grass roofs.

Smoke came only from one chimney, and the tiny village was deathly silent. Jun wondered why Noct had brought him to an abandoned place. But she wriggled her way into the hut with the active chimney, and Jun followed.

A girl huddled, scared, in a corner of the hut. A fire blazed in a pit at the center of the room, lighting the girl's young face. She still wore baby fat on her cheeks, and a white silk smock embroidered with colorful beads in the pattern of eagle feathers. Her hair was black and sleek.

Jun stared at her, uncertain. Noct squeezed in the small space, looked up him, opened her snout to shriek, but stopped herself. Instead of a sound, her red forked tongue flickered out of her mouth and gently lapped at the girl's forehead. The girl shrank down further, trembling with fear.

Jun took a step forward and realized the red gleam on the girl's skin and smock wasn't firelight, it was blood. He pulled the runestone out of the pouch at his waist and held it out to her. The girl's eyes lit with recognition, and she took a tentative step forward. Jun met her by the fire pit and handed her the stone. She clutched it hard to her little chest.

"Come," Jun said patiently. "Let's get you and your stone cleaned up."

After some coaxing, the girl followed Jun timidly out of the hut. When she spoke, it was in a language he did not recognize, so he communicated as best as he could with gestures. Noct extinguished the fire and followed them at a distance to a livestock pen behind the huts, where Jun found a watering trough full of clean enough water. He wetted his cotton jerkin and washed the blood off the girl's face. She didn't seem to be injured, which almost concerned Jun more. Whose blood did she wear? What carnage had she witnessed?

Noct revealed the answer presently. While Jun cleaned up the girl, she crept between the huts, and soon cried out for Jun with a series of bellowing shrieks. Jun left the girl by the trough and followed the sounds to a pit at the other side of the village. He took one glance inside the pit and turned away and retched.

The plateau was chilly, and steam still rose from the pit. Whatever violence had occurred was very recent. Jun felt a sense of being watched, and shivered. He had to get away from here. He had to get the girl away. He knew he should look for some kind of clues to what had happened, but he couldn't remain in this dead village any longer. He called for Noct to follow him, ran back to the trough, and scooped up the girl before she could protest.

*

They were almost to the ridge when the girl started to cry, wet tears pressing against the thin fabric of Jun's tunic. She struggled and shouted in her strange language, but he held her tight. Noct sailed down into the valley, circled Jun's bamboo stalk and landed on the platform he had rigged for her.

Inside the small hollow in the stalk, Jun lit a fire in his charcoal brazier and set a thimble-pot up on the tripod, filled with a savory broth to warm. He bundled the girl in a nuthatch-down blanket and lay her on his sleeping mat by the fire. She had ceased struggling and crying, but she did not sleep, only lay staring at the smooth pith coating of the inside of the bamboo stalk. Jun puttered around, adding this and that to the broth, but when he ran out of things to do, he took both the scroll and the rune stone from his knapsack and examined them by lamplight.

He still could not decipher the scroll, but the characters on the stone took on new significance, after what he had witnessed today.

"Danger is Imminent."

Jun thought of the pit and the stench of blood. He looked again at the girl, staring off at nothing. He thought of the rising, raging waters of the lake rushing over the river bottoms where his family had lived. At least he had not seen their bodies. Only a hat, a doll, a staff.

Jun rose and went to Noct. She was resting, but her golden eyes were open. "Watch over her?" he asked. She might not understand his words, but as usual she read his intent in his eyes, and ducked her head inside the door to keep an eye on the girl.

Jun went to his pottery cave and lit the kiln, then the lamps. Midday was near, and Jun was tired, having not slept the night before, but he heated himself a pot of tea and began to throw pots.

As he worked, his mind loosened and spun like the clay. He gathered the events in his mind and nudged them gently this way and that until they began to take shape. A woman in foreign clothes, from somewhere far away where they rode moon-boats had been mortally wounded. She bore a scroll with strange writings. Noct had sniffed at this scroll and flown off, then returned with a bloody rune stone carrying a warning, Danger is Imminent. When Jun went with Noct to the source of the stone, they found a massacred village and a lone survivor.

What if the woman in the moon-boat had attacked the village? Not alone, of course, but with a whole fleet of her people? What if she was part of a group of marauders, wounded in the act of attacking?

But if that was the case, where was the rest of the fleet? Would someone come looking for her? And what of the scroll, and the woman's warning? "They must know," she had said. That seemed a warning now, though Jun had not fathomed it at the time.

"They must know." "Danger is Imminent." Something had attacked the moon-boat woman's Folk, perhaps, and she had fled with a warning. Perhaps meant for the girl? If so, it was too late for the steppe village. The scene in the pit flashed in Jun's mind again. A jumble of bloody woolen clothes. He would have to alter something of his to fit the girl. Her silk smock was covered in blood.

At least the girl was safe. But there was the scroll, and the moon-boat woman's words, "They must know." Someone, somewhere, had not received the message. Someone out there might still be in grave danger.

Jun cut the vase off the wheel and carried it to the kiln. He inhaled the earthy aroma of the fresh clay before setting it in the firing chamber. Then he cleaned up his wheel and returned to his home in the bamboo stalk.

*

Noct had somehow wriggled all the way inside his hollow and was curled protectively around the girl—the whole bed, in fact. The girl, remarkably, was asleep. Noct slitted one golden eye open and fixed Jun with a look that said he'd regret waking her. Jun ladled up a cup of broth and went out to watch the glow of the sun fade into evening. He knew he must go down to the shore and sing the songs, but tonight he had little heart for it. Who would sing the songs to the Steppe Folk's ghosts?

From the platform outside his hollow, he could see the sparkle of the lake fade between the leaves. The valley felt safe. Even if whatever had destroyed the girl's steppe village came to the valley, Jun had infinite hiding places among the bamboo roots. He could cast the scroll in the kiln, toss the rune stone in the lake, and forget the whole matter. He could raise the girl, or perhaps send her with Ruan to the tiny folk in El Tal. Yes, that would be better. She should be raised among a whole community of people, not just by one mountain hermit.

Jun looked out over the lake. The darkening surface was stippled by the wind, a sign of restless ghosts. Somewhere down there, a new ghost walked on the lake bottom among the wreckage of bamboo huts and sacks of rice preserved forever by the cold water. Jun imagined her looking skyward through the water, yearning for the eyries of her people.

"They must know."

The memory of the woman's final words stopped Jun cold in his trail of thought. What if someone had flown in a moon-boat to warn Jun's family, before the lake swallowed the valley? It was too late for Jun's family, too late for the Steppe Folk, but what if the woman's family was out there, on a mountain top somewhere, still alive? What if the scroll was intended to warn them?

Jun still had the scroll. He might yet be able to save someone.

\*

The next day in midmorning, something large came stomping and shaking through the forest. Jun was sitting on the platform outside his house, poring over the scroll again, trying to see if any of the characters could lend themselves to some hint of a location for the moon-boat woman's origin. Noct had coaxed the girl out of the bed and was playing a gentle game of chase-me in the leaf litter below. When they heard the noise, Jun went on alert and all of Noct's spines stood straight up, but it was only Ruan.

Noct put the girl behind her and eyed Ruan suspiciously while Jun greeted the giant dwarf. Ruan's face was level with the platform. He boomed a loud greeting, and Jun asked him hastily what luck he had with the characters he'd noted from the scroll.

"In reading them, no," Ruan said, and Jun's heart sank, "But I met another peddler, from the east, beyond Roselake, coming from mountains east even of Rachdale. He said he has seen these characters among a group of tiny folk he trades with in those mountains. They ride golden eagles and steal treasures far and wide, which they trade to him for useful things. And he has seen them take to air in moon-boats, too."

"That must be her people!" Jun said. "I have to take the scroll to them."

But it was so far. All the way across Roselake and beyond Rachdale. Jun shivered inside at the thought of being so far from the grave of his family.

Jun told Ruan the story of the ruined steppe village and the pit. He spoke quietly, not wanting to awaken the girl's trauma again. "Can you take this girl to El Tal and find her safe keeping among the tiny folk there? She needs care, but I won't be able to watch her if I am to travel all the way beyond Rachdale."

Ruan agreed, and then he and Jun traded, pottery for provisions. When their business was concluded, it took an effort for Jun to convince Noct that it was safe for the girl to go with Ruan. In the end Ruan won the girl's trust with a giant round of hard candy and by making a show with a pair of puppets, one a goose and the other a horse, that made the girl crack a smile. When the girl warmed to Ruan, Noct relaxed.

Ruan stayed the night, sleeping on the forest floor on his bedroll, and early the next morning, he left with the tiny girl perched upon his thick shoulder, clinging to the red strands of his massive beard. Jun ached to see her go, and hoped the runestone would be enough to keep her safe in El Tal.

Then he checked his potting cave to make sure the kiln was fully extinguished, shouldered his own pack which held provisions, a bed roll and the scroll, and mounted up on Noct.

The lake was a golden eye in the glow of the rising sun as they crested the ridges flanking the valley. Its surface was restless, and Jun's heart sank as he thought of what would happen to his family's ghosts in his absence. But when they circled over the steppes, Jun knew he could not turn back, not if there was the smallest chance he could save lives.

They flew into the sun, its rays turning Noct's black scales gold. They passed over El Tal, and Jun thought again of how dreadfully he had wished to go there as a youth. Now he could go there, but he had no desire for it.

For a time, they followed the river that had swallowed his valley. Near midday, they reached its terminus in Roselake. Noct landed to rest on the gravelly lakeshore. They ate some dried fish and rice bread from Jun's provisions.

Crossing Roselake took the rest of the day and much of the night. It was a tired, bedraggled Noct and Jun who finally touched ground on the other side, in a wilderness of grasslands.

The grasslands seemed to go on forever. Jun lost count of the days Noct flew over featureless, waving blades of green. They flew and slept intermittently, not with the rise and fall of the sun but simply when exhaustion brought them to the ground. Jun began to wonder if they would arrive at the moon-boat woman's home in time to do her message any good.

*

Several days into the grasslands, when they were camped for a few hours at a small, placid lake, a dark spot appeared in the clear blue sky. Jun and Noct watched something winged sail down the edge of a thermal. The dot's reflection grew in the lake until it mirrored the belly of a small dragon with dark blue scales. When the dragon landed, ripping turf with its sharp talons, Jun saw that it was just a little larger than Noct. A tiny rider hopped off its back and confronted Jun with the tip of a metal spear.

"Who are you, and how came you by this dragon?" The tiny man's accent was strange, but Jun recognized his words, which were in the common tongue of Mirstone.

"I am Jun, of the Bamboo Valley tiny folk," he said, putting a hand on Noct's neck to try to soothe her low growl. He liked the spear as little as she did, but he was determined to be polite in the face of rudeness. "As for Noct, she came by me. Nesting in my valley, she asked my help to protect her dragonlings, and we have been fast friends ever since."

"Nonetheless, you are in violation of the Rachdale Hoard Folk laws of Dragon Binding. None but the Hoard Folk are allowed to bind and ride the Tiny Dragons. You must come with me, to be given a fair trial in the Heart of the Hoard. And this dragon must be repatriated, and bound to a Hoard man worthy of her."

"She is her own creature, and will go where she likes," Jun said, shifting his stance and tightening his grip on his staff.

The dark blue dragon raised his head, scented the air, and shrieked. Noct shrieked in harmony with him, and lifted herself with the beat of her wings. The blue dragon followed swiftly. They flew loop-de-loops through the clear sky while Jun and the Hoard man watched. Then the blue caught Noct with his jaws on her neck, and the dragon's bodies twined furiously around one another until Jun could not tell where onc began and one ended.

"He will kill her," Jun cried, terrified for his friend. "Please, call your dragon back! We will go peaceably!"

But the Hoard man laughed. "Don't you know a mating flight when you see one? When did you say she had her last nesting? Long enough ago that she is in season again. Come, let us be comfortable. It will be hours before they remember us and return. Stoke your fire, put up your staff. I have a flask of ale and a fresh-killed prairie wren to make a stew with whatever traveling tack you have. If you still want to resist arrest, you can do it when they return. Come. My name is Toman."

Jun disliked the idea of feasting with this rude person, but he saw little choice in the matter, and besides, he sensed an opportunity to learn something. He almost brought the scroll out, but some instinct stayed his hand. Instead, as he helped Toman pluck the wren, he asked about the Hoard Folk.

He learned that they lived deep within the Rachdale mountains.
They denned with Tiny Dragons, who stole tiny treasures from the
dwarf mines and forges and hoarded them in their caves.

"Does anyone try to steal your treasures in return?" Jun
wondered. A thought was growing in his mind, but it was still
hazy.

"Oh, aye, all the time!" Toman exclaimed, taking another gulp
of ale from his clay flask. "We most recently were raided by the
Eagle Eyrie tiny folk. They have troubled us for many years with
their theft. Recently, our new king declared it time to put an end to
them for good. And we are almost successful. A few of their royal
family have fled—they think they can hide from us, but there is
nowhere in Mirstone we Hoard Folk cannot fly on our dragons!"

Toman drank more ale. He had not offered Jun any, nor had he
helped with cleaning the bird or tending the fire. Jun went about
those tasks methodically. He was glad he had not shown this man
the scroll. He searched for the right question to keep him talking.

"Are the eagles very big?" he asked. "Big enough to match a
dragon in a fight?"

"Aye, and bigger. Though our dragons are fierce, sheer size is
on the eagles' side. But we are the more clever. There is only one
spring that the eagles drink from, and we sent a spy among them
and poisoned the spring, killing every single eagle in the eyrie.
Now the Eyrie Folk are trapped. They sent a few brats off in moon-
boats, but they have run out of silk even for that. Soon they will
starve, and that will be an end of it."

"But some of them escaped. Do you fear a counter-attack?"

"Aye, and that's why I'm out here, searching hill and dale for
them. Not that they can amount to much—they are children
mostly, but some are of royal blood, and royalty can be a rallying
point. Most likely they will worm their way into some other tiny
folks' sympathies, and bring them to war with us. You see why I

had to be cautious of you, especially with your stolen dragon."

"I see," Jun said slowly. He finished cutting up the bird, and began adding chunks of rice bread to the pot balanced on the fire. Toman continued talking, going on to describe the treasures of the Hoard in great detail. Jun tuned him out, grateful for a task to keep his hands busy. Outwardly he affected calm, but inside his heart and mind were racing as he put together the pieces of Toman's story with what he had witnessed.

The Eyrie Folk stole treasures to trade with the peddler Ruan had met. They had stolen from the Hoard Folk, and awoken a vicious vengeance in them, to the tune of total destruction. Somewhere on mountaintop eyries, an entire community of tiny folk were starving to death in the absence of their eagles. A few had escaped on moon-boats, carrying children to safety in hopes of saving some remnant of their tribe. One of those must have been the woman who died in Jun's valley. She did not have a child with her, so perhaps she had already hidden her charge.

What, then, was the scroll? A warning for someone. Not the Folk in the eyries; they already knew the danger they were in. One of the children and their keepers, perhaps? Toman said they would find them. What if they had, and the scroll was a warning that the cover was blown? The woman had an arrow through her, one that, in Jun's memory, looked a lot like the arrow he had just pulled out of the wren.

The child. The final piece clicked in Jun's mind. The girl had been wearing a silk smock beaded with a pattern of eagle feathers. Even stained as it was, Jun had seen that it was a fine garment compared to the rough wool clothes worn by the Steppe Folk. She must have been hidden among the Steppe Folk. The scroll was a warning that the Hoard Folk were coming, but it was never delivered, and the Steppe Folk had paid the price. But the runestone had kept the little girl safe. Did the Hoard Folk know she had escaped? Did they search for her in El Tal even now?

He would not find out if Toman took him to some farce of a trial, or if Noct was taken and imprisoned by the Hoard Folk. He looked up from stirring the stew and saw that the man was slouched back against his bedroll, sleeping lightly. Jun took a pouch of medicines from his waist. Earthensalve would induce a long, deep sleep in a patient. It was used when some pain was too great for the body to rest and recover.

Jun upended the whole pouch in the stew, then filled a bowl, dumped it in the lake, and set the dirty bowl and spoon beside the fire.

The stew bubbled away and Toman continued to sleep off his ale. Occasionally Jun heard Noct shriek in the distance. The shadows of grass blades lengthened as the afternoon ticked past. Eventually, Toman woke, rubbed his eyes with his fists and took a swig of his ale, which had gone flat. He rose wordlessly and relieved himself beyond a clump of grass.

When he returned to the fire, Jun said, "Have a bowl of stew. I've eaten my fill."

He rubbed his belly and handed Toman a clean bowl. Toman took it groggily and Jun watched as the Hoard man slurped bowl after bowl of the stew. He prayed the earthensalve would be strong enough. He thought he could best Toman with his staff, but he had no wish to fight, especially if Toman's dragon returned.

Toman muttered something about his mother's cooking as he ate. Halfway through his fourth bowl, he slumped over, dumping the stew on his lap. Jun cleaned him up and lay him down on his bedroll. He washed the dishes in the lake, dumping the rest of the stew into the water. Then he packed up and waited for Noct.

\*

Sunset was painting the little lake blood-red when she arrived, trailed closely by the blue dragon. Both of their scales were crimson with the fading light.

Noct looked drowsy and languid, but Jun managed to catch her eye. As she had gazed her desperation for him to come to the steppe village before, now he pierced her with his determination to be away from here. She glanced at the sleeping Toman, took in Jun's pack ready to go, and understood that he was fleeing.

The blue dragon landed near his rider and sniffed Toman with concern, but found nothing amiss but a deep sleep. Noct shrieked at him, and they shrieked and gurgled and rumbled at each other for a time. Then Noct came to Jun and crouched low for him to mount. She looked back at the blue dragon before taking to the skies again. Once aloft, she circled the lake, waiting for Jun's direction.

Jun had spent the long, quiet afternoon after Toman fell into his deep sleep thinking on where to go. Since it was too late to warn the Steppe Folk, as the scroll had likely been intended to do, he decided they might as well press on and try to reach the Eyrie Folk. He could bring them news of their dead kinswoman, and also news that the child they had stashed on the steppes had survived and was on her way to El Tal. And perhaps, with Noct's help, he could find a way to help them.

A few hours into the night, Noct's strength began to fail, and Jun recalled that while he had been somewhat at rest, she had been flying all afternoon. He asked her to land in the Rachdale foothills, and they slept concealed in a stand of low bushes for the night.

Jun woke in the dusky hour before sunrise to find Noct crouched over him, watching him intently. He jerked upright and gazed into her eyes, their golden sparkle dim in the greasy grey light of morning. And as always, when he gazed into her eyes he knew her mind, even though she could not speak his language.

He saw in her eyes the reflection of the lake-blue dragon and a yearning to return to him. "Come with me to Hoard Folk," her eyes said. "There is a life for us there. A warm nest for the eggs I must soon lay."

Jun shook his head emphatically, trying to impress on her with his eyes all that he had deduced from his conversation with Toman. "They are a bad people," he said aloud. "Violence, misery. Remember the Steppe Folk. We cannot go there. We must press on to the Eagle Eyries."

For a long time, they stared at each other, blue dragon in her eyes, golden eagles in his, until the first rays of the sun turned everything gold, and Noct looked aside, and Jun knew he had won.

*

So it was that they approached the Eagle Eyries at sunrise, sun shining through twists, spires and arches of sandstone carved by the wind. Jun thought he had never seen anything so beautiful as those lace cliffs.

But when Noct passed under an arch, an arrow whizzed by her wing, nearly slicing through it. She went into a spinning dive to get out of range, and Jun held on for dear life. They recovered and circled the cliffs from a distance. Jun stripped off his pale cotton undershirt and waved it over his head, whistling to Noct to try the approach again.

This time, they were allowed to land on a small platform, but faced a pincushion of knocked arrows when they did. Jun scrambled off Noct's back, holding his shirt above his head.

"Don't shoot!" he cried. "We're friendly!"

After a long moment, one of the Eyrie Folk stepped forward, releasing the tension on his bow. Jun saw that they were dressed like the woman in the moon-boat, in snow-white silk uniforms. He held out the scroll, and the man took it and began to read.

After a moment, he made a gesture and all the bows went

down. A woman stepped up to his side. She looked just like the woman in the moon-boat. She saw the scroll covered in blood, and the look in Jun's eyes, and began to weep.

"I'm sorry," Jun said. "I couldn't save her. But maybe I can help you?"

"You do us no help to bring one of those Hoard Dragons into our midst, to terrify my people anew," the man said sternly in the common tongue, but the woman wiped at her tears and said something scolding in a language Jun could not understand.

"We didn't mean to scare you," Jun insisted. "Noct is a friend. She can bring you food. Or deliver messages to your allies. Or something."

"I thank you for bringing news of my sister," the woman said. "But why would a Hoard Dragon help us? If you met my sister, surely you know we are war with them."

"I know," Jun said grimly. He thought of the Steppe Folk. "Noct is not a Hoard Dragon. She is a friend. Please, let us help you. Noct, you will bring them food, will you not?"

He turned to face her, but what he found in her eyes was alien and strange. The reflection of the blue dragon still floated against her golden orbs. *I have delivered you to your folk,* her eyes seemed to say. *Now it is time I go to mine.*

"No," Jun whispered hollowly.

Noct shrieked once, then again, and again, and to Jun's horror, she rose into the sky and flew away, leaving him stranded along with the Eyrie Folk. He called after her, but his words were lost in the whistling wind that scoured the twists and spires of the eyrie.

*

At first Jun held out hope that Noct would return swiftly, perhaps with food. That hope slowly dwindled as the day wore on.

Shortly after Noct flew off, Sirena, the sister of the woman who had died in Jun's valley, took him for a walk around through the nests. The nests were a series of south-facing hollows filled with piles of sticks. Several of them had unhatched eggs, which Eyrie Folk tended day and night in hopes that they might hatch and begin a new generation of eagles.

Jun told Sirena how her sister had landed in the lake and tried to pass on her warning. He told her of the Steppe Folk and the sole survivor, a girl he thought must be Eagle Eyrie royalty. Sirena listened attentively, then apologized that she could not offer him a meal. They had finished the last of their food two days before. Already, two youths had tried to make the perilous journey by foot to the ground, and died in the trying. The Eyrie Folk had always been able to rely on their eagles for transport, and had chosen the eyrie as their home in part because it was completely inaccessible by ground. Now it was only a waiting game until the end. Several of her fellow soldiers had suggested shooting Noct and eating her, and they might have if Sirena had not stopped them.

The day ticked past, and still Noct did not return. The stars came out over the twisted rock landscape, piercing in their brilliance. The setting of the sun plunged the plateau into bone-chilling cold. Sirena showed Jun to a sheltered hollow, a wind-scoured hole in the rock, and gave him warm garments made of eagle down. He lay awake in this little hollow long into the night, listening to the wind and thinking himself foolish to come here, foolish not to realize that Noct might turn tail after spending time with her kind. Of course she would choose them over him, he thought, imagining that she had flown off to join the Hoard Folk.

He thought back to how they had met. Noct had been alone in the bamboo forest, away from her kind. After her dragonlings hatched and left, she had stayed with him. Jun had never considered that she had a family that might miss her, or she them. He had thought of her as himself, alone in the world. Now, he wondered why he had never considered that she might be lonely with him, missing the company of other dragons.

Even though she had left him in a dire place, Jun felt regret that he had not thought more of Noct, or tried to inquire as to her wants. He had thought her a partner in his own loss and grief.

When the sun rose, the rocky cliffs swiftly warmed, but the new day revealed the depth of Jun's foolishness, as the light of dawn revealed the stark outlines of ribs and hips jutting out of the Eyrie Folk's starving bodies. The grim reality set in; intentional or not, Noct had left Jun here to die.

He could not comprehend it. Always before, they had understood one another. Sure, she must miss her kind, but could she not have helped him rescue the Eyrie Folk before she returned to them? No, Jun began to reason, his thoughts growing tinged with anger; Noct had not merely returned to her Folk because she missed them; she had returned because she was siding with the Hoard Folk. She had abandoned him here on purpose.

Jun's thoughts ran on like this, a burbling brook at first, then picking up speed and tumbling in a rushing, furious stream. The hungrier he became, the angrier he became. Ever since his family had died, he had been able to throw pots as a way to soothe himself. Now, he had no such outlet. He began to imagine greater and greater betrayals. Perhaps Noct had been a spy for the Hoard Folk all along, a plant meant to sabotage efforts by the Eyrie Folk to protect their young royals. Yes, that must be it, she had always meant to betray him. In some distant part of himself, Jun knew he was not making sense, but he could not stop the cascading thoughts that flooded his mind with hate.

*

Over the next few days, as hunger took its toll on the Eyrie Folk, Jun began to imagine wilder and wilder conspiracies, all revolving around Noct. On the last day, he was thinking so hard about a dragon army led by Noct coming to finish them all off, that when the dragons appeared in the sky, Jun thought he was hallucinating. But the Eyrie Folk saw them too, and lined up on the landing plateau, knocking and aiming their arrows.

The dragons drew closer. Jun saw Noct at their head. She had led the Hoard dragons to them! He could hardly believe her betrayal. His thoughts were flooded with fury. He wished for his own arrow.

Noct was almost abreast of the cliff. Sirena explained that the Eyrie Folk were letting the dragons come within range, to limit the loss of arrows and more accurately strike their targets. Jun could see Noct's eyes, huge and golden, bearing down on him like twin suns in a black sky. She was in range; at any moment, an arrow would strike her and pierce her ebony hide, but still, she did not breath fire and incinerate them all.

Jun looked up into her eyes and saw her clearly, as he had not seen her in a long time. He saw the blue dragon in her eyes, but also the valley, the lake, the fire in his kiln, and himself. He saw himself kneeling to wrap a poultice around the injury the stoat had done her.

And he understood, in that moment, as they had always understood each other before. She was not here to kill him or any of the Eyrie Folk. He did not understand exactly what was happening, but he knew he must trust her, as she was trusting him by coming in range of the arrows.

"Hold fire!" he cried to the Eyrie Folk. "They come to save us! Hold fire!"

Sirena was about to loose her arrow. Jun could feel the tension in her arm. "Hold fire!" he cried again, and knocked her aside. Her arrow fired, but it shot just over Noct's brow. Noct shrieked and dove.

Jun imagined her bathing the plateau in flames. But the flames didn't come, and when he righted himself next to a furious Sirena, he looked up to see that Noct had landed. She was crouching before him on the plateau, her snout stretched forward. In her teeth she bore a wriggling silver fish, a minnow that would have been tiny to the big folk. To Jun, it looked like a feast.

The other dragons circled behind Noct, just out of range of the bows. Jun yelled to Sirena. "She brings food! They are here to help us, not to harm!"

But Sirena had already risen, and was yelling commands at her fellows. Soon, bows were lowered all across the plateau, and the folk were moving aside to make space for the dragons to land. Several dragons brought wood to fuel the Eyrie's ovens, and soon a feast was in the making.

In the middle of this commotion, Jun approached Noct and stroked her scales. "I'm sorry I doubted our friendship," he said. His eyes swam in salty tears. "You risked your life to save us. But how did you do it? How did you get the Hoard dragons to come here peacefully?"

She shrieked, and the dark blue dragon sidled up beside her and eyed Jun suspiciously. For the first time, Jun noticed that he was covered in crisscrossing scars of a paler blue than his scales. The dragon pushed his snout into Jun's hand. Jun stroked him, feeling the ridges of the scars.

Their eyes met, and Jun understood the blue dragon just as he had always understood Noct. He saw the dragon's youth, a time when he was as wild and free as Noct. Then ropes and chains and beatings. He saw the lifetime of pain this dragon had withstood at the hands of the Hoard Folk. He saw how easy it had been for Noct to convince the Hoard dragons to rebel against their cruel masters and fly to the assistance of the Eyrie Folk.

"Sirena," he called. "Please come here. I wish you to meet

someone."

He knew from their conversations over the last few days how the Eyrie Folk had treated the eagles, before they were all poisoned. It was a bond just as deep as he shared with Noct. Perhaps the dragons, having known a life of trauma, and the Eyrie Folk, grieving the loss of their feathered kin, could offer each other solace and friendship, as he and Noct had done for each other.

Sirena stepped up beside him and looked into the blue dragon's silvery eyes. They shared a long gaze. Jun did not see what passed in that gaze, but he knew it was something like the understanding that usually passed between him and Noct. After a long moment, Sirena stepped forward and stretched her arms up, and the blue dragon curved his head down and laid it on her breast.

"His name is Lac," she said, wonderingly.

\*

They feasted that day, and the next day Sirena and Jun rode Noct and Lac west, to find the child Jun had sent to safety in El Tal. Another contingent of Eyrie Folk headed north on dragons to the seat of power of the big folk of Rachdale, to report the murder done to the eagles by the Hoard Folk and petition for justice.

Before they landed in El Tal, Jun asked Sirena and the dragons to take a detour and visit the valley. It had been days since anyone had made the offerings to the ghosts of his family, and he expected to see the surface of the lake enraged. But when they crested the ridge, the lake was placid, sparkling and golden in the afternoon sun.

They aired out the hollow and started a stew bubbling on Jun's hearth, then went to the lakeshore. Jun showed Sirena the rituals for the ghosts buried in the lake, and together they sang for his family and her sister. Jun told Sirena of his fears, that if he left the valley for too long, the ghosts would become restless and unhappy under the water.

"That's impossible," Sirena laughed. "Ghosts don't stay where they die, silly. Why, we leave our dead out for the vultures to feast upon, but we don't think their ghosts are flying around with the vultures."

"Where are they, then?" Jun asked, shocked at such a grisly custom.

"We carry them with us, here," she said, and put a hand over her heart. "Always, and everywhere."

The next day, Jun rose before anyone else. He packed up everything he wished to take. It wasn't much; clothes, a few pottery tools, a favorite set of bowls. Then he went down to the lake shore. He set his sister's doll, his grandfather's staff, and his father's hat into the shallows and watched the lake carry them out, over deeper and deeper waters. He put a hand over his heart. "Always, and everywhere," he said.

Then he turned his back to the lake, ready at last to go out into the world, knowing he would carry the ghosts of his family in his heart.

## THE END

# The Lost Dragons of Mirstone
Craig A. Price Jr.

Every last dragonrider in Arathor was dead, except for her.
Lyra Nightwing stood on the mountaintops, staring north to her
home now in ruins. It was a quiet island, surrounded by nothing
but forests; recluse, and not desiring to be a part of any worldly
conflict. However, that was not how the humans had seen it.

*Humans.*

Lyra spat on the ground. It was improper for an elf, but she
cared little. The humans had killed her entire family and their
dragons.

She was the last.

Lyra had never trusted a single human. Not even one. She had
a feeling, deep within her soul, that they were corrupt. Lyra knew
the humans would betray them all. It was in their character, and
she'd spent the last several years trying to warn everyone.

No one listened.

Not even the one she trusted the most.

An ache settled in her heart as she thought about Maradalo.
The one who was supposed to trust her judgement most of all. Her
soul mate, or so she thought. He hadn't listened but continued to
spend time with the humans despite her best judgment.

It was through him that the humans found out so much about
her home, Arathor. They used Maradalo to betray the elves. It was
as Lyra feared; the humans had taken advantage of Maradalo. He
hadn't listened to her, instead continuing to see the humans behind
her back.

And now Arathor lay in ruins.

Maradalo had tried to come to her, pleading for mercy and
begging for forgiveness.

Lyra turned her back on him. The same he had done to her

when she warned him about her discomfort toward the humans. Her concerns didn't matter to him. Not truly. Else he wouldn't have continued to see them. Especially not behind her back.

He'd fallen for the humans and their promises. Maradalo had claimed he hadn't realized their intention. He truly believed the humans wanted friendship between themselves and the elves, that it was only a moment of weakness and confusion, but Lyra didn't see it that way. All she saw was all the surrounding destruction— the repercussions of what Maradalo had done.

It had all started over a decade ago when Maradalo first met with the humans. At first, it was all innocent, but then he began hiding things from Lyra. He was telling the humans secrets about the elves they should have never known. It wasn't intentional, but with the relationship he'd built with the humans over the last decade, it was enough for them to put all the pieces together. Maradalo had betrayed her. And to top it all off, he hadn't broken his relationship with the humans. Even after he realized he had betrayed the elves—betrayed her, he continued his friendship with the humans—somehow still seeing good in them. Lyra couldn't comprehend it.

Her heart was shattered. Broken beyond repair. Even breathing hurt. She didn't even know how she continued to breathe any longer. All she saw when she closed her eyes were the faces of the humans. Especially the one in particular that always rubbed Lyra the wrong way. Even before he'd confessed to her what he'd done, he knew how Lyra felt about a few of them well before he made his decision, yet he did so anyway.

Lyra's face twisted in disgust as she thought about the human woman, Gwendolyn. She appeared to be the leader of the group that befriended the elves of Arathor. The cause of all of her grief. The one who led the humans into Arathor, and the reason Arathor fell.

Every time Gwendolyn had been around her, Lyra tensed up. She didn't trust the woman. Not a single bit. Lyra's jaw tightened, fists clenched, and eyes narrowed every time the woman's name was even mentioned. Maradalo knew her dislike toward Gwendolyn the whole while, but it hadn't mattered to him. In fact, he was also quick to defend Gwendolyn, asking what Lyra's issue was with the human. He claimed Gwendolyn was a nice person, who wanted to do good, and that there was no reason to dislike her.

And yet...

Maradalo defended Gwendolyn before the attack. A tear fell down Lyra's cheek. And he had even defended her after the fall of Arathor. Lyra couldn't comprehend how he could still defend her and the humans.

Whenever Lyra closed her eyes, she saw Gwendolyn's face. She even saw Gwendolyn's face while awake and her eyes were open. Lyra saw her face over and over again. She couldn't get it out of her head, and so when the confession came, she couldn't even look at him anymore, let alone let him touch her. He had betrayed his people—he had betrayed her.

Maradalo had trusted someone besides Lyra. He was supposed to trust her first. He confessed everything to her. And now, it was too late. It was too late to take back what he'd done to Lyra and their people, and definitely too late to take back the repercussions of all the dragons and their riders that fell as a causality of his ignorance.

Her body quivered. Tears streaked down her face, falling from each corner of her eyes, dripping from her nose and chin. Her eyes were bloodshot, and her nose congested. It was an ugly cry. She had been crying non-stop for hours. It wasn't a simple cry of defeat, but a cry of betrayal. Full betrayal. It went so much beyond a cry and into a wail as she screamed into the wilderness.

Lyra's knees were weak. She could barely stand as more tears fell at her feet. A small puddle formed on the ground. She knelt, gently placing a hand to balance herself. Chill bumps traveled up and down her body, and she shivered almost uncontrollably. She didn't even know how to go on with life any longer.

A dragon-scaled head rubbed against her hand as a gentle warmth pushed against her mind, trying to get into her thoughts.

Lyra almost caved. She almost opened her mind to him. But she pushed back against the walls of her mind, bringing them back up. She wasn't ready.

Lyra stroked her hand across her companion's head, scratching beneath his ear. Nightwing. She'd bonded with him, then took his name as her surname. They'd been together almost a hundred years, and she hadn't wanted it any other way.

At least he had stayed true to her.

"Humans are despicable creatures," she muttered.

She felt the warmth press against her mind once again, but she pushed it away, sniffling.

Humans had only recently come to the land in the last hundred years. For the most part, they had kept to themselves in the north, where the climate stayed warmer. They formed a few villages on the northern coast: Scorpionya, Aracnard, and Dradamar.

But they were greedy. They saw elves, dwarves, and even a few gnomes had dragons. And they wanted their own. However, they could not find them. The dragons showed no interest in bonding with the humans.

The elves had hoped that was the end of it, but it still wasn't enough for the humans. Since they couldn't get their own dragons, they decided to take them from the elves.

Lyra had underestimated them. Now, however, she would not make the same mistake again. She trained her whole life as an elven ranger. Lyra hoped she wouldn't see another war in her lifetime. The war against the dwarves had been enough.

Resistance still clouded her judgment, but she knew she had no other choice. She had to go to Dwarta Island and beg for aid. Lyra had already heard word from Myrolyna and Scartoya that they had lost their dragonriders. And even worse—all the eggs were stolen from the hatcheries.

With her fingers, she gently brushed her eyelids to remove all traces of tears as she turned away. As much as she wanted to sit and wallow in her pity, she knew there was work to be done.

"Nightwing, take me to Dwarta Island. It is time I swallowed my pride and asked for help."

*As you wish,* came the gentle, gravely response.

Dwarta Island wasn't far from Arathor. It took less than an hour of flight to arrive at the heart of the mountains. Lyra held onto Nightwing tight, eyes closed, in silence as she hoped her tears would dry.

Lyra and Nightwing descended upon Dwarta Island as the air crackled with tension, mirroring the tumultuous emotions roiling within Lyra's heart. With every beat of Nightwing's powerful wings, the weight of her mission pressed down upon her, a heavy burden she bore with grim determination.

\*

The dwarven city loomed before them, its stout walls and intricately carved structures a testament to the resilience and craftsmanship of its inhabitants. As they landed in the heart of the city, Lyra couldn't help but feel a pang of nostalgia tinged with sorrow, for she had once walked these streets as a friend and ally to the dwarves.

But now, as she approached the great hall where the dwarven elders convened, Lyra knew that she was no longer welcome among them. The memory of the not-so-long-ago war between elves and dwarves still lingered like a shadow over their relationship, a bitter legacy of bloodshed and betrayal that had left scars upon the hearts of both peoples.

With a heavy heart, Lyra stepped into the great hall, her eyes meeting the stern gazes of the dwarven elders gathered around the council table. Their faces were etched with lines of age and wisdom, but also with the hardness of those who had endured too much sorrow and loss.

"Lyra Nightwing," one of the elders spoke, his voice gruff and tinged with bitterness. "What brings you back to our halls after so many years? Have you come to ask for more of our kin to spill their blood in your endless wars?"

Lyra's throat tightened at the accusation, but she refused to falter. "I come not to ask for bloodshed, but for aid," she replied, her voice steady despite the tremors of emotion that threatened to overwhelm her. "The humans have stolen our dragon eggs, our future. We need your help to reclaim them, to save our kin from a fate worse than death."

The dwarven elders exchanged glances, their expressions unreadable as they deliberated amongst themselves. After what felt like an eternity, the eldest among them spoke once more, his voice heavy with regret.

"We remember the war, Lyra Nightwing. We remember the sacrifices made, and the lives lost. And we remember the dragons that once soared above our lands, their fiery breath lighting up the skies. But we also remember the price we paid for such alliances."

Lyra's heart sank at the refusal, a bitter taste filling her mouth as she fought back tears of frustration and despair. "I understand," she whispered, her voice barely more than a choked sob. "But please, I beg of you... If not for our past alliances, then for the sake of all that is good and just in this world. Help us save the dragons before it's too late."

As the words hung in the air, a heavy silence descended upon the great hall, broken only by the sound of Lyra's ragged breathing and the soft rustle of Nightwing's wings from the courtyard. And in that moment, as hope teetered on the edge of despair, Lyra knew that the fate of her world hung in the balance—and that the road ahead would be fraught with peril and sacrifice, but also with the glimmer of possibility and the faintest whisper of hope.

"How many elves remain? Do you even have enough to wage a war against the humans? Or are you depending on us to fight this war for you?" The council all murmured in agreement.

Lyra's eyes met the floor. "I do not know. They have laid Arathor to ruins."

"Arathor has fallen?" an elder asked.

Lyra's eyes pressed tight. She didn't want to shed any more tears, but she had a hard time keeping them at bay. Lyra took a deep breath, then met the council's eyes. "Word is Myrolyna and Enyatora do not fare well, either."

"So, you have no army?" The dwarf shook his head. "Yet you want us to sacrifice ours? We have no ill will toward the humans. Should we fight them only to become destroyed ourselves?"

Tears could no longer hold themselves back. The betrayal. The hurt. The pain. She went through it all over again. Memories flashed back into her mind. She could no longer contain the sorrow.

"Lyra..." The dwarf sighed. "There is no ill will toward you. Even during conflict between our peoples, you've always showed compassion toward us."

Lyra wiped a tear from her face. "Will you do the same?"

The dwarf tilted his head.

"Show compassion?"

The dwarf tugged at his beard. "I cannot send an army of dwarves to their death."

Lyra dipped her head, turning away from them. If they would

not help her, then… What was then? Was there anywhere else she could turn? Gnomash Island? Would the gnomes even care? They were even deeper into their mountains than the dwarves. Gnomes didn't get involved in anything.

"Lyra…?"

Lyra spun around, her eyes downcast, shivers traveling all the way down her spine, and bile in her mouth. If the dwarves wouldn't help her, she'd attempt it all on her own. She knew she wasn't going to survive, but survival didn't matter to her any longer. In fact, death felt like a sweet release after the torture of betrayal she'd recently gone through.

"Yes?"

"I cannot send an army with you… but I can send someone."

Lyra tilted her head, a single eyebrow raising. What could a lone dwarf do? "Who?"

"Tomas Ironsteel."

Lyra's eyes widened. "He's still around?" She brushed a strand of hair behind her pointed ear. "He's a legend."

"Yes."

"Even so—" Lyra bit her lip. "What can the two of us do?"

"Find the eggs. Bring them back to us, and I promise you, we'll keep them safeguarded. No human will ever find them."

The tension in Lyra's heart lessened slightly. It wasn't a solution. Nor was it what she wanted. Lyra wanted the humans exterminated off the face of the land. Her hurt ran deep, and she didn't want to see another human alive to cause any additional harm to her people. Yet, she knew that was her own selfishness over her betrayal. She needed to think of what was best for the dragons, what was best for the elves in the future.

Humans had short lives. They were lucky to even live a hundred years. Elves and dwarves lived for hundreds to thousands of years. Eventually, the humans would die out, and then what would remain? At least the dragons would survive. Any elves who went into hiding could survive.

"Will you open your homes to the elves?"

The dwarf's eyes hardened before he took a deep breath. "We'll hide the dragons."

"And what? Condemn the elves to their deaths?" Lyra took a step toward the council. "If we're successful, they'll come after all of us."

"The decision is made."

Lyra's head fell to her chest. "Fine. I accept."

She no longer cared if she lived or died anyway. Part of her wanted to ensure the safety of her kin, though with how adept the elves were in the forest, perhaps they could hide from the humans. At least now they knew they needed to hide.

Lyra returned to her dragon, who had curled up in the courtyard. A handful of dwarves lingered nearby, watching with awe at the magnificent beast. A few children, still young enough to not have a full beard, passed a ball near the dragon, laughing all the while as they played and admired the beast.

A dwarf strolled up to her, wearing leather armor over a cotton shirt. His hair and white-flecked beard were gray. A small axe was strapped to his back, and he looked up at her with a stern expression.

"Tomas Ironsteel?"

He grunted.

"How much do you know?"

He grunted again.

"The human kingdom is in the north. Dradamar is the capital. I can only assume they took the dragon eggs there, but I am not certain." Lyra licked her lips.

"We need a tracker."

Lyra titled her head. "Where are we going to find a tracker?"

"Gnomash Island."

"You cannot be serious? A gnome?"

"The best." Tomas crossed his arms.

Without saying another word, he climbed atop the dragon and sat on the back of the saddle. Lyra looked from him to the dragon for a long moment before shrugging, climbing on top, and sitting in front of him.

"Nightwing, to Gnomash Island."

Nightwing soared gracefully through the skies, his wings slicing through the crisp mountain air. Below them, the sprawling landscape of the continent unfolded like a patchwork quilt, dotted with forests, rivers, and rolling hills.

As they approached the island, Lyra marveled at the sight of its towering peaks and lush valleys, shrouded in mist and mystery. Gnomash Island was a place of legend, home to the reclusive gnomes who dwelled deep within the heart of the mountains, their vast underground cities hidden from prying eyes.

Descending into the island's verdant forests, Lyra and Tomas made their way toward the entrance of one of the gnomish settlements, a bustling hub of activity nestled amidst the towering trees. The air was filled with the sound of tinkling laughter and the hum of machinery, as gnomes went about their daily tasks with boundless energy and ingenuity.

When they entered the settlement, Lyra couldn't help but feel a sense of wonder at the sight of the gnomes' intricate inventions and contraptions, from steam-powered automatons to clockwork contrivances that whirred and clicked with mechanical precision.

Tomas led the way through the bustling streets, his keen eyes scanning the crowd for any sign of their quarry. Finally, they came upon a small workshop tucked away in a corner of the settlement, where a lone gnome tinkered away at a peculiar device that resembled a cross between a compass and a sextant.

"This must be the place," Tomas muttered, nodding toward the workshop. "Let's see if this gnome can help us."

Approaching the gnome, Lyra cleared her throat to get his attention. The gnome looked up from his work, his eyes widening in surprise at the sight of the elf and dwarf before him.

"Greetings," Lyra began, her voice warm and friendly. "We're in need of your expertise. We're looking for a tracker to help us locate something of great importance."

The gnome eyed them suspiciously, his bushy eyebrows furrowing in thought. "And what, pray tell, is this 'something' you're looking for?"

Lyra glanced at Tomas, who nodded in silent agreement. "Dragon eggs," she replied simply. "Stolen by humans. We need to find them before it's too late."

The gnome's eyes widened in astonishment, and he leaned in closer, his curiosity piqued. "Dragon eggs, you say? Fascinating! I've always been partial to dragons myself. Well, in that case, you've come to the right gnome! I happen to be the best tracker on this side of the mountains."

With a flourish, the gnome produced a small device from his pocket, a complex array of gears and lenses that gleamed in the sunlight. "This, my dear friends, is my latest invention—an egg tracker! With this device, we'll have those dragon eggs back in no time!"

"Have you tracked dragon eggs with it before?" Lyra asked.

"Of course not." The gnome patted his belly. "I've only tracked quail eggs."

"But you're certain it will work?"

"Quite." He stuck out his hand. "Name's Ralph."

Lyra couldn't help but smile at the gnome's enthusiasm, her heart swelling with hope at the prospect of success. "Thank you," she said sincerely. "We're grateful for your help."

"Lead the way." He grinned.

When Lyra led him back to her dragon, he stumbled. "You telling me you want me to ride that?"

"We don't have enough time. We need to reach the human cities before it's too late."

Ralph grunted. "That creature better not drop me."

"Nightwing would never."

With a slight reservation, Ralph finally accepted Lyra's help to climb atop the saddle between her and Tomas.

Nightwing leapt into the air and soared through the skies. Lyra, Tomas, and Ralph clung tightly to his back, the wind whipping through their hair and filling their lungs with the exhilarating rush of flight. Below them, the verdant landscape of the continent unfurled, reminding Lyra again of a patchwork quilt, bathed in the golden glow of the setting sun.

During their journey north, the trio remained cautious, constantly on the lookout for signs of human presence, anxious about crossing paths with the egg thieves. Despite Nightwing's swift flight and Ralph's assurances that his egg tracker was working perfectly, there was a palpable tension in the air, a sense of impending danger that lurked just beyond the horizon.

"We'll need to find shelter for the night," Lyra called out over the rushing wind, her voice tinged with urgency. "We can't risk being spotted by human scouts."

Tomas nodded in agreement, his gaze scanning the landscape below for any sign of a suitable hiding place. "There." He pointed toward a dense thicket of trees nestled in a secluded valley below. "We can camp there for the night."

After Nightwing descended into the sheltered grove, Lyra and the others dismounted, their feet sinking into the soft earth as they made their way toward the cover of the trees. The air was thick with the scent of pine and earth, and the sound of nocturnal creatures stirring in the underbrush filled the night with a symphony of sound.

"We'll need to set up a watch," Lyra said, her voice low and tense as she scanned the surrounding forest for any signs of movement. "We can't afford to let our guard down, not with the humans in this territory."

Ralph nodded solemnly, his eyes darting nervously from shadow to shadow as he fiddled with his egg tracker, adjusting its settings in the dim light of the campfire. "Don't worry," he said, his voice tinged with determination. "I'll make sure we're not caught off guard."

As they settled in for the night, the crackling of the campfire and the rustle of the wind through the trees filled the air with a sense of tranquility, a brief respite from the chaos and uncertainty of their journey. And as Lyra, Tomas, and Ralph huddled together beneath the starlit sky, Lyra's heart filled with hope and determination. She knew that no matter what dangers lay ahead, they would face them together, united in their quest to save the dragons and reclaim their stolen future.

*

As the first light of dawn cast its gentle glow upon the forest, Lyra stirred from her slumber, her senses alert to the world around her. Beside her, Tomas and Ralph were already awake, their faces etched with determination as they prepared for the day ahead.

"Morning," Lyra greeted them, her voice rough with sleep as she rubbed the tiredness from her eyes. "Any sign of trouble during the night?"

Tomas shook his head, his gaze scanning the surrounding forest with the keen eyes of a seasoned warrior. "Nothing to report," he replied, his voice steady and reassuring. "But we'll need to remain vigilant. The humans could be close on our trail."

Ralph, meanwhile, was busy tinkering with his egg tracker, his brow furrowed in concentration as he adjusted its settings with deft fingers. "I've recalibrated the tracker," he announced, his voice muffled by the whirring of gears and clicking of mechanisms. "It should lead us straight to the dragon eggs."

Lyra nodded in approval, impressed by the gnome's ingenuity and determination, though admittedly not fully understanding how such a device worked. "Thank you, Ralph," she said sincerely. "We're lucky to have you with us."

The gnome grinned up at her, his eyes sparkling with mischief as he tucked the egg tracker back into his pocket. "Don't mention it," he replied, his voice laced with a hint of pride. "Just doing my part to save the day, as usual."

Lyra couldn't help but feel a sense of camaraderie and unity with her unlikely companions. Despite their differences in race and background, they shared a common purpose, and a shared determination to see their quest through to the end. She didn't know them too well yet, but from the brief conversations she'd had with them, it was clear they too were fond of dragons, and resented the humans for stealing the eggs.

"Let's get moving," Lyra said, her voice firm with resolve as she mounted Nightwing's back once more. "We have a long journey ahead of us, but together, I know we can succeed."

Lyra stroked her dragon behind the ear, whispering, "How do you fare?"

*Better than you*, Nightwing replied in her mind.

"Our companions. Can we trust them?" Lyra glanced at the dwarf and gnome as they began climbing up Nightwing's tail to reach the saddle behind her.

*They seem genuine. They care about the dragons. I believe that is all we can ask.*

Lyra nodded, then checked behind her to ensure everyone was

secured. "Let's ride."

With a flap of his powerful wings, Nightwing took to the skies once more, Lyra and her companions clinging tightly to her back as they soared into the boundless expanse of the morning sky.

The landscape shifted beneath them, transitioning from dense forests to rolling plains and craggy mountain ranges. The trio traversed valleys and crossed rivers, always keeping a wary eye out for any signs of human presence.

Throughout their travels, Lyra found herself growing closer to Tomas and Ralph, learning more about their backgrounds and the experiences that had shaped them into the individuals they were today.

"Tomas, tell me about your life before joining me on this quest," Lyra prompted one evening as they made camp beneath a canopy of stars.

Tomas settled himself beside the crackling fire, his weathered face softened by the flickering light. "I was born and raised in the dwarven city of Ironhold," he began, his voice tinged with nostalgia. "I come from a long line of warriors, but I always felt drawn to the art of smithing. I spent my youth honing my craft, forging weapons and armor for my kin."

"Your name is legendary. I've heard many a tale of your adventures."

"Many dwarves dislike adventure. Seldom do dwarves leave the mountains." Tomas pulled his beard. "I was never one to stay in any one place for too long. I always felt there was something I could do to make a difference."

"Is that why you decided to come on this quest?" Lyra asked.

"A dragon saved me long ago. I did not know her name, nor have I seen her since. But that compassion…" Tomas gulped. "I will never forget it. All of my previous adventures are pale in comparison to what difference I can make today. I have a debt to repay."

Lyra smiled. "I will never repay all my debt to the dragons. That is why I am here. I cannot condemn their future to slavery if there is anything I can do to prevent it."

"Aye."

"And what about you, Ralph?" Lyra turned her attention to the gnome, who was busy tinkering with his inventions nearby.

Ralph glanced up from his work, a mischievous twinkle in his eye. "Ah, where to begin?" he chuckled. "I come from a long line of inventors and tinkerers, a family of gnomes renowned for our ingenuity and creativity. From a young age, the inner workings of machines and gadgets fascinated me, and I spent countless hours experimenting and tinkering with various contraptions."

Lyra couldn't help but marvel at the gnome's enthusiasm and zest for life, his passion for invention evident in every word he spoke. "And you, too, have a passion for adventure?"

Ralph set his invention down. "This is the first time I've left home. Truth be told, I've always wanted to see the world."

"How much further is it to Dradamar?" Tomas asked.

"You won't make it to Dradamar," came a cold voice from behind them.

Lyra spun around to find a woman with golden hair grinning back at her. The woman held two scimitars and wore full chainmail. A hood attempted to hide some of her features, but it wasn't enough to fool Lyra. It was *her*.

"Gwendolyn," Lyra spat.

"Lyra. Oh, how nice it is to see you again."

Lyra's blood boiled. Her body tensed, beginning to shake. She could barely contain her rage. All Lyra wanted to do was strangle the woman. "Where is he?"

Gwendolyn laughed. "He chose us."

"No. He came back to me."

"If he truly chose you… he would have never come to me in the first place."

Lyra clenched her jaw. Tears wanted to fall, but she held them back with all her might. She wouldn't give the woman the satisfaction. Instead, she bled out with anger.

She reached for the bow over her shoulder.

A dozen more humans appeared, all wearing armor and wielding swords.

"Where are the dragon eggs?" Lyra snarled, drawing an arrow from her quiver.

"Like I would tell you."

Lyra nocked the arrow and aimed it for Gwendolyn's throat. "I won't hesitate."

"You're not woman enough. You weren't woman enough to keep your man from us… and you're certainly not woman enough to kill me."

Gwendolyn was wrong. Killing the woman had been at the forefront of Lyra's mind since Maradalo had first told her. She wanted to hurt all the humans. However, she was not a cold-blooded killer. Until now. She had an excuse now. Lyra released the arrow.

Gwendolyn's eye twitched before she spun to the side. She hadn't believed her.

Lyra nocked another arrow. Gwendolyn ran for cover, attempting to cower behind the other human warriors. Lyra loosed her second arrow. This one rang true, imbedding itself in Gwendolyn's shoulder.

Gwendolyn screamed, dropping to the ground and crawling away.

It wasn't enough. Lyra nocked a third arrow. Before she could release, the other humans charged. Lyra had to alter her aim. She released. It embedded into the throat of a human warrior, and he fell to the ground, lifeless.

Ralph and Tomas wielded their axes and stepped between the humans and Lyra. Metal clanged against metal as sword met axe.

Lyra no longer held back. She pulled another arrow from her quiver and released. It struck the human attempting to overpower Ralph. The gnome jumped on top of the human in victory as he swung his ax at the next human, catching him off-guard and knocking him to the ground where the gnome had a level playing field.

At first, Lyra had wanted to protect the two of them, but she realized they were both more than capable of holding their own. Instead, she focused on ensuring they weren't overwhelmed. They were still outnumbered.

Loose. Nock. Loose.

The warriors dropped. They were fast, but she was faster. She nocked her next arrow and paused.

There were no more. She looked over to Ralph and Tomas. They each had an opponent, but seemed to be handling themselves well.

She glanced at all the bodies on the forest floor. One. Two. Three. Seven. Nine.

One was missing. She counted the bodies again. Her eyes widened.

*Gwendolyn.*

Lyra rushed forward, running past Ralph and Tomas. She only had one thing on her mind. One person.

Leaves brushed across her face as she dashed through the bushes, desperately searching for any sign of the woman.

Sunlight exposed a fletching in the bushes. Lyra ran over to it, pulling it out from the bush. It was her arrow, and the arrowhead was stained crimson.

She took another step forward, scrutinizing the ground. A drop of blood caught her attention. She knelt and scanned further, licking her lips. She found the trail of blood.

Lyra ran. She didn't look back. For a brief moment, nothing else mattered. She needed to find Gwendolyn.

Her mind buzzed with one thought. She moved faster— desperation fueling her. Lyra could no longer see anything around her. She didn't care what was behind her. All she cared about was moving forward.

After a few more paces, Lyra finally found what she was desperately searching for. Gwendolyn cowered in a bush; a piece of cloth tied to her arm to prevent further bleeding.

Lyra nocked an arrow.

"Please. Have mercy," Gwendolyn begged.

"People like you do not deserve mercy." Lyra loosed the arrow.

It penetrated Gwendolyn's other shoulder. She screamed out in pain.

Lyra nocked another arrow.

"If you're going to do it, then just do it already," Gwendolyn begged.

"You don't deserve a quick death. I need you to feel a fraction of what I feel." Lyra gritted her teeth.

"Please," Gwendolyn begged.

*Lyra, don't!* came a voice from inside of her head. She suppressed the voice.

Lyra released another arrow. This one pierced Gwendolyn's thigh.

"Lyra!" Someone called her name in the distance.

She glanced over her shoulder. Who was calling her name? Her eyebrows furrowed. She felt like she was supposed to be doing something. Why was she here? Was there something other than revenge?

"Lyra, there you are," came a gruff voice.

"Tomas?"

The dwarf appeared through the bushes. Lyra smiled as she saw him, followed by Ralph. She recognized the two of them— even knew their names but she couldn't place why or how she knew them. Was there something she was supposed to be doing right now? It felt like there was, but all she could see in her mind was darkness... and Gwendolyn's sinister grin.

"What are you doing here?"

"We discovered the location of the dragon eggs." Tomas planted the butt of his axe in the ground and leaned on the knob.

"Dragon eggs," she whispered. She had nearly forgotten. No, she *had* forgotten. "How did you find them?"

"We interrogated the remaining warriors."

"We?" Ralph asked.

Tomas shrugged. "Fine. Ralph did. It turns out he has a few gadgets that can be a bit... persuasive."

"They told you exactly where they are?" Lyra asked, dumbfounded.

"Not quite," Ralph admitted. "Turns out, they didn't know exactly, but they knew where the entrance was. The rest—" Ralph patted his egg tracker secured to his belt. "I'll use this lovely to track down."

"We don't have much time," Tomas added. "The human army will return tonight. We have a small window of opportunity."

Lyra turned back around. She looked from the nocked arrow to the empty space on the ground. Gwendolyn had escaped again.

Part of her didn't want to go. She wanted to find Gwendolyn. Lyra wasn't done with her yet.

*Lyra, let her go.*

Lyra clenched her teeth. *I cannot just let her go.*

*You would condemn all of dragonkind for revenge?*

The tension in Lyra's shoulders relaxed a little. No, she

couldn't do that. Her dragon was right. She closed her eyes, trying not to see the two of them as she attempted to collect her thoughts. *You're right. Lead the way.*

With her heart still pounding, Lyra nodded and followed Tomas and Ralph into the depths of the forest, the dwarf guiding them on a winding path through the dense thicket of trees and undergrowth. Ralph, who had been silent up until now, finally spoke.

"Are you all right?" Ralph asked Lyra, his voice barely audible over the rustling of the leaves. "You seem different."

Lyra's eyes flashed with anger, but she quickly suppressed it. "I don't know what you're talking about. I'm here for one reason and one reason only, and that's to retrieve those dragon eggs."

Tomas stopped in his tracks and turned to face Lyra. "Listen to me, Lyra. You cannot let your desire for revenge cloud your judgment. We have a mission that is greater than any personal vendetta you may hold. The fate of the dragons rests on our success tonight."

Lyra felt a jolt of realization shoot through her as Tomas' words sank in. The weight of their quest pressed down upon her, heavier than the bow in her hand.

She took a deep breath, squaring her shoulders and meeting Tomas' gaze. "You're right," she said, her voice low but resolute. "I won't let my personal vendetta jeopardize our mission."

Ralph nodded approvingly, a glimmer of admiration in his eyes.

With renewed determination, they continued their journey deeper into the heart of the forest. The air grew thick with magic as they approached the site where the dragon eggs were rumored to be hidden.

As they crested a ridge, a breathtaking sight unfolded before them. Nestled within a clearing and bathed in moonlight was a massive cavern, its entrance hidden by a waterfall that cascaded down like a shimmering veil. The water glistened with hues of silver and gold, and the earthy scent of old growth mingled with the crisp, cool air.

"This must be it," Tomas whispered, his eyes wide with anticipation.

The gnome nodded in agreement, his small fingers tracing a pattern in the air as if to summon the power of the earth itself. Lyra felt a surge of energy flow through her, and she could feel the dragon eggs calling to her deep within her core.

With the passage of time almost imperceptible, the group approached the cavern, their senses heightened as the magic of the night lay heavily upon them. The waterfall parted, revealing a tunnel that spiraled down into the heart of the cavern.

With meticulous care, they stepped into the darkness, the sound of rushing water fading behind them. The air grew warmer as they descended deeper, and a faint, otherworldly glow illuminated the path before them.

As they ventured further into the depths of the cavern, they began to hear a low, rumbling sound echoing off the walls. Lyra's heart quickened with each step, eagerness and trepidation warring within her.

At last, they reached a chamber bathed in an ethereal light that emanated from a cluster of colossal dragon eggs nestled on a bed of shimmering crystals. The eggs pulsed with a gentle energy that seemed to harmonize with the very heartbeat of the earth.

Tomas and Ralph stood in reverent awe at the sight before them, but Lyra felt a deep connection stirring within her soul. She approached the nearest egg, her hand lingering above its surface.

Lyra placed her fingers upon the egg, feeling its cold, smooth surface. Suddenly, a surge of warmth flooded through her, and for the first time on their journey, Lyra felt relief.

"Hurry, pack up the eggs in Nightwing's saddlebags." Lyra didn't wait for the dwarf or gnome to start as she wrapped her fingers around the egg to grip it, feeling it consume the entirety of her hand.

It felt warm, and stranger than that, she could sense a heartbeat within. A feeling of hope came over her, and she didn't believe it was coming from within herself but instead from the egg. Biting her lip, she rushed it back over to her dragon and stuffed it in the large saddlebag.

There were at least fifty eggs. Lyra inspected the saddlebags. It would be close, but they had to save them all.

"You won't escape," came a voice.

Lyra placed another egg in the saddlebag, now over halfway full, then spun around, drawing her bow once more.

Gwendolyn stood with over two dozen companions now. She had bandages over both shoulders and her thigh, but she looked determined.

Once again, Lyra regretted not killing her. The woman had broken Lyra over and over again now, and it was time to finally end it all, one way or another. She glanced over her shoulder to find Tomas and Ralph surrounded by another dozen warriors. They had almost finished securing all the eggs in the saddlebags. This couldn't happen now. Nightwing growled, clearly ready to strike.

*Stand down,* Lyra said. *You have dragon eggs to worry about. Lyra... don't.*

A sad half-smile crossed Lyra's face. *I do not have a choice. It was always meant to be this way.*

Lyra rapidly loosed two arrows at Gwendolyn, then spun around and charged toward Tomas and Ralph. She released another arrow, striking one of the warriors in the back of the neck. Tomas and Ralph took up the fight, and Lyra loosed another arrow, again striking true. Her third arrow bounced off the plate armor of a warrior, but she barely noticed as she released a fourth.

Tomas and Ralph each took out three warriors, leaving only three remaining. However, the final three ganged up on Ralph, knocking the gnome down and leaving a slice across his cheek.

Lyra charged toward the offending warrior and tackled him from behind, rolling to the ground and stabbing an arrow into his throat before turning to nock and release it at one of the warriors attacking Tomas. Her arrow struck true.

The final warrior knocked Tomas to the ground. Lyra struggled to nock her next arrow as the warrior slammed his sword to the ground for the killing blow. Lyra tensed, her body shivering, and her teeth grinded as she rushed toward the warrior. Tomas, however, rolled out of the way, avoiding the strike, then slammed the butt of his axe into the warrior's groin. The warrior's head dropped forward as he reached for his groin, and Tomas took that opportunity to slam the toe of the axe into the warrior's head. Tomas rolled out of the way again, as the warrior dropped to the ground, lifeless.

Lyra rushed over and held her hand out to the dwarf, helping him to his feet. "Finish packing up, then get back to the mountains. It's imperative we get the eggs to safety."

Lyra licked her lips and looked at her dwarf and gnome companions. "Finish packing up, then get back to the mountains. It's imperative we get the eggs to safety."

"What are you going to do?" Tomas asked.

She bit her lip. "Whatever is required to give you time."

"You won't survive."

Lyra gulped. "As long as the dragon eggs survive… that is all that matters."

There was another thought in her mind that she did not speak aloud. *As long as she goes down with me.*

Tomas nodded. "I'll ensure their safety."

Lyra clasped a hand on his shoulder and smiled. Ralph waddled over to her with another dragon egg in hand, his head drooping to his chest. She placed a hand on his shoulder next.

"Go."

Without saying another word, she turned around to meet Gwendolyn's eyes. The woman and the remaining warriors were close now. Lyra drew her bow, aimed for Gwendolyn's skull, then loosed. The arrow didn't meet its target but struck a warrior behind her when Gwendolyn moved out of the way. Lyra didn't blink before she had another arrow and released. Every arrow aimed at Gwendolyn. None struck true, as Gwendolyn either moved or used another warrior as a shield.

"Stop them!" Gwendolyn yelled.

Tomas and Ralph had successfully packed away all the dragon eggs and climbed atop Nightwing. The warriors rushed toward the dragon, rushing past Lyra on their way. She spun around and released arrow after arrow, felling several of them. Nightwing spread his wings and began his flight. Three warriors clung to him, but Lyra made quick work of them with her bow.

With Nightwing safely away, the other warriors turned their attention to her. She released another arrow, then another. When she reached for a third, she discovered her quiver was empty.

Lyra dropped her bow and unsheathed her short sword, prepared to take down as many as she could before a sharp pain sank into her side. She gasped, her sword clanging to the ground as she fell to her knees. Lyra reached behind her to feel a dagger hilt protruding from her side. She collapsed the rest of the way, falling onto her back.

Gwendolyn stepped over her, a widespread grin on her face. "I told you that you wouldn't escape."

Lyra began to laugh. Gwendolyn grabbed a throwing knife from her belt and stabbed it into Lyra's abdomen. Lyra gagged as blood spurted out of her mouth, yet she continued to laugh.

"Why are you laughing at me?"

Lyra coughed up blood, trying to clear her throat. "The eggs are safe… you failed."

Gwendolyn crouched on top of Lyra and punched her in the face. Lyra yanked the dagger out of her side and plunged it into Gwendolyn's chest. "And I told you I would kill you."

Gwendolyn choked, blood pouring from her mouth as she collapsed on top of Lyra.

Pain ran through Lyra's entire body, but she pushed it aside. A large smile came across her face as she relished in her victory. Then she closed her eyes for the last time.

## THE END

# Dragon Unchained
## Keith Robinson

Wyst paused to rest in another subterranean passage. She dropped lightly onto the sloped rocky floor and stood still while she acclimated to normality. The nausea passed in seconds, and then she straightened and picked her way across the smooth, hard incline until she found a suitable ledge to sit on.

She blinked, trying to pierce the darkness. Her night vision was already fading. With a sigh, she unhooked the lantern from her belt, twisted the knob, and held it high as the soft glow illuminated her surroundings.

The silence was absolute. Nothing unusual there. What troubled her was the fact that this passage, like all the others she'd come across on her descent, was short and narrow, barely tall enough to stand in. Any smaller, and there would be nowhere to rest. And without rest, she might perish.

"Not far now," she told herself again. "One last push."

Standing, she faced the wall and stashed her lantern. In darkness again, Wyst placed her hands on the cold rock and pressed against it.

In seconds, she became intangible.

Ghosting into the rock, she pitched forward and began another descent—straight down, falling at a steady pace, chilled by cool mineral deposits passing through her body. She preferred soil; it had a warm, welcoming feel about it, soft and pure. Rock struck her as abrasive, harsh, and unfriendly. Especially deep below the surface. She doubted many had traveled deeper than this.

Her night vision revealed another set of layers in the igneous rock. And once again, it felt like she bumped past every striation. She ground her teeth and suffered through it, knowing she'd be aching in the morning. Then again, if this were a simple ride through nothing but soil, she doubted the dragon would have been trapped for long.

*The dragon.*

Excitement coursed through her veins as the descent came to an end at last. She dropped from the ceiling of a cavern and gasped as she began to plummet toward the treetops below.

*Treetops?*

*And where's the light coming from?*

She focused on her slow, ghostly fall. Midair descents were tricky. She could easily die unless she kept her wits about her. Gritting her teeth, she maintained her incorporeal state as she fell among the treetops. Sinking painlessly through dozens of branches all the way to the cavern floor, she dropped onto the ground and halted, buried up to her waist, her legs still in an incorporeal state. She carefully solidified her upper body and arms, pushed herself up and out of the ground, and finished the transition to her fully tangible self.

Wyst took a moment to wiggle her bare toes in the pine needles. She breathed long and deep, waiting for the nausea to pass. Then she allowed herself to take in the surroundings.

"This has to be it," she whispered. "Come on, Wyst, you *know* this is the place. A gigantic cavern deep underground, crammed full of trees, and—is that a waterfall in the distance? It's magical! How is this place even possible?"

Some vegetation was to be expected. After all, the legendary scrolls read, "... *and a place too green to be Hell*..." However, the pages didn't go so far to say that the cavern would be thick with lush ferns and healthy trees.

The scrolls also read, "... *will not survive on the water alone*..." She'd always imagined a narrow stream gurgling through gaps in the rock, but the thunderous noise in the distance was definitely more than a stream.

As for the light…

"… *will forever look upon that which it despises…*"

There was no explanation for the illumination, but according to the stories, this place was a form of Hell for the prisoner. A cavern deep underground should be pitch-black and featureless, nothing but rock. Yet here she was in what could only be described as a pocket of enchantment deep within Mirstone, lush and beautiful and eerily lit. Any rational person would guess the presence of bioluminescent fungi or insects, but the hazy light reminded her more of a typical murky morning on the surface. Only… a rocky ceiling loomed far overhead.

Shaking her head in amazement, she focused on which way to go. A light mist hung low and silent, and she saw nothing but trees. The waterfall seemed like a logical place to start. She could follow its sound. When the dragon had been trapped down here hundreds of years ago, it too would have gravitated toward that sound eventually. Perhaps it had laid itself down to die there, when escape seemed futile.

If she were to find the final resting place of the legendary Magma Demon of Mirstone, it would likely be there by the falls.

\*

The forest was bigger than it had any right to be. Every so often, Wyst stopped to peer up through the canopy. The cavern roof hung overhead, partly obscured by a haze. *Where* did the mysterious daylight come from? How could the sun's rays penetrate so deep below ground?

She paused as a new noise permeated the woods, distinct from the waterfall. It sounded like…

Like what?

Wyst frowned. Chains?

The sound came again—the unmistakable rattle of iron links

accompanied by heavy thuds.

It was a while before Wyst resumed her trek. She found herself tiptoeing, cautious about being heard. Who could possibly be here in this forest with her? The answer was nobody, except perhaps another of her kind, which she highly doubted. The rattle of chains made her think she'd managed to get hopelessly lost and wound up back on the surface.

*Some gnome you are.*

"Part gnome," she muttered.

As she stepped around thorny bushes and struggled through a dense patch of ferns, it occurred to her that she could be walking into terrible danger. Chains indicated someone or something restrained, which begged the question: should she fear the captive or the captor?

More to the point, who would be down here, deep underground, in what she'd thought was an inaccessible burial ground? There could only be one answer. Dragon seekers had found and uncovered the original tunnel. It seemed unlikely but the only logical answer. According to the stories, the dragon had been defeated and restrained, then dragged down the steep tunnel by a thousand orcs commanded by elves—a rare moment of unity to rid Mirstone of the threat.

And that tunnel had been blasted by explosives and hexed by witches. None should be able to find it, let alone traverse it.

The rattle of chains came again, and she froze. "That's really close," she whispered, scouring the vegetation for a hint of movement beyond the forest. But she saw nothing but trees. She'd have to keep pressing on.

Not long after, Wyst stumbled out of the trees into an expanse of open space surrounding a colossal monolith of rock. It rose like a small, narrow mountain but was too angular to be naturally formed. Maybe an earthquake had shoved a massive shard out of the ground. It reminded her of an injury she'd suffered as a child, when a broken bone had protruded from her shin.

She judged the monolith's base to be fifty paces across. The surrounding forest shied away from it, leaving a swath of lush grass that would make it easy to circle the oddity.

Just then, the sound of rattling chains filled the air from around the other side of the monolith. A huffing sigh suggested the captive was huge. A small number of possibilities bounced around in Wyst's head. Could it be that the prison remained accessible and was still used to this day, in absolute secrecy? She doubted that very much, yet clearly *something* was here with her...

"Here goes nothing," she muttered.

Long grass swished around her boots as she walked. The chains rattled again, small *clink* noises and occasional thuds. She gave the monolith a wide berth, circling on the very edge of the clearing, just inside the treeline.

Movement caught her eye—the tip of an enormous crimson tail, scaly and ridged.

"No," she whispered. "It can't be."

But as she continued, more cautiously now, the rear half of the great beast slowly came into view. There could be no doubt that this was a dragon. Her mind reeled with questions. How could another dragon be down here in this ancient place? Who had access to the entry tunnel? Why go to such lengths to trap a dragon when it could simply be slain? And why in secrecy?

She couldn't see the creature's front half yet. But she saw enough for now. The dragon's jagged spine rose as high as the roof of her humble home. That ugly crest was the deepest of reds, again reminding her of a terrible injury where bones had punched through the flesh and stuck out. The scales on its flank looked tattered and worn as though the dragon were malnourished—which might well be the case. Powerful thigh muscles rippled as the captive shuffled about, dragging lengths of chain across the bald patch of ground it was confined to. Its black claws raked up piles of dirt.

It had raised its wings overhead, spreading them wide, perhaps to air them out or to stretch a few cramps. The thick, leathery skin had dozens of holes, but none serious enough to hamper its flight if it ever broke free.

Wyst realized she'd pulled out her knife. Sharp and vicious though the blade might be, it was a laughable defense against a monster this size. She slowly pushed it back into its sheath and continued circling until the dragon's shoulders, neck, and head came into view.

All at once, it twisted its head around and spotted her. Wyst prayed the chains were short enough to restrict its movement, but still she retreated toward the trees, one foot after another, her gaze locked on the dragon's unblinking yellow eyes.

It turned suddenly, paws stomping and tail swinging. The wings spread farther, and the head snapped forward—and halted as the chain snapped taut. The sturdy links were attached to a giant iron manacle encircling the dragon's throat.

Wyst breathed a sigh of relief.

Then jumped in terror as the dragon's mouth opened. She was easily within range of its fiery breath.

She turned to run for her life into the trees—

"Wait."

The deep, booming voice echoed in her skull, making her flinch and duck. She shook herself and spun about.

When no blast of fire incinerated her, Wyst's terror gave way to confusion. She retreated a little more, feeling for the nearest tree trunk, wondering how a forest would fare in protecting her against a dragon's full-on assault.

*Not well*, she concluded.

"Do not run." The booming voice in her head sounded male.

"Wh-what?"

"If you run, I will burn you. You are here now, and you will stay awhile."

Wyst had heard of dragons using mindspeak. Mirstone had plenty of brave dragon riders who boasted long conversations with their companions. But a dragon sparking up a conversation with a humble gnomish girl who'd stumbled upon its lair? That had to be rare.

"Where exactly am I?" she asked once her heart settled and her throat relaxed enough to get the words out. "Am I where I *think* I am, or…?"

The dragon tilted his head. "That depends on where you think you are."

*I'm in a dream*, Wyst thought. *Or a nightmare.*

"Is… is this the resting place of the ancient Magma Demon, deep under the ground?" When no immediate answer was forthcoming, she added, "Are the bones by the waterfall? I feel like a trapped dragon would… would gravitate toward a drinking hole before it…"

"Before it died?" The monstrous beast pulled back a little, his unblinking steely glare fixated on her. "The Magma Beast was offered no such courtesy. It was simply chained to this monolith and left to rot."

Wyst's mouth fell open. Her gaze immediately flitted about the long grass, trying to spot signs of a long-dead creature. "So it's beneath our feet?"

The dragon chuckled softly, a low, huffing noise from deep within. "No. Do you want to see the Magma Demon? Let me show you."

With that, the dragon rose up high, his chest swelling as he inhaled long and hard. Yellow light flared inside his throat, growing brighter.

Wyst knew her time had come. Running was futile. "Please—" she begged.

The dragon opened wide and thrust his head forward, rattling the chains as he did so. A stream of yellow and orange liquid fire shot forth, raining hell on the forest some distance from where Wyst stood. She felt the intense heat and cringed away from it, stumbling and falling on her hands and knees.

Trees blackened and exploded. Fire spat and leapt from branch to branch, destroying everything in its path. Black smoke rolled upward. The stinging fumes reduced Wyst to a coughing fit, her eyes streaming with tears. Waves of heat threatened to melt her skin.

Abruptly, the stream of liquid fire ended. Through teary eyes, Wyst peered at the dragon and gawked at the bright-yellow molten drops falling from his mouth as he lowered his head and turned his glare on her once more.

"Do you see now?" he rumbled. "Do you recognize my uniquely *wet* fire?"

Wyst slowly climbed to her feet. Aware that charred and smoking trees still cracked and fell not too far away, she hacked a little more until she could speak her answer.

"You're... you're the Magma Demon."

Again, that soft, huffing laughter. "Such a dramatic name. Most dragons breathe liquid fire, you know. Mine is simply... well, wetter than most. And that makes me a *demon*?"

"H-how are you alive? You were brought down here hundreds of years ago!"

"Really? Time moves so fast when you're so thoroughly entertained." The dragon sank to his belly, making a great play of shifting and squirming until he'd found optimum comfort. His wings slowly folded and became still. "Come closer, whoever you are."

Seeing no good reason to think the dragon would suddenly melt her when he could have done so already, Wyst took a deep breath and emerged from the trees. She walked slowly across the grass, glancing over her shoulder at the blackened destruction. Small fires still raged, but it seemed to have burnt itself out for the most part, despite an entire forest of burnable material around its fringes.

"Oh, don't worry about the carnage I wrought," the dragon grumbled. "Those trees will sprout anew in a short while. Before long, there will be no trace of burns. Such is my curse."

Wyst paused about halfway. Any closer, and she'd be within reach of his outstretched claws if he decided to make a grab for her.

"Who *are* you?" the dragon rumbled. His mouth remained firmly closed as he boomed in her head, reminding her that he spoke with mindspeak. An eavesdropper would hear exactly half of the conversation.

"I... I am Wyst, from the town of Algaran. In the east," she added helpfully.

"You are unlike any human I've ever seen."

Wyst sighed. She got that a lot. "I'm also unlike any gnome you've ever seen," she said, the much-practiced words flowing from her tongue.

The dragon gave a nod. "You are a half-breed."

"The best of both." She couldn't keep the defiant tone from her voice. A lifetime of prejudice against her dubious origins had bred an impertinence that her mother had been unable to tame.

"Indeed. And how, Wyst the Half-Breed, did you manage to reach this unnatural place that no others have bothered to seek?"

"Others *have* looked. The entrance was destroyed, and its exact location is lost in history thanks to a memory hex. This place was meant as a tomb for one of the most dangerous dragons in Mirstone."

Questions surged in her mind. They jostled for priority, and she hardly knew where to start.

The dragon seemed to be in deep thought. "Yet here you are. How so?"

"Because I'm a half-breed," she said in a sardonic tone. "All my life, people have scoffed at my looks, saying I'm too ugly for a human and too pretty for a gnome, and neither here nor there for anyone but an orc. They call me a mistake-child, or worse. They laugh and jeer at my mother, wondering how any normal human could even *consider* romantic relations with a gnomish man. They claim that no such law exists where a child like me could ever be legitimate, and some even call me an abomination fit only for a swift death to put me out of my misery."

Wyst paused as tears welled up. She swallowed and shook her head. Why in Mirstone was she telling a *dragon* all of this? How pathetic she must appear to such a monster.

When the dragon remained silent, she composed herself and went on. "To answer your question, I have a talent that few can compete with. Some gnomes can move through earth and rock. It's not a skill you learn. It's an ability you have or don't have, like being artistic or musical or athletic. I can move through earth and rock better than anyone I know."

Again, that defiant tone. Sometimes it morphed into conceit.

If the dragon recognized her bragging, he failed to say as much. "Are you suggesting," he said slowly, "that you passed through earth and rock to arrive at this place?"

Wyst nodded. "I am. Nobody else could have attempted it."

She sensed a shift in the air. Perhaps a tingle of restrained excitement from the dragon. He peered at her with those unblinking yellow eyes with not the slightest inkling of kindness, yet she didn't feel unduly threatened—well, except for the casual *"If you run, I will burn you"* it had thrown into the conversation earlier.

The dragon's wings creaked a little as they lifted and unfolded. "Wyst," he boomed, a little softer now, "may I ask you a question?"

Surprised, Wyst nodded. "Of course."

"My question is this." After a pause, the dragon said, "Are you able to extend your ability to those in contact with you?"

\*

"If we're to do this," Wyst said, "then I need to give you a name. I can't just call you Dragon or Magma Demon." She frowned. "Or... do you have a name already?"

The dragon lowered his belly to the ground. "Call me whatever you wish."

After a moment's thought, Wyst shrugged. "Well, how about Mag? It's short and—"

"It will do. Now, let us get this done."

Steeling herself, Wyst climbed on the dragon's back, finding the scaly hide slicker than a tile roof but as solid as a mountain. When she reached the bony spine, the rock-hard protrusions proved useful for handholds. She worked her way forward to the shoulders, then sat, straddling the thick neck.

*What are you doing? Have you lost your mind?*

She ignored her inner voice of wisdom. That inner voice had kept her out of a lot of trouble back in Algaran; her urge to respond to insults with her fists would get her nowhere. But being passive also got her nowhere. That was why she'd come here, to find the Magma Demon—to take a bone or two back to the village and take great delight in the resulting astonishment. "Where did you find these?" they'd cry. "Did you really find the resting place of the legendary dragon?"

Just for once, they'd *see* her.

Now she desired more than simply being recognized as a useful explorer. The fiery streak in her heart told her that Mag was what she needed to prove her worth as a half-breed: not just an explorer but a *dragon-rider*. It was time to make a stand and wipe the scorn from everyone's faces. Nobody would mock her again, at least not to her face.

Just an arm's length away, the manacle around the beast's neck glinted in the curious daylight. It reminded her again of the strangeness of this impossible place. "Why is there light?" she asked again. "Why is there a forest? How is any of this possible?"

The dragon sighed. "It is *not* possible. It is not real but an illusion cast by witches, designed to antagonize me for eternity— my own personal Hell, which ironically is the exact opposite of yours. Where you fear eternal flames, I loathe perpetual serenity. Now, focus!"

They'd discussed this matter at length earlier. In that time, Wyst had found herself relaxing around the deadly Magma Demon. He could have drenched her in liquid fire a hundred times by now, if he so wished. And he still might. But if she refused to help, he would anyway. At least by helping him, she stood a chance.

And if they escaped this place together, her life would be forever changed for the better.

She rejected notions that he was merely using her. Should they escape to the surface, her usefulness would be at an end, and so might her life. But what if they could become friends along the way? What if she could be the first gnome-human to ride a dragon?

"Wyst," the dragon growled, "I am waiting."

She nodded and focused on the giant manacle. Like the chain itself, it remained untarnished by time, her first clue that it was forged from adamantine ore. "I really don't know if this will work," she said. "Traces of iron, copper, and adamantine in rock are common, and I pass through them all the time. But this chain is solid *metal*."

"So is the buckle on your belt, yet you still manage to pass through rock."

"True, but adamantine is one of the hardest metals in Mirstone, worked by skilled dwarves for armor and weapons. It's unbreakable. There's a good reason why they used this metal to imprison you, Mag."

"Regardless of how hard the metal is, it is forged from the *natural ore* found in rock," the dragon insisted. "It contains more minerals than your clothing, yet here you are, deep underground, fully dressed and carrying a lamp and a knife."

"Our winter coats have mineral wool in the lining," Wyst mused, growing puzzled. "And blacksmiths use basalt fibers, which originate from volcanic rock—"

"And these trace amounts, Wyst, appear to be enough to allow your magic to work." The dragon chuckled softly. "I suspect it is no accident you gnomes carry a scattering of minerals at all times. It enhances your magic."

Wyst opened her mouth, then closed it again.

"I put it to you, young Wyst, that your magic is far more powerful and versatile than you give credit. If you can pass through rock and earth carrying all manner of objects, then why not impart your magic to an ornery dragon and allow me to pass through a simple collar?"

Mag seemed to have a persuasive way about him. "I… I suppose you're right."

"Then let us not waste any more time. Say the word, young Wyst, and I will pull free."

She set to work. Being in direct contact with the dragon, she might be able to *impart her magic*, as it were, and grant him the same ability. And, truth be told, she'd managed the same trick with animals before. The first time was at a young age, with a mouse. It had been in her pocket—a fleeting pet—and she'd dropped into the ground to avoid one of many bullies in her town. Too late, she'd remembered her mouse. Luckily, it had survived unscathed, and she'd realized she could extend her talent to organic material as well as inorganic.

It made sense, when she thought about it; after all, she'd carried a wooden sword in those days, as well as a slingshot carved from a stick, both of which were organic material and had traveled with her as she passed through earth and rock.

Of course, the dragon was much bigger.

She slowed her breathing, emptied her mind, focused. The dragon she sat upon would become like her, incorporeal and unhindered. As the familiar tingle of energy surged from her core and spread throughout her body, she willed it to expand and leech into her new companion.

To her horror, something else happened first. She began to sink into the dragon's scaly shoulders. Before she knew it, she was waist-deep in muscle and sinew, her feet kicking as though treading water in a warm bog. Disgusted, she struggled to the surface and climbed out, much as she had after arriving in this strange place.

"What are you doing?" Mag rumbled.

"Nothing!"

She resumed her work, this time willing herself to remain atop the dragon's shoulders—and it was this conscious effort that set her on the right track, for in order to avoid sinking into flesh a second time, her magic infused the dragon so that it was of equal substance to her—and intangible to the real world.

She watched, fascinated, as the sturdy adamantine manacle

began to slide through the dragon's neck. Though slow at first, it picked up speed—then snagged—and finally dropped all the way through. The giant metal collar clattered to the ground along with its chains.

Mag jerked and recoiled as if encountering a snake on the path. He stared and stared, slowly backing away and emitting a low rumble. Wyst sensed the surprise, the *shock*, and the rising elation.

"Young gnome," he said at last, "I cannot thank you enough. You have freed me!"

"Not yet," she answered, trying to suppress her wave of pride. "We have a journey ahead of us—to the surface."

\*

Mag refused to fly straight up through the roof of the cavern, protesting that the gnome's magic may fade at a crucial moment and result in a terrible collision. And to be fair, that was a strong possibility.

So, putting on a show of grumbling, Wyst remained perched on the dragon's shoulders as they headed through the woods toward the nearest cavern wall. This short trek proved to be useful to them both. Passing through trees with ease showed them the magic worked.

The dragon said very little. He seemed intent on his outspread wings, looking from one to the other as the leathery sails ghosted in and out of bushes and tree trunks without hindrance. Nothing stood in their way.

"Loathsome foliage," he growled.

"Why do you hate trees so much?"

"Because I was born inside a volcano. Because I breathe lava. Because wherever I lay down, I turn the vegetation into a comfortable bed of igneous rock. It would seem the people of this world do not appreciate my trail of destruction."

"And they imprisoned you," Wyst muttered. "I'm surprised they didn't slay you."

"Oh, but they tried. And they paid for their efforts."

His ominous words hung in the air.

Wyst told herself that the legend of the Magma Demon was exaggerated, that the dragon hadn't murdered innocents and had instead been poorly treated. It wasn't his fault he dripped lava and ruined the landscape.

But those final words gave her doubt.

"Why are my paws not sinking into the ground?" he said at last.

"They probably are," Wyst admitted. "It's one of the hardest aspects of my magic—being in this phantom state while my feet remain partially solid. Or *your* feet, at the moment. It's like slogging through mud."

"Indeed it is," Mag agreed. "The cavern wall is near. How will we climb to the surface? I assume we must be in an entirely phantom state for the duration?"

"It's more like swimming than climbing." Wyst couldn't help chuckling at the image of a dragon paddling in a lake. *Could* they swim? "It's much easier to descend. Rising to the surface takes effort."

Mag stopped before the solid rock wall and gazed at it. "And I simply… enter?"

"It would be a start."

Wyst was probably as nervous as the dragon. She felt an enormous responsibility. Mag's life was in her hands. If her magic failed halfway up…

And what about when she needed a rest? Finding narrow crevices was fairly easy, but one large enough for a dragon would be a challenge.

"Mag," she said as they continued to stare at the wall, "I should warn you that—"

"Stop." The booming command echoed in her head. "I believe in you, Wyst. And if the worst should happen, well, that would be a blessing compared to an eternity chained to a monolith staring at a picturesque forest."

Making up his mind, Mag heaved a sigh, shook his wings, and marched forward.

Wyst had done this a thousand times, and now was no different. She plunged into the rockface, into a strange darkness that illuminated somewhat as her night vision kicked in. Layers of substrate came into sharp focus, and a feeling of weightlessness settled on her.

The dragon, on the other hand, floundered and gasped.

"Relax," Wyst said. "Everything is normal."

"I cannot see!"

That was interesting. "I can see for the two of us. All you need to do is aim high. Lift your chin, think of being underwater, and strive for the surface."

It was strange not being in control. As a passenger, she could only navigate. However, it meant she didn't have to tire herself out. She could concentrate on remaining intangible and let the dragon do all the physical work.

With a growing sense of confidence, she urged the dragon onward and upward, describing what little she saw ahead, constantly telling her companion that all was well.

*I'm reassuring a nervous, lava-spitting dragon*, she thought. *I never could have predicted this would happen. I came to find ancient bones and instead made a giant new friend.*

"You never explained how you're still living after all this time," she said in an effort to keep the dragon engaged in conversation. "It's been hundreds of years since you were banished. Do all dragons live that long?"

"As I understand it," Mag rumbled, "my body regenerates more than most dragons, perhaps because of the magma in my veins."

Wyst laughed. "I doubt it's in your veins. But I see your point. You're constantly burning up inside, and your body heals nonstop?"

"More than usual, yes."

"What's that monolith? What did you do all this time? What did you eat and drink?"

"You ask a lot of questions, young gnome."

"To which I deserve answers," Wyst griped.

The dragon was silent for a moment, focusing on his ascent. His wings pumped as though he soared in the air, and Wyst said nothing to distract him. Whatever worked. They'd made good progress so far.

"Powerful magic surrounds the monolith," Mag said after a while. "It was here before any of us. I believe the witches harnessed its energy for their illusion. I understand this place is really nothing but darkness and rock. Or... perhaps they exaggerated their skills. Perhaps this place has always been shrouded in illusion. Perhaps the forest is real. Ah, the ponderings of centuries."

The mind-boggling concept of a magical monolith deep under the ground inside a cavern caused Wyst's mind to wander. As a result, her hold on intangibility weakened. Abruptly, the dragon winced and halted—then roared in pain.

The savage noise jolted her back to the task at hand, and she buckled down to restore their ghostlike state. "So sorry!" she gasped. "I was just— Are you all right?"

But Mag seemed shaken. "My tail. It felt like a mountain had shifted on top of me. I was unable to move." After a second or two, he rumbled, "My tail is damaged. It will take time to heal. And it will not heal until I breathe lava."

"Don't do that here!" Wyst exclaimed. But, the moment she said, she wondered if that would really matter. A phantom dragon would breathe phantom fire. It wasn't like it would splash off walls and cascade back on her.

She kept her thoughts to herself for a while, allowing the dragon time to resume its ascent through the gloom. When the wings were beating as before, she ventured another question— cautiously.

"How many did you... kill?"

To her surprise, this caused the dragon some mirth. "As many as necessary."

"What does *that* mean?"

"Wyst, do you suppose I kill indiscriminately? That I fly around vomiting lava on humans and gnomes and dwarves and elves?"

"Well, you *are* a dragon..."

"Indeed. One that will be surfacing into daylight shortly."

He'd changed the subject again. Still, Wyst tried to picture the dragon rising out of the ground and blinking in the glare of the sun. She couldn't imagine it would be easy for anyone to transition from hundreds of years of blackness to sudden daylight.

The image of the dragon emerging above ground sent a flutter of fear through her body. Where would he go first? What would be his objective?

Dark thoughts invaded her mind. Why in Mirstone had she thought a friendship with such a beast was anything more than pure folly? The dragon had been imprisoned for a good reason. Who was she to release this damned creature? What if he immediately went on a rampage, burning every nearby village and town to the ground?

Wyst suppressed a shudder as a terrible feeling swept over her.

*

They were nearing the surface, and Wyst felt like she might burst. Like holding her breath for too long underwater, the need to solidify increased by the second now. Perhaps it was *because* they were near that her resolve was crumbling. She'd steadied her mind the whole way up, paced herself—but now an urgency kicked in.

Mag must have sensed it, though he said nothing. He flew faster, or rather swam—or neither. The most common gnomish word for ghosting through rock was *phasing*, but that was more a state of being and didn't really describe the frantic motions of waving legs and arms about. Or indeed wings.

But perhaps the panic Wyst felt wasn't about losing her grip on intangibility. Perhaps it was the opposite. Worse than embedding a deadly lava-spitting dragon deep in the rock was allowing it to *escape*.

"I must rest!" she yelled suddenly.

Her exclamation caused Mag to skip a beat. His wings froze, and he swung his head sideways, unable to fix his steely glare on her in the darkness. "Are we not close?"

"We are, but... I can't make it!"

Wyst was already looking for a bolthole. They tended to be everywhere; there were far more fissures under the ground than anyone cared to imagine. Still, her frantic search revealed nothing suitable for a dragon.

*Maybe that's a good thing.*

Mag began ascending again. "I will keep going."

"No, I..."

Wyst entertained the idea of simply rolling off the dragon's back. She would tumble free and take her magic with her. The dragon would solidify and be one with the rock, a permanent feature and probably an interesting fossil for future generations.

Even Mag couldn't survive that. Wyst had the power to put an end to her foolish adventure and avoid unleashing a monster on the world.

And yet… how would she sleep at night thereafter?

"If you are doubting our union," Mag said after a moment, "then please be assured that I mean your people no harm."

"I find that hard to believe," Wyst muttered, her face heating up.

"Because I am a monster," the dragon said in a matter-of-fact tone. "The—what did you call me?—ah yes, the *Magma Demon*. I destroy for pleasure, kill without remorse. Is that it?"

"Do you deny it? Why else would you be locked away underground for hundreds of years? Dragons are revered in Mirstone—"

Mag snorted. "Revered? Enslaved, I think you mean. Enslaved or hunted. And a dragon like me, with particularly deadly lava fire that splashes down from the sky, would be a powerful weapon, yes? Failing that, then I would be dead—for it is better for me to be dead than an ally for the wrong side."

Wyst felt a moment of doubt. "Convince me that you've simply been misunderstood all these centuries, cast as a monster for everyone to despise."

"There is little point in trying to convince you, young gnome. You will believe what you will believe, and you certainly should not take my word for it. I could be lying."

If nothing else, the turn in conversation had distracted Wyst from her growing urgency to rest. She felt more relaxed now, at least physically. Besides, they'd be emerging above ground any moment now.

She forged onward, her mind made up. The dragon would see the daylight again.

"We're here," she announced. "Shield your eyes—and fly!"

A second later, they burst out of the rock and earth. The daylight dazzled her for a moment, but she was used to adapting quickly. Meanwhile, she focused on her state of being. Normally, she'd have to solidify the top half of her body so she could haul herself out of the dirt, but this time was different. This time, the dragon's momentum carried them both soaring into the air— though only for a moment. Despite flapping his wings with vigor, a ghostly creature had no way to capture the air and create lift.

*Yet they work underground...?*

Even as Wyst's inner mind wrestled with that logic, she worked to restore the dragon's wings to normal so they could indeed capture the air. The bulk of the body remained a partial phantom for a while longer, so there was very little weight to get off the ground. In a surprisingly short time, Mag was climbing into the sky for real, fully restored and breathless with excitement.

Wyst clung tight, suddenly realizing she hadn't considered this eventuality, at least not fully. Here she was, *riding on a dragon's back*, holding on for dear life, the landscape opening up around her. She was completely at the mercy of the legendary Magma Demon.

She grew cold very quickly. The dragon climbed and climbed, and Wyst's ears popped with the increasing altitude. She wiggled a finger in one, then grabbed tight again as Mag banked hard to the left. To her horror, he started to corkscrew, and she hunkered down and prayed to the gods that her life wouldn't end so pointlessly— slipping off a dragon's back because he'd forgotten she was there.

"Stop!" she gasped.

Mag immediately leveled off and laughed a throaty roar that simultaneously boomed inside her head. "I apologize, my friend. But it feels good to be free. The rush of wind is invigorating. Wyst, you have saved me, and I cannot thank you enough."

Wyst felt a swell of pride. "You can thank me by respecting

my wishes. Do no harm, Mag. Show the people of Mirstone that your reputation is unfounded."

"Ah, but is it?"

The way he said that sent a chill down her spine. "Well, you tell me," she said, gritting her teeth. "Is the legend right or wrong? Are you or are you not a murdering monster that should be slain?"

Instead of answering, Mag began a steady descent, aiming for a valley.

Thoughts spun in her head. What if she made the dragon intangible again? Would that render his lava fire ghostly as well? Or was that expecting too much of her gnomish talent? Regardless, without the rush of air under his wings, he'd sink to the ground like a hapless ghost and continue his descent into doom. While she remained seated on his shoulders, she held a certain degree of power over him. Or at least until he corkscrewed again and threw her off.

To her horror, rooftops appeared on the horizon ahead. Faint wisps of smoke rose from chimneys. She was far from home and didn't recognize the village, but it didn't matter; lives were lives. "Mag," she warned, "what are you doing?"

"I am going to show you what kind of dragon I am," he rumbled.

"Please don't do this," she begged. "If you burn this village—"

"And then what? Finish what you were saying, Wyst. Tell me you'll use your magic to drop me deep into the ground. Ah, but what if I throw you off first?"

*He can read my mind.*

"Mag, please, we can be allies. Friends. We can do so much good in the land."

The rooftops grew closer. In the streets, people began to scream and run. She could well imagine the terrible sight of a dragon swooping in. And while they may not know it yet, stories would spread about the return of the deadly Magma Demon—with a small gnomish-human girl on its back.

"Make a choice, Wyst," the dragon said. "I may or *may not* be the murdering monster you think I was centuries ago, but I certainly could be now, if the people of this world refuse to see me as anything else. So make a choice. Either trust me to pass over this village without releasing hellfire on these people—or use your magic and try to defeat me while you still have a chance. I need you to choose, and quickly."

"But *why*?"

"Because friendships are built on trust. What kind of dragon do you think I was before? Perhaps I razed dozens of settlements and burned thousands of innocent lives. Or perhaps those stories were fabricated. Use your judgment, Wyst. What kind of dragon am I? *Choose*, Wyst."

They were seconds away. Men, women, and children ran for cover—not that it would do much good. Wyst imagined the dragon's jaws opening, the chest and neck flaring orange, careless drips of lava spilling into the air... and the deep inhalation right before the deadly blast.

"Choose, Wyst."

What should she do? Act now and try to kill the Magma Demon? If she failed, she would have succeeded in angering him and perpetuating the myth that he was a murdering monster.

Or do nothing and trust this was merely a test of her faith?

"Choose!" the dragon roared.

Wyst squeezed her eyes shut. "I've chosen."

## THE END

# Dreams of the Lost
## Justin Turpin

Sylen looked over his shoulder as he trudged through low brush. The thatched roofs of the village disappeared behind the thickening copse of trees. If his mother caught him, he'd be in deep trouble. She was too cautious and superstitious to approve of the night's adventure.

"Do you think it's actually haunted?" Tonna asked, following Sylen's gaze back to the village before gesturing deeper into the forest. "I've never actually seen the stream."

"Don't be scared, it's just water. Hurry up," he told the boy.

"That's not what Nadya said. She said if we cross it then evil creatures from the forest will eat me, and then my family."

Sylen groaned and quickened his pace.

"If you are gonna be a coward about this, then go back. I'll just do it myself."

Tonna's eyes went wide. He'd been called a coward too many times. This was his chance to prove the others wrong. Scared as he was, Tonna remembered his grandmother's stories about the pact with Fae, recited so often at bedtime over the years that he could recite them by heart.

> *The Fae's forest, with magic dark and vast,*
> *A pact, upon the stream that must not be passed.*
> *Bad children go wandering, with curious eyes,*
> *Beware the Fae's realm, where danger lies.*
> *You shan't cross the stream, or you'll find your way,*
> *Lost to their world, us all til death to stay.*

He knew the grownups had only said those things to scare him into behaving.

"No, no, I'm with you Sylen. All night, on the other side of the stream. Then you can tell Ryder and his bullies that I'm brave, like a warden."

Sylen rolled his eyes at the younger boy.

"Don't worry, I'll tell Ryder. He'll believe me," Sylen replied.

Soon a soft gurgle filled their ears, broken only by the snapping of twigs underfoot. At each snap, they both froze, listening for other movement in the forest before continuing on. Around a large knobby tree, they stopped at the edge of the bubbling stream. The water looked pure and clean, like a long flowing, solid pane of glass. Strange that something so peaceful would carry so much fear.

A few steps away, the stream narrowed enough for the boys to step across. Sylen hesitated for a moment. If the pact were real, to take that one step across the stream would mean their pact with the Fae would end. The unknown mischievous creatures would be able to cross into the village and wreak havoc on everyone he'd ever known. He steeled himself. It was all fake. No one had ever seen a Fae creature in the woods. It had to be blustering parents trying to keep their children close to home. He wouldn't go back on the dare either, not ever.

"I can't do it," Tonna's soft voice said, his eyes wide at the dark forest beyond the stream.

Sylen turned around and gave Tonna a look that would have skinned a cat.

"Are you really going to back out now?" Sylen kept his gaze fixed on the smaller boy. Tonna was pale and shaking. He tried to meet Sylen's eyes but faltered.

"I'm sorry, Sylen. I just can't!" Tonna said as he turned and ran back towards the village. "I'm sorry!" He yelled as he disappeared into the woods.

"Coward!" Sylen yelled after him. "Everyone will know!"

Tonna's crunching footsteps in the underbrush of the woods faded until the only sounds that remained were the bubbling stream and Sylen's breathing.

Doubt began filling Sylen as loneliness settled over him. He could always blame Tonna for going back, say that he cried and begged for them to go back. But would the other boys believe it? Would Ryder see it that way? Of course not. He was already on the outside of that circle, and this was supposed to prove he was tough enough to get in.

He'd do it.

"I'm no coward," he whispered to himself. Hearing the words out loud steeled his resolve and he turned back to the stream and stepped across.

As he believed, nothing happened. He took a few more steps on the other side. The grass felt the same, and the trees looked no different. Nothing popped out of the woods to eat him. It was all made up, he told himself.

He sat down. There was no reason why he'd need to go deeper. He'd just need to spend the rest of the night here and the dare would be complete. He watched the stream gently bubble past as his eyelids grew heavy. He yawned and laid back, listening to the lullaby of the gentle rustling of leaves and closed his eyes.

On the edge of consciousness, he heard soft footsteps on the ground. He pushed through his sleepiness to open his eyes, just for a moment, to investigate the sound. Standing above him was a short, plump creature with large yellow eyes that stared at him blankly. It had an oversized head attached to a thick torso with small, yet muscular arms and legs. Its skin was deep navy blue and thick straight black hairs protruded an inch or so out the top of its head that could have been porcupine needles. It cocked its head to the side, letting a long, split tongue slide out of its mouth to lick its lips. A wide smile revealed sharply pointed yellow teeth.

Sylen screamed.

*

The sun shone through the front window of the narthex and cast long shadows across the tables and chairs, turning the furniture into monsters and demons.

Memories had strange powers. They invaded the mundane and laid siege to the otherwise peaceful afternoon. Was he right to continue on after all these years, fulfilling the directive of the Empress even though he knew his best days were far behind him? To give up his role would be to give up his bond with Solarien. The thought formed a lump in his throat. She'd been his companion for decades and was like family.

"Your tea, Sir," Benedict stated dryly, interrupting his thoughts. The servant laid down his copper tray and placed a small teacup on the low wooden table.

"Jasmine?" Clive asked, reaching out for the half-filled cup. He was grateful for Benedict's attention to detail, as he grasped the cup's handle while he tried to ignore the tremors.

"Yessir," he responded. "Purchased this morning from a peddler traveling from the coast."

"Thank you, Benedict. Do we have many petitioners this morning?" Clive sipped on the hot tea, burning his tongue slightly, but embracing the warmth it spread down his body as it made its way into his belly. He closed his eyes and savored the sensation.

"Just a few rural villagers," he said as he placed a napkin– neatly folded–where the tea cup had been. "Would you like me to send them in?"

"Please do," Clive responded, placing the cup of tea down on the napkin.

Benedict walked the length of the room and opened the two large doors that served as the main entrance to the compound.

Sturdy yet ornate, the doors had been crafted with care and attention. The wardens' motto was carved across the top in the ancient dialect of their people: *Peace of the Empress.*

Two middle-aged men, one balding and wearing a long dirty blue cloak, and the other in a green shirt and orange pants in similar condition entered the narthex.

"Warden Clive Sionodell, let me introduce Farmer Varda Clemens and Cobbler Donan Harten of the village of Dali, in the northernmost reaches of the Eastern Ward. They wish to petition the appointed hand of the Empress."

Clive sighed at the formal introduction. No matter how many times he had tried to get Benedict to work less stiffly, the man had refused to budge.

Clive gestured to the seats across from him. "Please have a seat. You must be weary after traveling such a long distance. How long did it take you to get here? Two weeks?"

"It took us 15 days, your lordship. We have the most urgent matter to discuss with you."

"Please tell me why you have traveled such a distance," Clive asked.

"Our children, sir!" Donan yelped, already holding back tears. "They've disappeared! We've searched and searched and can find no sign of them."

Clive sat back into his chair, crossed his legs, and placed both of his hands across his lap.

"How many children are missing, exactly?"

"Ten," Varda replied in his gruff, gravelly voice.

"How long have they been missing?"

"The first disappeared a week before we left," Donan chimed in quickly. "Once it started, a new child or two would go missing almost every day. At first, we thought it was just a case of youthful antics. It's common for children to get lost in the woods from time to time… lost to wild animals or teenage hazing."

"But never this many," Varda cut in. "They seem to always go missing in the middle of the night, their parents having put them to sleep only to find their bed empty in the morning."

Clive went through multiple scenarios in his head as the men talked. Former similar petitions had ended several ways. An angry relative, a sadistic killer, a hungry monster, and many more flashed through his mind.

"What have you done to prevent these kidnappings?" Clive asked, trying to piece together the details.

"We've increased the town watch in addition to parents and guardians locking their doors and windows. Nothing seems to work," Donan replied.

"Have you ever seen any signs of a struggle? Any evidence of disturbance?" Clive asked.

"No. They are there one moment, then gone another."

"One by one we are losing the next generation," Varda said. He leaned forward. "You serve the Empress and have solved many terrible cases in the past. Will you please find our children? We beg you, Warden. Please."

Clive stood and walked over to one of the windows overlooking the busy street. It had been more than a year since he had been required to go more than an hour outside of the city. He could send a few marshals, and perhaps the wizard.

*You need to go on this one,* Solarien sent through their bond. The dragon pressed on his mind, sending emotions of love and encouragement. *It will be good for you, don't just delegate. You need to be out in the field.*

*I know that's how you feel. But I'm getting old. My hands shake, and my vision sometimes blurs. You and I both know I'd be a liability.*

He heard the dragon roar in the sky above the city. The two

men behind Clive shifted in their seats.

*Clive, Warden of the East, defender of Cheshaven, a liability? A dragon rider a liability? You discount yourself and your abilities greatly. Besides, you'll have me.*

Clive bowed his head. *I need to retire, to pass your bond to someone younger. I just don't know who to trust.* He could feel her try to mask the sadness she felt.

*Then bring your candidates with you and use this last quest as a proving ground for discerning which would make the best Warden,* Solarien replied.

It was a good plan, he knew, but he felt at odds with himself. A part of him didn't want to give up the bond, or the mantle of Wardenship. He enjoyed being the arbiter of the Empress's law, and he couldn't imagine life without his connection to Solarien. How could he pass her on to someone else? She was a part of him and had been for decades. They'd been through war, grief, joy, and loss together. He loved her in a way no one else could really understand.

*Ok, I'll bring them. But I'm going to need you to keep an eye on me,* he insisted.

*I always do,* she replied enthusiastically.

He turned back toward the villagers who sat perplexed, watching him. Varda sat stone-faced, bracing for whatever decision Clive had come to, while Donan sat fidgeting, anxiety strewn across his face.

"I'll come. I'll bring a crew and we'll figure out what is going on. You have my word," Clive said.

Donan looked like he melted in relief. He sunk back into his chair and smiled broadly before thanking Clive over and over.

Varda nodded and asked, "How soon until we leave? Every day of delay costs us dearly."

"We'll leave in the morning. If you need accommodations,

please speak with Benedict." Clive bowed his head to the men. Both bowed back deeply and approached Benedict who was standing stoically at the side of the room.

There were many preparations that would need to take place if they were to meet in the morning.

Clive left the narthex and headed back to his workshop. Abaro sat at the middle of a long, thick wooden table which had been filled to each edge with a collection of books, loose papers, strange artifacts and gadgets. The wizard was wearing strange goggles under the wide brim of his blue hat that made his eyes look magnified as he looked up at Clive.

"Good to see you this morning, boss man," Abaro said. "Interested in seeing my new self-sealing envelopes, or translation tonic?"

"I've got a new assignment for us. Field work."

"You sure you don't want to hear about these?" Abaro held an envelope and a small vial of green liquid in his hands.

Clive relented to the man. He knew the wizard wouldn't let it drop until he did.

"Just the translation tonic? How does that work?" Clive asked begrudgingly.

"Same as the spell, with one advantage… and one drawback." The man stood and lifted the small potion into the air between them. "With this, you won't need a Wizard to speak and hear different languages. I'm sure it'd be very handy for the traveling diplomat. However, while active, you forget your mother tongue so perhaps a bit more situational than I intended."

Clive couldn't help but crack a smile and said, "That might have been useful during that flood in Cabybog,"

"For sure. It's still a work-in-progress," Abaro chuckled. "So, what's this field work?"

"We'll be traveling to the far North on the border of the ward.

A string of kidnappings has been committed in the village of Dali. What can you tell me about the place?"

Abaro held out a finger and pulled the goggles down around his neck before scurrying over to one of the many bookshelves that lined the walls of the room. He pulled a large tome from the middle of the bottom shelf and thudded it down on the table. He flipped through the pages quickly before stopping on a page with the tip of his index finger.

"The Faeon forest, a dangerous wood. Dali is the only village to endure in the region. It's historically been a hotbed of Fae activity. The aether—or in layman's terms, magic—is strong there. A millennia ago, the Fae Queen ruled the forest. Back then, this whole ward down to the ocean was part of the wood. She was eventually overthrown by her sons who split her domain before our Empire tamed the land. Strange artifacts have been recovered from the region. The scouting guild recommends caution when traveling to the region and encourages travelers to stick to main roads."

Clive crossed his arms. "I'm going to need your expertise on hand for this one. Departure in the morning," he ordered.

Abaro nodded his head, "At your pleasure, Warden."

"Do you know where Weir and Bix are?" Clive asked.

"Maxen told me they were hogging the sparing field. Might check there first. I'll get my things together for the trip."

Clive left the workshop behind and turned down the hall, passing a handful of servants and a few Marshals going about their daily chores. Each of them saluted him with a crooked finger to the forehead.

Outside the rear of the Warden's complex, Clive found the two Marshals sparring in front of a small cheering crowd of initiates. He folded his arms and stood a few paces back, watching as the two swung their blades in flashy arches. He could see they were both grinning broadly.

Bix pulled both arms back in an obvious prelude to a thrust and gave a loud grunt as she lunged at Weir dramatically. With a spin, Weir deflected the blow and continued his turning into a low swipe at Bix's feet which she adeptly leaped over. The initiates gasped and cheered in delight at the display. To their eyes, the duel was an impressive display of skill. To Clive, it was infuriating.

"Enough!" Clive yelled, surprising the initiates who hadn't seen him join them. A few of them involuntarily stood at attention, heels clicking together as their hands went to salute. Bix and Weir let their swords drop down to their sides as they turned in their clanking practice armor to face the Warden. A look of horror shot across Weir's face, while Bix locked her jaw and held her chin high.

"That sort of display would get you both killed in actual combat. Stop wasting your time and stop leading these young ones astray with such theatrics. Initiates, back to your chores, now!"

The group dispersed, leaving Bix and Weir alone in the yard with Clive.

"And you wonder why I hesitate to leave you in charge," Clive said sternly. "Don't you understand you are setting an example? Some of those initiates lack the judgment to discern those kinds of movements are impractical and dangerous to use in real combat. Leadership means putting others' needs ahead of your own, and preparing those you are responsible for with what is to come."

Weir sheathed his sword and bowed.

"My apologies, Warden. It won't happen again. You have my word," he said gingerly.

Bix followed suit, joining Weir in his bow and adding, "We've missed the mark. Tell us our penance and we'll gladly pay it."

Weir flinched at the mention of a penance.

"Your word will suffice for now," Clive sighed. He knew he'd come down perhaps a bit too harshly. In his younger days he had shown off for attention, too. The constant discipline and regimen of life under a Warden could suffocate, he knew, and having fun was one of those ways they'd adapted. The voice of his teacher, the warden before him, was hard to ignore, though. Tough and unyielding, the former Warden, Balthasar, had exacted strict adherence with liberal penance.

*You don't want to be like him, so don't be like him,* Solairen said across the bond. Clive could feel her approaching the compound. She was coming in to rest.

*Balthasar was a good man, and you served with him. One of the best Wardens in the history of the Empire,* Clive responded. He could hear the flaps of her wings as she slowed her approach to the yard.

Bix and Weir moved back toward the outer wall of the complex as the large red dragon landed in the grass more gently than a creature that size should be able to. Clive walked forward as Solarien lowered her large head down to him. He reached out and scratched the side of her head, right where he knew she liked it.

*He may have been impressive, but he didn't have your heart. And to me, that is equally impressive.*

Bix and Weir circled around to the front of Solarien and saluted before turning to the compound. Clive stopped them mid-step.

"I need you both to pack. We're leaving tomorrow morning at dawn. Equipment for a standard excursion, enough for a few days," he instructed, suppressing a grin as the two spun to attention facing him, both with wide smiles on their faces. Oh yes, he remembered those early days and the eagerness to be chosen by a Warden for deployment. It was the action they craved. It was the action he had learned to fear.

The rest of the day ended uneventfully, besides a brief argument between Bix and Weir about who would be taking second-in-command. Clive ended the argument by informing them that neither would be second, and that Abaro would assume command if anything were to happen.

When the next morning broke over the city, a group of initiates were preparing the basket for Solarien. It was a long wooden container, sized to hold up to six adults sitting side by side on low benches. A sturdy iron bar, wrapped in thick sheets of bound leather, was affixed to two opposing sides of the basket and rose above the center of the construction for Solarien to hold onto. Clive had ridden in it himself back in the day, always a little frightening at first but a very efficient way to travel. He was glad that he now rode in the saddle.

Solarien was already being tended to in the large shelter house at the other end of the yard. The large entrance, thirty paces high and forty across, revealed the red dragon lying down and patiently being strapped with the leather saddle. She nodded to him as he approached.

*Ready for the long trip?* Clive asked over their bond as he inspected the work of the grooms. The leather saddle sat properly on her back, and three long dragon spears were clipped in their proper place within reach of the rider. He ran one of his fingers across the shaft, remembering back to the last time he had needed one of the weapons. Their long mithril tips, freshly polished, shone in the morning light.

*Of course,* she replied, bringing one of her eyes up to him. *I'm confident we'll solve this for them.*

Clive rubbed his sore shoulder, tight even after all these years from an old injury.

*You're going to be fine, Clive. We're not going to war, we're going to find some missing children.* Solarien brushed the top of her large head gently across his chest. Even now, after all the years together, he was in awe at the amount of control and grace the large creature held.

*I think this will be my last one, Solarien. I'm afraid I'll be a liability.* Clive placed a hand on top of her head.

*None of that now,* Solarien said. *The Marshals and I are too reliant on you for you to be worrying about being a liability.* She said the last part with a snort for emphasis.

A part of him appreciated her confidence in him, but the seed of doubt within him was too powerful to be snuffed out.

*At least keep an eye on me, would you?* Clive asked, trying to avoid a prolonged argument.

*Always,* she responded, letting the topic pass.

A short time later Bix, Weir, Abaro, and the two villagers Varda and Donan arrived. The three marshals climbed into the large basket without hesitation, each checking that the others' packs were sufficiently secure. Varda and Donan on the other hand stared bleakly, Donan's face going white as he looked from the basket to Solarien, then back to the basket.

"You mean for us to ride in that thing?" he asked, pointing.

Solarien plodded out of her shelter, each step sending small tremors through the ground.

"Do you doubt her strength to carry us?" Clive asked while Solarien stretched her wings wide, covering almost the entirety of the yard in shade. Donan watched in fearful awe as he lost balance and fell onto his back.

One of the Marshals snickered while Varda helped his companion up.

"Come now, you don't truly think the Warden would put his own Marshals in harm's way?" Varda asked, pulling the man up to his feet. He didn't let go as he half-dragged the man into the basket. "Just think about how much faster we'll get home than if we were on foot."

"How much faster will it be?" Donan asked wearily.

"We should be there by late afternoon," Abaro responded.

Donan nodded slowly and sat down on the bench, closing the basket's side door behind him.

With the passengers ready to go, Solarien bent down to where Clive could climb into the saddle and he mounted. With a bounding leap, Solarien lifted into the sky, throwing up dust and dirt across the compound's yard. Varda and Donan, who had been sitting wide-eyed in the basket, began to cough and rub their eyes. Solarien beat her wings and disappeared, flying out of view.

"Did they forget us?" Donan asked, almost relieved.

"You should probably hold onto something," Abaro replied.

Donan yelped as Clive and Solarien appeared behind them, large talons grabbing the basket by the top supporting bar. The quick acceleration knocked both villagers off their low benches and onto the wicker floor beneath. The Marshals held tight to the edges of their bench until Solarien ended her ascent and began a gentle glide. Bix reached down and helped both of the villagers up.

"Sorry," she said, brushing off Varda's coat. "We probably should have given you more of a heads up."

Varda grumbled something under his breath as Donan stared out over the side of the chest high basket, taking in the passing city. A look of awe morphed into fear, then sickness flashed across his face before he spilled the contents of his stomach over the side.

The city gave way to farms, which gave way to rolling hills before the first trees of the great forest were seen. They traveled quickly, the air current working with their course.

Clive kept a close watch on the horizon. Having lived so long and explored every bit of the ward for food, Solarien wouldn't need any help finding the village. Clive busied himself by scanning the skies and terrain. It had been a few months since he'd ridden Solarien so far from the compound and the joy of it hit him anew. He felt young again, too stimulated to worry about the pestering aches and pains of age. The wind rushed against his leather armor, finding small creases and gaps to send cold air across his body. It was one of those sensations draped in nostalgia for him, and he fully embraced its thrill and beauty.

As the sun started to set in the west, casting purple and orange hues over the seemingly unending canopy of trees, a set of small lights and plumes of lazy smoke signaled their final destination. Solarien descended, making a wide circle around the village. The forest here had been cleared enough to fit thirty or so thatch-roofed buildings, small fields filled with vegetables, and small pens for chickens and goats. It was a picture of a quaint rural village.

Solarien descended slowly, whipping up a small cloud of dust. The dragon waited until the basket was a few feet above the ground before dropping it to the side of the lone dirt road that led into the town, then landed a short distance behind. As Clive climbed out of the saddle, he scanned the village. A collection of wide eyes watched from the corners of buildings and small gaps in the window shutters. A few of the older villagers were coming their way, recognizing Varda and Donan climbing out of what must seem like a giant's knitting basket.

One man with white hair thinning on top and adorned with a long green embroidered tunic stepped up to meet Clive, wary eyes watching Solarien. Around his neck, a large necklace of shiny silver discs marked him as a higher status than the rest of the people wandering over to gawk at the dragon.

"The village of Dali welcomes you, Warden, and your company. I'm Harvor Mallen, mayor here. Would you all care to join me for some refreshment? I'll have lodging prepared for you."

"I'd like to speak to the families that have lost their children," Clive said, removing his helmet and gloves.

"I will arrange for a community meeting first thing in the morning…" Harvor began.

"No, I want to meet with them now," Clive interrupted. "If the children are disappearing at night—and night is fast approaching—I want to get as much information as I can before then."

Harvor's face flushed at the quick denial.

"It will take some time. You see, some of the children's parents have already begun their preparations for the night," he explained, straightening his necklace.

"Be quick about it then. The longer you take, the more at risk the children will be," Clive said as he removed his gloves.

"It will be as you say, Warden," Harvor muttered through his clenched jaw, offering a quick bow. He returned to the gathering crowd of villagers and began barking orders as a few villagers stepped forward and others ran off.

"Marshals, with me!" Clive commanded.

The three marshals approached and huddled together, intently listening to the Warden's direction.

"Abaro, Solarien, and I will interview the parents. I would like you two," he gestured to Bix and Weir, "to fan out and look for disturbances or any evidence left by the kidnapper."

"Would you like me to use compulsion on them?" Abaro asked. "Or I could have them sample one of my truth serums." He grinned as he opened the flap on the leather satchel at his side. Inside, over a dozen diffcrent bottles and tinctures clanked against each other.

"I'm sure that won't be necessary," Clive responded. "Let's try just speaking with them and see how far that gets us."

Bix and Weir nodded to each other before saluting, then marched off in opposing directions.

Abaro laid out a blanket in front of a resting Solarien as a group of timid villagers approached. A few paces away, the group bowed in reverence, and one of them even approached and laid a flower where the dragon had laid her head. Never one for formalities, Solarien yawned, her teeth bared as her maw opened to its full capacity, causing the gift giver to let out a short squeak before recovering.

Clive and Abaro sat down on the wool blanket cross-legged and gestured for the group to come closer.

"One set of guardians at a time, please," Clive said as he waved to the first pair.

The large man sat down with a thump, while his wife hesitated, watching Solarien warily.

"Now tell me, what do you remember about the night your child disappeared?" Clive asked, eyeing the pair.

The wife sat down next to her husband and began.

"Warden, it was three days ago when our little Bari was taken from us," she began, tears welling up in her eyes. Her husband reached over and placed a hand on her back, and she continued. "With all the disappearances these past few weeks, we'd been keeping him with us all day, everywhere we went."

"Had him in the field next to me all day," the husband added.

"After dinner, we put him to bed and checked all the windows and doors. We made sure that no one could get in, and we even took shifts standing guard in his room." She motioned for her husband to continue as she pulled out a handkerchief and wiped her eyes.

"It was around midnight when it happened, I remember looking at him and thought I heard a sound outside. So I stood and faced the door, ready for whatever might come. Then I glanced back to the bed and Bari was gone. No cry, no nothing, just gone." The man's face went red, and he locked his jaw for a moment before continuing. "I'm telling you it has to be the Fae," he said, ending with a growl. "I'm telling you, they're the only ones who could do this."

At the mention of the Fae, Solarien exhaled audibly and shifted slightly, now more interested in the conversation.

"Have you been having trouble with the Fae?" Clive asked, making a quick glance at Abaro. The wizard had pulled out a notebook and was scribbling notes as the couple spoke.

"No," the wife replied, shifting slightly away from her husband as he crossed his arms. "Everyone in this village blames the Fae for anything from a broken dish to the death of a family member."

"Do I detect a slight accent? Mogavian?" Clive asked.

The wife nodded, and gently reached out to grasp her husband's hand. They leaned back toward each other.

"She doesn't believe it, but this forest was once ruled by the Fae, and if it wasn't for the pact our ancestors made with them, we'd have been chased off a hundred times by now," the husband insisted.

*The Fae would be a dangerous foe. And few other magical creatures would be so subtle,* Solarien reminded Clive.

A similar story was repeated as they interviewed family after family. Clive had seen many different disappearances, and typically with children it was more familial in nature. Or in the more rural areas, one or two children might get lost, or killed by creatures. He'd never had a case with so many missing, and never one with such little evidence. They spoke of a small sound heard outside or a scratch on a wall as the only warning.

As the sun fell below the horizon, Bix and Weir returned, frustrated and empty-handed.

"There was nothing. We checked all the ways an intruder could make it into those homes and nothing adds up," Weir said. "We didn't find anything to suggest the perpetrator was able to get into the homes. I'd expect some sort of broken window, scratched up lock, something."

"I'm detecting some strange anomalies in the aether," Abaro said, rummaging through his bag of potions. He grabbed one and downed it quickly in one gulp. Closing his eyes, he lifted his head into the air, sniffing loudly several times. "That's better... it's faint, so very faint I didn't detect it at first, but now I'm sure. There has been a spell cast in this village in the last day or so. I can detect a residue."

"A residue? What do you mean?" Bix asked, eyebrows raised.

"Imagine you cook up an omelet," Abaro began, opening one of his eyes and peering down at the shorter of the two Marshals. "Now I mean a tasty, delicious omelet filled with mushrooms, bacon, cheese, the works."

"That hardly seems relevant," Weir chimed in.

"When you're done cooking, do you put the pan back in the cupboard? No, you put it in the sink. There's residue on the pan. It's like that. Except different, but essentially the same," Abaro explained.

Weir scoffed.

"I want us doubled up on shifts while we patrol the town tonight. No one should make their way in or out of town unnoticed," Clive said, picking up his bedroll.

"With all due respect, sir," Bix interjected. "I think we should move all the children into a single location, to make it easier to keep an eye on them."

"The only place large enough would be the mayor's home," Weir responded, eyeing Bix, Abaro, and Clive in turn. "I'd hate to be the one to have to tell him."

"Go tell him," Clive ordered with a grin.

Weir's face contorted before frowning.

"I set myself up for that one, didn't I?" Weir asked.

"Yes, my friend, you did," Bix replied, patting him on the shoulder.

The mayor reluctantly agreed and word spread quickly around the village. More than twenty children joined together in the mayor's great room, huddled together in small groups and speaking in hushed tones. Their parents and guardians continually shushed them. It was a tight fit, and they would have to sleep close together, touching one another on both sides, but Clive agreed that Bix was right. It was a smart idea. Unfortunately, the home was not big enough for all of the parents to tag along, and many decided they'd camp around the home, encircling it in parental protection. They gave Solarien a wide berth, the as the dragon took up the space between the mayor's home and the forest. Tired from the long journey, her deep snoring announced her slumber.

"We should take turns patrolling tonight, see if we can catch any potential kidnappers in the act. Weir and Abaro, you take the first shift. Bix, you and I will take the second. Four-hour shifts, and keep your wits about you."

"Yes, Warden," Abaro and Weir both responded in unison. Weir saluted and Abaro nodded before they marched off.

"This home has two doors. I want you at the front, and I'll take the side. Get what rest you can, but be ready," Clive said, rubbing his shoulder. He could tell night was settling in from the ache in his joints.

"Ugh, I guess that means I should probably sleep in my armor," Bix said with a sigh as she hefted her bedroll over her shoulder and marched off to the front door.

Clive made his way to the side of the home and laid next to some decorative bushes lined up beside to the home's side entrance. Laying on the ground, he could feel a hundred small injuries from his years of service protest his every move. Sleep would be fitful tonight, if he got any.

Clive habitually checked on Solarien through the bond as he drifted. He could feel her exhaustion. Carrying five people in full gear for that long was taxing. In response to his probing, she released a wave of emotions instead of formed words; relief and exhaustion mixed with a confidence about their task. It was one of the special ways they were able to communicate over the bond. It had startled him when he'd first become the warden. In the beginning, when Solarien had first sent a surge of emotion through the bond, Clive had been overwhelmed, unable to distinguish between his own emotions and hers. In those days, he had asked her to refrain from communicating that way, but now, after years of service together, he was able to easily distinguish her emotions from his and appreciated the intimacy it brought them. The intimate connection with Solarien lulled him into sleep.

He was running through the dense forest, no longer an old man but instead a young child, and he was being followed. Broken twigs warned of something approaching. Above, the canopy of trees blocked all but a faint light from a waxing purple moon. The leaves rustled in the darkness that seemed to loom and cackle as he tried to escape.

He tripped, his foot catching on emerged roots and he tumbled forward. Pain erupted along his arms as he caught himself. Face down, he frantically pulled at his foot, but the root of the tree had seemingly wrapped itself around his ankle and was refusing to let go. He rolled back and forth to rip the tree root free. It cracked and creaked, loosening its grip on his leg. The canopy above lowered and melded into a damp and dreary cave, and the tree root disappeared.

The oppressive force of claustrophobia pressed in on him until a single, waning candle appeared in his hand. He stood up and listened. The slow drip of water echoed from somewhere in the cave. He tried to discern its direction as something large swished across the cave, stealing his attention. At the edge of his light, a form materialized. It was the face of a decrepit old man, with oozing lesions leaving stripes of blood across his gaping face.

*Clive...*

From behind, thick cords wrapped themselves around his legs. The cords climbed up his body and pinned his arms, causing him to drop the candle which flickered and waned on its side. He fought desperately, but was only a boy and not strong enough to break the bonds that held him. The face changed as it approached, shifting between different people he had known throughout his life.

*Clive, I need you...*

His mother. His brother. Then a thousand other faces he had met over his decades of service before settling on the face he knew best of all. His own.

*Now, Clive!*

The maw opened wider than seemed possible. He could feel its hot breath as it approached. He screamed, pulling against the cords, unwilling to give in to despair. His scream turned into the familiar roar of his companion as Solarien surged into his consciousness.

*Wake up, Clive!*

He sat up in a sweat, his breath coming in heaves. A feeling of relief slid across his body as he stared at his veiny wrinkled old hands. He had never been so grateful for the sight.

*I need you out here now, cut me out of this!*

The desperation in Solarien's voice moved him to action and he hurried around the building, sword unsheathed and ready in his hand. A chorus of shouts all around him was not enough to disrupt his well-practiced focus. He found Solarien pinned to the ground and wrapped in a thick web of green vines.

*How did this happen to you?* Clive shouted between thwacks with his sword.

*Very quickly,* Solarien snapped back through the bond. She snorted hot steam out of her nostrils. *I'd take care of it myself but I didn't want to catch the village on fire. We're under attack, look to the north.*

Far to his left, illuminated by the faint moonlight, towering wooden moss-covered creatures marched forward in an unruly group. Clive hacked faster, each severed vine giving Solarien more and more leeway under her bindings. Panting with one last heavy cut, the mighty red dragon was able to stand, finally able to utilize her large leg muscles. She ripped through the rest of the vines, pulling them up out of the ground and showering Clive and the mayor's home in clods of dirt. Clive covered his face against the rain of earth and the dragon leapt into the sky with a roar that shook the air around him.

*See if you can take care of any of those creatures as they first appear out of the forest,* Clive commanded through the bond. *Let the marshals and me handle those that have made it to the village proper.* He felt the pulse of a confirmation; a telepathic head nod in response.

Clive took stock of the battlefield as he jogged to join the fighting. Each of the creatures stood a good foot or more than he and possessed anywhere between four and eight thick, sinewy appendages that they wielded like clubs. Groups of villagers huddled together between houses, stabbing with spears and swinging axes at any creature that tried to enter the village proper. Farther into the fields, Bix and Weir wielded flaming swords that danced across a dozen creatures approaching in the open. Floating above, sitting cross-legged in the air twenty or so paces high, Abaro hurled bolts of lightning that blew off large chunks of the creatures.

"Abaro!" Clive yelled as he ran to join Bix and Weir. He held his sword above him as he approached his first adversary. Right before he struck, his sword erupted in a magical fire summoned by the floating wizard. The strike bit deep into the cord-like bindings holding one of the creature's appendages in place. As the tree-creature's arm caught fire and went limp, it took its other arm and swiped at him. Clive ducked under the strike and lunged forward, slicing the thing across its hip joint. It toppled over and writhed on the ground as the flames consumed it.

Clive turned just in time to see the night light up around him. Solarien spewed fire across the treeline in a tight cone. A handful of the tree-creatures exploded into a shower of flames as Solarien's fire ravaged them. A few others stopped at the forest's edge and hesitated as the fire began to spread through the farmers' crops. After a few moments, the remaining nearby creatures turned and ran back into the forest. There were some caught between the fire and the village, but they were quickly dispatched by the marshals, the final one falling to the sound of villagers whooping.

Abaro floated to the ground as their group huddled together.

"Should we go after them, sir?" Weir asked between breaths. Muck and blood were streaked across his face.

"No, our priority is the villagers. We can't leave them unprotected," Clive responded. "I suspect our presence was the catalyst for this tonight. Are you all alright?"

"Just a graze," Weir said, pointing to a cut on his temple. "You know how it is with head wounds."

Bix checked herself over, the adrenaline from the battle fading. None of them were seriously hurt.

"Floating? That's a new one, eh, Abaro?" Bix asked.

"I thought you could only do one spell at a time? How'd you float and hurl lightning bolts?" Weir followed up.

Abaro hopped off a small wooden plank he had been sitting on that now floated on its own next to him.

"Nothing particularly ingenious. Just an enchanted piece of timber I brought with me thinking it might come in handy." He grinned widely and tapped the side of his head, mocking thoughtfulness. "And I can do more than one spell at a time, it just depends on the level of concentration required. Don't you remember the swords?"

Bix and Weir both laughed as their sword fires vanished when Abaro snapped his fingers. Clive frowned and pointed to the fire that was spreading.

"Can your magical abilities do something about that?" Clive asked, cutting through the group's jovial post-battle bravado. The wizard picked up the front of his robes and began running toward the fire. "While Abaro saves what crops he can, you two check on the villagers. I'm afraid it's going to be a long night."

Clive inspected his blade as his orders were carried out, somehow cool to the touch even though it was hot just a few minutes ago. Abaro's talents had always amazed him, and he counted himself lucky that a wizard of his talent was interested in being a Marshal at all. Most wizards, especially of his caliber, went on to research at one of the great libraries or to serve one of the noble bloodlines, or even in the Imperial palace itself. He sheathed his sword and called to Solarien through the bond. A few moments later, he felt the whoosh of her wings as she drifted down gracefully next to him, landing softly despite her large size.

*There is more to this than a simple kidnapping,* Solarien said, bringing her head down to meet his. He reached out and scratched her, and she rumbled a soft pulse in thanks.

*Those were Green Men, weren't they?* Clive asked through the bond. *The animated guardians of the forest. Something must have summoned them here, only a great threat or a great power can do that. This village has been here for generations, so I can't imagine it's suddenly a threat to the forest's ecosystem.*

*Then a great power summoned them,* Solarien responded.

*The same power that is behind the disappearances.* Clive watched as Abaro worked his spell, creating a low cloud that dropped rained and slowly drowned the fire. Clive turned back toward the village and began walking.

*Did you experience that nightmare I was having?* Clive asked, sending Solarien the memory and sharing the terror he felt.

*You were having a nightmare? I just thought you were exceptionally tired,* Solarien responded. *Strange, I can always sense your feelings as you sleep. It is a constant connection, yet I felt nothing. I assumed you were sleeping peacefully.*

*What could mask our bond?* Clive asked before being interrupted by the wide-eyed mayor.

"What were those things, Warden? Thank the Empress that you were here to stop them." He clutched his robes close to his body. The danger had passed, and the early morning's chill pressed into their bodies.

"Green Men, guardians of the forest. Summoned by someone," the warden replied. He folded his arms across his chest as he looked past the man toward the rest of the villagers who had congregated into a throng and spoke in hushed tones. "My apologies for the lost crops. I'm afraid it was the only way to stem the creatures' advance, but luckily it ended up driving them back."

The mayor frowned, then closed his eyes and let out a heavy sigh.

"Without your intervention, none of us would have survived. Our people are tough. It is a grave loss, but not all the crops were destroyed and we are a hardy people. The forest has always provided. Even during the leanest times, we've been able to rely on its abundance."

A shuffling boy, being pushed forward by his mother, approached cautiously from behind the mayor.

"Go on, show the warden what you found," the woman said, encouraging the young boy. He averted his gaze but pulled out a strange crystalline disc from a small satchel hanging from his shoulder.

"I found it on the ground next to the mayor's home…" he said timidly, holding out the disc to Clive. "I was hiding and another little boy dropped it as he ran off into the forest."

Clive inspected the disc. While solid, its surface was fractured. The cracks formed an intricate spiral pattern. Its coloration moved from a pearl white across the outside and faded into a milky emerald toward the center.

"Do you know who it was that ran into the forest?" Clive asked, his knees popping in protest as he crouched down.

The small boy looked to his mom for support, who gave him a serious glare in return.

"No... I couldn't tell who it was," he said, fidgeting.

Clive put a hand on the boy's shoulder reassuringly.

"Any details you can share could be important in unraveling this mystery. Is there anything else you want to tell me?"

The boy gave his mother a side glance before speaking out in a quick avalanche.

"I couldn't tell who it was because the face was moving and melting. It kept shifting, and sometimes for a moment it looked like ma, then Georgie, then grandpa, but never stayed as one face. I've never seen anything like it!"

The mother smacked the back of the boy's head with a wide frown.

"Now don't you go wasting the Warden's time with that nonsense. Being scared doesn't give you the right to make things up. My apologies, Warden," she said.

He studied the woman as she bowed and pulled her child away, hunching over and speaking sternly into his ear. He replayed the conversation in his mind and considered the mother's actions. The simplest answer to her trying to hide the boy's experience was indeed that she thought it was all nonsense. More often than not, the simple answer really was the truth, but too many odd things picked at his brain and a suspicion was rising that he didn't want to admit.

An hour later, the village had calmed down as the sun rose into the sky. A group of men were piling up the vegetative carcasses of the Green Men onto fires, and columns of smoke billowed into the crisp air.

Clive gathered his team of marshals next to the well in the center of the village. Solarien landed, dwarfing those gathered and taking up most of the village proper. They did their best to cleanse themselves using rags, and Clive showed them the disc and what he had learned.

"Two things bother me. The first is the nature of the disappearances in context to the summoning of the Green Men. And the second is the boy who reportedly ran off into the forest." Clive paused for a moment, considering his words. "The nature of this mystery had already led to the suspicion of magic playing a key role. I believe with the summoning of the Green Men, it must be treated as confirmed that a powerful magic user is at play, likely our culprit or an accomplice."

"How powerful of a magic user does it take to summon that many Green Men?" Weir asked, pulling out a pipe and stuffing it with tobacco.

"I wouldn't be able to do more than one on my best day," Abaro said. "It's incredibly difficult to control the will of a magical creature."

*It would take an Archmage or an Ancient Dragon.*

Clive relayed Solarien's words to the group.

"There can't be more than a handful of those in the world, then," Bix offered. "Seems unlikely one would be out in the backwater of our district."

Weir struck a match, lighting his pipe, puffing quickly at the beginning to get an ember going. He coughed after a moment before recovering.

"How do you think this boy is connected?" Weir asked.

"Most likely, he's one of the few remaining children from the village who legitimately was scared for their life and ran into the forest to hide. Not a particularly sound strategy when the threat is the actual guardians of the forest, but nonetheless understandable. If that is the case, then we need to send a search party to find the boy and bring him back to safety."

Weir cocked his head to the side.

"I'm not sure anything about this case has been the likely scenario," Weir said before breathing in a dose of smoke.

"I agree. It is also possible based on the boy's description that he is actually another kind of magical creature, separate from the Green Men, but in league with this powerful magic user," Clive said, looking at each of them in turn. "Two leads, both dangerous, and the five of us to follow where they go."

"What about this disc, then? How does it factor in?" Abaro asked, holding it up to the light.

"I have a strong suspicion, but admittedly it's out of my expertise. I would like your thoughts," Clive said before unscrewing the top of his canteen and taking a sip of water.

Abaro eyed the thing, then tapped it with his finger. He gave the thing a puzzled look before sniffing it vigorously.

"The pattern suggests a mark of passage. A physical manifestation declaring the touch of another realm. I've seen this pattern before." Abaro abruptly sat and pulled a small book out from his pack and began flipping through the pages. "You should know, the possibility for transportation between the realms is frightening. It's forbidden and costly magic," he said with a tut-tut at the end. "Wouldn't want to be the one providing that spell. One mistake and you can be ripped apart into multiple dimensions of reality... Ah, here it is. That pattern marks the realm of dreams"

Clive screwed the cap back on to the top of his canteen and

gave Abaro a flat look while Bix and Weir looked at each other in confusion. Weir just shrugged his shoulders.

"You shouldn't have said anything, Abaro. Now Clive knows you know. You know what he's going to ask you to do next," Bix said with a grin.

"I know a little bit about everything. Occupational hazard of being a wizard," he replied, lifting his chin before continuing. "But really, Warden, this is a bad idea. I would very much like to keep my appendages attached and in the same version of reality."

"So you think the culprit has been getting into the children's rooms through the use of this disc?" Weir asked.

"Yes, and I believe the children have been taken back to this dream realm as well, but for what purpose remains unclear," Clive responded, crossing his arms and bowing his head. "If they are in the dream realm, they are in grave danger. I've read that the realms outside the material have strange rules and unique dangers. I fear the culprit's ultimate motivation."

Clive looked up at Abaro and held his gaze.

"Do you think you can get Solarien and I into the dream realm with that thing?" Clive asked pointedly.

Abaro hesitated, a rarity for the man.

"You do understand, that this could kill you, me, and Solarien?" Abaro asked.

Clive nodded and held a stoic look.

"If the wizarding guild hears about this, they'll seal my magic and keep me from ever practicing again," Abaro said gravely.

"Those children are as good as dead if we don't try," Clive replied.

Abaro breathed out a heavy breath and dropped his head to peer at his feet.

"I'm never having children," the wizard said, relenting.

He held the disc in front of him, peering intently, then spoke quietly to himself. A faint glow surrounded the item. He let go of the thing and it stayed where he had held it, free-floating in the air. He used his now free hands to dig into his bag of tricks and produced a small vial of pink liquid that went down in a single gulp.

"What was that?" Bix asked with a concerned look on her face.

"I was having some indigestion," Abaro answered before producing a second tonic, this one a dark blue that glowed faintly. "This one I brewed up specifically for the identification of magical items. It should help me see how it was enchanted and the proper inputs and limitations."

He downed the second vial and grunted, bending over in pain. He closed his eyes and pressed his hands to his temples. The group stood there watching with concerned looks on their faces before Bix stepped forward, then back, unsure of how to help the man.

After a few moments, he stood up straight again and lowered his hands. He opened his eyes and sighed.

"Better than last time, for sure," Abaro said. "What are you all looking at?"

Weir's pipe fell from his mouth.

"Your eyes, Abaro, they're… different," Clive responded.

Abaro's brown eyes were gone, and in their place swirled pools of starry blackness. It was beautiful and unworldly.

"You don't expect me to be able to dissect the intricacies of magic with mortal eyes, do you? I'm borrowing a celestial's for a few moments."

Clive's brow furrowed in confusion at the comments.

"It's consensual. The celestial was actually pretty intrigued by the prospect, and didn't ask for anything but a straight swap," Abaro added. "Imagine what my eyes are looking at in his head right now."

Through the bond, Clive could feel Solarien laughing at the

comment.

Abaro lifted his hands as he spoke in an ancient tongue. His words became a cadence, a rhythm of power that sent small hair-like threads of white energy flowing out his fingers and into the disc. Small beads of sweat began to appear on the wizard's forehead as he explored the intricacies of the magical enchantment attached to the item.

"I see. Hmm, yes," Abaro muttered as he examined. "The difficulty isn't the strength of the user's magical power, it's how accurate they can be. This object demands absolute precision from the user. Interesting."

A few minutes passed as the group allowed Abaro to focus on his task. Around them, a few villagers had gathered to watch the strange sight, some looked on in amazement as others looked apprehensive. Magic was rare enough a gift that these smaller villages may go generations without seeing someone with the aptitude and gumption to learn.

"Here's what I think I can do for you, to both keep myself whole and to get you to the dream realm," Abaro started before licking his lips. "I can transport you to this exact spot in the dream realm."

"What do you mean 'this exact spot'?" Clive asked.

"Have you been to another realm before?" Abaro asked.

"You know I haven't. Have you?"

"Just once, during my studies at the academy. The instructor had us visit a rather tame realm where everything weighed one-tenth its normal weight but was otherwise a mimic of this realm that we live in. Each realm is a reflection of ours. This village exists across all the realms. It may be different, bent, twisted, have new rules or properties, but fundamentally, it is the same."

"The makeup of this magical item, this fractal disc, takes some of the load off of the spellcaster by acting as a bridge between the realms of existence. The challenge is on the caster to keep the destination exactly straight through the whole of the spellcasting process. Honestly, it's a clever little thing. I'd like to keep it when we're done here."

"Very good then," Clive said. "Is there a tolerable risk of us all getting maimed?"

"The odds of sending your body simultaneously into a hundred different realms is probably less than one in twenty, with the aid of this disc," Abaro said with a nod at the end.

Bix and Weir looked at each other and mouthed the word 'probably' before eyeing Clive. The Warden stood there, a look of determination on his face. The personification of resolution.

"Bix, Weir. When Abaro is finished sending Solarien and I to the dream realm, I want you three to find the missing boy who ran into the woods. With no parents or friends reaching out to us for help finding their newly missing friend, be wary that the child may be more than he seems. Have each other's back." The three marshals all saluted. "When you're finished, join Solarien and I in the dream realm. Who knows what awaits us there. I'd rather go knowing I have you all as backup on the way."

"No need to worry, Warden. We won't forget you there," Abaro replied. "It might be easier to send you if you were mounted on Solarien's back. Turns you into one target instead of two."

Clive turned to face Solarien.

*This is going to be something new for me. In my five centuries, I've never traveled to another realm. I'm a bit nervous to be honest,* Solarien said.

Clive hesitated in response. Nerves were a rare occurrence for Solarien, and in his decades of service she'd only spoken out about being nervous a handful of times.

*I'm nervous, too. I've read terrible things about the other realms. And in the dream realm there are few limitations to what we might face. Whatever it is, we'll face it together,* Clive said. He tried to sound as confident as he could. His determination traveled across the bond.

*Yes, together,* Solarien echoed softly as she bent down to help Clive reach the saddle. He climbed up with a grunt and settled atop her back.

"Whenever you are ready, Abaro," he called.

The wizard reached a hand out toward them and clutched the disc with the other. He spoke in an ancient tongue, but instead of whispering, he spoke with gusto and intensity. Clive could feel something happening. It was similar to the pressure he felt when diving underwater, and it pressed in on him from all sides, causing his ears to ring. The compression increased continually, blurring his vision. He reached out through the bond, hoping for the security it offered and found Solarien doing the same. Their minds met and they held tight to one another as their world changed. All around him, his view took on a purple tint before both he and Solarien were surprised by a sudden drop that almost lifted him out of the saddle. The few seconds that passed felt like hours before the pressure finally evaporated and both Solarien and Clive again sat in the tiny village's town square.

Instead of the clear early morning sun above though, the sky was cloudy, giving only brief glimpses into the deep black sky beyond. In those gaps, he saw thousands of impossible stars shining brilliantly overhead in constellations he had never seen. He wondered how it would look on a clear night.

The purple tint to everything remained, almost like a haze. They were alone as far as he could tell, no sign of any villagers or marshals who had been standing right next to them just moments before.

The village looked the same. The buildings were arranged in the same manner, but a short distance into the forest stood a tall stone tower. At its top, an orb of blue light shined harshly.

*Do you think you could get me a closer look at that?* Clive asked.

*Certainly.* She leaned back and jumped into the air.

As they rose above the canopy of trees, somewhere beyond the tower a deathly human shriek filled the air, followed by a murderous roar of delight. Concern shot through their shared bond as they drew nearer to the tower's ramparts.

The top of the tower was about a hundred paces wide, and had several long wooden boxes arranged in a wide circle around the glowing orb. It hung in the air about 10 paces above the floor, and a hooded figure stood beneath it, watching them as Solarien decided on the safest place to land. Off in the distance, another terrible roar echoed through the trees.

*I need to know what made that roar,* she said, perching on the edge of the rampart and peering back out toward the forest. She lowered her head as Clive slid to the floor.

*Then let's make this quick,* he replied before turning and walking toward the hooded figure.

The figure responded in kind, and seemed to travel an impossible amount of distance with each stride. Clive's attention was distracted though, as Solarien jumped back into the air behind him, reading a threat approaching quickly from deeper within the forest.

"This is no place for a weak and feeble old man," the hooded figure said in a deep voice, venom dripping in its tone.

"Are these the children?" Clive asked, pointing to the boxes.

The only response he got was the sound of a sword unsheathing.

"Very well, then." Clive pulled his own sword.

The two met their blades and began the deadly dance.

Clive began by testing the hooded figure's defenses, thrusting, then parrying, then coming at him from a different angle. He used the stance of the Three Rivers, a flexible base that would allow him to weigh his opponent.

The hooded man, both taller and broader than he, matched his stance and for a few moments, they tested each other.

*Clive, that roar we heard? I found the source and it's not good,* Solarien said. He could tell she had traveled some distance away, trusting that Clive could handle himself with the sword and judging the creature a bigger threat. *It's an umbral dragon and it's headed your way. I'm going to slow it down, but I don't think I'll be able to stop it without you.*

Clive's opponent shifted into a Rush of the Bulls stance and began a flurry of attacks. Clive was forced onto his back foot as he fended off each attack, one after another. He countered by assuming the stance of the Shattered Rock, a combination of deft dodging and expert parries that put the two back onto even footing.

A thought trickled down the back of Clive's mind, a tug of memory as the two continued to meet swords. He decided to follow the thread and shifted his stance to Pouncing Tiger to go on the offensive. His opponent quickly shifted into Dance of the Frogs which kept him always just out of reach. His opponent's choice of response was familiar, so he tried one more time, wanting to be certain of who he was fighting.

He slid back into Slithering Snake form, and the hooded opponent jumped forward with a downward cut which he transformed into a forward lunge. Charging Horse. Just like old times.

"Balthasar, how are you here? You were dead. I saw you lowered into your grave," Clive said, confused but continuing his defensive posture and stepping out of range.

"Finally figured it out, eh? You never were the brightest in the bunch," Bathasar replied, removing his hood and revealing the weathered but sturdy face of his old Warden.

"This is impossible," Clive said as he backed up, sweat running down the side of his face. Balthasar seemed to grow as he stepped toward Clive.

"The rules are different here. No one truly dies until we are forgotten in the material realm, which means I'll be here for quite some time," Balthasar said with a grin.

"Why did you kidnap children?" Clive asked, anger boiling up inside of him. "That's not who you are."

"I've done nothing to them. I did not bring them here. I didn't even come here willingly," Balthasar responded. His eyes changed, glowing softly at first, then brighter until a red mist began seeping out of the corners. "The creature here cast a powerful spell, a trap triggered when someone finds this place. It summons the trespassers' fears, which, apparently for you, is me."

Clive stood dumbfounded. Balthasar had been a tough master, but he had never feared the man. He feared Balthasar's discipline in his youth, perhaps, but not the man himself.

"I don't understand. Why fight me, then? If you're really... you?" Clive asked. "You see me, you know me. I'm serving as Warden of the East in your stead and am here to rescue these missing children. That's something you would be doing yourself if you were still in my shoes."

Tendrils of mist continued to float from Balthasar's eyes, drifting into the night sky as he responded, "Because the rules are different here, and I've been compelled by the summoner to stop you. My will is irrelevant. Let us both hope you've surpassed your old master in your years of service."

*It's coming your way!* Solarien sent through the bond.

Balthasar's last words struck home as a fearsome roar split the air. Balthasar turned and ran, jumping off the tower. A few moments later, he was soaring through the air on the back of an enormous gray and black dragon, its mouth dripping with green acid.

*Your turn to jump,* Solarien said.

Clive responded his agreement through their bond, sheathing his sword. He looked out over the canopy of trees swaying softly in the hazy purple breeze and saw Solarien quickly approaching. He timed the approach and leaped off, falling a short span before reaching out and catching one of the holds on the saddle. With a grunt, he pulled himself up onto Solarien's back and strapped his feet securely into the stirrups, buckling his waist strap.

*If we survive this, I'm going to feel that one,* Clive said.

He looked around the sky, trying to find their adversaries. At the last moment, he saw them descending from above.

*Bank now!* Clive urged. Solarien felt his urgency and immediately banked to the right. A moment's hesitation would have brought gallons of green acid across Solarien's back, surely killing Clive and maiming Solarien. In the bank, Solarien peered under her left wing and got a sight of Balthasar and his dragon pulling back up. The leafy canopy below writhed under the wind from the umbral dragon's powerful wings.

Clive reached down under his right stirrup where his dragon spears were securely mounted. He undid the fastener and brought one of the heavy weapons to bear. Its tip was a four-foot span of sharpened mithril, strong and sharp enough to pierce even the toughest dragon hide. It was too unwieldy for regular combat, but upon the back of a dragon, all he had to do was hold it at the right angle and coordinate with Solarien. She'd do the maneuvering, and he would aim and thrust.

Solarien rose higher as the umbral dragon and Balthasar gave chase.

*I'm going to swing above them and turn. You'll have a chance to strike.* Solarien said before performing the acrobatic maneuvers.

Clive held on tightly to the saddle with both feet and his left hand as he tucked the spear under his right armpit for extra stability. He followed their target with his eyes and watched as they gave direct chase. He could see the glint of Balthasar's own dragon spear and made sure Solarien knew of the danger. She pulsed her acknowledgement through the bond and inverted their position into a tight turn. Clive breathed out as he aimed and thrusted his spear at the exact moment Solarien spun. His spear was deflected by Balthasar's own thrust, the umbral dragon squealing with delight as it banked and continued to give chase.

*We're going to have to try something a little more unconventional,* Clive said.

*I have an idea, but you're probably not going to like it,* Solarien replied, the exhilaration of the fight giving her voice an edge.

A blast of acid sprayed to their left as the umbral dragon screeched behind them.

*They are gaining on us!* Clive shouted, peering over his shoulder.

*Not for long. Hold on,* Solarien warned, lifting straight up into the sky. *Here's what I'm thinking.*

Clive received a set of images through the bond, detailing her plan.

*You've got to be kidding me,* Clive said, mouth agape. *What if I miss again?*

*Don't miss,* Solarien demanded. *It's this, or going toe-to-toe with Balthasar, one of the greatest dragon riders of our time. I'm faster than that umbral dragon, but it's more powerful. One good splash of acid on my wings and it'll be over.*

*Let's roll the dice, then. If I have to die, at least it'll be a quick one,* Clive responded. *Wait until we hit a cloud; it'll give us the best chance.*

He unbuckled from the saddle, grabbed another dragon spear, and carefully stood. Using his spear as a balance pole, he walked across Solarien's back. He waited, crouching above Solarien's hips until they had cloud cover. At Solarien's command, he advanced halfway down her tail and counted. On three, Solarien launched him high into the air. He clutched his spear with both hands as he watched Solarien blast fire at Balthasar. It was quite a spectacle for the few moments he floated weightlessly. Streams of fire and acid shot back and forth through the gaps in the clouds.

He began his descent, hurtling faster and faster toward the ground. For this to work, Solarien had to get the umbral dragon in just the right position at just the right time. The wrong timing would cost him his life. He angled his body to take advantage of the air currents and stabilized himself enough to keep the spear point aimed in the right direction.

Below, Solarien began another ascent, her blasts of fire infuriating the larger dragon, goading it into a chase. She headed straight for Clive, trying to gain enough distance from the umbral dragon to buy herself time to catch Clive out of his dive.

*Now!* Solarien yelled.

Clive summoned his strength and threw the spear straight down at Solarien before changing the angle of his body to create more drag and slow his descent. Solarien stopped beating her wings and slowed her ascent for a moment before twisting in mid-air, allowing the dragon spear to slip just past her underbelly before catching Clive with her talons.

Clive watched as his spear shot toward the umbral dragon, who tried to move out of its trajectory, but caught sight of the weapon too late. The spear embedded more than half its length under the beast's left shoulder. The dragon shrieked in pain as its momentum halted and it began tumbling end over end. Balthasar and his dragon fell like a meteor, crashing into the forest below and toppling trees with loud cracks and booms.

*Let's never do that again,* Clive gasped as his adrenaline faded. They'd done aerial maneuvers in the past, but nothing so reckless. It was the kind of risk taking that Balthasar had tried to train out of him. Never roll the dice, always control, and make your own luck.

*It worked, didn't it?* Solarien responded as she descended back toward the tower which was nothing more than a dot in the forest scape. *Today you were greater than even your old Warden.*

*Drop me back on the tower, then go make sure that dragon is dead,* Clive ordered, digesting her last comment. *I don't need to be greater than Balthasar. What truly matters is the bonds we've all forged with each other. That's a real legacy. And when the day comes that I do retire, I'll still spend my days doing what I can for those I care deeply for.*

Solarien rumbled in delight as they approached the tower. For a moment, she hovered in place and dropped Clive off near one of the wooden boxes.

*Be careful, Clive. Remember, Balthasar was the trap that was sprung, not the villain himself. Danger still lurks,* Solarien reminded him.

She turned and flew off to find where Balthasar and the umbral dragon had fallen.

He looked around and found himself alone on the top of the tower. He unsheathed his sword and walked up to the closest box. It was long and rectangular, made of a dark wood that was almost black, polished and finely crafted. He reached down with his free hand and tried to lift the top, but it was securely fastened. Clive crouched and stuck his blade into the seam between the side and top pieces of wood. He strained until the top popped off with a loud crack.

Inside lay a small child. A pale blue aura surrounded him and led to the floating orb. The boy's chest rose and fell, and Clive let go of the breath he didn't realize he'd been holding. He truly had found them, and they were alive. He leapt over to the next box and pried its top off as well. Another child in the same condition, and then another, and another as he progressed around the circle.

*We found them, Solarien! They are alive!*

Clive stood, sheathing his sword as he inspected the last child. Solarien didn't respond.

*Did you hear me?* Clive asked, focusing on the bond. It was silent, peaceful, almost as if she was sleeping. The bond was present, but that was it, nothing else manifested from the connection besides its existence.

"You found them. Good," a familiar voice said from behind.

Clive spun, hand on the hilt of his sword.

Abaro stood there, arms crossed. Staring.

"Finally, the mystery is unraveled. Let's grab these children and be off, then," the wizard said as he started to rummage through his pack.

"Where are Bix and Weir?" Clive asked, hand still clutching the hilt of his sword.

"Oh, once we found the missing boy, they agreed to take him back to the village. We can pick them up after we take a few of these kids home with us. It'll take us a few trips back and forth to get them all," Abaro said, leaning over one of the boxes to inspect the child inside.

Clive relaxed, taking his hand off his sword. He reached into the nearest box and tried to grab the sleeping child within but froze in place as invisible strands wrapped tightly around him. The binds pulled him backward and knocked him off balance. He rolled and saw Abaro standing, hands extended toward him.

"You'll be the final piece of my machination, Warden. Your dreams will be extracted as well, just a few more of you will do the trick," Abaro said. As he approached, Clive watched one of

Abaro's eyes shift down toward his nose, his skin shifting awkwardly, almost like it was melting.

"You are the abductor," Clive said angrily.

"You'd be surprised how easy it is to bring someone here while they are sleeping. Especially when they are in a nightmare. I've wondered why that is. Perhaps the desire to escape the terror?" The changeling continued to morph. "The children were the easiest targets, and their imaginations are so vivid… a very powerful magic source here in the realm of dreams."

"Let them go, changeling!" Clive shouted as he struggled against the bonds, testing them for any weakness. No matter how he tried, they would not budge.

"Bah, your human names for us Fae are so ugly. No respect, no beauty," it said as the shifting slowed. Its face was perfectly smooth, showing no blemish or wrinkles. The only potential mark of age was the long silver hair that hung loosely to its shoulders. The changeling was short and stocky, not elegant, and had an air of brutal sophistication. It had a long and wide nose dominating above its small mouth. As it continued talking, Clive could see short, sharply pointed teeth behind thin lips. "You can call me Prince, as I'm the true heir to the forest."

"A descendent of the Fae Queen, then. Were you one of her offspring that betrayed and overthrew her? Or one of their progenies?" Clive recalled Abaro's briefing on the forest. He tried to reach out through the bond again, but it still hung quietly. It would only be a matter of time before she returned. He just needed to keep the Prince occupied until then.

"Ancient history, and not something I'd like to rehash with you, Warden. I'm more interested in what can be saved and returned to the Fae. Now that the pact with that cursed village has been broken, I'm free to unleash my power on the material world and reestablish my dominion," the Prince said with a cackle. "I'll unleash nightmares into your world and reconquer my lands. Soon, even your Empress will bow before me! And now my dear Warden, sleep. Sleep and never awaken!"

With a wave of his small hand, Clive felt his eyelids clamp down heavily, and his eyes began to roll back. He fought the urge. It was his body, his eyes. If he could just resist, outlast the changeling's power, he'd be able to find a way to escape. As he fluttered on the edge of sleep, he heard Abaro's voice speaking in a strange tongue. Clive was comfortable and tired. He'd done so much in such a short time, perhaps he deserved his rest. The sound of ringing metal and claps of thunder sounded at his periphery. A small part of him called out, *danger!* The sounds meant something, a call to action to join the fray.

Like a tide receding, the compulsion to sleep disappeared and the invisible bonds loosened. His eyes opened wide as he saw the Prince turn and raise a hand toward the sky. Solarien spewed a tight stream of fire that flickered across a round blue shield that surrounded the Prince. Clive felt woozy as he tried to stand. Beyond the prince he saw Abaro, Weir, and Bix charging forward. Abaro hurled a bolt of lightning that cracked the Prince's blue shield. A second strike brought the shield down completely, and Bix and Weir sprang forward, swords in hand. They never reached the Prince. Without the magical shield, Solarien's stream of dragon fire consumed the changeling, leaving a husk of burnt flesh where the creature once stood.

"You all saved me," Clive said, his mouth feeling dry and sluggish.

"Yes, Yes, we did," Abaro said, not taking his eyes off the changeling's husk. "Do you think they all looked like that?"

Clive processed the question for a moment. Was he really asking that at a time like this? Of course he was. This was the real Abaro, always inquisitive.

*Are you all right?* Clive asked Solarien.

*Only terrified that I had lost you,* Solarien responded. *I couldn't feel you. It was like you were masked as before when you had your nightmare.*

*He must have been the source of the masking,* Clive concluded. *Were Balthasar and the umbral dragon dead?*

Solarien landed and snorted. *No, I saw no sign of them.*

*Without the Prince compelling them, I can't imagine they'd be a threat any longer.*

"What is that thing?" Bix asked, pointing to the glowing orb.

Abaro cocked his head to the side as he studied it. He touched the thing and it bobbed up and down like it was floating in water.

"This is a glorified jar," he said flatly. "Nothing immediately dangerous, just close to full with magical potential."

The wizard walked over to one of the slumbering children and placed his hand on the child's forehead. The blue aura around her vanished and she awoke with a deep inhalation.

"Honestly, it's all pretty standard stuff. You can think of all these kids like they're dripping spigots, and that orb is just collecting the water."

The child sat up and looked around, eyes wide with fright. Weir ran over and knelt next to the kid and tried to comfort and explain what had happened to her.

"Magical potential? Sounds dangerous. Can you get rid of it?" Clive asked.

"Well, no. Can't really destroy energy," Abaro mused as he walked to the next child. "But I can take it with us, make sure it isn't misused. Perhaps it could be a nice reading lamp in my workshop."

Clive rolled his eyes.

"We want to make sure it can't be used," he replied before rounding up the rest of the children.

\*

They departed the small village of Dali with wreaths of flowers around their necks and promises of gifts, of future children named after them, and of prayers for blessings. They left as they had come, flying high in the sky, Clive riding in the saddle and enjoying the view his life had afforded him. Below, the marshals elbowed each other and joked.

*So, have you decided?* Solarien asked, interrupting Clive's peace as they glided across the sky.

*Decided what, exactly?*

*Have you decided who you are going to pass the mantle of Wardenship to? You were considering hanging up your saddle before we left.*

Clive sighed and sat up, rubbing his aching shoulder.

*Perhaps I was being too hasty to call this my last outing,* he said. *But the time is coming. Tell me, have you ever considered bonding with a wizard?*

He could feel her pleasure at his words.

*I can still serve some time longer, and give the marshals a little more time to grow,* Clive added.

*I was hoping you would say something like that,* Solarien replied warmly as she skimmed across the bottom of a cloud. Clive reached out, touched the white puff, and laughed with delight.

## THE END

# Riders Rebirth
Andrew McDermott

## Chapter 1

Bjorn lay back as he surveyed the vast expanse of verdant splendor below. Layers of green, lush foliage stretched as far as his eyes could see, a mesmerizing display of isolation away from the machinations of man. Towering trees stood like sentinels, their canopy creating a cover for a myriad display of fauna. Bird's and insects hummed, filling the air with a symphony of nature's song. In the distance he could see mist rising from a cascading waterfall, adding an ethereal touch to the breathtaking panorama. He felt a slight rumble behind him and turned to his companion.

"You feeling any better this morning?" he asked, looking back at Shifa, her red scales shimmering like rubies under the sun's rays. With sinuous elegance for a creature so large she left the cave, gracing Bjorn with her presence on the cliff top. There was silence for a moment before the voice sounded in his head.

*Not really. The bile build up has been increasing at night while I rest, and as you are well aware, when I awaken, the hacking cough bring up the most foul-smelling poison.*

"Too much information, Shifa, my friend. All the same, I have a deep hope that somewhere on this island we will find a cure for you."

The dragon stretched, before crawling forward to nestle her head beside Bjorn's leg.

*Beautiful, isn't it?* she asked

"I can take it or leave it." Bjorn rested his hand on the dragon's head, giving the beast an uncertain grin. "Too often we place value on a nice view without knowing the quality underneath." He pointed to the vast landscape before them. "From this clifftop, the land looks amazing and fertile. However, there is a reason not many, if anyone at all lives here."

*Care to enlighten me?*

"Because underneath that beauty lies something so powerful or so evil that men tremble before it."

Shifa nudged Bjorn before turning and once again stretching.

*I think you make it up as you go along,* she said. *The day moves on quickly, it's time we got moving.*

Bjorn nodded as he rose to his feet. Taking a moment, he looked at Shifa, examining her for any change in the disease that had blighted her in recent months.

*Well?* she asked. *Will I make it much longer?*

"You shouldn't joke."

*Who said anything about joking?* Shifa turned, swiping her tail close to Bjorn in a playful tease.

"I'm serious. I've no intention of coming this far just to lose one of my closest friends."

*You don't have friends,* she replied. *You said they all end up using you for their own purposes. But it warms my heart that you call me your friend.*

Bjorn drew closer to Shifa, resting his head on her jaw.

"Stop teasing. In the years since I found you, I've experienced things some men can only dream of."

*Come, stop being so dramatic.*

"Fine, I'll keep the compliments to myself," he said, patting her on the neck as he reached up. Shifa let out what sounded like a grunt as Bjorn climbed on her back.

"The sooner we get you healed, the better. I sense that carrying me is a burden to you now."

*Maybe you've put on a little too much weight,* she replied.

As they launched into the air and ascended into the cloudless sky, Bjorn surveyed the way ahead. The guide had been vague.

Travel to the isolated isle of Ospa, and somewhere in the dense overgrowth was a woman that knew the old ways. A fear jabbed at his heart. What if the disease was too far gone? What if this was yet another dead end on a journey to heal his friend.

As Shifa's wings undulated, the deep undercurrent of discontent continued to gnaw away at Bjorn's heart. It had been five years since he had met Shifa. She was young then, and even now still a youth by dragon standards, yet large for her age. She had rescued him from himself. His family dead, his clan wiped out, and Bjorn a drunk.

Through their travels together, the dragon had shown Bjorn the beauty of the world beyond his grief-stricken heart. She guided him to hidden valleys adorned with flowers of every hue, to towering mountains that kissed the heavens, and to tranquil lakes where the reflection of the stars shimmered like diamonds on velvet. With each new sight, Bjorn's spirit began to heal, and the weight of his sorrow gradually lifted. The bond had somehow made Shifa his silent confidante, listening to his every whispered fear, and offering silent solace in return.

*You saved me, as much as I saved you.*

"Stop reading my mind, Shifa. Is there no privacy between us?"

*You think so loud, it gives me a headache sometimes.*

"Be careful or I'll start thinking loudly about my bowel movements."

*If I remember correctly, you thought about bowel movements the moment we met.*

"You remember too much, Shifa. It's one of those annoying qualities that makes you adorable." Bjorn chuckled for the first time in as long as he could remember, briefly losing his grip on Shifa before righting himself.

## Chapter 2

Hours had passed since they left the cliff view, scanning endless miles of verdant valleys and thick forests, intermingled with several small tributaries that seemed to feed into a much bigger river a few miles further north. The pair had flown in silence, not a word spoken since their jesting earlier that day. As Bjorn sat on the back of Shifa, her wings coursing through the air with less energy than usual, he noticed a dark vein stretching from the end of her skull, running haphazardly across her back, then out across her wing.

"Shifa?" he asked. "There's something you need to see." There was no response. "Shifa?"

Bjorn patted his hand on her back, trying to nudge a response out of her. Still nothing. He stretched forward, aiming to get a better view of her.

"Open your eyes, Shifa!"

Shifa's head drooped, jaw slack, her wings folding mid-air. "Shifa! Wake up! You must wake up!" Down they dropped as Bjorn struggled to keep hold of his dragon. Again and again, he pounded on her back in a vain attempt to awaken her. As the ground rapidly drew near, Bjorn reached back, grabbed his axe, and jabbed the end of it into Shifa's side. The dragon jolted with a roar, her eyes wide with madness. She spun, flames ready to pour from her maw.

"It's me!" Bjorn cried out. Shifa paused for a moment as they plummeted, her eyes opening wide.

*Forgive me.* Her voice echoed through Bjorn's mind. *I can't seem to right myself. Something is wrong.* Shifa spun, her wings flapping furiously, slowing their decent. *If only there was a little more time.* Bjorn saw the trees approaching like giant arrows before he felt the first branch crash into him. He couldn't tell if the cracking sounds were from him, Shifa or the tree branches. As he dropped the final twenty feet to the forest floor, he braced with what energy he had left. A sharp pain shot across the back of his head and darkness consumed him.

*

Bjorn grimaced as pain shot through his body. A *thunk* sounded nearby, jerking him awake as darkness covered the canopy of trees above him.

"Shifa?" he grunted, attempting to pull himself upright. Pain shot through his back as he staggered to his feet, his stomach churning as dizziness pushed him down to his knees before he emptied the contents of his stomach onto the grass beneath him. Another *thunk* sounded further in the distance, startling Bjorn. As he spun to look, pain shot through his arm causing him to scream out in pain.

"I have to fix this."

Reaching out to a nearby tree, he took hold and yanked with all his might. He groaned like a maddened dog as a loud pop sounded, pulling his arm back into place. Bjorn turned, sinking down to collapse at the base of the tree.

"Shifa?"

There was no response, but he found himself distracted as another *thunk* sounded closer, followed by another two *thunks* not ten feet away. Bjorn straightened, a shiver running up his spine. A multitude of beady, black eyes glistened in the moonlight, staring out at him, edging ever nearer. His hand froze as he reached for his axe, finding nothing where it was usually strapped to his back. Frantic, he glanced around the forest, looking for any sign of Shifa or his weapon.

The eyes paused for a moment, and a chittering echoed through the forest.

"How many of you vile creatures are there?" Bjorn spat.

As if it read his mind, the nearest stepped forward from the shadow, revealing itself in the light of the moon. One by one, eight dark, hairy legs brought forward a bulbous body, with a wicked looking stinger at the back.

Bjorn gasped at the sight. "Arachins," he mouthed. Never before had he laid eyes on the vile creatures, nor had he wished to. Attempting to scramble back he found the base of the tree a sentinel, keeping him captive.

As the Arachin drew closer, more similar looking creatures stepped out of the shadows. Bjorn drew in a deep breath.

"One chance," he muttered, eyeing for any way to escape the menace. He leaped forward towards the giant spider, feinting to leap over the creature before sliding under. His foe raised up, missing the feint, but bringing the stinger down mere inches from his face. Scrambling to his feet he darted through trees as one after another Arachin charged towards him. Finally, the moonlight revealed a clearing not twenty feet away. The pain in Bjorn's shoulder returned as he charged forward, his heart racing.

As the last tree passed his field of vision he stopped dead in his tracks. Agony seared through his chest as he felt himself lifted from his feet. His head drooped to see a giant stinger protruding from his chest.

"Shifa," he gurgled. "Help me."

*

*Wake up.*

Bjorn jolted awake, screaming as he found himself wrapped in webbing. "Take a moment," he said to himself. "Breathe."

*Bjorn.*

Shifa's voice echoed in his ears.

"I hear you," he replied.

*I need you to listen to me Bjorn, you don't have much time. I'm hanging ten feet from you.*

"Can you see?"

*I've managed to burn a small hole in my webbing, but I can't free myself enough to get a full belly of fire. When I came to, I was already wrapped in this prison.*

"I'd help, but I'm kind of stuck."

*Stop talking and listen to me. There's no time. The Arachin's seem to be on some routine. They guard, then they feed, then disappear for what seems like thirty minutes. As far as I can see, we are the last meal they have. I need you to do me a favor.*

"Name it," he said.

*There is a pile at the corner of the clearing, I believe your axe is there. I need you to get it and cut me out.*

"What manner of magic do you think I possess in order to get out of this cocoon?"

*Do you trust me?*

"I don't like this."

*I'm going to direct a small burst of flame at your midsection. It's all I have, but it should free your hands. I'm too tightly wrapped to move my head, otherwise I'd be able to get myself out, but you hang directly across from me.*

"Shifa, there has to be a better way." Bjorn wreathed, trying to free his hands.

*Now.*

"Shifa!" Bjorn shouted, as the webbing round his midsection began to flame. Heat permeated the entire web as he felt the insufferable burning sensation cover him from head to toe. "Stop! You're taking the skin off me."

*Better that than having your insides sucked out by overgrown spiders.*

Bjorn felt the webbing round his hands singe and fray,

allowing him to pull against it, opening a hole as Shifa stopped her assault. As he pulled through the cocoon, he eyes lighted on the familiar face of his friend. The dark vein had spread, covering what he could see of her head.

*Over there,* she said, nodding in the direction of the pile. *Be careful, the arachin venom still runs through your veins.*

Bjorn staggered as he made him way, lurching from branch to branch before finding stability on the ground below. Rarely before had the warrior tiptoed so light as to avoid conflict. He rubbed his hand over his face, trying to focus on the pile before him. His vision blurred as his body fought against the arachin toxins. Squinting, he finally came upon his axe, buried just below a nobleman's cloak.

"Poor end for a rich Lord," he muttered to himself before coving his mouth and watching lest he give himself away.

*Quickly now, get back up here and free me.*

The forest echoed with the ominous chatter of unseen creatures as Bjorn pushed himself onward, determination burning within his heart. With each step he took, the tangled branches of the ancient trees seemed to reach out to ensnare him, their twisted limbs serving as a sinister reminder of the danger that lurked within the shadows.

With a surge of adrenaline, Bjorn leaped forward, his muscles coiling like springs as he propelled himself through the underbrush. But the forest seemed to conspire against him, each branch and vine a barrier to his progress. Time and time again, he found himself ensnared in the off-cast webs of the Arachin, their sticky strands clinging to him like the grasp of death itself.

With a growl of frustration, Bjorn struggled as one web after another worked against him, his breath coming in ragged gasps as he fought to break through. With each passing moment, time grew short, the arachins return imminent.

Determined not to be defeated, Bjorn renewed his efforts, his eyes fixed unwaveringly on the distant figure of Shifa. With a mighty push, he summoned every ounce of strength within him, launching himself into the air with a desperate leap.

For a moment, it seemed as though time itself had frozen, and the world around him reduced to a blur of motion and sound. His outstretched fingers found purchase against the rough bark of a nearby branch, his momentum carrying him ever closer to his goal.

With a burst of adrenaline-fueled energy, Bjorn reached out once more, his hand closing around the limb with a vice-like grip. With a grunt of effort, he pulled himself upward, his muscles straining against the weight of his own body as he climbed ever higher into the tangled embrace of the trees.

There, suspended within the heart of the Arachin's web, hung Shifa, her form shrouded in a veil of shimmering silk, her jaw barely visible. Bjorn pulled out his axe, launching himself forward to free her from the prison.

*If you can slice open the webbing on my chest, then I should be able to do the rest.*

As the webbing pulled apart, he gasped, staggering back.

"What have they done to you?" he whispered. Puncture wounds criss-crossed with black veins covered the majority of Shifa's body.

*Look out!*

The dragon's cry came a second too late as a web caught Bjorn's arm. He spun around, arm held in the air as he came face to face with the monstrous shape standing before him. His breath caught in his throat as he beheld the creature, its grotesque form illuminated by the faint moonlight filtering through the dense canopy above.

The Arachin stood tall and menacing, its bloated abdomen pulsating with a sickly glow. Its eyes gleamed with a malevolent intelligence, fixing him with a stare that seemed to pierce straight through to his soul.

For a moment, time seemed to stand still as Bjorn and the arachin faced off. Fear coursed through Bjorn's veins like ice, threatening to paralyze him where he stood.

Summoning every ounce of courage he possessed, Bjorn opened his hand, dropping his axe and catching it with his free hand. With a defiant roar, he swung forward, catching the beast across one of its putrid eyes. The arachin let out a squeal as it flung him into the air before catching him and piercing his chest over and over with its stinger. The forest rumbled as Shifa let out a blood curdling roar, pulling the remaining web to pieces. The spider paused for a moment before flinging Bjorn against a tree and charging Shifa.

As the poison seeped through his veins and delirium threatened to overwhelm him, he saw a swath of flame bellow from Shifa's maw, purging the arachin to nothingness. He caught the dragon's gaze for a moment, her eyes flaming red. As one, the arachin's returned in force, meeting the fury of his friend. Bjorn sunk back, the smell of charred flesh and burnt tree permeating his nostrils.

Suddenly, he felt his body lift, rising into the air before landing on soft green grass.

*Stay with me Bjorn.*

"I am always with you, my friend."

*It's there. The temple is there, Bjorn. Get up. I can see the temple, but I need you to walk the last few feet.*

"I am too tired," he said, his hands vainly stifling the blood gushing from his chest wounds. "I think my time is complete." He smiled as his hands grasped his bloodied chest. "Out of all the dragons in the world, I'm glad I met you."

*Bjorn!* Shifa's voice screamed in his mind.

*

*Is this what death feels like?* he thought, as Bjorn felt hands tugging him this way and that.

*Too late.* A voice reverberated near him.

*Never too late,* said another in a deep hiss of a whisper.

A rumble sounded nearby before he felt the cold, hard touch of stone.

"Shifa?"

*He lives.*

*For now.*

"Shifa?"

*He speaks of the dragon.*

*He loves the dragon, doesn't he?*

"Love?" he asked.

*He loves what the dragon brings,* the voice snapped, sending a shock of pain through Bjorn's bones.

*No, he loves the dragon. See the tears in his eyes.*

*Tears for his own life.*

A hand touched his arm and he could feel a presence near his ear.

*Tears for a true love, a sacrificial love...*

The stone floor below him seemed to move, yet as Bjorn sought to open his eyes, he saw only darkness. The deep voice spoke out to him, sending terror through him.

*Would you die for it?* the voice asked.

Blood poured from Bjorn's mouth as he gasped out the words. "I already have."

*So be it.*

He felt his skin burn from his bones, and in his writhing agony, his mind flickered with images of his father, telling him stories of a punishing afterlife. How he wished he'd listened. The burning feeling left, replaced by a thick, cool sensation working its way up his body. His pulse raced, and his breathing got quicker. Finally, the thick sensation covered his head, filling his mouth with a sickening, suffocating texture, causing him to writhe and heave.

*Hold him still,* the whisper said. *You must hold him still.*

Heavy hands clamped on his head and chest, the weight almost crushing his skull as a sharp pain struck his heart. All feeling left his body, leaving him paralysed before his captors. A glimmer of light flashed before him, and for a second, he could have sworn he saw his own heart held before him.

*His eyes are open.* The deep voice came from behind him. *Quickly, we must settle him.*

*So, I'm not dead yet?* Bjorn thought as a sharp pain jabbed his skull, and darkness overtook him.

## Chapter 3

Bjorn awoke with a start, his heart pounding in his chest as he struggled to make sense of his surroundings. Disoriented and confused, he found himself standing in the midst of a dimly lit chamber, the air heavy with the scent of herbs and incense. As he attempted to push himself upright, a surge of pain shot through his body, causing him to cry out in anguish.

His movements caught the attention of an old woman who had been sitting in the shadows, her eyes fixed intently upon him. With a voice like the rustle of leaves in the wind, she spoke, her words sending shivers down his spine.

"It was prophesied that you would come," she said, her voice carrying an otherworldly resonance. "But your arrival has come at a cost."

Bjorn's brow furrowed in confusion as he struggled to comprehend her words. What prophecy could possibly involve him? And what price had he unknowingly paid?

Before he could voice his questions, the old woman continued, her gaze piercing through him like a blade.

"You both were ready to pass on, we did what we could to save you both," she said cryptically.

"Shifa?" Bjorn asked.

The woman raised a placating hand.

"Adapt to your own circumstances before you look any further." She walked over to Bjorn, resting a hand on his arm before leading him into the next room, to a pool of water. "Gaze upon the water."

Bjorn obeyed the old woman's command, stepping forward to gaze into the still liquid before him. As his reflection shimmered on the surface, he beheld a visage that was both familiar and foreign. Gone was the pure human form he had known all his life; instead, staring back at him was a figure transformed. His features were no longer wholly human, his eyes now bearing a glint of otherworldly wisdom, and his skin adorned with faint scales that seemed to catch the light in a mesmerizing dance. Yet, despite these physical changes, there remained a semblance of his former self, a reminder of the humanity that still resided within him.

As he continued to gaze into the depths of the pool, a mix of emotions welled up within him. Fear mingled with awe, uncertainty with acceptance. What was he?

"What did you do to me? Where is Shifa? If you harmed her..."

The old woman seemed to sense his confusion, for she leaned forward, her eyes locking with his in an unyielding gaze.

"You are no longer purely human, Bjorn," she said softly. "And Shifa is alive, but... is no longer purely dragon. You are no longer your own, you belong to another, and she to you for we— *I*— have made you into something new."

"What has become of her?" he asked, his voice barely above a whisper.

The old woman's lips curled into a sad smile as she spoke, her words heavy with sorrow.

"Shifa is now part human, and you are part dragon," she explained. "Her fate is now intertwined with yours, bound by the same thread that connects your souls."

As the weight of her words settled upon him, Bjorn felt a surge of grief and guilt wash over him. Was this the fabled cure? Would he go through life as some sort of beast? And what of Shifa?

"But why?" he demanded, his voice filled with anguish. "Was there no other way?"

The old woman's eyes softened with compassion as she reached out to touch his trembling hand.

"We did what we had to do to save you both," she said gently. "But now, you must face the consequences of our actions."

"Where is the man that helped you?"

"There is no man, there is only myself."

Bjorn shook his head. "I heard a deep voice. There has to be someone else here."

"No, no one else. Just myself."

"Who are you?"

The woman smiled and met Bjorn's gaze.

"I have had many names. But you can call me Accord."

Bjorn gritted his teeth.

"Enough of your games, woman. Where is Shifa?"

"You must calm yourself, there is much to learn about yourself before you go any further."

Dragons were known for their pride, especially in their appearance. How would Shifa react to the transformation? Bjorn clenched his fist, his voice shaking as he spoke.

"Take me to her."

The woman sighed, turning away and muttering to herself.

"He wants to see her."

Bjorn paused as the deeper voice resonated from where the old woman stood.

"As you wish."

## Chapter 4

With a sense of urgency, the old woman guided Bjorn through winding corridors and chambers until they reached a large dimly lit room. At the far side was a pool similar to the one he had seen moments before. This time, however, a woman was standing before it.

Bjorn felt a hand rest on his back as the old woman turned to leave them.

"I will be back in a moment. Take a moment to recover, you both have been through a lot. Help her adapt," she said, her voice fading as she shuffled down the corridor.

He stepped forward, beholding his companion. As he took in her visage, a gasp escaped his lips, for she was no longer the majestic dragon he had known. Instead, she stood before him as he was, part human, part dragon.

She gazed upon her reflection in a nearby pool of water, and he could sense her trepidation. The sight filled her heart with turmoil.

Her once majestic form had been altered, transformed into a strange hybrid of human and dragon. She clawed at her skin, dragging scores along her soft human flesh.

"What am I?" she said through clenched teeth, her voice trembling. "My kin will kill me." She hissed at her reflection.

A whirlwind of emotions swept through Shifa's mind as she grappled with the reality of her new existence. How could she show her face to any dragon kin? She would be rejected, an outcast. How could she ever hope to be accepted in the presence of other dragons.

A moment passed as Bjorn stood in silence, listening to her thoughts. Shifa bolted to her feet, her body transforming before his eyes. Her shoulders pulled apart, her skin becoming red scales once more. Amidst the turmoil of her thoughts, a glimmer of hope flickered within her heart. Once again, she held dragon form, the dark vein that had so prominently covered her, now a light shadow in places. Yet there was something different about her form. Bjorn stepped closer, noticing her shape was softer, less pronounced. More human. Her scales were a lighter tone, and her head and jaw less pronounced.

*Bjorn. If you live...* Her thought echoed through his mind. *I need you.*

*I'm here,* he said, his mind reaching out to hers.

She spun, turning her gaze to him, seeing that he too had been changed, his once-human form now bearing the unmistakable traits of a dragon.

In that moment, Bjorn could feel a peace wash over her heart. She transformed back to her hybrid form. Her dragon form was once more gone, leaving in its place a woman that seemed so foreign and at the same time so familiar. Time seemed to stand still before she leaped toward him, wrapping her arms around him.

"I thought you were dead," she said, the words coming out as a croak as she learned to use her voice rather than her mind.

"As I did you."

She nuzzled her head in his neck, noticing the new hardness of his scaly skin.

"What will we do?" she asked

Bjorn took her hands in his, holding tight.

"As we always have done. We stay together."

She pulled away from him, concern etched on her face.

"We will be hunted, by dragon and man alike."

Bjorn smiled and chewed his lip for a moment. He ran his hand down her arm, taking in the transformation.

"And yet we have each other."

Shifa nodded before nuzzling back in his neck.

"I hope you're right. I have all these… feelings. More, deeper." She once again pulled back, looking him in the eye. "I have fear, Bjorn. Real fear. Dragons have fear, but not like this." She paused. "And there's more, but it's not bad. I can't put my finger on it, but there's more."

The old woman's voice echoed through the chamber as she re-entered the room. Bjorn and Shifa turned to face her, their eyes still wide with disbelief.

The old woman nodded solemnly, her eyes shining with a wisdom that seemed to transcend the ages. "Long ago," she began, her voice tinged with reverence, "there was a prophecy foretelling of a great upheaval, a time when two hybrid dragons would emerge to shake the very foundations of the world." She smiled for a moment. "They weren't called hybrids. What did they call them…" She tutted to herself before raising her hand like a school master quieting a student. "The Coalesced shall shatter the…"

Bjorn and Shifa listened intently as the old woman recounted the details of the prophecy, her words weaving a tapestry of destiny and fate. According to the ancient texts, the two dragons would possess powers unlike any other, drawing strength from the depths of their souls to wield a power that could potentially reshape the world itself.

"And I believe," the old woman continued, her gaze fixed unwaveringly upon Bjorn and Shifa, "that you are the ones foretold in the prophecy. You, Bjorn, with your strength and speed drawn from Shifa's dragon soul. And you, Shifa, with your empathy, heart, and passion drawn from Bjorn's human soul." She drew closer to them, concern etched on her face. "Be wary, you are not two. You are one. One soul, one flesh, one life force. If one dies, the other dies with them."

Bjorn and Shifa exchanged a glance, confusion heavy on their hearts with the weight of their newfound destiny. They had never asked for this burden, never sought to wield such power. And yet, it seemed that fate had chosen them for a purpose greater than they could have ever imagined.

But even as doubt gnawed at the edges of their minds, a spark of determination flickered within their hearts. For if they truly were the fulfilment of the prophecy, then it was up to them to decide how they would use their new found abilities. Would they embrace their destiny and forge a path of righteousness, or would they succumb to the darkness that threatened to consume them?

Shifa met Bjorn's gaze, hope filling her eyes.

"Together?" she asked.

"Aye."

## THE END

# Rebirth
## Alfred Muller

Raffin stood on the side of the sleek ship carrying him over the crashing waves on the way to the fabled Shimmering Cliffs. He shuffled the papers in his hands, crumbling and smoothing them out, unable to let go. A gruff sailor shoved him, almost taking Raffin and the papers overboard. The captain warned at the beginning of the adventure he would not be going back for anyone who fell off the ship. Their fate would be up to the water drakes. Not real drakes, Raffin knew. Those were extinct. These were serpentine-like creatures that had fins similar to whales and jaws like dragons. They didn't need to breathe air and could perpetually lurk beneath the surface. Raffin wasn't sure what was worse. Stepping away from the ship's edge, he stuffed the papers back into his pocket and made himself useful. He found a bucket and was bailing some of the water on the deck of the boat when the captain found him.

"Not thinking of jumping, are ye?"

"Who, me?" Raffin asked.

"Yer the only scrawny knave wanderin' 'bout my ship lookin' over the side as if a trip to the depths is more suitable than braving the drink's fit," the captain said, taking the bucket from Raffin's hands. "What were ya doin' at the bow?"

"I'm just—I was trying…" Raffin sputtered. He wasn't a small fellow as the captain suggested, but compared to the tall men with arms as large as his head he supposed he did look scrawny. He was easily intimidated under the best of circumstances. Alone and isolated on a boat with no land in sight made everything sound like a threat to him.

The captain took Raffin's sputtering as a sign of lying and drew his cutlass.

"Yer a tax collector?"

That made Raffin laugh. If the captain knew his story, he'd laugh too. Instead, he narrowed his brow in confusion.

"Yer part of the crown? Come to arrest us for poaching?"

"No," Raffin said, wishing he hadn't spent the last of his money on this fool's mission. A bribe would probably end the encounter fast. The truth would do no good, so he lied. "Letters from my cheating wife. I can't seem to let them go."

The captain looked at him for a moment and raised an eyebrow, then partook in the laughter.

"Lubber, ye ain't got no worries of lasses out here. Only the drink and her clutches," the captain said, patting Raffin on the shoulder. He made his way along the ship with Raffin coming up behind him, trying to grab the bucket back.

Quick as a snapping sail line, the captain spun with his cutlass in hand and pressed the tip against Raffin's throat.

"Go near the railings again, spooking my crew or threatening yer own life, and I'll drain ye on the beach when we get to the Shimmering Cliffs. I need every man, including ye, thinking of the task at hand. Understood, lubber?"

Raffin nodded slightly, afraid to move his head.

"Glad we understand one another."

Raffin plopped down in the water, soaking his pants and adding to his misery. He needed to survive this trip. He gambled a life in debtors' prison for a single mission. If he succeeded, his problems would be solved. If he failed, well, his problems would be solved in a manner of speaking. For the same reason he didn't leap over the edge of the ship, he didn't want to fail.

Raffin slept fitfully the whole trip in a cot swinging below a deformed plank from the main deck. The ocean spray crashed over the railings before slipping through the deformity and dripping onto his head. When sleep did find him, he was hauled up from the hammock shortly after to perform chores. All the crew and some of the travelers on the ship seemed to enjoy the labor and adventure. Raffin tolerated it but saw this only as a way to solve a problem. The trouble it brought was far less than what he had to look forward to, so he stayed away from the ship's railing. Even the unhappy and unwilling aboard the ship didn't mesh well with him.

A trip to hunt dragons was a common alternative to military or jail time. Most port cities frowned on hunting dragons, but the Shimmering Cliffs were an isolated island chain with no allegiance to any one kingdom. Dragon scales were inherently valued because of their supernatural resiliency and were often used to make armor. The danger of taking on a small kingdom and its dragon inhabitants was another matter altogether. Still, a vessel like this with a daring crew sprung up from time to time, and it was just Raffin's luck it happened to be when and where he needed it. He wouldn't call it *good* luck, but it was some kind of luck.

"First dragon I sees you know whats I'm gonna do?" one of the men said. His jaw stood out, giving him an underbite, and he spat when he spoke.

"What?" another man said. He was larger than most of the other sailors and spoke slowly.

"I'm gonna guts it and take all the scales back to Betsy the tavern wench," Underbite laughed.

"I'm gonna find an island girl and lay down the hammer," the slow one said, slamming his big meaty fist on the table as he laughed.

Raffin stopped midway to their corner, hoping for a friendly conversation. They spotted him as he was turning away and hollered after him.

"Oi, you. Whats you was doin' spyins on us?" Underbite asked.

"I wasn't spying," Raffin said. He made the quiver in his voice more pronounced to play up his fear. It wasn't much of an act as Raffin was frightened. These men weren't here for adventure. They might have been sent on a suicide mission as opposed to jail time, which wasn't far from Raffin's own reasons.

"He is lying," the slow one said.

"Have either of you ever seen a dragon?" Raffin asked. Many from his town knew of someone or another who rode dragons, but no one had ever seen one in person. A few scales were the closest he ever came to them.

"What?" Underbite asked.

"Dragons. The creature we're going to slay? I was just looking around and noticed you two were the right ones to ask," Raffin said, laying down the only cards the gods seemed to bless him with. "Most of these men are just sailors, more at home surrounded by water and taking orders. You two on the other hand are planning, strategizing. I hoped you would help a newbie like me to the game."

Raffin didn't expect them to help or know anything about strategy. Most dragon hunters were new as death was a common occurrence. His only hope was they might beat him and leave him rather than shank him and toss him overboard.

The slow one took his meaning in the wrong direction, accidentally stumbling into the truth of the matter. Raffin blinked and shook his head absently.

"Youz makin' fun of us."

"Is e?" Underbite asked. He glared at Raffin with his good eye, squinting with the other so the eyelid covered its milky film.

"No, no," Raffin said, attempting to salvage his only move, raising his hands in front of him. "I overheard your conversation. I'm sorry, it's my first time on a ship and my mind wanders into conversations it shouldn't. I just thought this time my bad habit blessed me with a little luck."

Underbite thought that one over. Raffin's words did their job, confusing the slow one into looking back to the gaming table and cheating while his friend was otherwise occupied.

"Alright. Alright. We'll help you for a share of your cut," Underbite said.

Raffin's shoulders sagged. That wasn't something he expected. He maintained his composure by drawing on his remaining sliver of bravery.

"That's fine. Twenty percent," Raffin said. He needed all the money this suicide mission would give him, but he didn't expect them all to survive.

"Eighty."

"Forty."

"Seventy," Underbite countered.

"Eighty," Raffin said, attempting an old trick.

"Thirty," Underbite said.

"Deal."

Underbite cocked his head, staring intently at his hands. Raffin pulled away before the realization dawned on the man and he decided to take out his frustrations. With any luck, they'd reach land in a day or two. Until then, he'd give those two a wide birth. The ship wasn't large compared to the galleons and warships that traversed the sea, but for someone like Raffin who was used to hiding in alleys and taverns, it was large enough to avoid unwanted attention. In the meantime, Raffin found a quiet place at the back of the boat, behind the helm where gear was stored. The Quartermaster was asleep and drunk, so Raffin was left alone. A fog crept in, blotting out most of what would have been a calm sea.

Raffin gave up everything to come on this venture. Not that he had anything of worth. In truth, he probably had a net negative in value, but that didn't stop people from harassing him or threatening to throw him in jail. The life he left behind wasn't much different from the one he was headed for. He could either live in fear of someone breaking his knees or confront fear head on. Neither was ideal, but at least this option had the potential for profit. Raffin pulled out the papers in his pocket again. Every day of his life seemed to be a trial. All he wanted was to find a way to live free of fear and constricting debt.

*

The day finally came when the Shimmering Cliffs came into view. The gloomy trip broke that morning, the sun cresting over the waves. It hit the cliffs, shattering the orange glow into twinkling orbs of blue, bronze, gold, and red. The crew and passengers respectively stopped what they were doing to watch. Only when the orbs of light started to move did the gathered men realize the dragons on the cliffs caused the shimmering that gave the rockface its name.

As the ship coasted into view of the island, Raffin noticed a merchant sail had been rigged to the mast, and it hung low near the deck. The current drifted the ship towards land. Raffin wasn't a sailor, so it hadn't dawned on him that an island nation might need supplies from outside to survive. It seemed masquerading as merchants was the approach the captain was taking. Near the horizon, crystalline light sparkled with the sunrise.

"To yer stations. Every last one of ye will earn yer passage. Ye there, get to the rigging! And ye, drop that bucket and get to the crow's-nest. As for ye," the captain looked to Raffin. "Go with them fer the weapons."

Raffin looked over to who the captain indicated. The slow one and Underbite grinned at him. It was only yesterday that the two realized Raffin's deception. It was longer than he expected it to take them, but he was delighted at the time. Raffin had done a good job avoiding the two by busying himself near the rest of the crew. It was a risky ploy because he didn't think the crew cared if he was killed. But if those two interrupted their work or killed the helper who was alleviating some of their labor, it might make the crew angry. He thought that would save him from being attacked. Now he would be alone with weapons and the two who were looking for him.

"Uh, captain" Raffin said, but the man had already moved on to give the rest of the crew instruction.

"Come on, smart-boy. Let us show you where the weapons be," Underbite said.

The two grabbed Raffin by the arms and dragged him down below deck. Crewmembers raced to positions Raffin couldn't begin to understand. It looked like they were all doing the same job, pulling ropes or adjusting things along the railings. The sail was raised high and cannons covered in the process. Several ran past the trio, oblivious to Raffin's peril. He didn't have a death wish in spite of his current course of decisions, but he did have a fondness for adrenaline. It was why he loved to gamble. Winning was fun, but the risk was his favorite part. He was meek in the face of physical pain, but risk was another thing entirely. The threat of being beaten up or worse wasn't appealing to him, but he saw no way out just yet.

"We should stuff 'em in a cannon," the slow one said.

Raffin wasn't a fan of that, but before he could voice his opinion, the slow one punched him in the stomach, knocking the wind out of his chest.

"We'd have to cut 'im a bit," Underbite said.

"I could pull him apart," the slow one said, yanking on Raffin's arms for good measure.

"You'd have to uncover a cannon. It would give us away," Raffin said.

Underbite glared at him.

"Okay smart boy, I wonder what toys they have down 'ere?" Underbite asked of no one. He fiddled with a few crossbows and rapiers, giving Raffin time to catch his breath.

"Friends, I thought we had a deal. Why so much hostility?"

"I don't know 'bout yankin' 'im apart, but feel free to rip out 'is tongue," Underbite said.

"He talks pretty, but smells like dung," the slow one said.

"Please, we can work this out. I don't like pain," Raffin said.

"That's too bad. Shouldn't 'ave tried to cheat us," Underbite said.

"I had to. I already owe a lot of people a lot of money. Giving you half of my earnings from this job would land me in the gallows," Raffin argued.

"You ain't surviving this trip. None of us is," Underbite said.

"Then why did you come?"

"I was forced. If not, I was to be hung," Underbite shrugged. "Going out by dragon seemed fun."

Underbite pulled out a wickedly curved dagger with serrated edges and a sharp tip. He held it to Raffin's throat. The slow one held him tight to make sure he didn't move. He sucked in some drool leaking out over his bottom lip and grinned.

The boat rocked hard, throwing the trio around. The slow one let go and sat on his haunches, but Raffin and Underbite were tossed about the bottom deck. Underbite fell into the weapon storage, clanging and rattling filled the air until he stopped moving, and Raffin fell on some liquid he didn't think was water. A loud crack sent splinters rattling over the floor, and a loud thud rolled over the floorboards.

"Cannons?" Raffin asked, getting to his feet and positioning himself near the stairs to the main deck and away from the knife. His shoulder pulled at him uncomfortably, but it was the least of his concerns.

"Ain't noffin but natives there," Underbite said. He climbed out of the storage cabinet with a few minor wounds.

The slow one cried out, seeing a large splinter in his stomach. Underbite helped him remove it. After soothing him, another projectile came crashing through the hull. Underbite grabbed it, holding it up to the lantern that swayed on its hook.

"A rock?"

Raffin scrambled up the stairs to see what was going on. A battle was unfolding, one that would chill the blood of the hardiest warrior. Men and women on dragon back hurled rocks at the ship; diving down before releasing the projectiles at extreme speeds. Raffin ducked out of the way as a larger rock crashed into the ship.

"Look out!" Raffin yelled to the two men below.

Underbite and his companion grabbed crossbows and quivers of bolts, darting up the steps and leaving Raffin hunkered down. Several minutes passed, and the ship lurched and rocked over the waves as larger boulders crashed into the ship. Raffin buried his head below the deck, covering it with his hands and begging for the violence to stop. The crash of waves and yelling of sailors mingled with guttural roars that not only vibrated the boards of the ship but strummed in Raffin's chest. How anyone thought it was possible to kill a dragon, he couldn't fathom. How those people convinced him and others that it was possible, he didn't want to think about. What he did think about were the stories sailors told at the gambling tables off the docks about ships going down and men being trapped on the lower decks. Coupled with a sick curiosity and desire for adventure, Raffin stood up and found his way to the top deck.

Much of the crew was dead, smashed by rocks or burned. Charred wood smoked as waves crashed over the sinking ship. The mast and sails were on fire. Underbite was at the railing holding onto something on the other side. The captain remained at the ship's helm. They sat low in the water, slowly sinking. Something had gone horribly wrong in the captain's plan.

"What are you doing? Jump overboard," Raffin yelled.

"Ye know nothin' of a captain and his ship," the captain spat.

Raffin looked again and saw he intended to beach it.

"You'd rather die than let your ship go down?"

"Without my ship I'm nothin," the captain said.

Raffin barely heard it above the chaos, but he was not about to die because of the captain's stubbornness. Raffin ran and leapt over the side of the ship. He splashed into the water as a large boulder missed the ship and splashed into the water, nearly taking Raffin down to the bottom with it. His head broke the surface in time to see the ship beach itself and a host of warriors descend on it. The Underbite's slow companion fell to the sand as Underbite's strength gave out.

A wave crashed over Raffin's head, pushing him closer to the beach. Raffin kicked, trying to get out of the water. There was nothing he cared much about to risk dying to protect it. The papers weighed heavy in his pocket. His shoulder hurt the more he used it, and he wondered if he'd been hit by a rock after all.

The warriors gathered up the remaining crew, forcing them onto their knees in the sand. Raffin was surprised to see how many crew members survived. The captain was the last to be pulled off the ship and thrown to the sand. Blood dripped down his forehead from a large gash. Raffin washed up on the shore a few moments later, and a trio of warriors with spears and bows pulled him out of the water. They weren't gentle, but it was their rough handling that made him realize he had something stuck in his shoulder. One of the spear wielders wearing leather armor and war paint across his face asked him something in a language he didn't understand. The spear wielder repeated himself, and it took Raffin several seconds to realize he was speaking in a different language. The man rotated through several until he spoke one Raffin recognized.

"Are you a slave or a warrior?"

Raffin took so long to answer the spear wielder that he moved on to another language. It was one he was less familiar with but they registered as the same general question. Raffin wasn't fond of either title, but went with the lesser of the two.

"Slave," he said.

The warriors dragged him away, separating him from the rest of the crew. In total, thirteen of the fifty-person crew remained. The captain was killed on the spot. Someone who must have been the leader directed the trio to bring Raffin in line with the rest. A small discussion went on, but ended when Raffin was placed on his knees with the rest of the crew. In the trauma-filled moments, Raffin didn't notice the hulking beasts surrounding them.

Dragons.

Raffin locked eyes with one that snorted smoke from its nose. He didn't look away from the creature, both terrified and mesmerized all at once. He felt sorry for the members of the crew, but at the same time, they all signed up for this. He expected to go out in a more mundane fashion and hoped this wouldn't hurt.

Then the dragon did something so human, so unexpected, that Raffin was shocked and looked away. It tilted its head in a quizzical manner. Something akin to a seagull's caw with the force of a whale's moan projected from a reptilian throat, the sound barking across the beach. The warriors stopped. The leader turned to face the dragons. Nothing verbally passed between them, but it was obvious a silent conversation took place. The man spun and addressed the warriors and prisoners.

"You are condemned to death. You have one way to avoid this fate," the leader said. Raffin perked up at that. "Participate in the Ceremony and live."

Ceremony? Raffin didn't know what that meant. The first

person to hesitate was stabbed in the arm with a spear. He took the ceremony option. Several in line also took the ceremony option, until some dumb youth tried to be brave. He died in the sand. Underbite and his companion took the ceremony.

At that the dragon stepped in and spoke with the leader again. Something akin to a caress passed between the human and dragon. It wasn't romantic, but something as strong. A nuzzle, maybe? Raffin was still putting it together when the slower man was hauled off. Underbite tried to protest, swinging one of his arms wildly. Two warriors restrained him, forcing him back to his knees. The dragon barked again, the sound rattling in its throat. It locked eyes with Underbite. Again, Raffin was sure a conversation took place between the two. Afterward, Underbite cried in relief.

No one opted for death after that. Then the question was posed to Raffin. The same dragon who he locked eyes with appeared to be measuring him. He didn't hesitate.

"The Ceremony," Raffin said. Only a brave idiot chose death when life was an option. All Raffin did was spend his life jumping from one risk to the next. This was just another day.

The ship was torched by a firing squad of dragons. Lightning, fire, and acid ate away at the wood until the debris washed out to sea. The captain's blood seeped into the sand, mingling with the water from the crashing waves.

*

The crew members were brought to a solid looking structure open to the elements on a stretch of land a short hike away. To their back was a cliff and a rocky shore below. On the other three sides was grass and at least a dozen dragons circling overhead. Wooden beams were spaced wide enough that a determined individual could slip through, but a wild animal would have a hard time getting in. Raffin had no idea if there were other wild animals on the island other than dragons, but the scratches in the wooden beams made him think so.

The wooden door slammed shut, followed by the lock bolting into place. Pointed tips jutted up towards the sky from the beams, holding up a thatched roof. It didn't regulate temperature, but it might hold off some rain. Compared to the homes he passed on the way up, these was poor constructions. Realization settled in. It was a jail cell. Not long after they were locked up, a few individuals came and saw to their wounds. Everyone who approached was accompanied by a dragon.

The physician, or whatever this group of people called their healer, pulled a long splinter from Raffin's shoulder. The relief was instant. He sat down beside Underbite once the healer left and laughed to himself.

"What's so funny?" Underbite asked.

"Just thinking of home," Raffin said.

"Oh?"

"Most of us came here to avoid this fate. When posed with the question, we all chose life in a jailcell over death."

"This is helluva lot different than the cells back home," Underbite huffed.

"Where's your friend?" Raffin was afraid of the man, but they were all lost here. There were no weapons, and Underbite's friend was more of a threat than their captors.

"They took 'im. Said he wasn't needed."

"Who said that?" Raffin asked, wanting to hear if the man's experience with the dragon was the same as his own.

"The dragon. She... well, I don't know if she *said* it. I felt—" Underbite stopped abruptly, unable to finish his train of thought.

"Like images pressed into your head?" Raffin asked.

"Aye. And through that, she said he'd be cared for."

The two shared a moment of silence. Coughs and moans

echoed off the walls, and the one who'd been stabbed in the arm cried out for whiskey to numb the pain. The healers treated them all, but they did not offer any comfort. Despite their differences, Underbite and Raffin shared a sympathy with one another.

"I'm Vyncent. My mate is, well, I don't know what he is, but his name's Lugh."

"I'm Raffin. How'd you meet him?"

"We was orphans together. He took a mean knock on the head when we was kids, and he ain't never been right since. Took this gig to get him some help. Might 'o failed, but at least he gets some help."

"We'll see. We don't even know what this Ceremony is," Raffin said.

"You joined up right quick," Vyncent replied.

Raffin remembered deliberating, but it could have been the dragon doing something to him, just as she did with the others.

"I'm a gambler. I like bets. I win more than I lose, but when I lose, I lose big. Recently I've lost a lot and have the wrong kinds of people after me. It just seemed like the easiest solution. Gamble on myself."

Vyncent didn't respond. Instead, he rolled over and went to sleep. Raffin leaned against the wooden beams and stared through the wooden beams at the moonlit sky. Stars sparkled overhead, occasionally blotted out by dragon wings. The beasts spiraled and summersaulted in the air, resembling a practiced dance. Raffin's eyes grew heavy, and in his fading consciousness, he wondered if they were communicating with one another. Raffin drifted off to a shadow puppet show of dragons darting across the moon.

In the morning, a dragon's roar woke them. Gathered outside the cell were dozens of warriors led by the same man from the beach. He spoke to them in the common tongue.

"We have discussed the conditions of you participating in our

Ceremony. Within your hearts lies the true test. You came here to claim the lives of our dragon companions and their young. Now, you will need to prove you worthy of their trust or you will die. It was Syldraina who spared you." The warrior pointed to the silver dragon behind him. Raffin looked up to see the same dragon who stared at him yesterday. "She thinks this will be a just punishment. Make no mistake, you wanted to take our lives, so we return the favor. Unlike you, who come from the sea and try to poach our friends, we will give you the chance to live."

"Are there any who oppose?" a female asked. She was older than the warrior who spoke, but they shared a resemblance that was undeniable.

No one objected. After the demonstration yesterday, Raffin would be surprised if anyone was brave enough to voice their dissent. Before the warrior moved on, Vyncent stood and stepped up to the bars.

"Is my friend okay?"

"The slow one? Yes. He is being cared for by the dragons. Our shaman will look at him soon. For now, her attention is on the coming Ceremony."

Syldraina turned her head slightly to take in Vyncent. Raffin thought he saw a brief nod from the dragon, but couldn't be sure.

"What is the Ceremony?" he asked. Many of the surviving crew stopped talking amongst themselves to hear the answer.

"It is tradition for our people to relive our beginning, when the first of our people came across this island and made it our home."

"But what does it consist of?" another sailor asked.

The elder woman smiled. "We will tell you in due time. For now, remain here. If you try to run, our dragons will stop you. Food and water will be provided. We are giving you a chance to succeed. If you leave your mouths closed, you might just see how gracious we can be."

The group of warriors left, and no guards remained to watch over them. Some of the more vocal of the remaining twelve crew members started to rile one another up to the point that two slipped through the bars and made to jump into the water below. At the last second, their nerve gave out, but before they could find an alternative escape, two dragons swooped in. One exhaled a burst of fire on the escapees while the other shot a bolt of electricity from its mouth. There was nothing left of either crew member, and no one else tried to escape.

Raffin stood much longer than the rest, admiring the skill and precision of the dragons and their riders. At first glance, he thought they were wild dragons, until they pulled up and flew away. He caught a glimpse of two individuals riding on their backs, situated between their spines. That wasn't the only example of the two species working together. Man and dragon pulled wagons of materials, food, water, and waste to and from the city. Together they built homes, or repaired damage caused by previous storms. The crew experienced one of those tropical storms over the course of a few days. They were soaked day and night during that time, and exposed to the wind coming off the ocean, forcing them to huddle together for warmth.

"This is balls. They want us dead," Vyncent grumbled during the second night. He hadn't said much of anything to Raffin since the first night of their captivity, and the outburst was uncharacteristic.

"Maybe, but why feed us?" Raffin asked.

"Stale bread and half rotten fruit isn't food," Vyncent said.

"We survived on the ship's rations. I think we can make it a little longer," Raffin replied. Maybe it was due to the initial bad blood between the two, but his optimism was new. For some reason, Raffin wasn't convinced the natives of the island wanted them dead. He viewed it as a test. Even if they didn't care if the crew lived or died, Raffin thought Syldraina wanted him to live. "I think it's a test. Weed out the weak."

"To the locker with that," Vyncent cursed.

"You gonna let a city boy like me last longer than you?" Raffin asked. "I'll wager the amount I owe you that I'll last longer than you."

Vyncent looked up at him as rain pelted his eyes, the droplets sliding sideways across his face from the wind's force.

"Deal."

After the storm passed, Raffin and Vyncent spent their days watching the movements of the people. One of the benefits of being so high up was the vantage it provided. The city was simple, but it was sprawling. Smoke billowed from the fireplaces of hundreds of homes, even far into the woods. Each person had a purpose and performed daily tasks. Vyncent pointed out over the ocean towards a dozen dragons and their riders fishing.

"I could eats some fish," Vyncent said.

"When we are freed, we can eat all the fish we want," Raffin said.

"When that'll be?" Vyncent asked.

"I don't know, but I've noticed Syldraina flying nearer the last few days."

"So?"

Raffin wasn't sure why he said it. It was just an observation. He changed topics.

"I think those dragons out there gave us away on our approach."

"How's ya figure?" Vyncent asked.

"How else would they know we were coming? And about our purpose?"

"Thems dragons ain't normal," was all Vyncent said before sitting down.

Raffin found the island society fascinating. It was nothing like his own, and maybe that was why it interested him. His pocket was heavy and he reached for the notes there. A group of guards came to stand around the cell once Syldraina flew off. Raffin was preoccupied and hadn't noticed the dragon's absence. He leaned into his natural gifts of observation and listened in on the guards' conversations.

The number of days that passed since their capture was anyone's guess. None of the crew were particularly good at counting, and while Raffin's grasp of numbers was good, he hadn't thought to keep track of them until several days in. He figured they were about two weeks into captivity. The guards' conversations gave up very little helpful information except that Alowin was the chief, and Wulfa was his mother and matriarch of the clan. After chatting up one young guard, he learned the island people grew a connection with the dragons that many couldn't understand. The guard explained that it stemmed from how his people came to the island, but wouldn't say anything more.

"It shouldn't be long now. We're all excited because it's been some time since an outsider tried their hand at the Ceremony," the young guard said.

Vyncent grabbed Raffin and pointed to the Shimmering Cliffs. "Look there," he said. The two watched as dragons were pushed off the edge of the cliff and forced to fly. Several times Raffin gripped the wooden poles of the pen expecting the worst, only to see tiny wings spread and a new dragon take flight.

"I bet that's the ceremony," Raffin said.

"Youngins?"

"Yes. It's got to be some kind of celebration for newborn dragons."

"Theys the best to catch," Vyncent said. "Their scales ain't the shiniest, but once you polish 'em, they is passable."

The remaining crew seemed to remember their purpose for being on the island then. The lifeless stares burning bright with purpose again.

"Once I get out of this hell, I'm going to break every last one of their necks," a crewman said.

"We'll be rich off their scales," another one laughed.

"You have to stop them," Raffin said to Vyncent, but the man just shifted his under bite and shrugged.

"Theys just blowin' off steam."

"You started it," Raffin said, but the man didn't budge. He just turned back to watch the baby dragons take to the sky and warm their new wings on the sun.

"It only the runt guarding us, we can take him and be off. The dragons can't get us all," one of the crew began.

Narder, the young guard, turned around when he noticed the commotion.

"Shut up," Raffin said. The papers in his pocket were like weights pulling on his heart. Why did he feel the need to stand up and argue? Every fiber of his being was screaming for him to stay away from confrontation.

"You got a problem?" the first crewman said. He had blonde hair that was tied up in a bun using fibers from the wooden poles of their prison cell.

"You takin' a likin' to these beasts that trapped us in 'ere?" a second one asked. His face was covered in a long black beard. His broad nose and dangerous eyes added to his unfriendly demeanor. Spittle flew from his lips as he spoke.

"I just think maybe we made a mistake trying to kill the dragons. Why don't we just try to join them?" Raffin suggested.

"And live in poverty? Why do ya think we came out 'ere in the first place, boy? We ain't lookin' for scraps. If these people are dumb enough to let us live, we'll show 'em."

"What's going on?" Narder asked. The inexperienced boy made the mistake of getting too close to the cell. One of the larger crewmen grabbed him by the scruff and pulled him against the poles. More hands grabbed at him, forcing him through the bars. Several of the men threw punches at the boy. The spear was useless in close combat, but Narder held firm, not wanting to give the prisoners a weapon.

Something came over Raffin in that moment. He didn't enjoy conflict, but this felt right in his bones.

"The hell you are," Raffin said.

The two loud-mouthed crewmen stopped to see who spoke. The rest were caught in a frenzy. Raffin knew he had to help Narder or the crew would kill him. He knew the consequences if that happened would be something to fear. Raffin screamed within his mind for help, praying to anyone listening that a guard or dragon would see what was happening and come to his aid.

"You're the kid who barged 'is way on, ain't ya?" the first one asked. He balled his fist and pulled back, primed to strike.

"Almost got throwed overboard he did," the second one said.

"May haps we take care 'o the trash now?" the first one added.

Raffin didn't fare well in a fair fight. The few times his words didn't get him out of a brawl usually ended with him bloodied and bruised in a back ally. He'd already involved himself, so he reared back and kicked the first one between the legs. The man dropped, clutching his nether region.

A meaty fist caught Raffin in the jaw, sending him sprawling and tasting dirt. The second man was on him in seconds, punching the back of his head. Spending most of his adolescence and adult life on the receiving end of beatings, Raffin was used to losing. The man stood over Raffin, ready to pound his face into the ground with the heel of his boot when a whip cracked, catching him in the chest. He scrambled backwards, recoiling from the pain until he was up against the far side of the cage. A couple arrows flew into the mass of men, killing a few and wounding others.

"What is the meaning of this?" a female warrior asked. She was holding the whip. If Raffin remembered correctly, Narder said her name was Aerils.

No one said a word. They were too frightened. Those holding up Narder released him and stepped away, blending back into the bedraggled group. Narder fell to the floor, unconscious.

"Summon the Shaman, get the chief, and call Syldraina!" Aerils called. The warriors with her raised their bows. "Against the wall, all of you."

The group complied. Yet again, they were on death's doorstep. It wasn't the first time in his life that Raffin wondered if there was an hourglass ticking away, counting down his remaining time in the world. He'd have to wait to find out. The chief showed up, and the surrounding warriors stepped back to allow him access. The Shaman, an elderly lady with pin-straight gray hair and a hump, approached Narder. She didn't speak, but several warriors carried the boy away. Syldraina was circling overhead, crashing to the ground in a gust of wind once Narder was a safe distance away.

When she exhaled, the air around them burned at their flesh, the heat worse than the hottest day Raffin had ever experienced. The dragon's eyes locked on them each in turn. If Raffin could have dragged his eyes away, he would have seen the chief staring at Syldraina's face, slowly nodding in agreement. As it was, Raffin was stuck in a mental parade of images. Ships from far off lands coming to the island. Naïve dragons welcoming them, only to be captured and slaughtered. Another group arriving on similar ships who joined the fight, but instead aiding the humans, they sided with the dragons. Every ship that arrived afterward was repelled by the power of the two combined groups. Whether outnumbered or not, the dragons and their riders were victorious. His heart thundered in his chest, startling him and ending the torrent of images. Syldraina still watched them.

"We will start the ceremony now. You two first." The chief glanced at his dragon briefly before pointing to two of the men who attacked Narder.

That was the last Raffin and the crew saw of them. They watched from the cell, but they weren't forced. Their vantage point was great for breadth, if not the details of the events. There was a scuffle, and a small shadow fall from the cliff, though it was impossible to tell which one it was. As for the other, they didn't see anything that confirmed his fate. As the day progressed, half of the crew attempted the trial. None returned. Each time the chief chose a new duo to attempt the Ceremony, the female warrior smiled. Syldraina ceased superheating the air after the first two failed and took flight near the end of the day, circling overhead above the cell.

"If you don't mind me asking again, what is the Ceremony?" Raffin asked. He was the first to speak since the fight, and the three remaining crewmen, which included Vyncent, slipped away from him as he did. It wasn't an easy task. It took a lot of willpower to speak up, but in the end it was apathy towards his future that leant him the courage.

"I am not deaf, nor am I stupid, Outsider."

"What?" Raffin asked.

"You have potential. I might actually enjoy having you as a part of our community, but you have a lot to prove," the female warrior said.

"What do you mean? I thought we were free to leave if we passed the Ceremony?" The parchments in his pocket clung to his sweaty skin as he touched them.

"No. You were given your lives. That is the mercy the chief has bestowed upon you. In return, you will attempt the Ceremony.

If you pass, you will pledge your life to our community."

"I have a life outside of here. I have plans," Raffin said.

"You will need to change them," Aerils retorted.

"What was Syldraina showing us?"

Aerils didn't answer, but the chief did.

"Our community fought beside the dragons when your kind were praying on them for their scales before they knew what mankind was. Half of our people were killed in the initial attack. Dragons are trusting by nature, relying on their size and mastery of elements to intimidate potential threats. We aimed to help them from the start, but it took them time to notice our efforts were aiding them. We accepted the losses and fought alongside them, pushing the raiders away. That is what Syldraina was showing you."

"I didn't see that," one of the remaining crew said.

"No. I imagine you didn't. You are the threat. Our people and the dragons know this. You must prove yourself in other ways. How you do that is up to you. Some outsiders who have come here tell remarkable tales in our drinking halls, but to join them, you must pass the Ceremony. We will end here for the night. Tomorrow, it is your turn." The chief pointed at Raffin.

*

Raffin pawed at the notes all night and cried tears for a life he had intended to live. They slid down his dirty cheeks, leaving behind evidence of their existence. He half expected the crew to try to kill him, but whatever they had seen in their visions kept them quiet and still. He crumpled and uncrumpled the papers. A family business he would never reopen. It would fall to some rich noble back home, the owner of his debts most likely. He rested his head against one of the poles. He wanted to feel failure, or a sense of despair, but for the first time in his life he was truly excited.

Perhaps this would be a good change. There was something special about this place. Was it possible to find hope in the pits of hell?

Standing on the beach the next morning, he pulled the notes out from his pocket. He had considered tossing them into the sea back on the ship that night in hopes someone would find them... a remnant of the memory that his family once owned the greatest bakery in the city. He never expected to survive the trip. After seeing the beauty of the island and the creatures that inhabited it, he couldn't care less about his debts. The loss of his family's bakery stung, but he'd never been a good baker and knew he would gamble it away again. That was who he was. Or at least, it was who he'd been. He crumbled up the papers and tossed them into the waves. They washed back onto the shore, but Raffin was long gone.

The sun was high and warm, baking the sand at his feet. He could see himself living here and even wanted to prove Aerlis's confidence well founded. He couldn't fight, at least not well, but perhaps his ability to beguile would come in handy here. The chief motioned for him to follow.

The community of the island enjoyed a sprawling village. As he traversed the streets, he forgot about the prison cell was. Shops, homes, businesses, and training grounds were everywhere. Raffin saw no money exchange hands, though. Livestock ambled along the road, slowly following their watchful shepherds. Some kids played while others did chores. The village was more like a city, stretching from the beach and wrapping around the cliffs. The most shocking part of his excursion was the lack of walls. It seemed there was no threats for the community to worry about, not until they reached the section of the city that butted up against the cliffs.

"To keep the dragons out?" Raffin asked.

"To keep the drakes out," the chief said.

"Drakes? Aren't they extinct?"

"I do not know about the rest of the world, but drakes spawn here, though not frequently. We patrol the beach vigilantly. This helps us be aware of their presence in case one comes around," the chief said.

Raffin felt his knees lock up momentarily.

"Are you okay?"

"Why would you tell me that?"

"My father told me of our ancestor who first arrived here, and of how he handled seeing his family slaughtered by the dragons before siding with them against the other humans. Why do you suppose he reminded me that dragons were the ones who killed my people?"

"I don't know," Raffin said, answering before he took the time to consider the question.

The chief smiled. "Perhaps you will come to the conclusion and it will aid you."

"What now?" Raffin asked.

"The gates will open and you will attempt the trials of the Ceremony. Good luck," the chief said, then turned and started the long journey back.

"Hey," Raffin called after him.

The warriors shuffled unhappily with the disrespect Raffin showed. It wasn't intentional, but it was blatant. The chief showed no offense, turning to look at him with the same smile.

"Yes?"

"Why not fly back?"

"Dragons are allies, not pets or domesticated tools."

With that, the chief continued on his way. Aerlis shoved Raffin out of the gate and it closed behind him. She offered him some parting words.

"Don't get eaten."

The island mass was too large to see the ocean from his current position, but he knew if he braved the woods, he would make it to the ocean on the far side. From there he had nowhere to go. He was excited, but also scared. He could die, and he expected to. Every time he'd faced death before, he'd had a plan or a skill that helped him. Here, he was outskilled and outmaneuvered. A worn dirt path cut through the grass, leading up to the rocky cliffs. Dragons barked, somewhere between a screech and a growl, and he knew that was only a portion of their language.

An arrow struck the ground behind him and he took that as a warning that it was time to get moving. He trekked onward and the grass gave way to rock. It wasn't slick, but seemed polished and gleamed under the sun. The brightness of the sun and the reflection off the rocks forced him to squint. The whoosh of wings made him drop to his knees, and he crouched behind a rocky outcropping. Shielding his eyes with his hands, he watched a bronze and a blue dragon spar in midair, their riders hanging on, unfazed at being upside down. The movements, while sparked by necessity, were streamlined. There was no hesitation or jerkiness to them. The rider and dragon knew what was expected, performing their moves flawlessly.

Raffin wasn't sure if they always spared over the cliffs or if it was for his benefit. Regardless, he slowly made his way to the cliffs. A small path led to where he saw the baby dragons learn to fly. He followed the trail, hugging the walls of the cliff, unwilling to look over the edge. A new fear rose within him. It wasn't something a kid from a wealthy family ever got used to. As an adult, he slept in gutters, not in high-rise buildings. What was he supposed to be looking for?

He spotted some cracked eggs and tiny bones, but it wasn't obvious what they were doing there. He didn't know if dragons were cannibalistic. Eventually, the pathway tunneled through the rocky cliff, forcing Raffin into darkness. This was more familiar territory for him, spending most of his time scouring the poorly lit streets and relying on his silver tongue to get him out of situations if he got caught. The light filtered through the porous rock walls and from the tunnel entrance, reflecting off something wet.

Curious, Raffin bent down and touched what he thought was water. His hand came away slick. Blood. He rubbed the dark liquid between his fingers and could just make out an egg shell with cracked edges. A newborn's first kill? There wasn't any blood on the previous eggs or bones to indicate a kill.

Something blocked the light from the entrance, its growl echoing through the tunnel. A small light shone at the other end of the tunnel. Raffin didn't hesitate. Finally, something he was good at. He ran for the light, never letting it out of his sight. He figured if it was visible to him, nothing impeded his path. Unless the impediment was shorter than the height of the light. Raffin felt hard, unmoving stone crack into his shins, sending him summersaulting and slipping into a fissure in the darkness.

Heavy breathing echoed above the fissure. Reaching out, Raffin caught the edge of something sharp. The rock dug into his hands, but he didn't let go. He couldn't see below him. It felt as though there was nothing but open air. He overheard a scholar once talking about how the heart stopped in free fall. He decided that was better way to go than being eaten alive. Hot breath warmed his neck and Raffin found the courage to let go. There was a short drop and he hit something solid, rolling along a path until he came out onto a ledge only wide enough to fit his feet. He caught himself before he tumbled over the edge.

A cry vibrating in the throat of a reptile cut through the rushing wind. Raffin turned his head to see a four-legged beast with no wings ruffle its feathers. Drakes were supposed to be extinct. They were the bastard offspring of dragons born from eggs that hatched in the water. Dragon eggs were sturdy and difficult to break, and falls to the sand and water rarely ended in broken shells, but drakes had the strength of a dragon and could easily crack the shell and eat their properly formed cousins. Raffin hadn't believed the chief when he told him of their continued existence. Seeing one now barely registered, but it made sense why the eggs he saw were broken open, not hatched.

The creature growled, anticipating an easy meal. Raffin scanned the ledge below him and saw another landing. It surprised him the creature was able to follow him from the upper cave. Hoping he would make it, he let go and fell through the air, hitting hard on the next landing. He looked up. The drake slithered like a serpent across the rocks, darting to a slope that connected the two levels.

Raffin had no weapon he could use. The rocks scattered at his feet would be useless on such tough scales. A powerful gust of wind blew both him and the drake against the cliff face. Raffin grabbed the rocks tightly, injuring his wounded hands even more. Unfazed, the drake made its way closer to Raffin. While dragon eggs were their main diet, any meat they found was devoured just as voraciously.

How had he let this happen? He knew that death was a possibility, but he never gave up fighting it. It wasn't enough for him to just accept his fate; he had to confront and overcome his fears first. The anticipation ate at him, causing him to sweat. Once the object of his terror was in his face, all of the immobilization vanished. Unfortunately, he'd put himself in a tight spot to get out of. His only hope was to tackle the creature over the edge and hope they crashed into a rock spire. While similar to dragons, the feathery scales were weaker than normal scales, meant to help the beasts glide through the water rather than offer any sort of protection. Still, a fall to the rocks might not do the trick.

Hearing the same throaty sound, Raffin mistook it as a drake's call before noticing the cooing behind him. The two sounds were similar, but this one was different. Raffin couldn't risk taking his eyes from the drake. If the dragon approaching from behind him wanted him dead, it wouldn't have announced itself. His shins hurt, he couldn't run, and there was no lower ledge to descend to. He would either have to attack the drake or dive off the ledge. The dragon cooed again. He knew it was trying to communicate, but he didn't understand it. He barely knew what the silver dragon had said when it imparted its images into his head.

The drake snapped its jaws, approaching quickly. Raffin leapt up as the drake pounced. It scraped a jagged claw along his thigh. Meat tore and skin parted. The pain took Raffin's breath away. A hungry moan gurgled in the drake's throat, and the dragon barked. Raffin couldn't think. The pain in his leg consumed him. He was afraid to look at the wound, barely noticed the barking growing louder. The growling sounds and snapping jaws of the drake faded away. Raffin tried to get up and his instincts told him to use his legs for assistance. The pain lancing up his thigh shocked him into letting go and he crashed back down, feeling a *pop* within his ribs.

Through pain-filled eyes, he saw the drake and dragon battling. The fear of rolling off the edge hit Raffin in the chest. It was an alien feeling. He brushed it off, unable to focus on much other than the pain. He vaguely wondered why the dragon didn't use its advantage of flight.

As the two fought, Raffin noticed the dragon wasn't as young as he first thought. Its scales had a shimmer of blue under its opaque scales, like water under the thin sheets of lava glass. It fought hard, avoiding bites and slashes from the drake. Still, it refused to fly, keeping its wings close to its back. Raffin felt blood trailing down his leg. The scent excited the drake. Its attacks grew eager, throwing itself against the dragon, pushing it back a step before whipping around and coming at Raffin. Rocks fell away as the dragon's foot slipped on the edge. The fear of falling electrified Raffin's nerves. Placing his elbows onto the rough ledge, he backed up as fast as he could, but he was no match for the drake's speed.

It stood over Raffin, thick saliva dripping in globs onto his face and chest. The stench of rotting flesh made him gag and his eyes watered. It reared back, ready to bite. Raffin grabbed the nearest thing he could and swung. The jagged edges of the rock cut into Raffin's fingers and palm, doing more damage to him than the drake. Something heavy struck the drake, and it disappeared from the ledge. He rolled over and saw two shapes plummeting to the sea below. He laid back with a pained sigh, staring up at the cloudless sky. He'd survived... for now. He knew the dragon would be fine, but the flashing image of rocks approaching caused fear to constrict his chest. There would be no survival high this time. Both shapes were still falling.

"Open your wings," he shouted, but the words were weak.

What was he feeling? It couldn't be the fear of falling. He was safe on the ledge. *Don't,* he thought. He wouldn't tempt fate, but it wasn't time to rest. His nerves were on fire. *Scared,* he thought. The words were unbidden.

Why hadn't the dragon flown up yet? He cursed himself and leapt over the side. His heart didn't stop, and his chest didn't explode. He squinted against the wind, making himself as small as possible. The dragon on the other hand flailed in terror.

Raffin tried to scream, but air rushed down his throat. Not wanting to feel that again, he closed his mouth and kept his eyes on the dragon. Images of splattering on the rocks below entered his mind. At first, he wasn't sure if the thoughts were his own or the dragon's. He soon understood. The dragon was imparting feelings to him. It wasn't old enough to have mastered the ability as Syldraina had.

As he continued to fall, the thoughts grew more frantic. Raffin had less of an idea on how to communicate with the dragon. He tried to push his thoughts out to tell the dragon to spread its wings. If he was successful, he couldn't tell. The dragon kept falling, getting closer to the rocks as images of death kept flooding Raffin's mind.

For what felt like an eternity, he slowly closed the distance until he felt the scaly skin of the dragon and could clearly see the brilliant blue of its scales. He grabbed at its wings, yanking upward and spreading them as wide as he could. They flipped out like the spring of a catapult, nearly knocking Raffin off its back. The force of the thin membrane catching the wind pressed him against the dragon's back, and he watched as the drake impaled itself on the rocks below.

A single word passed between Raffin and the dragon. Thoceada.

Thoceada and Raffin soared across the bay, both feeling the freedom of flight and knowing no obstacle could impede their passage now. He could travel wherever he wanted, outrun any enemy, escape for peace amongst the clouds. The freedom he craved was at his fingertips. Thoceada started to drop, heading for the beach. Concern washed over him. He looked out over the ocean and saw an armada of ships headed towards the island.

Thoceada hit the sand and Raffin slid off her back. His injured leg buckled before the warriors could catch him. His bloodied hands clenched the sand, and he felt trapped again.

Aerlis, the chief, and his mother were waiting for him and Thoceada. The Shaman was summoned. As the ancient woman worked on his wounds, the chief approached. Thoceada watched over Raffin protectively. The chief drew close, placing a friendly hand on the dragon's side.

"It seems your life has been spared, only to postpone your

death."

Raffin had a better look from the air at the size of the navy coming in. It didn't look any better from the beach.

"If you will stay and fight alongside us, as you have earned?"

"Survival is my way of life. It's just another day," Raffin said without hesitation.

## THE END

# Wings Across Realms
Jay Reace

"Alaric!" Jotar, Alaric's father calls as he stands in the threshold of their quaint cabin. The high sun touches his dark complexion as he moves out of the doorway. His hand flies up to shield his brown eyes from the sudden light. "Alaric!" he shouts again, before saying to himself, "Where is that boy? Alaric!"

*

Alaric blazes through the forest, with the sound of wild galloping gaining behind him. His bare feet pounding against the woodland floor, his chest screams in pain. A burning sensation radiates from his core, spreading through his whole body. But he sees his chance, an open field. Alaric powers through and pushes himself faster, making it into the field. He quickly turns to slide on the soft grass until he stops and faces his pursuer.

An apep dragon bursts through the forest canopy, with its cobalt black scales and a fiery red underbelly glistening for all to see. Alaric looks on in amazement as the winged beauty shines under the sun's rays before blocking the light with its glorious wings. Alaric stands ready as it descends, divebombing toward the ground, only pulling up at the last minute, like arrow now aimed at Alaric. It hurtles forward but Alaric sees his chance and runs in its direction, summersaulting and flipping onto its back. Alaric slaps the back of its neck and says, "Tag! Got you, Nightfire."

The gentle beast glides to a soft landing and turns its cobra-like neck to face Alaric and licks him furiously.

"Okay, okay, that's enough," Alaric says with laughter and gently pushes Nightfire back.

"Alaric!" He hears the faint calling of his father and looks into the sky before realizing he's about to be late and says, "Dad's going to be mad, let's go."

Nightfire gets a running start before flapping his wings and taking off over the forest and into the sky. Alaric lets his arms stretch outward before Nightfire makes his descent near their cottage. Jotar stands waiting with his arms folded. He marches forward once they land. "Where have you two been?"

They both hang their heads as Jotar continues scolding them.

"You know it's the day of your bonding ritual and Nightfire, you should know better." Nightfire moves forward meekly and nudges his face against Jotar's gently. Jotar smiles. "All right, I'm not mad. Sometimes I wonder who you're actually paired with, me or him?"

"Baba," Alaric says. "Nightfire was only helping me train for the ritual." Jotar exhales loudly. "I've told you, and Nightfire knows this, there is no training for the ritual. It's a series of trails the source gives you, based on what you need to grow and connect to your dragon."

"Didn't you say there were three trials, Baba?" Alaric asks. Jotar places a soft hand on Alaric's back, to motion him forward as they begin to walk.

"I did, but you shouldn't look at them like that." Jotar notices Nightfire following behind them and turns. "It's okay, old friend. We'll be fine. You stay here and rest." Nightfire rubs his head against Jotar and does the same to Alaric. But there is a sudden sadness in Nightfire's soft purple eyes.

"Can't he come, Baba?"

"It's best if he stays here. We wouldn't want your future dragon smelling the scent of another on you. That usually doesn't go well."

Alaric hugs Nightfire and briefly watches him head back to their cabin before continuing with his father. They stroll for a moment, admiring the natural beauty of the forest before Jotar says, "You have been wanting to go through with the pairing ritual for a very long time, my son. I haven't been completely honest with you."

Alaric listens intently. Jotar pauses and says, "I can't tell you what you will see and face during your ritual, but what I can say is that the pairing ritual is three phases, with various trials within each phase. Phase one is a journey of self, where you prove you are worthy of being paired with a dragon. Phase two, once you find a dragon, is to earn that dragon's trust." Jotar stops and becomes quiet as they near several stone pillars that separate the forest from the vast valley.

"How do I earn my dragon's trust, Baba?"

With a warm smile, Jotar says, "By using your heart." Jotar hugs his son tightly before sending him on his way. Alaric starts to walk but stops and turns.

"Aren't you coming with me?"

Jotar fights against the moisture behind his eyes. "I almost forgot the third phase. You and your dragon must go out into the world together."

"Baba?" Alaric chokes out.

"I have faith that I will not see you again as you are now, my son, but as the man I know you can be."

"Baba," Alaric says with a tear. "What if I can't?"

"Then you try again." Jotar smiles. "Now go. The priest is waiting on you."

Alaric stands tall as he turns away from all he's known and gazes into the foreign beauty of the lush valley. Taking in a deep breath, he exhales and moves forward with his head held high. He walks forward between the stone pillars and vanishes.

*

Alaric appears among the Floating Peaks, a sacred site of ethereal beauty. Floating blue mountains with snow covered tops surround him as celestial wonders dance above in the sky. A path of still water reflects his image. Alaric moves forward, causing the image to dissolve into ripples.

"What is this place? Where am I?"

"You are where you need to be, Alaric," a voice says. Alaric looks around until he sees an old woman sitting cross-legged on a rock floating towards him. Alaric's eyes widen.

"Are you the priest?"

Her face begins to let a small smile peak through before sending it away.

"I am what you need me to be. Would you like me to be a priest?"

Alaric scratches his head and shrugs his shoulders.

"Come, sit." She smirks and motions for Alaric to sit beside her on the rock. He climbs up and takes a seat in front of her, rubbing a hand on his tan shirt sleeve. He notices her staring intensely into his brown eyes. Her head tilts from side to side as she analyzes him.

"What is it you seek?"

Alaric perks up with enthusiasm. "I want to be a dragon rider."

She throws down a pinch of dust from her pocket that sparks violently, causing Alaric to scramble backward. A small fire ignites between them, illuminating her old face as she leans in close.

"Everyone comes here to be a dragon rider! To undergo a transformative experience, forging an unbreakable bond with a dragon that will be their lifelong companion… This ritual is not merely a passage; it is a profound communion between rider and dragon, a harmonious blending of destinies. So, I ask again, what do you seek?"

"I want to be a…" Alaric starts to say but stops to consider the question. He takes a deep breath and exhales slowly. Then, as if lifting a huge invisible burden, he says softly, "My mother. I seek my mother." He wipes a tear from his eyes.

"Very good, now drink from the water below."

He looks down at the watery path and back at her, unsure. Before she can say anything else, Alaric hops off the rock and kneels beside the water. He scoops out some of the water with his hand and takes a sip. He starts to stand but his vision begins to blur, and the world starts to spin around him. He finds it hard to stand and falls flat back down to the ground and passes out.

*

Alaric is roused from his slumber, emerging into a wonderous dreamscape surrounded by a forest with a cosmic vista that stretches into the boundless reaches of the universe. He looks around and finds himself alone.

*Where am I? he wonders.*

He moves forward and ventures through the otherworldly realm until he stumbles upon a solitary lion-hog. He swiftly backsteps into a retreat but the lion-hog's big soft eyes quickly become narrow upon seeing Alaric. The serene tranquility is shattered as the lion-hog's massive hooves dig deep, leaping forward to attack Alaric. He dodges while keeping his eyes on the beastly animal. Alaric cross-steps to the side and back to see if it will mirror him, but the lion-hog simply hunkers down with its long golden ears pinned back, watching its prey.

Alaric works to steady his heart as he keeps the animal in his gaze, careful not to look it in its eyes as he tries again to back away slowly.

"Nice kitty-piggy. Nice…" Before he can finish, the lion-hog tries to leap forward again but stumbles with a whimper. Alaric raises a brow.

*This could be my chance,* he thinks.

Alaric takes a big step back and the lion-hog pounces unsuccessfully forward with a crash. Alaric turns to run but stops several steps away as he looks back at the helpless lion-hog. He discerns that the lion-hog is hurt. Moved by empathy, Alaric swiftly crouches down.

"Are you hurt?"

The lion-hog begins growling low, causing Alaric to stop. He extends his hand and the lion-hog snaps at him. Alaric falls but raises back up.

"I just want to help. May I help you?"

The lion-hog's eyes soften as if understanding Alaric. He continues forward slowly and sees a gash on the animal's hind leg.

"I don't have anything to put on your wound but maybe…" He rips his shirt sleeve startling the lion-hog. "Easy there, I'm just going to wrap it." He gently places the torn piece onto the gash and ties it to the animal's leg. The lion-hog looks back at Alaric and his work, touched by his kindness. The lion-hog begins to shift and morph, evolving into the familiar form of the woman priest. To Alaric's astonishment, he realizes that the entire sequence was a fantastical reverie.

"Was this all a dream?"

She offers an enigmatic smile and says, "This was a test. And you have passed." Guiding him towards the second segment of his quest, she stops. "This is as far as I go. The mythical dragon you seek awaits at the summit of the Floating Peaks. But be warned, it is surrounded by floating snow-capped mountains, where trouble also lies waiting."

She vanishes, as does the cosmic scenery around him. Returning to the foothills of the Floating Peaks and blue mountains, he gazes at the celestial wonders dancing in the sky before looking up at the mountain that seems to touch the heavens. He begins to climb.

*

As he takes step after step, grasping onto the side of the mountain, the jagged terrain makes each move difficult and painful. Thoughts of returning home flood his young mind, but his father's voice whispers to him.

"There will be times you want to quit, but just keep going, keep pushing forward."

Alaric keeps moving, only stopping momentarily for rest, but soon his fatigue from climbing turns to burning pain throughout his bones and nerves. Sweat beads down his face as he looks up for hope. And there, high above him, is an edge that may be where he can find his dragon.

With new determination, Alaric finds his strength and continues onward. He moves steadily, keeping calm so as not to slip before making it to the top. Once there, the soft cushy grass welcomes his back as he falls from exhaustion. The cold, crisp air cools his warm body as he takes in the low-hanging sun dancing within the cosmic ceiling above. He begins to dream of Baba's warm maple squash, with garbanzos, cranberries, and kalic.

*Actually, forget the kalic,* he thinks to himself.

Alaric can barely hold back salivating as his stomach begins to rumble with hunger. Before he can address it, he hears the clatter of a few pebbles falling in the distance. Quickly sitting up, he scans the surrounding rocky terrain but only sees the jagged cliffside that stretches upward.

He scans higher and sees them, three ferocious dragons. A Ngoubou creepily descends toward him, lurking to the side with its scaly hunter-green spikes protruding down its muscular body. A Kongamato claws forward, seemingly made of pure fire, its scales shades of red, orange, and yellow. And the third, a Ninki Nanka, its dark, earthy scales accented by blood red specks scattered along its face, neck, limbs and tail. It slinks between the others as they all slowly assess their prey.

Standing, Alaric sees the threats before him and feels panic setting in. His heart pounds and his hands tremor, but he stands tall with his head high, as he knows not to run. The dragons continue down until they surround him. They hiss and growl, working to intimidate Alaric.

A misty rain begins to fall, highlighting the Kongamato's claws as they cut through growing heavy rain, swiping at Alaric. He evades with a quick step back and pivots to avoid a sudden snap of sharp teeth.

Thunder cracks the sky, catching their attention. They inch back from Alaric, moving toward the mountain.

"What's the matter? Scared of a little thunder?"

Lightning flashes, and Alaric turns sharply to see a dragon launching up into the sky. His eyes go wide as the sterling grey dragon spreads its wings with a thunderous roar that echoes across the heavens. Lightning arcs from the tips of its wings before it soars down and lands on the edge of the plateau. Alaric stands in awe as he realizes it's an Aido Weido, a god of dragons. He is quickly taken from his trance as the three dragons rush past him to attack the Aido Weido.

The Ngoubou is quickly thwarted as the Aido Weido swats its massive talons and knocks it back. The rain sizzles as it strikes the scales of the Kongamato, who leaps onto the back of the Aido Weido. It shakes furiously to launch the Kongamato off the mountain's edge. The Ngoubou charges and is caught in a death grip with the Aido Weido. They grapple, twist, and shuffle back and forth before the Aido Weido finally lifts the enormous green beast over its head and tosses it over the mountainside.

It looks around, searching for the last threat as Alaric peeks from around a boulder. Summoning his courage, he moves toward the monstrous silver beauty, inching forward, but stops in his tracks as the dragon whips its head in his direction and stares with a narrow gaze. Alaric is entranced with the dragon's deep navy-colored eyes but keeps his distance as it growls at him.

Alaric admires the simple beauty of the dragon. The silver scales shimmer with electricity. Its large wings have subtle shades of red underneath them. And its eyes shine like sapphires. Alaric finds his nerve as he crouches low with his hand out and eases forward. The dragon snarls but Alaric moves closer in hopes to gain its trust.

The Aido Weido tilts its head before cautiously sniffing Alaric's hand. Its massive wings shift forward as its talons dig into the dirt. Alaric carefully reaches out to pet it on its long snout. He can't help but notice the contrast of his rich brown skin against the surprisingly soft pearly scales. The dragon nudges against his hand, encouraging Alaric to continue petting. Alaric goes to rub higher but soon finds himself and the Aido Weido launched into the air as the Ninki Nanka bursts from the ground.

Alaric regains his feet near the mountain's edge. The Ninki Nanka quickly pounces onto the Aido Weido, biting and clawing. The Aido Weido roars in agony, unable to defend against the attack. Alaric scans the area and finds several rocks before picking them up and hurling them at Ninki Nanka, gaining its attention when a few hit it square on the head. With a sudden flip, it kicks the Aido Weido back against the rocky mountain side and sets its sights onto its new prey.

Alaric is frozen as it charges toward him. Its massive teeth consume Alaric's view as it draws closer. It leaps, and Alaric can see his destiny down its enormous throat as its mouth stretches to swallow him whole. Its jaws snap shut inches from his face before its drug backward. It fights to move forward, clawing at the ground for purchase, but it continues moving away before being lifted into the air. Alaric sees the Aido Weido has grabbed the Ninki Nanka's tail with its mouth and twirls it around before launching it off the mountain.

With no time to react, Alaric barrel rolls out of the way. He stands up before looking down the side of the mountain. A sea of monstrous clouds and three angry dragons clawing their way back up lay below him. He turns, looking back at the Aido Weido, and begins to feel the ground beneath him shift as gravity pushes him down. His hands reach to grab the dissolving earth below him but it crumbles as he frantically claws at it. Alaric feels his weightless body falling.

Fear overtakes him, his heart pulsating in his ears, his life flashing before his eyes. The Aido Weido whooshes past him, extending its wings and catches Alaric on its back. Alaric holds tight as they soar high into the air. He often wondered what it would feel like to ride a dragon. Sure, he rode Nightfire for quick spurts around the forest, but nothing like this. High in the sky, with nothing holding him in place but the sky above and the freedom below.

Most people never ride a dragon, and the ones they encounter are paired. It is forbidden to ride someone else's dragon, though his father allowed him to break that rule. Once that dragon is paired, the bond cannot be broken, even in death because if one of the two dies, so does the other. But Alaric didn't worry about that now. Now, he felt freer than he ever had. The sun beamed on him, and he smiled wide, stretching his arms out and mimicking his new found friend.

*

They land softly, high atop a snow-covered mountain. Alaric hops off the dragon's back and looks at the gentle giant. It gazes at Alaric, and for a moment, Alaric hears a faint sound in his head. Instinctively, he listens closely as the sound grows louder and clearer. A firm and masculine voice breaks through.

"Can you hear me?"

"Who... are you speaking to me?" Alaric replies as he points at the silver dragon.

"Yes, what is your name, young one?"

Alaric's eyes grow wide. "Baba said the connection between a dragon and its rider is strong but—"

"I am not an it!" he proclaims. "My name is Stormwing."

"My apologies, Stormwing. I didn't mean to... I just—can we start over? Hey Stormwing, my name is Alaric. It is a pleasure to meet you."

"It is a pleasure to meet you, too, Alaric," he says with a tilt of his head.

"How can I hear you? It's like you're in my head."

"Our pairing has begun. Did they teach you nothing, young one?"

"Riders don't speak of what happens during their ritual or what is shared between them and their dragon to non-riders."

"I see. Well, let me educate you, then. The stronger our bond grows, the more abilities we will share."

"I understand, but how does our bond grow?"

"Like any other, over time. But for now, there is somewhere we must go."

Alaric's tilts his head. "Go where?"

"In order to complete the bonding, we must go to Tyranthia."
Stormwing lowers his head in a motioning fashion. Alaric takes
notice and climbs onto his back.

"Isn't that where the Silent Peaks of Sobat are?"

"Yes. They are protected by the walking mountain. He is who
we need to see."

"Will he have food? I'm starving."

Stormwing flaps his enormous wings and launches them into
the air.

"I'm sure we can find food along the way. Hold on."

Alaric grips tightly as they soar through the air and into the
cosmic sky.

*

Alaric and Stormwing have soared past the serenely wild
floating mountains, and are on their way to the Silent Peaks of
Sobat. Stormwing was nice enough to stop near a forest grove to
let Alaric pick various vegetation to eat before continuing their
journey. They glide through the air as Alaric struggles to munch on
his food.

"Why are we going to Tyranthia?" Alaric asks.

"I told you, to see the walking mountain."

"But why?"

"He will be able to guide us on how to complete our bond."

Alaric finishes crunching on an apple-berry before asking, "I
thought we were bonded?"

"Our bonding started when you entered the cosmic plane but
because I am not like other dragons and you are not like other
humans, our bonding has not been cemented yet."

"What do you mean we are not like others?"

"Being an Aido Weido, my connection to the elements is
greater than others of my kind, just like your…"

A spear whizzes past them, causing Stormwing to barrel roll out of the way. Alaric briefly losses his grip but quickly regains it and holds tightly to Stormwing's scaly mane.

"What was that?!" Alaric looks back to see several dragons and their riders behind them. "We've got incoming!"

"I see them," Stormwing says. "Hold on!"

Stormwing pivots through the air to turn sharply, avoiding a barrage of arrows flying past. He darts and turns but is unable to evade the onslaught of persistent pursuers. Alaric holds on tightly as Stormwing maneuvers but feels his grip loosening.

"I'm slipping!"

"Old on!" Stormwing replies, but Alaric's fingers can't keep their grip.

"I'm trying!"

Stormwing swerves within inches of each oncoming attack. "I can't seem to get them off of us. I'm going to try something."

Before Alaric can respond, Stormwing launches them up high, his wings spread wide, and lets out a thunderous roar before shooting massive bolts of lightning from his wings. Several hit various dragon riders pursuing them but in the eternity of that moment, Alaric feels numb and can only look on as he sees Stormwing flying away as he plummets through the air. In a silent cry, he calls out, "Stormwing!"

As he falls and watches the continuing battle in the sky, Alaric is unable to breathe. Immense pain fills him as Stormwing cries out after taking a spear to the back. The wind begins to tickle Alaric's skin as it cuts through his clothes and his feeling begins to return. Stormwing does his best to avoid spears being hurled at him, but they hinder his flight.

Four dragon riders proceed to fly an enormous net over Stormwing. Alaric screams as he continues to watch, and Stormwing realizes he's lost Alaric. The dragon turns frantically until he sees Alaric plummeting down. But it's too late, the dragon riders have him in their net. Stormwing struggles to fight but the more he struggles, the tighter the net gets until he's unable to move.

Alaric watches helplessly, paralyzed by fear. Suddenly, he lands on the back of one of the riders' dragons. Alaric sits up to see a savage looking woman with long blond hair, a deep scar over one eye, and a twisted grimace that displays rotting teeth. Alaric rolls back as the woman swipes at him with a jagged staff. She missed and swipes again but Alaric is able to grab and pull it towards him, jerking the woman off balance. Alaric takes the staff but immediately feels pain radiating throughout his head as he is met with a swift punch to his jaw.

Alaric shakes off the pain and quickly swats his neck as he feels a pinch. The sky becomes fuzzy as his eyelids grow heavy. He tries to look at the woman, who is now smiling as she lowers a blow dart, but blackness creeps in, causing him to pass out.

*

"Alaric! Alaric!" He hears his name and he slowly moves his throbbing head. "Alaric, if you can hear me, don't speak out loud." It takes him a moment, but he soon realizes it's Stormwing speaking.

"Where... where are we?" Alaric starts to look around before Stormwing says, "Don't move. We are being watched." Alaric stays still. "By who?"

"By Battle Trolls."

"Battle Trolls? Baba use to tell me bedtime stories about them as I'd fall asleep."

"These are not like the ones your father would tell you about. These are vicious parasites," Stormwing says with disdain. "No doubt living off of the walking mountain."

"Are we on the walking mountain? We're not moving." Alaric continues to stare into the tranquil forest before him.

"You may not see it, but behind you are the Silent Peaks of Sobat and I can feel the mystic energy crackling through the air. It's electrifying." Alaric frowns slightly.

"Don't speak of electricity, my fingers are still tingling from whatever it was you did up there."

"I'm sorry Alaric," Stormwing says softly. "I thought our bond had grown strong enough."

"For you to electrocute me?"

"For you to handle my abilities."

Alaric's eyes go wide. "Wait, you're saying I'll be able to withstand lightning?"

"When our bond is strong enough, you will be able to produce it along with many other things. We need to get out of here before they eat us."

"What do you mean?"

"What part of 'eat us' isn't clear? Battle Trolls will eat anything, including dragon. The dragon riders of Tyranthia must be working with them. However, we have two things in our favor."

"Which are?" Alaric asks impatiently.

"They only eat at sunrise."

"Okay, not sure how that helps and..."

"They enjoy the chase" Stormwing says. Alaric takes in a deep breath and exhales. "I still don't see how that helps us."

"Humans," Stormwing says as a slight. "They are watching us through the bush but won't move unless we run or fly away. I will stay here while you find the head of the walking mountain."

Alaric's face scrunches. "You forgot some things. I'm tied up, and I can't leave you."

"If you want us to survive, you will. The dragon riders that dropped us off must be working with the Battle Trolls for some reason. But more importantly, they must be using some sort of blood magic to keep me tied down. You were tied with ropes. See if you can break them."

"How? And won't the Battle Trolls rush us if I break free?"

"You're wasting time, Alaric! Sunrise is only a few hours away, and you may need that time to find the head of the walking mountain. Break your bonds and stand slowly."

Alaric starts to protest but holds his mental tongue. He twists his wrists, feeling the course rope against his skin before flexing his muscles. The rope fights against his efforts.

"Harder Alaric."

Alaric ignores Stormwing as he puts all his might into pulling the ropes apart. An exhilarating feeling begins to pump in his chest and radiate throughout his body. A newfound energy courses through Alaric's body. He continues to pull until there's a sudden snap and his arms whip around. He looks down to see pieces of the rope torn and dangling from his wrists, and the skin where the ropes are tied has a silver tint like Stormwing's scales before they fade back into his normal mocha color.

"That felt amazing," he says with wide eyes. "Is that how you always feel?"

"Yes. Now stand slowly and don't turn towards me. Just walk naturally toward the rising sun."

"It's still dark. Where's the sun?" Alaric asks.

Stormwing sighs loudly. "Focus, and you will see what I see."

Alaric's eyes narrow as he concentrates. The forest begins to come alive before him, muted greens of pine and basil leaves flourish into vibrant colors of lime, fern and chartreuse. The early darkness of dawn glows bright, illuminating the lush forest.

"I—I see everything," Alaric says. "But what is that smell?"

Stormwing chuckles. "That would be the Battle Trolls. I see you have gotten my sense of smell now, too. You must hurry, we don't have a lot of time."

Alaric gazes through the trees to see sunlight peeking just over the horizon and starts to walk toward it. He keeps his head high as he walks cautiously through the brush, grass and dirt crunching underneath his feet. Alaric continues on as he becomes aware of the growing threat around him. The Battle Trolls watch his every move, and he glimpses them from his periphery as he walks. The stench is ever-present, and continuous grunts remind him he's not alone.

He hastens his steps but soon hears Stormwing's voice saying, "Battle Trolls like to chase, do not run." Alaric pushes forward at a fast walk but soon sees the edge of the sun peaking, creating a dark red and orange edge along the horizon. Alaric bursts forward into a mad dash.

He can't stop now. A hoard of ravenous Battle Trolls scream and howl from behind, chasing him like shadows.

"I told you not to run."

Alaric runs anyway, ignoring the monstrous sounds behind him. He looks forward, knowing there is no point in looking back. His only option is to keep running. Spears and other projectiles fly past his head, but he continues on. It appears as if death may come before he reaches his destination, and ahead, he sees the edge of the cliff and there is nowhere else to go.

"Run Alaric, don't stop!" Stormwing says.

Alaric feels that thumping into his chest again, as it radiates throughout his body. His feet dig deeper into the dirt as he blazes forward. The cool breeze ripples past him as trees whiz by. The edge nears, and he leaps without thought.

He free falls to a small plateau before landing on the balls of his feet and rolls forward. He turns, clawing at the lush grass as his momentum carries him closer to the edge. Stopping with his lower half dangling off the cliff, he holds on tightly and glances up. No Battle Trolls. He breathes a sigh of relief.

"Do you mind?" A booming voice sends vibrations through Alaric's body. "Your feet are in my eye."

Alaric pulls himself up, then peers back over the edge. He sees what appears to be the ridge of a nose. "Are you the walking mountain?"

"I am. And who might you be?"

"My name is Alaric. I need your help."

"Perhaps you can help me as well?"

Alaric's eyes widen. "I'm sure Stormwing and I can help…"

"Stormwing! I would do anything to help Stormwing! But first… you must get rid of the dragon riders of Tyranthia. They have me immobilized with some sort of blood magic."

"That's holding Stormwing, too," Alaric blurts out.

"If you can free him, then you should be able to free me as well. I need to keep moving before the Silent Peaks begin to clash."

"Clash?" Alaric asks.

"I must continue my trudge to keep the Silent Peaks moving so they don't collide with one another. The dragon riders from Tyranthia want that to happen so it will create what they call geraas matumbi. They believe it will bring about a rebirth of the world."

"How do I free you and Stormwing?"

"Blood magic can only be defeated with blood magic."

"But I don't know any magic."

"All you need is a clear ruby of Sabot," the mountain says. Alaric quickly replies, "The sun is almost up. How do I find the clear ruby and save Stormwing before sunrise?"

"Within me is the path to the ruby and to Stormwing."

"I don't think there is time for me to dig."

"Climb down and enter through my mouth. I will give you a direct path to a clear ruby and then back to Stormwing." Alaric raises an eyebrow, hesitating.

"Through your mouth?"

"You need not worry. I do not have a digestive track as you would imagine."

Alaric's face holds a grimace as he slowly starts to climb down the face of the walking mountain. Alaric inches past his eye and nose to rest on his top lip.

"And you're sure you won't eat me?"

"I will not eat you," he replies, filling Alaric's nose with damp air. Alaric flares his nostrils before taking in a deep breath, quickly exhaling before entering the giant opening of the walking mountain. "To activate the ruby, it will need some of your blood," the mountain says. "The greater the offering, the more the ruby's power."

*

Alaric steps out from a small cave with a clear ruby in hand. He sees Stormwing still subdued by a net in the distance and calls out with his mind.

"Stormwing, can you hear me?"

"Alaric, it's almost daybreak," the dragon says with uneasiness. Alaric gazes around to see several Battle Trolls scattered about in the tree line, just beyond Stormwing.

"There are trolls hiding near you. What should I do?"

"I don't know, but you must think of something—and fast."

Paralyzed, Alaric clutches the clear ruby tightly in hand. Thoughts run through his head and he dismisses all of them. His nostrils flare as the scent of the Battle Trolls grows, and without hesitation, he turns and raises his arm defensively as a huge club arcs down upon him.

Alaric's eyes widen as the club breaks against his arm. He notices that familiar sensation flowing through him and quickly launches his fist into the center of the troll's chest, causing the Battle Troll to cry out in pain as it's launched backwards. Monstrous cries fill the air, gaining Alaric's attention. He turns to see a host of Battle Trolls coming towards him.

"Run!" Stormwing shouts, but Alaric stands his ground.

"I will not leave you."

He swiftly kicks the first assailant and turns to the next, dodging a vicious blow and punches the troll in its gut, causing it to gasp and fall to the ground. Alaric continues his assault against the onslaught of ghastly warriors. He feels his connection with Stormwing growing as he punches, tumbles, kicks and dodges through his opposition with surprising ease.

"Stormwing, this is amazing," Alaric says. "How am I doing this?"

"As our abilities merge, they will continue to—look out, Alaric!"

The warning is too late, and Alaric screams in agony from the pain of a razor-sharp javelin as it pierces his shoulder. He falls to his knees and the clear ruby tumbles out of his hand and clatters across the ground.

"Alaric! Get up, Alaric!" Stormwing pleads as Alaric struggles to his feet. "Alaric, you must go!"

"I told you; I'm not leaving you," Alaric replies as he scrambles to the ruby. He reaches forward but a troll keeps him in place as it tugs on his leg. Alaric kicks at it repeatedly until it finally lets him go. He gets to his feet using the help of only one arm and runs to the precious stone, falling on top of it as he's tackled by a Battle Troll. He works to get up as the troll pummels his back. Stormwing fights to break free of the net but notices the ruby, now red from absorbing blood from Alaric's shoulder.

"Alaric," he shouts. "Use the ruby!"

Alaric fumbles to find it underneath him. The course dirt and grass is all he finds until he bumps against a smooth surface. He grabs it quickly and manages to turn around. The hideous monster, with its yellowish-green skin and beady brown eyes send repulsive sensations through Alaric's whole being. Warts that bubble the stench of a thousand unwashed socks fill his nose as he holds the beast back with his good arm. Alaric works to raise the now fully red ruby with his injured arm but struggles to lift it.

"Stormwing, I can't!" Alaric pleads as jagged teeth from the Battle Troll snap in front of his face.

"You must! Find the strength within you and channel it into the stone, Alaric."

Alaric fights with all his might to keep the Battle Troll at bay as he finds the strength within to raise his arm. At the bend of his elbow, his arm begins to raise and he points the ruby towards the savage creature. Fury burns inside Alaric, and a primal yell escapes him. The ruby illuminates with the intensity of Alaric's scream. The area is engulfed in a blood-red light that fades into white, and the Battle Trolls are gone.

Alaric slowly stands with wide eyes and surveys the area.

"Alaric," Stormwing says, causing him to turn. "I'm free." The dragon tackles Alaric, and he gasps in pain.

"I'm sorry," Stormwing says, backing away.

"It's okay." Alaric groans as he stands. "By any chance, are there healing roots on the walking mountain?"

Stormwing thinks for a moment. "I don't know, but hold still..."

"Wait, what?" Before Alaric can move, Stormwing yanks the javelin out of Alaric's arm with his teeth. Alaric screams in agony. "That hurt!"

"The clear ruby should be able to heal your arm."

Alaric, now nursing his arm, forgot he was still holding the stone. He looks down and places it in his good hand before examining it at eye level. Its dark red hue has been replaced with a pale rose color. Alaric continues to stare at it as he asks, "What do I do?"

"Place it near your shoulder and do as you did before. Just think about what you want, and the clear stone will fulfill that desire if the blood sacrifice is big enough."

Alaric holds the stone close to his wound and thinks of his shoulder being healed. It begins to radiate a rose-colored light. A tingle works its way up and down Alaric's arm as the gaping wound reduces in size until it vanishes. Alaric lifts his arm and swings it around, showing its healed.

"Wow, my shoulder. It feels like new."

"Thank you, Alaric. That couldn't have been easy."

"You're welcome, Stormwing." Alaric smiles. "We're in this together, right?" Stormwing returns the smile and says, "Yes, I believe we are, Alaric."

Alaric's face lights up before he remembers something. "The walking mountain needs our help. He said the Dragon Riders of Tyranthia are using blood magic to keep him bound like they did to you."

"If that is so, we need to hurry before the Silent Peaks of Sabot collide."

"We can use the ruby again," Alaric says as he lifts it up, but sees the clear ruby has turned to ordinary stone. "Wait, what happened?"

"A ruby can only be used until the blood sacrifice has been used up."

"How do we find another one to reverse what the Tyranthia riders have done?"

Stormwing pauses for a moment. "Where did you retrieve that one?"

"The walking mountain opened a path within for me to get it. Do you think he'll do that again?"

"Unlikely," Stormwing replies. "He can be very helpful but he often doesn't help again until you have completed the task given. But… I don't see him helping those who bound him, so either they were able to find a large ruby to hold a great sacrifice, which is unlikely, or they had help."

Alaric's eyebrows scrunched together. "So, what do we do?"

"We need to find their stone, and hope their sacrifice wasn't completely used up".

"And if it was?" Alaric asks.

Stormwing's eyes narrow. "Let's cross that bridge later, if needed. But right now, let's fly."

Alaric climbs swiftly onto Stormwing's back. Stormwing takes a running start and extends his wings. Within a few strides, the dragon launches into the sky and pivots back around to glide to the base of the walking mountain. Alaric holds tight as Stormwing cuts through the air effortlessly, and he looks ahead to see a vast mountain landscape as the Peaks of Sabot float before them.

"It looks like the peaks are getting closer!" Alaric shouts.

"No worries, we are almost there. Look! Can you see them, Alaric?"

Alaric looks down between what he thought were pillars but are the walking mountain's legs to see the camp of the Dragon Riders from Tyranthia.

"Yes," Alaric says. "And there's the ruby!" He points to the middle of the camp.

Several of the dragon riders awaken and catch sight of them. One scrambles up and mounts his dragon. Grabbing a horn out of a satchel, he blowing into it, alarming the others. The sound carries on the wind, and Stormwing says, "I guess they know we're here."

"What do we do?" Alaric asks.

"Hold tight!"

Stormwing barrel rolls downward toward the oncoming threat.

"What if they use a net again?"

"You can only surprise me once, Alaric."

Stormwing pulls in his wings to gain speed, twisting and turning to avoid spears flying towards them. Alaric tightens his grip before Stormwing latches onto another dragon and bites its neck, shaking furiously until Alaric shouts, "Look out!"

Stormwing lets go and uses his hind legs to push off the ghostly pale dragon, avoiding the snare of another net. It whizzes past them to entrap the other dragon. Stormwing flaps his enormous wings, hovering as he surveys the area. Hundreds of riders and their dragons are closing in on them.

"I need you to trust me," Stormwing says.

"I do," Alaric replies.

"Let go."

And without thought or hesitation, without fear or worry, Alaric lets go. He falls, watching Stormwing soar above their enemies. He spreads his wings and issues a thunderous roar. Massive bolts of lightning shoot from tips of his wings. The bolts crackle through the air, causing dragons and riders to spasm as they are hit by the lightning.

Alaric looks on as dragons and their riders fall from the sky like flies. He turns his gaze to Stormwing, who descends towards him. Alaric twists to face the ground with his arms out wide before

Stormwing swoops underneath and catches him on his back. Alaric holds tight as they fly but notices a dragon rider soaring away from them.

"Stormwing! One's getting away!"

Stormwing smiles. "It's okay. We need to unbind the walking mountain before it's too late."

Alaric nods his head in agreement and Stormwing takes them down to safety. They land a few yards from a gigantic clear ruby stuck in the ground.

"I hope it has enough magic left," Alaric says.

"Me, too. Go ahead, Alaric. Unbind the walking mountain."

Alaric touches the large ruby and thinks of the walking mountain being free. The gem illuminates softly until it blinds them both with a sudden flash of light. Alaric covers his eyes, peaking at the stone through splayed fingers before fully opening his eyes. He sees the ruby has become an enormous boulder.

"Do you think it worked?"

"I don't know," Stormwing says. "Wait, do you feel that?"

Trembling from the ground causes their bodies to shake. Alaric looks over and sees one of the massive legs of the walking mountain beginning to move.

"It worked!" he shouts. "It worked!"

"Hurry Alaric, get on my back! We don't want to be down here as he stomps around."

Alaric quickly climbs onto Stormwing's back and holds on as the dragon takes flight. Stormwing flaps his wings, taking them higher into the air, soaring over the forest and climbing above the walking mountain. Stormwing circles around until he finds the walking mountain's face and lands gracefully on his head.

"Thank you," a booming voice says.

"Thank you as well, my old friend," Stormwing replies.

"I thought I was the only one you could speak to?" Alaric asks, interrupting.

"I can speak to everyone, but humans tend to have a harder time listening."

Alaric nods. "Walking mountain, may we ask you one last thing before we go?"

"Anything, my new friend."

"How may we cement our bonding ritual?"

He can hear the walking mountain groaning as he thinks. "You must find the one named Locita."

"That was my mother's name."

"Correct," the walking mountain says. "She is the one you seek."

"But sir," Alaric interjects. "She died when I was very little."

"Not true, young Alaric. Follow the one-eyed man and he will lead you to her."

"What one-eyed man?" Stormwing asks.

"The one that flew away. He will be your guide. Just follow the sun and you will find him in Tyranthia."

"I don't understand, sir," Alaric says. "My mother... she is alive? How?"

"Yes, now go, before you miss your chance to find her."

Stormwing nudges Alaric's arm with his head. Alaric ignores him for a moment, lost in his thoughts, then swiftly hops onto the dragon's back.

Stormwing takes a few steps forward, flapping his wings and soaring into the sky. The two make their way westward, following the sun, gliding toward their destiny.

### THE END

# ABOUT THE AUTHORS

**Alison Reeger Cook** (A.R. Cook) is the author of THE SCHOLAR AND THE SPHINX young adult fantasy novels, THE SCALE SEEKERS high fantasy series, and short stories found in CHRONICLES OF MIRSTONE (Dragonfire Press), WOMEN OF THE WOODS (Fabled Collective), WILLOW WEEP NO MORE and SHADOWS OF THE OAK (Tenebris Books), and THE KRESS PROJECT (Georgia Museum of Art).

Her theater plays have been performed and work-shopped at the University of Iowa in Iowa City; Western Springs, Illinois; and Atlanta, Georgia. She has placed as a finalist in various screenwriting competitions, including the Austin Film Festival, Screencraft, The Script Lab, and The Launch Pad. She resides near Chicago, IL, with her husband Dave and their furry diva, Daisy May.

Visit her at www.scholarandsphinx.wix.com/arcook, or visit her on Facebook (www.facebook.com/ARCookAuthor) and Twitter (@arcookauthor).

—

**Richard Fierce** is the author of over 30 fantasy and sci-fi books, including his bestselling series Dragon Riders of Osnen. A recovering retail worker, he now works in the tech industry when he's not busy writing.

He's married with 3 stepdaughters (pray for him!), 3 grandchildren (he's young!), 3 dogs (huskies!), and 2 ferrets. Basically, he has a zoo.

His love affair with fantasy was born in high school when a friend's mother gave him a copy of *Dragons of Spring Dawning* by

Margaret Weis and Tracy Hickman.

You can check out all of his books at www.richardfierce.com

Follow him on Facebook, Twitter, or Bookbub.

—

**Jeremy Hicks** is an archaeologist, author, and the co-founder of Broke Guys Productions. Alongside long-time friend Barry Hayes, he co-authored *Finders Keepers* and *Sands of Sorrow*, the initial installments of the *Cycle of Ages Saga*, first as screenplays and then novelizations. *Delve Deep*, the third installment, is Jeremy's first novel as a solo author. He has published a number of short stories in various anthologies, including the Amazon #1 best-seller *The C.A.M. Charity Anthology – Horror & Science Fiction.*

You can visit Jeremy's website at https://jjeremyhicks.com/

—

**David Alan Jones** is a veteran of the United States Air Force where he served as an Arabic linguist. A 2016 Writers of the Future silver honorable mention recipient, David's writing spans the science fiction, military sci-fi, fantasy, and urban fantasy genres. He is an author, a husband, and a father of three. David's day job involves programming computers for Uncle Sam.

You can find out more about David's writing, including his current projects, at his website: davidalanjones.net

—

**pdmac** spent a career in the US Army before transitioning to education as a university Academic Dean. He transitioned again and now writes fulltime. He has a MA in Creative Writing and a Ph.D. in Theology. He is a member of the Blue Ridge Writers Guild, the Steampunk Writers and Artists Guild, and the Georgia Writers Association. A diverse author, writer, and editor, he has also edited a Literature anthology, served as managing editor of an archaeology magazine, ghost-written an autobiography, and has had poems, short stories, articles, and editorials published in various literary journals, magazines and newspapers. His most recent short stories appear in the *Short Story America* anthologies III and IV, *Poets in Hell*, *The Mulberry Fork Review*, and the Fantasy Anthology *Chronicles of Mirstone*. He has also sung back-up for Broadway plays, provided voice for radio plays, and acted and directed theater stage productions. In his off time, he and his wife enjoy cycling, kayaking, and occasionally backpacking sections of the Appalachian Trail. Additionally, he and his wife love to travel, their favorite place so far being Crete, Greece.

You can visit pd's website at
http://www.pdmac-author.com/

—

**A.G. Porter** is the author of The Darkness Trilogy, a YA Paranormal Thriller, and two poetry collections, Pieces of My Heart and Pieces of My Soul. She is currently writing a spin-off of her The Darkness Trilogy characters, as well as a new YA Paranormal series, The Sacrifice of Ava Black, and her next poetry book. When she isn't writing, she's either busy being the coolest mom on the planet, crafting, or reading. Mrs. Porter lives in Alabama with her husband, Billy, and her amazing boys, Brenton, William, and Garrett.

You can check out her website here:
https://agporterbooks.wixsite.com/author/n

—

**Selah J Tay-Song** is living proof that if you persevere, you'll catch your dreams. She decided to be an author at the age of six. Today she is the author of the Dreams of QaiMaj series, an epic fantasy series described as magical, poetic and engrossing. When she's not writing, she's stalking the urban river otters that live less than a mile from her home in the Pacific Northwest.

You can check out her website here: www.selahjtaysong.com

—

**Craig A. Price Jr.** is a USA Today bestselling author of Claymore of Calthoria Trilogy, Dragon's Call Trilogy, Dragonia Empire Series, Space Gh0st Adventures Series, and several other titles available in alternate realities. He loves to read, write, cast spells, and spend time with his beautiful wife and three children. He dreams to one day become a full-time wizard, but until then, he'll settle for being an author. With more than a dozen novels under his belt now, it's only a matter of time before he settles for world domination, but until then, you can follow his author journey as he takes over one reader's soul at a time.

Visit him at https://www.craigaprice.com/

—

**Keith Robinson** is the author of 30+ fantasy, sci-fi, and spooky supernatural books primarily for middle-grade readers but suitable for all ages. Though best known for the Island of Fog fantasy books, he's also the author of the Sleep Writer sci-fi adventures and, more recently, the Darkhill Scary Stories. He wrote the dark fantasy *Quincy's Curse*, and co-wrote the two-book *Fractured* tale with Brian Clopper. He typically writes three books a year while drinking hot tea.

Visit him at https://www.unearthlytales.com/

—

**Justin Turpen** is a fantasy and science fiction writer from Indianapolis. He is a husband and father of two. Inspired at an early age by the writings of Tolkien, Weis and Hickman, Herbert, and later Sanderson, he writes to inspire others with wonder and imagination.

You can connect with him via his website, www.justinturpen.com

—

**Andrew McDermott** is an author and narrator from Northern Ireland. When he's not writing or narrating, he's hiking in the Morne mountains. He is also somewhat antisocial, but one of the nicest anti-heroes you'll ever meet.

Visit him at https://www.robertmcdermott.info/

—

**Alfred Muller** hated reading growing up for multiple reasons. Writing always sought him out, whether it was picture books or short stories. His imagination was never quiet. His mother would tell him stories growing up at bedtime while they camped in upstate NY, building the foundation of his creative instincts. His father would play G.I Joes with him, which only furthered his desire to create. It wasn't until he found the Percy Jackson series that he found his love of reading.

From there his future was set. He devoured every book he could get his hands on. He also realized he didn't read anything he was interested in as much as the mythos around religion and death. Many fantasy books piqued his interest and grabbed his attention, but he couldn't find the kind of stories he wanted to tell. With the roiling of his imagination to contend with, he started writing. In the end, he came up with the epic novel The Water Crystal: Deal With the Devil.

Visit him at https://alfredmuller44.wixsite.com/alfred-muller-books

—

**Jay Reace** is an extraordinary superhero of words and life. As a published author, devoted husband, and proud father, he has embarked on a journey to inspire through storytelling. A vegan with a heart for kindness, Jay is also a veteran who blends strength with compassion in his writing. Collaborating with renowned speaker Les Brown, he has learned firsthand the power of words. From experiencing the glitz of HBO's "Boardwalk Empire" to DJing across New York, Jay's diverse experiences span 28 U.S. states and numerous international destinations. His mantra? Doing his best with as little harm to others as possible.

Connect with him on TikTok at
https://www.tiktok.com/@iamjayreace

As always, thank you for supporting the writing community!

Printed in the USA
CPSIA information can be obtained
at www.ICGtesting.com
LVHW092019100524
779541LV00002B/9

9 781958 354742